THE
LAURENTIAN
CHANNEL

Other books by Christopher Knight:

St. Helena
Ferocity
Bestseller

Visit www.audiocraftpublishing.com

The
Laurentian
Channel

Christopher Knight

AC AUDIO CRAFT

PUBLISHING, INC.
PO Box 281
TOPINABEE ISLAND, MI 49791

This book contains the complete
unabridged text of the original work.

THE LAURENTIAN CHANNEL

An AudioCraft Publishing, Inc. book
published by arrangement with the author

ISBN: 1-893699-06-4

AudioCraft Books are published by
AudioCraft Publishing, Inc., PO Box 281, Topinabee Island, MI 49791

PUBLISHER'S NOTE
This is a work of fiction. Names, characters, places and
incidents are the products of the author's imagination or
are used fictitiously. Any resemblance to any person
living or dead is purely coincidental.

Printed in the United States of America
First printing, November 2001

Many thanks to the numerous people that became involved in this project in one way or another. Thanks to Lauren Henderson for getting the ball rolling, to Maureen MacLaughlin, Cindee Rocheleau, Rhiannon Seybert, Jeri Long-Vermillion, and, of course, the lovely and talented Mrs. Knight.

Although this is entirely a work of fiction, the setting of this story takes place in Cheboygan, MI. My thanks to those in the community who offered their assistance with this project. The reader, however, is cautioned to beware of any similarities drawn from the characters in the book, and any persons living or dead. Should a reader discover such similarities, they are most certainly the work of their own imagination.

-the author

chapter 1

"Kari, come and look at this." Eric Randall pointed to the inky, jagged lines on the depthfinder. He followed the moderate up and down waves on the tiny screen with his finger, until the cursor suddenly shot up in a steep incline for about an inch, moved horizontally for a moment, and then plummeted back to the bottom of the green screen. He scribbled the coordinates and cut the boat engine. *Whatever it is*, he thought, *it's big. And it's deep.*

Eric and Kari had spent most of the day on Lake Huron, sunbathing, taking it easy, and looking for a new dive site. They did this often throughout the summer, cruising slowly in their boat with the depthfinder on, hoping to come across the remains of a sunken ship. There were hundreds of wrecks strewn about the floor of the Straits of Mackinac alone, and they'd already come across a few earlier in the summer. Some were too deep to sport dive, but a few had been in water as shallow as thirty feet. Most of *those* wrecks weren't much more than a tangled pile of rotted, decaying boards on the bottom. Worth a short dive, but not much more.

Yet, there was always the possibility, however remote, that a diver might stumble across an undiscovered wreck. Remote, but possible. It was this slim chance that made every dive exciting, every dive more adventurous than the previous.

Probably another false alarm, Eric thought, studying the jagged lines on the screen. In most cases, even a hint of excitement from charting an object on the bottom of Lake Huron would be premature. Usually what was charted wasn't much of anything.

But not today.

Kari climbed up from below deck, her legs, arms, and face aglow with freshly-applied sun block. She lowered her sunglasses and peered at the depthfinder. A tanned finger reached out and traced the up and down lines. "Couldn't that be a sediment formation or rocks or something?" she asked, brushing her hair back from her face.

"It could be, but I don't think so," Eric replied, shaking his head. "It's too conspicuous, sitting at the bottom of the channel like that. It's about one hundred sixty, maybe one hundred seventy feet down. That thing is *deep.*"

Brilliant diamond nailheads flashed on the water in the hot afternoon sun. Jimmy Buffett crooned lazily from the stereo in the cabin, and Eric wiped his brow with the back of his hand. His light brown hair was sweat-soaked, and beads of perspiration trickled down the back of his neck and spine. It was hot. Hotter than usual, anyway. Waves of heat shimmered in the distance, obscuring the far off shoreline. Two miles to the west, Bois Blanc Island lay like a burnt pancake in the sticky July afternoon. To the south, the Michigan mainland was barely visible through a steamy haze. Not far off, a carnival of seagulls rode invisible rollercoasters of air, the white birds swirling and whirling in their ferris wheel and corkscrew patterns.

The thirty-foot cabin cruiser sat motionless in the calm waters of Lake Huron. Eric and Kari had purchased the old, wooden-hulled Sea-Ray two summers ago, and had spent month after grueling month on her restoration. Kari chose the name, and the restored cruiser was christened the *John Galt* after the character in a novel she'd read years before. Painted deep blue-and-white and looking more like an old fishing trawler than a pleasure craft, the *John Galt* sat low and moved like a sloth through the water. Water-skiing would be out of the question, but for Eric and Kari Randall—the *perfect* boat.

chapter 2

The waters of Lake Huron were docile, as if sleeping in the searing afternoon heat. Although Michigan wasn't known for its high temperatures, this summer had been a hot one. A few billowing white clouds were slowly making their way east, occasionally blotting out the sun for a moment or two. The air was dry and arid, despite the massive body of surrounding water.

Eric began putting together his dive equipment, glancing occasionally at the squiggly lines on the depthfinder. He had to admit the chances were, whatever lay at the bottom of the lake *wasn't* a shipwreck. The depthfinder charted anomalies like this all the time. They usually turned out to be rock formations, changes in the sediment level, or other natural features.

Only one way to find out, Eric thought, his youthful wonder and excitement growing like a balloon. The search alone, the hunt, the anticipation—made it all worthwhile, whether they found anything or not. At the very least, he was *diving*.

He connected his regulator to his tanks and did the same with Kari's, checking the air levels carefully. One hundred feet plus was not the place to encounter any surprises.

He helped Kari with her wetsuit and weight belt, and she with his.

"Finally get to try out your new mask," Eric said. He smiled.

"Yeah," Kari replied enthusiastically, affixing the black *Zeagle* mask over her hood. It fit well, and replaced the old *SeaQuest* mask that had finally seen its last dive.

"How do I look?" Kari said nasally. She struck a quick modeling pose, one hand on her hip, her lips pursed in her best *Victoria's Secret* pout.

"Like a skinny black frog," Eric teased. "With yellow feet."

"Shithead," she shot back playfully, losing the pose and swatting his butt with her gloved hand.

The wetsuit, complete with gloves and boots, were a must. The surface temperatures were warm, but deeper, when the divers reached the thermocline, the water temperature plummeted. It was colder than cold. *Dangerously* cold. Without the protection of a suit, diving would be near impossible. Not so, for some of the warmer, tropical areas that Eric and Kari had dived, but Lake Huron was about as tropical as Alaska.

Kari finished suiting up, fins on, weight belt firmly around her waist. She was the first to plunge into the refreshing water, as only a few minutes in the ninety degree heat had made her very uncomfortable in the confines of the cumbersome dive gear.

Warm, greasy sweat oozed between her skin and her wetsuit, and the cool, invigorating water of the lake was a welcome feeling. Even with eight pounds of lead belted around her waist, her wetsuit was buoyant enough to keep her afloat.

Reaching over the gunwale, Eric lowered her bright yellow BC vest affixed with two tanks to the water below, where Kari was able to easily slip into it. She bit down on the silicone mouthpiece as Eric finished putting his gear on, and then he too dropped feet-first into the lake.

An endless, greenish-blue expanse opened up below them. Here, the world stopped. Time slowed. Movements decelerated, motions were sluggish and inhibited.

And it was *breathtaking*. This time, and every time Eric and Kari dived. It was that all-powerful, oh-so-sweet blend of nature's most addictive drugs: mystery, adventure, excitement and adrenaline, all wrapped up nicely into one tasty libation. Life's most powerful cocktail, yessiree, on the rocks or straight up. Two shots of adrenaline, if you could handle it. And there is no cure. No half-way house, no Betty Ford Recovery Center, no outpatient clinic or 12-step programs. Not for this one, no sir. Once you're hooked, you're *hooked*. Bottoms up, folks. Might as well belly-up to the bar, take a big swig, and enjoy the ride.

Eric double-checked his computer gauge for proper air pressure in the tanks, made a note of time, water temperature, depth. The usual stuff, the necessary stuff. The *important* stuff. Kari checked her own gauges, then re-checked everything. There is no margin of error at the bottom of Lake Huron, or any lake for that matter.

Their eyes met. The two gave one another the 'all okay' sign and began to follow the anchor line into the darkening depths of Lake Huron.

chapter 3

At eighty feet, visibility was limited to vague images. Sometimes it was better, sometimes it was worse—but it was always dark this close to the Channel. In some areas in the Great Lakes, diving to depths of nearly two hundred feet without a light was possible. Not so in the Laurentian.

Weightless, neutrally buoyant, the two divers stopped and held the line, and Eric produced a flashlight. He clicked the light on, and a pale white shaft penetrated the darkness like a laser beam. The two divers made eye contact, and Kari instinctively touched her index finger with her thumb.

A-okay.

Eric acknowledged with a nod and they continued their descent, following the white anchor line down into the black depths. Down, down, down. Deeper and deeper. Darker and darker.

Bottoms up, folks. Take a big swig and enjoy the ride.

A large brown trout gave Eric a start when it materialized right next to him. A hooked jaw and protruding belly indicated that, indeed, this was a *big* brown. The fish was a dark auburn color with black spots on its side and back, each nearly the size of a dime. The black spots were ringed in beige and orange, and its belly was a rich titian, the color of a desert sunset. It cruised close to the motionless divers, wary, curious. Wide eyes inspected the two strange invaders. It was as if the fish was a watchman, a look-out, the reigning sentinel of the icy deep.

Yep, just doin' m' job, fellas, the trout seemed to say. *Just doin' m' job.*

Seconds later, after another suspicious examination of the divers, the fish broke its circling pattern and slowly faded out of sight, vanishing into dark catacombs of Lake Huron.

Kari checked her dive computer. Ninety feet. Below her, the white anchor line spiraled down like a javelin.

Down, down, down. Easy and smooth movements, slow and unhurried, controlled. Deeper and deeper. Each diver inhaling through their regulators, smoothly exhaling. Expelled bubbles billowed up and swirled about like expanding flying saucers, beginning their slow rise to the surface.

At one hundred twenty feet, Eric slowed and checked his gauges. Both divers cleared the fog from their masks. At this depth, they would use air much more rapidly than they would in shallower water, and once they made it to the bottom of the lake they wouldn't be able to spend a lot of time there.

Eric shined the light along the anchor line as they approached the bottom of the Channel. The surrounding atmosphere was dark and still, crypt-like. There were no shadows, nothing for the light to train upon. The white swath jutted into the depths, piercing a needle-like hole, only to be swallowed up by the carnivorous darkness. Without the aid of the flashlight, it would be like swimming in a bottle of ink.

At one hundred sixty feet, they reached the anchor. The bottom of the lake was a mixture of fine mocha-colored sand and silt, which was easily displaced by even the slightest movement. There was a moderate current, just enough to lightly stir the debris without creating thick clouds of sediment. A few plate-sized rocks peppered with small, triangular-shaped zebra mussels were scattered about. Nothing else.

Holding her compass in front of her, Kari cruised a few feet above the bottom, with Eric at her side holding the flashlight. Their movements were slow, dreamy. Kari had calculated that the charted object should be slightly north of the anchor line. But the flashlight beam penetrated only about a dozen feet, and they could literally be right on the wreck and not see it if they weren't careful.

This thing has gotta be right around here, Eric thought. *The boat was right on top of the thing, whatever it is.*

Fifty feet north of the anchor line the search was still fruitless. Eric and Kari made a quick routine check of their gauges. It had been nearly twenty minutes since they had left the surface, and the air in their tanks was rapidly diminishing. During their ascent they'd need to stop every fifteen feet and wait a few minutes to decompress. The undesired result of failing to allow the nitrogen in their bodies to normalize was called *the bends*, which was painful and sometimes fatal. Divers that got 'bent' suffered varying degrees of pain and illness, depending on the victim's reaction to the nitrogen bubbles in their body. The more serious cases could only be treated by going to a special hyperbaric decompression chamber. The nearest one for Eric and Kari was at the University of Michigan in Ann Arbor, over two hundred miles away. They had never had to use it, and prayed that they never would.

Nitrogen played another factor in deep dives: narcosis. Breathing in such large amounts of nitrogen is toxic, and diving to thirty three feet was the equivalent of drinking a single manhattan. Two drinks at sixty six feet, three drinks at ninety-nine feet, and so forth. The effects on the brain could be euphoric—and *deadly*. Many divers had ignored the drunken effects of nitrogen narcosis and hadn't lived to tell about it. A diver that became 'narced' would feel the effects through various maladies such as disorientation, a feeling of well-being, and other afflictions. However, simply ascending only a foot or two could drive the symptoms away. Skilled divers knew when the nitrogen was affecting them. They watched for the warning signs and took corrective steps.

The divers had completed a fifty-foot perimeter around the anchor. *This thing has to be here*, Eric thought, his frustration growing. He shined the light on his air gauge and tapped it with his hand. Kari understood. They had been searching nearly four minutes already, and they'd have to begin their ascent to the surface soon. In the leaden gloom Eric pointed, signaling that they would go a little farther northwest, and then return to the anchor and begin to start back up.

Damn. I can't believe there's nothing here.

They started forward, Eric slowly swinging the light from right to left, and back again.

Gotta be here. Gotta be around—

They had gone only a short distance when the beam of light suddenly stopped four feet in front of the two divers, cut short by some unseen knife. The pale white disc illuminated a solid wall of aged, decaying wood, covered with a layer of dirty-green, algae-like substance.

But the definition—the planks, the structure, the corroding wooden slats—were unmistakable.

Eric and Kari froze, breathless. Hearts pounded. Adrenalin raged. Bells clanged, sirens shrieked. Glass shattered and thunder exploded. The past screamed in painful defiance, howling with the dead of a thousand seas, as if crying, begging.

Pleading.

No, no, no, no . . . .

The divers exhaled, and a vortex of air bubbles whirled about in their double and triple helix patterns, spiraling up in their journey to the surface.

No, no, no, n—

Above Eric and Kari, a massive, dark shadow loomed like an enormous sleeping dinosaur.

A ship.

chapter 4

The ship is docked in a busy harbor. A rickety wagon pulled by two massive horses stops next to it, and the young driver jumps down and begins unloading the wooden crates stacked in the back. Soon, he is helped by several other men, and they work to load the crates onto the vessel and store them below deck.

It is Chicago, 1859. It is a bustling time, an optimistic time. The city, on the doorstep of the industrial revolution, is teeming with an undercurrent of excitement and confidence. A certain particular hopefulness can be felt throughout the rapidly growing city. There is a genuine earnest, collective progression, a massive moving ahead toward the promise of the future. It is, as many would agree, the proverbial 'best of times'.

The ominous clouds that darkened the sky earlier in the day are beginning to disperse, and the afternoon sun is quickly drying up the puddles on the docks. Finally, three of the men gather to review their preparations and, satisfied that they have covered *every detail, they walk down to the Dockside Saloon. 'Spirits Lifted Inside' is written in smaller letters below the name on the sign.*

The bar is smoke-filled, and the air is garnished with the odors of cigars, pipes, and stale beer. The oak floor is sticky from years of drunken patrons spilling their libations, and a few saucer-sized dents in the wall and a shoddily-repaired broken window are proof that not all disagreements have been friendly. The tiny pub is cluttered with nautical memorabilia. Haphazardly, someone has strewn a large net on the wall and attached carved wooden fish and large wooden fishing lures to the skeins. A cane pole with a line and cork bobber and the enormous, gaping jaws of a twelve-foot shark complete the décor.

The three men—Captain Nathan LaChance, Jack Malloy, and young Daniel Hawthorne—discuss the journey. If all goes well, they will reach their destination in about twenty days. Of the seven persons that will be aboard, only the three of them are experienced sailors. The other four, the passengers, two men and two women, are more problematic. Captain LaChance has tried to dissuade them from the journey, but the four are unrelenting in their desire to go by water. At least there is one good thing about having women on board, the men agree . . . they can cook and clean.

LaChance unfolds a map from his pocket and spreads it out on the table. They look closely at what promises to be some of the more dangerous areas of their journey. Shoals and rocks are the worst hazards, stationary and often unseen until the last tragic second when it is always too late. A rock could rip the wooden hull of the ship wide open, leaving a gaping hole for water to come pouring in. There are several such areas on the map and the men look them over, circle a few of the more treacherous areas, scribble a few notes, and finally put the map away. The men agree that they will sleep on the ship that night while it rests in the harbor.

Christopher Knight

The four passengers will arrive early in the morning, and the long journey will begin.

That night, they sleep easily, except Captain Nathan LaChance. He stands at the stern of the ship looking over the harbor. Stars flash and twinkle on the water, reflecting the panoramic heavens above. The city is quiet, and the only sound comes from a mild breeze that lightly whispers in the captain's ears. It slithers through the ship, slinking through cracks and around dark corners. A dog barks somewhere in the distance, then stops abruptly. Beyond the docks the city is dark, except the dotting of a few gas lights here and there. LaChance strokes his beard and ponders the journey, now only a few hours away.

In the darkness, he walks quietly below deck, being careful not to wake the other men. Wood planks creak beneath his heavy boots. Lighting a lantern, he walks between the stacks of boxes and crates until he finds the cabin that holds what he was looking for. He peers inside, ever so cautiously, ever so carefully. Shadows sweep and bob as he raises the lantern, looking, looking—

There. LaChance feels a tinge of relief.

Still here.

But of course it is still here. How would one man . . . how would ten men . . . be able to move it?

Captain LaChance closes the door, walks as quietly as he can to his cabin, and climbs into bed. It is a long time before he is able to fall asleep.

The sun rises and the men awake, complete last minute duties, and ready the vessel. The four passengers arrive ahead of schedule and board the ship carrying small bags containing their personal belongings. An early morning westerly breeze fills the ship's sails as it departs, on schedule and on course, out of the harbor and into the shimmering waters.

chapter 5

The phone rang in Phillip Keanan's murky motel room. The curtains were closed, and the air conditioner hummed beneath the cloaked window.

The phone rang again.

A groan, a shuffling beneath the sheets. An arm flopped to one side of the bed. Another groan.

Ring.

Phillip's head thumped painfully, and he wrapped a pillow over his face and ears to try to make the awful noise go away. *Who the hell is calling at this hour, anyway?* he thought. *And why do they make motel phones so obnoxiously loud?*

Ring.

Shit. Can't people call at a decent hour?

Ring.

Keanan swatted the air, as if the phone were a mosquito and he could shoo it away with a careless snap of his arm. He had spent a good portion of the previous night at *Goodtime Charlie's*, intending to have only one or two beers. One or two had become three or four, then six, then eight, and finally, it was last call. *Last call for alcohol.* There was some song that used that line. Maybe a couple songs. Phillip couldn't remember. He was still nursing a Budweiser when the bartender had flashed the lights.

Last call, fellas. Last call for alcohol.

Phillip had a hard time remembering if he'd partaken in just one last beer, but he knew that chances were better than average that he had.

Ring.

He reached to the side of the bed and fumbled for the phone. Dropped the receiver to the table, then cursed as he pawed it onto the bed, where he finally picked it up.

"Yeah, *what?*" he groaned into the receiver. He made no effort to conceal his annoyance for the rude interruption. Slapping his hand to his forehead, an *oh-shit-what-next?* kind of motion, he let out with a moan. "You're calling me at this hour of the morning to tell me *that?*"

He groaned again, announcing his foggy stubbornness, stood up groggily, stretched, stumbled to the window, and drew open the blinds just a crack. Light seized the room; darkness scattered. Outside, the afternoon sun burned the black pavement of the parking lot, baking the cars like potatoes in a microwave. Phillip backed away from the window, phone pressed to his ear, one hand on his hip. Listening to the caller, he suddenly glanced, wide-eyed, at the clock on the bedside table. "Shit," he replied, shaking his head slowly. "I guess I *did* oversleep." His voice was raspy and hoarse, and he cleared his throat. There was another long pause while he listened, hand on his brow, as if this action would cure his aching body.

Suddenly, his body went rigid. His eyes glowed, and he pressed the receiver to his ear. "In the Channel?" There was alarm in his voice. "How do you know? Are you sure they're in the Channel?"

Long pause. Listening . . . .

"All right, all right," he finally heaved in annoyed exasperation. The caller himself was becoming increasingly hostile, and Phillip didn't want to rile him up any further. "All right. I'll go check it out. It's probably nothing. They're nobody. Probably just somebody fishing." With some effort he returned the phone to its cradle.

He stumbled to the bathroom, and a check in the mirror revealed puffy, swollen droops below reddened eyes; even more evidence of a late night. His black hair was unnaturally disheveled; nothing that a quick shower couldn't fix. The eyes, however, would need a dose of Visine to bring them back to life. Maybe an entire bottle.

Shit, he thought, leaning closer to the mirror and examining the inflated pouches beneath his eyes. *It looks like I picked up a couple of carry-ons.*

And the bottle of Motrin was empty, for crying out loud. He swore beneath his breath and tossed the orange and white bottle into the small waste basket beneath the sink.

At twenty-seven, Phillip Keanan had a seemingly recognizable look, an almost star-like quality. A rigid, chiseled jaw line and firm, pronounced cheekbones. A nose whittled from the catalogs of J.C. Penney or Eddie Baur or J. Crew. He was tall, fit, and carried himself with a finely-honed confidence. Phillip had a boyish, telegenic appearance, a look that caused many to wonder if he might indeed be, well . . . *somebody*. A look that helped him learn (successfully, at that) the very skilled art of manipulation. He was good at this game, and he wielded his expertise to suit his needs whenever necessary.

In five minutes he had showered and dressed. The eye drops had indeed done their work, and sunglasses would conceal the two carry-ons. He would just have to bear with the constant pounding of his head until he could pick up some aspirin.

chapter 6

The blue Dodge Dakota cruised south on US-23. The snaking highway cut a swath through acres of hardwoods, generally following the lakeshore from a distance. Occasionally the highway trimmed closer to the huge lake, and a slim, sandy shoreline was all that separated water and road. Five miles out of town only a few houses interrupted the woods, and Phillip Keanan turned left onto Highbanks Drive and followed it to where the pavement ended and the water began. Highbanks Drive was sparsely populated, with only a few houses sprinkled here and there, and a few *FOR SALE* signs scattered about, mostly on vacant lots, beckoning tourists and retirees. *The vacation home of a lifetime!* they screamed. *Perfect for that weekend getaway!* It wouldn't be long before the vacant lots were filled with cottages and homes.

At the end of the road there were no houses at all. The

pavement ended abruptly at a crude, natural boat launch in a small field surrounded by towering maple and pine trees. The ground was ruddy and uneven, and golf ball-sized rocks popped and crunched beneath all-weather tires. Jagged, six-inch deep trenches spider-webbed across the ground, created by heavy rains and their subsequent run-off, searching for the their homeland: Lake Huron.

Phillip stopped the truck at the waters' edge, cut the engine, and gazed out over a crystal-blue titanium sea. He squinted in the bright sunshine and cursed his throbbing head.

In the distance, he could make out the shimmering line of trees on Bois Blanc Island. Although the island lay only a few miles from the mainland, it was barely visible in the afternoon haze.

He raised the binoculars, and his view of the island cleared. But on the water . . . *nothing*. He swept the area southwest of the island, scanning the flickering blue waters, until—

There. A boat. Faint, but it was a boat, alright. Even with the binoculars, he had to squint to make out any details.

Well, how about that, Phillip thought. *A fishing boat. Probably illegal gill nets, too, being right in the Channel like that.* He relaxed a little. Although Ed Belmont's phone call was a rude awakening, the thought of other divers in or near the Channel concerned him. He was glad to see that whoever was moored out there was only doing some fishing.

Thanks, Ed. Thanks for the fucking wake-up call. Really appreciate it. He was just about to lower the binoculars when he saw it. *Oops. Hang on uno momento.*

Just off the stern of the boat, floating in the water, a small red-and-white flag bobbed on the surface, and the second alarm of the

day raked his head.
  A dive marker.
  Son of a bitch.

chapter 7

Phillip couldn't be sure that they were diving *in* the Channel. Lots of divers skirted the edge, and with so many other popular dive sites in moderately shallow water, not many divers were adventurous or daring enough, let alone *skilled* enough, to venture into the Laurentian Channel with its unpredictable currents and extreme depths.

The Laurentian Channel was the ancient bed of the St. Lawrence River that had, years and years ago, extended through Canada, Lake Ontario, Georgian Bay, and Lake Huron, passing under where the Mackinac Bridge now stands, and into Lake Michigan. When the last Ice Age ended ten-thousand years ago and the Great Lakes were formed, the river flooded, and its old berth now lay at the bottom of the Lakes. The Laurentian Channel was three hundred feet deep below the span of the Mackinac Bridge, although depths of almost five hundred feet could be charted in Lake Huron near the mouth of Georgian Bay.

Most would say that only fools bent on suicide dived the Laurentian, like the crew that had set out to find the wreck of the schooner *Nightingale* in 1993. They thought they had located her in the Channel a few miles from Spectacle Reef, in two hundred fifty feet of water. The three divers were very experienced in wreck dives, deep dives, and underwater rescue. They were, as they say, *masters* of their *craft*.

On their second descent to the wreck, none had returned. There were no clues as to what went wrong, despite the fact that they had taken an underwater video camera to film the dive. On the surface, an excited crew watched in awe and fascination as ghostly images glowed on a grainy television screen. When the screen suddenly went blank and the images were replaced by fuzzy snow, they suspected electronic malfunction. Their initial annoyance became concern, then, as the minutes ticked by, it turned into a gut-twisting fear—followed by all-out terror when the divers still had not returned forty minutes into the dive. The Coast Guard was called in, but all searches ended in vain. Attempts to find out what went wrong were fruitless.

Then, nearly a month later, a body washed ashore in Milwaukee, Wisconsin, hundreds of miles from the original dive site. The bloated, badly-decomposed body was found on the beach by Tyler Pratt, age six. The happy child had been playing on the beach with his dog, Booper, a black lab, when he noticed what he thought was an abandoned, semi-inflated dinghy washed ashore. The boy ran as fast as he could towards it, longing to feel the warm rubber beneath his feet, wanting to hear the final dying whooshes of air escape as the raft collapsed beneath his weight. He ran, jumped into the air, and landed smack dab into the middle of the very late Walter P. Middleton. The squishy flesh collapsed easily under the weight of the boy, who quickly discovered that Mr. Wally Middleton was not a discarded beach toy, and certainly wouldn't be doing any floating in the near or distant future. In terrified fascination, the boy flung back part of the torn wetsuit and stared in horror at the grotesque, disfigured face. Puffed-up, pale-gray cheeks engulfed the dead man's nose. His neck was swollen, and it was impossible to tell where his chin began. The eye sockets had receded and one eye seemed to float about on invisible strings, glaring blankly up at the boy. The man's other eye had been eaten away by crayfish, leaving only a small piece of swollen, creamy sclera and a gaping, dark cavity. The corpse had no hair (which the man hadn't had much of when he was alive) and part of his forehead had been gnawed away, leaving a section of dirty white skull exposed. Booper the black lab, entranced by the scent, had enthusiastically rolled in the remains of Mr. Middleton, legs upended and bicycling in all of his doggie glory.

An autopsy of Middleton determined death by drowning. Superstitious divers had their own explanations, and the stories grew and changed in pubs and bars with every tilted ale. *'Lake Huron takes what she wants,'* they said, sipping beers and lagers, *'and never gives back what's hers.'* Toasts were raised in honor of the dead, families were remembered, history was respected and revered. The *Nightingale* had not been dived upon since.

Holding the binoculars to his eyes, Phillip watched the boat for a moment. It was too far off to tell if they actually *were* in the Channel. But one thing was for sure.

They *were* diving.

Probably sport divers screwing around on the edge of the Channel, Phillip thought. *But, then again . . . .*

He lowered the binoculars and stroked the gritty, day-old growth on his chin.

Can't be too sure, he thought.

Phillip fired up the Dodge and headed back into town.

chapter 8

Kari and Eric stared up at the ship in astonished excitement. Eric guided the flashlight beam up the hull until it illuminated the bow of the wreck. The sunken ship sat upright, but listing to her starboard side. He checked his gauges and then held the dials under the beam of light for Kari to see. He flashed two gloved fingers, then motioned a thumbs-up sign. Kari understood. Two minutes; then they would have to begin their ascent to the surface.

With slow, deliberate kicks, Eric and Kari rose along the hull to the deck of the foundered wreck. A film of heavy silt covered the entire deck, and the motion created by their fins fashioned small, wisping clouds. The two divers distanced themselves from the wreck, not wanting to stir up any more of the fine loam and make visibility even poorer in the dark depths.

They scanned the ship with the bright beam of light. The vessel lay still and silent. It appeared to be in immaculate shape, the kind every diver dreams of finding. The slim masts jutted up and dissolved into the darkness, and haunting shadows jumped as the beams of light danced across the wreck. The grim silence spoke the language of the long forgotten. It rang with the voices of the deceased, echoing through the deep underwater prison.

Kari pulled her small Nikon underwater camera from her vest. The shutter clicked several times, capturing images of the cabin and the main mast. The flash lit up the darkness for an instant, but she was ten feet above the deck, and wasn't sure how well the pictures would turn out. She turned on her own flashlight and gently glided to the deck and over the gunwale, following the hull down. Two beams pierced the underwater night, spotlights sweeping to and fro. Kari spotted an open space in the hull where the planking had splintered. She shined her light through the small interstices, but saw only dim shadows. Nevertheless, she held the Nikon lens to a crack and aimed it into the depths of the ship. She took one picture and was dismayed to hear the whirring sound that told her the roll was finished.

That'll have to do, she thought, gently easing back from the ship. *Maybe they'll turn out, maybe they won't.* At this point, it didn't matter. They'd found a wreck, an undiscovered gem of history.

Eric, still hovering near the deck, pointed his flashlight towards her and clicked it off, then back on again. Reluctantly, Kari tucked the camera back into her vest and ascended towards him, and together the two divers floated effortlessly back to the bow of the long-lost ship. Following Kari's compass, they returned to the anchor and began the long ascent to the surface, stopping every fifteen feet for five minutes to decompress. By the time they reached the surface, neither had much air left in their tanks to spare.

chapter 9

Phillip's movements were sluggish as he worked on the deck of the Bayliner docked in the Cheboygan marina. His head thumped again, rudely reminding him of the phone call at his motel room. True, there had been divers in or near the Channel. *Their* Channel. But there were hundreds, maybe thousands of wrecks in the Straits of Mackinac. Fishermen charted them all the time on their depthfinders and never paid them any mind–although there were a few notable exceptions. When the *Sunset Queen* had been found, it was in pristine shape: a plunderer's dream. Phillip had tried to persuade the others to go check it out. But Ed and Jimmy had maintained that they shouldn't waste time on it because it would only distract them from their real goal.

He stood at the bow of the Bayliner and scanned the parking lot, then turned his attention toward the lake. A few boats speckled the horizon, and he looked wishfully at the lightly churning waters. He knew Huron, he felt, like he knew his own home. The three of them—Ed, Phillip, and Jimmy—had been up and down and back around every square foot of the Channel.

So why hadn't they found it? Already they'd probably discovered more uncharted wrecks than any other divers in the Straits.

They just haven't found *the* one. The search would continue, until . . . well, until they found the ship they were looking for. There had been a few heart-stopping moments when the *Cheyboygan Tribune* reported that a shipwreck had been found south of Bois Blanc Island. The divers who had made the discovery refused to disclose the name of the ship or its exact location. This development had caused a lot of anxiety among the three men. They decided to follow the divers out to the location to get a rough idea where the ship had been found, and make their own dive at night to find out if the wreck might be what they were looking for. If it was, they'd have to act fast. However, in the next day's edition of the *Tribune*, a front-page article, complete with pictures, showed the schooner *Newell Eddy* in one hundred eighty feet of water. The location was not disclosed, but that no longer mattered. To their relief, it wasn't what they were looking for. The three men had set their sights quite a bit higher than the *Newell Eddy*.

chapter 10

Phillip had just finished preparing the Bayliner when an enormous monster of a man walked towards him on the dock. The man spoke, his voice bellowing above the sound of seagulls, wind, and lapping water. "You look like shit. What the hell *did* you do last night?" It was Ed Belmont, a case of beer under one arm and an open beer in the other, and it was not at all an unfamiliar site. Although alcohol could seriously incapacitate a diver, Ed never paid much more than a casual observance to even the most basic rules.

Such was life for Ed Belmont.

He was a mammoth hulk of a man, carrying not one, but two all-weather radials around his waist. It was a wonder he could even fit into a wetsuit, let alone dive. On a scale, he hit a whopping three hundred seventy earth-shattering pounds. A colorful tattoo of

Mickey Mouse, outfitted with mask, snorkel, and fins, and sporting an extended middle finger, covered most of his right shoulder. Ed's gray hair had receded on top to the point of near extinction, but where it grew abundantly on the sides, he wore it about four inches long. Ed had no need for a barber or hair stylist . . . when he needed a trim he did it himself, using scissors from the kitchen drawer or sometimes even his dive knife. Phillip thought that Ed resembled an evil clown because of the way the hair on the sides of his head stuck out, swirling madly in the breeze. A fat, evil clown with gray hair and a Mickey Mouse tattoo. But this was sure as hell not something you'd mention to Ed Belmont. Phillip was sure that one of these days the dock would simply collapse under Ed's weight.

But Phillip knew one thing more: don't cross Ed Belmont. If Ed was about to go off, get out of his face, get out of his way, and leave him the hell *alone*. He was napalm, nails and gasoline, and when the fuse was lit, brother, *look out*.

Ed Belmont had had a life marred by turmoil. When he was six, both of his parents and his sister were killed by a burglar. Ed's father had accidentally caught the intruder in the act, and was shot in the head at point blank range. Young Ed watched through a tiny crack in his bedroom door as his father's head exploded, mangled and twisted like a watermelon tossed from a moving car. The intruder showed the same mercy for Ed's mother as well, and when Ed's nine-year old sister opened the door to investigate she got it, too, twice in the chest. Little Eddie Belmont had escaped the same fate by hiding in his room in the closet, but not before witnessing the three brutal, violent deaths. That was back in the fifties, and the story made headlines all across the country. The killer was convicted and sentenced to death, but soon after, the death penalty was repealed and the killer was re-sentenced to life in prison.

After the murders, Ed went to live with his grandparents, only to run away at sixteen. He did whatever he could for money or food. Often, he worked on ships doing odd jobs, and when he got sick of that, he'd jump port somewhere and do what he could to get by. By the time he was twenty, Ed had been all over the world. He got hooked up with some treasure hunters—divers—in the Florida Keys in the early seventies. In 1974, they located a galleon in fifty feet of water. When two of the divers got sick, Ed, who knew nothing about diving, volunteered to go down and help the other divers out. He quickly became comfortable using the regulator and equalizing the pressure in his ears while descending. When he reached the wreck and found Spanish doubloons littering the bottom of the sea, he was *hooked*. The coins glittered in his eyes and set his mind afire. Salt-water stocks and bonds. Wall street, just off the coral reef. His share of the payoff was almost $75,000. "Not bad for a shit job," Ed muttered to the bank teller when he opened up an account with the $75,000 check in hand.

From that day forward, Ed never held a 'real' job. He sailed the seas with various dive companies and treasure hunters in search of the next big jackpot. Money would just about run out and they'd strike it rich, or at least find something of value, allowing Ed to continue his lifestyle. A lifestyle that included a voracious appetite for food and drink. Many searchers, broke and tired after years of finding nothing, gave it up and headed for more stable working conditions. Ed kept it up as long as the money held out, borrowing when he needed more. So far he had been lucky enough to find enough treasure to keep him going.

In 1984, he and a few other hunters were paid $80,000 apiece just for finding the *Galileo*, eleven miles east of Marathon in the Florida Keys. There was no treasure on board, but an historical institute wanted the entire ship raised for an exhibit. Ed stayed on to help with the salvage and restoration, earning himself another $60,000 in the process.

And it was in Florida that Ed Belmont committed his first murder.

chapter 11

Ed Belmont had never really planned on killing anybody. It just kind of . . . *happened.* Growing up, he had often wondered what it would be like to kill someone. He tried to imagine what it would be like when the man who murdered his family would die. He anticipated the final few burning seconds of the man in the electric chair, hands coiled in charged convulsion, his body stiff and shaking. Ed saw the smoke rolling out of his ears, his eyes bulging, and he could hear the dull *pop! pop!* as they exploded like little ripe tomatoes. He could see the hot blood trickling down the man's face, over his cheeks, lips, and down his chin. And he would *enjoy* it. Every second of it.

When the death sentence was repealed and the man was re-sentenced to life in prison, Ed directed his malevolent thoughts elsewhere—to girls who refused to go on dates with him, to people who made fun of his steadily increasing weight, or to people who cut him off on the freeway. But these were simply 'wish lists'—he knew that he'd never actually follow through with his ideas.

Wish lists. *One of these days, I'm gonna . . . .*

No, he hadn't *planned* on killing Paul Sprague. It just kind of *happened.*

At least that's the way Ed thought of it.

The original *Galileo* search team included six men: Ed Belmont and Paul Sprague were the divers, another two men were electronics specialists, and the last two, the captain and the first mate, owned the boat. The captain was a scrawny middle-aged man who made his living charter fishing around the Florida Keys. The first mate was, of all things, the captain's lover of nearly ten years. Ed Belmont couldn't stand gays, and the thought of spending any time at all with them on a boat repulsed him. His paranoia kept him a safe distance away, and Ed never even shook hands with either the captain or the mate. But the job was too easy and the money was too good to pass up. He could handle the two gays, and stayed well away from them. Nevertheless, he never missed the opportunity to whisper some homophobic verbal assault under his breath when the two were out of earshot.

The two that handled the electronic searching gear were very knowledgeable in their field. Every time a dark, obscured image was charted, Ed and Paul dived on it to determine what it was. For the most part, the wrecks they searched never lay deeper than one hundred feet, and they encountered relatively few dangers. Sharks often patrolled the waters, but had never been a problem. This particular wreck had been located in three months, which was one hell of a stroke of luck. After Ed and Paul confirmed that the wreck was the *Galileo*, the two electronics men took their checks from the historical institute and departed. The captain and his first mate opted to head back to Key West and do some more fishing charters, and Ed couldn't have been happier. He and Paul were placed in charge of the raising and restoration project, which really only meant hiring the right people to do the job. When the job was complete, Ed picked up another $60,000 in addition to the original $80,000, as did Paul Sprague. The two celebrated one evening at a bar in Key Largo.

"Easiest sixty grand I ever made," Ed boasted, as the thick smoke from his cigarette swirled from the corner of his mouth. "Just too friggin' easy." By now Ed was a whopping three hundred forty pounds, and his massive bulk took up an entire corner booth.

Paul smiled and lifted his glass for a toast. "Here's to easy money and lots of it! I'm gonna buy me a little bungalow in Weeeezeanna." Paul never said 'Louisiana.' It was always 'Weeeezeanna,' putting emphasis on the first syllable and dragging the 'eeee' as if he was experiencing fond memories of a childhood home. He had, in fact, been born and raised in Pittsburgh, and the only things he knew about his beloved Weeeezeanna is what he saw in pictures. "You know . . . one with them big willow trees out front by the ocean. Gonna sail that little boat a' mine out there all the way to Weeeezeanna and take 'er easy for a while." Paul had a small twenty-two-foot Catalina sailboat docked at Key Largo on which he and Ed had spent the afternoon sailing and drinking.

"Yep! Me an' this sack." Paul dropped his voice to a hushed whisper. "Me an' this sack o' cash is gonna be partners for the trip." Paul motioned to a dark blue duffel bag that he had kept close to him throughout the day. Ed hadn't thought too much about it, as Paul often kept spare clothing in a duffel bag he carried with him. Now Ed crushed out his cigarette and pulled another from the pack sitting on the table. He glanced at the blue bag, then up at Sprague.

"Sack of cash?" Eyes flashed. "You've been carrying around your cash in a duffel bag?" Ed asked incredulously.

"Sure enough," Paul replied. "I don't trust them banks. One day your money might be there, the next, well, who knows? My uncle in Connecticut lost almost half a mil at a savings and loan that went belly-up. I'm not taking any chances 'til I get to Weeeezeanna, no sir."

The cigarette dangled from Ed's lip. "I know what you mean." *What a dumbshit,* he thought. Ed lit the cigarette, took a long drag, then exhaled the thick, hazy smoke as he spoke again, laying it on thick and heavy. "I mean, that's what I almost did," he continued. His voice hissed like a snake. "Almost kept all my money in a paper sack in my apartment. Nobody around here is gonna steal a paper sack."

Paul sipped his beer, placed it on the table, and fingered the condensation on the bottle. "Why didn't ya?"

"Fire," Ed replied, matter-of-factly. "If my house burned down, 'poof!' There goes all my money. Nope. I thought I'd put it in the bank 'til I find a nice safe place for it. But you mean to tell me you got $60,000 in cash in that bag you've been dragging around all day?"

Paul Sprague shifted, a bit uneasily, in his seat. "Well, no." He turned and looked around, first to the left, then to the right, to make sure no one was within earshot. His voice quieted to a whisper again. "I got a hundred grand in this bag. I still had some left from the first paycheck from the historical society. And I'm gonna . . ." But big Ed Belmont was no longer paying any attention to what Paul was saying. *A hundred grand in a duffel bag? What an idiot!* It wasn't an incredible amount of money, but it was a chunk. A *nice* chunk.

"Well, Paul . . . whaddya say I pick up a bottle of Dom Perignon, and let's go for an evening sail . . . kind of a 'last sail together' before you head up to Louisiana. How 'bout it?" Ed continued to lay it on as thick and heavy as he possibly could, laughing and slapping Paul on the shoulder now and then as the two men walked along the dock to Paul's boat.

chapter 12

The sun had set and the night sky was speckled with millions of tiny, flashing stars. Paul Sprague's boat, the *Sea Lady*, sat idle about a mile off Key Largo.

Minus one passenger.

Ed didn't really relish what he had just done, but all the same, he didn't feel particularly guilty. *You gotta get what you can while you can, as soon as you can*, he reminded himself.

Ed and Paul had sailed well past dusk and had gotten into a mild argument about who was the better knot-maker. "I can make knots that would hold two trees together in a hurricane," Paul's liquor bragged.

"Well, I was an Eagle Scout," Ed lied.

Thick.

"We were trained to make knots that are impossible to untie,"

Ed continued. "In fact, I know how to tie a knot that only *I* know the secret of untying."

Heavy.

By now, the bottle of Dom Perignon was long gone, and Paul had pulled out a bottle of Skyy vodka and made up a couple of screwdrivers. Ed had drunk little of either.

Paul waved his drink. "If you can make a knot that I can't untie, I'll—"

He had to think about that one for a moment. It had been a long time since his last high school dare, and he wasn't sure what to offer up. He and Ed both had plenty of money. He thought for a moment, and then a smile flashed as an idea came to him. "If you can make a knot that I can't untie, you can have my truck. Lock, stock, and barrel." Paul had a red 1983 Ford Ranger that didn't get driven much at all, since he spent most of his time on ships or beneath the water.

"Well, then," Ed replied confidently. The fat man let out a chuckle and lit another cigarette, and continued. "I can tie your feet together so good that you'll be beggin' for me to untie the knot, just so you can walk again."

Thick and —

"You're on," Paul exclaimed.

—heavy.

Ed picked up a rope lying on the deck and began to tie Paul's ankles together. "Now don't rush me," he warned, the cigarette drooping from his lips. "It's been a while since I've done this and it's kind of dark." Ed's fleshy hands whirled in the dim moonlight. Finally, he sat back, puffing on his cigarette and inspecting his work. Paul reached down to begin untying the knot. "Hold on, hold on," Ed said with a laugh. "I wanna look at this and make sure I got it right. I *want* that truck of yours."

"Oh sure! You think *that* knot is gonna hold me? Guess again, Eddie boy." By now, Paul was totally intoxicated. Ed had never considered Paul Sprague very bright, but he was amazed that he hadn't figured out what the hell was going on.

Or what was *about* to go on, anyway.

With one giant heave, Ed pushed the very drunk and totally unsuspecting Paul Sprague overboard. Arms spun like pinwheels, and his head bobbed in rooster-fashion as Paul tried, quite unsuccessfully, to regain some sort of balance. His drink flew out of his hand, ice cubes tinkling on the fiberglass hull of the boat and landing in the dark water. Paul Sprague hit the water a split-second after the ice, in a cacophony of confused splashing and swearing.

"What the . . . dammit, Ed!!" Paul sputtered. "What the hell you doin'? What in the *hell* you doin'?"

"Geez, I'm sorry Paul," Ed said contritely, his disembodied voice drifting eerily over the dark water. Water lapped and babbled as Paul struggled to tread water. "I gotta watch what the hell I'm doin'. Here, I'll toss you a life preserver." More shuffling came from the boat, and in the darkness Paul heard a heavy splash next to him.

"Ed! Don't . . . please *don't* . . . ." A suddenly sober Paul realized what had happened, but by now, it was much, much too late. *That crazy bastard tied the anchor line around my feet!* In the next instant, the sinking anchor abruptly snapped Paul's body below the surface. Quickly finding it hopeless to stay afloat with a forty-pound weight tied to him, Paul tried to reach down and untie the knot that bound his legs together. It was impossible. The alcohol, the darkness, the sudden vertigo was too disorienting.

The anchor hit bottom. Nearly out of air, Paul reached down in a frenzy and found the knot that held his feet in a death-grip. In the complete darkness he had no idea where to begin, and the liquor buzz only added to his confusion. His need for air was immediate. His lungs were ready to explode and his thoughts were frantic and distorted. His hands and fingers wove back and forth, churning and whirling. *There's gotta be a way . . . gotta be . . . a way. Gotta be something—*

In a final, panicked effort to make it out alive from his saltwater coffin, Paul sprang up from the bottom and began swimming desperately for the surface.

Maybe I can . . . gotta kick . . . harder! Maybe—

Five feet from the bottom the anchor jerked him to an abrupt stop. It was the end of the line, in more ways than one.

It was the end of the line for Paul Sprague.

Paul's body convulsed violently as the seawater filled his mouth, his nose, and his lungs. He felt a sudden, searing pain as his lungs burst, and then—*nothing*. Paul's lifeless form sank down, down, and came to rest, his face burying in the soft ocean floor. In the dark depths, only a few feet away, a glass tumbler lay sideways in the sand.

Eighty feet above the lifeless body of Paul Sprague, Ed stood on the bow of the sailboat and listened in the darkness.

Nothing.

Only the low wash of water on the *Sea Lady's* hull as she rested calmly in the water. In the distance, the lights of Key Largo wavered in the night heat, and the stars above twinkled and danced. *Plip-plip. Bloop. Plip-bloop. Baloop.* The last gasps of Paul Sprague reached the surface. *Bloop-lip. Blip-loop.*

"Good luck in Weeeezeanna," Ed whispered smugly, tossing his cigarette into the water. He cut the anchor line, started the sailboat's motor, and headed back to Key Largo. He did feel a slight twinge of remorse for poor Paul, but the feeling left him as he glanced at the dark shape of the blue duffel bag on the seat. An extra hundred grand would suit him just fine and dandy. As well as a Ford Ranger and a twenty-two foot Catalina sailboat. He lit another cigarette, and the smoke drifted against his cheek and dissipated in the light breeze. *You gotta get what you can while you can as soon as you can*, he thought with greedy satisfaction.

He hadn't really thought much about where he was going next. Maybe he'd take a while off, but he doubted it. He loved it too much. Like a gambler always waiting for that next big stroke of luck, Ed Belmont needed the rush of high adventure. He loved the mystery, intrigue and excitement of treasure hunting. But most of all, he loved the lure of big, big money. And that's what had brought him to the Laurentian Channel six years ago.

chapter 13

Captain LaChance is nervous. Although he is a seasoned sailor, occasionally the weather makes him a little edgy. But it isn't the atmospheric conditions that he is nervous about tonight. He has a special cargo to worry about, and the faster they can make it to their destination, the better.

The others have gone below deck, and LaChance stands alone at the helm as the last rays of sun dip below the horizon. It has been a good day. The weather has been favorable, and everything has gone smoothly.

But still . . . .

A few stars appear, and a bright, silvery moon hangs overhead in the darkening sky. LaChance takes another sip of the whiskey that he has tucked away inside his thick overcoat. The breeze is just enough to move the ship and put a slight chill in the air. He pushes the cork stopper back into the mouth of the bottle and replaces it in his pocket.

Six miles to the east, the coast of western Michigan is visible, even in the rapidly fading daylight. He knows these waters well, and, as long as he is able to see land under the light of the moon, the sailing will be downright pleasant. But he has a hunch, a slight twinge, that tells him that all is not well. Over the years, he has learned never to deny or ignore such feelings. It is a comfort to him that they are actually under way, that the long journey has finally begun, but he knows that he will need to be on his guard until they reach the safety of New York harbor.

LaChance is not a greedy man. But when Richard Merman had asked for his help, Nathan could not say no. Richard had been his childhood friend. Although they had drifted apart in their late teens and the years had spun by without the two men seeing each other, they have kept in contact. So when Richard suddenly appeared at LaChance's front door in the middle of the night, Nathan was surprised. Folks don't come calling at three o'clock in the morning, and Richard had received one hell of a shock when he was greeted with a ten-gauge shotgun. At the kitchen table, in the glow of an oil lamp, Richard told his old friend an unbelievable story.

LaChance recalls that night over in his mind. He puffs thoughtfully on his pipe as he stands at the helm, guiding his ship through the dark waters. Below deck, the six others are sleeping.

Or, at least, five of them are sleeping.

chapter 14

The twenty-eight-foot Bayliner cruised smoothly across the water. Phillip and Ed were the only crew because Jimmy was in Detroit and wouldn't be back for another few days. Ed had outfitted the boat for fishing, including downriggers. None of the three really liked to fish, but the fishing gear provided a perfect cover, and it helped to keep a low profile during the busy summer tourist season. Ed had purchased an air compressor so that they wouldn't have to go to the local dive shop to fill their tanks with air. When they did need dive equipment or repairs, they were careful to go to Traverse City or have Jimmy make the four-hour drive to Detroit. When the weather grew too cold and fall and winter storms threatened, the men went their separate ways. Jimmy returned to Detroit, Ed to the Keys, and Phillip to Telluride, Colorado, where he worked repairing bikes.

But not for long. The three men were certain that, soon, they would find the ship—and, more importantly—what was on the ship.

Phillip slowed the boat and glanced back at the downriggers. They had put all four lines out, not because they wanted fish, but because it perpetuated the lie. The only things attached to the end of the lines were empty beer cans and a broken transistor radio.

Phillip pointed to a boat off in the distance. Ed raised the binoculars to get a better look. "Looks like they're done diving. Yeah, they're moving. They're following the Channel west."

Ed handed the binoculars to Phillip, who raised them to his face. "Yeah, that's the boat I saw earlier today. A blue-and-white cruiser . . . and there is a dive flag on deck," Phillip confirmed gloomily.

"Hey, no big deal," Ed said, nonchalantly throwing up his enormous arms. "So they're divers. So maybe they are diving in the Channel. So what? We've been looking for this thing for six years. The chances of them coming across it are zero. Even if they *knew* what to look for, which they *don't.*"

In all the years Ed, Phillip, and Jimmy spent looking, they'd only encountered one other boat diving in the Channel. Four men, fresh with their open-water dive certificates, had decided to dive the ledge of the Channel to a depth of about one hundred twenty feet. Not deep for experienced divers, but for the four rookies, it was a stupid idea. One got bent, suffering decompression sickness when he ascended too rapidly, and had to be flown to the hyperbaric chamber in Ann Arbor. Another forgot to breathe on his way back to the surface while trying to help Mr. Ascending-Too-Rapidly, and the air in his own lungs expanded, causing one of his lungs to literally explode. He almost died. The Coast Guard had to come and get them, and the TV, radio, and newspapers covered the story and warned of the dangers of diving the Laurentian Channel.

All of this hoopla could not have made Phillip, Ed, and Jimmy happier. They almost jumped for joy when the Coast Guard Commander was interviewed on television, reminding everyone that the *"Laurentian Channel, with its unpredictable currents and extreme depths, are for master divers only, if for any at all. This post highly recommends all divers stay away from the Channel, and instead, explore the many sites and wrecks to be found in much safer, shallower water."*

Ed tossed his cigarette into the water and put his hand to his brow to shade his eyes from the sun, and squinted off into the distance. "It looks like they're coming in. Let's head back. We can get a closer look at them at the marina."

Ed's probably right, Phillip thought. *Probably just sport divers along the ledge.*

Ed put his sunglasses back on and pulled a white T-shirt over his tanktop. Even the extra-large didn't fit him, and one entire radial hung below the shirt and above his massive shorts.

Phillip generally got along with Ed Belmont. Ed could be a royal pain in the ass at times, but then so could Phillip when he wanted to. He and Ed had never directly crossed each other and Phillip wanted to keep it that way. Of course, Phillip had no idea that Ed had murdered one of his friends by tying his feet with an anchor line and tossing him overboard. He did know that, like himself, Ed usually got what he wanted.

What was it that Ed was always saying?

Oh, yeah.

You gotta get what you can while you can as soon as you can.

That sounded just dandy to Phillip Keanan.

chapter 15

The *John Galt* slowed as it passed the breakwall and reached the mouth of the Cheboygan River, welcomed by a single, unmanned red-and-white lighthouse. Kari made preparations for docking while Eric, at the helm, glanced back longingly at the pristine blue waters of Lake Huron. He had lived in northern Michigan most of his life. The time he'd spent in large metropolitan areas now seemed a tremendous waste, and he wondered now how they could have lived in the traffic, smog, and noise of a city for more than a week. It just wasn't *home*. Home was the river gently caressing the banks, the crickets calling for mates in the late evening, and the serene peaceful quiet from dusk until dawn. Rarely did a siren pierce the night in Cheboygan. True, there were times that both he and Kari longed for the fast-paced action of the city night, the squealing of tires on hot pavement, the loud music in bars, and the close heat of many people crowded into one area, laughing, talking, and drinking—but more than one or two nights in a row and its allure wore off.

His reflections were rudely interrupted by two jet skis, impatient with the sluggish pace of the cabin cruiser. The sounds of the personal watercrafts were poisonous, filling the air with their shrill, toxic whine. The two crafts suddenly whizzed around the *John Galt*, ignoring the 'NO WAKE' signs posted along the banks, and zipped recklessly up the river. Eric grimaced as the two jet skis buzzed by without even looking to see if another boat was coming from the opposite direction. He had to struggle to keep his finger from gesturing on its own.

Kari was below deck, stowing the dive gear and checking to see which tanks needed filling so they could drop them off at the dive shop on their way upriver. The shop had been there since the 1970s, right around the time when diving in the Great Lakes was just becoming popular. '*Conveniently ocat d on the Che oy an iver*' read the dilapidated red-and-white sign out front of the weathered wood building. No one had bothered to replace the missing red letters that had fallen into the water years ago.

Eric turned his attention back to steering the *John Galt* upriver. He and Kari had left Cheboygan seven years before, moving first to Chicago, then to Galveston, then back to Chicago. While contemplating yet another move, this time to Detroit, Kari had become pregnant. She had only been three months along at the time of the accident.

chapter 16

Kari had been jogging through a park near their apartment complex in Chicago. She often ran the winding, paved path, as did many other people. If there was anything different about this day, it was the fact that a heavy drizzle was falling that had kept most other runners indoors. Only a handful of diehards had braved the cold chill and the damp air that soaked to the bone.

Squish squish squish squish. Kari's shoes were sopping wet before the first mile, and her feet felt heavy as she ran along the sidewalk that wound through the park. She passed a few other runners, coming from the other direction, and she waved to the ones she recognized. Ahead of her, the lofty, full branches of a dozen maple trees, leaves shiny and wet, spread their sheltering arms over the sidewalk. *A quarter of a mile,* she thought. *Those trees will be a nice break from the rain.* A few runners had already stopped and were standing in the cover of the trees, chatting with one another, running in place, waiting for the rain to lessen.

Squish squish squish squish. She ran under the trees, relishing, if only for a moment, the break from the rain. In a few seconds, she would be back in the full force of the downpour, which was now creating small streams and rivers on the cement beneath her feet.

Squish squish squish squish. Home in another mile.

She didn't see the bicycle approaching from around a sharp corner. And, quite obviously, the cyclist didn't see Kari. At least, not until the last moment, as he rounded the hairpin turn. He had been going faster to get home himself and perhaps the rain clouded his vision or maybe the pavement was too slick to control the thin tires of the racing cycle around the corner.

Squish squish squi—

The collision wasn't that severe, except for the fact that Kari was pregnant. The force of the impact knocked her backwards nearly twelve feet, and as she tumbled through the wet grass, she had an awful knowledge that it was over. There was severe pain, unbearable aching cramps, and then it was gone, the pain was gone, everything . . . gone. She remembered waking up in the ambulance, an oxygen mask over her face, and the worried expression of the EMT as he hovered over her.

She had wept for nearly a week. Eric had been away working at the time of the accident and couldn't be reached until the following day. He immediately flew home and the two spent the following days in agonizing grief, alone in the confines of the lonely, still apartment. The sounds of the city that drifted up to them—the honking horns, the wailing of sirens, a shout from the distance here and there—only added to the haunting emptiness. The curtains had remained closed, as if the light of day was too bright and too happy. But the darkness only multiplied the seemingly unending sorrow. They had both so very much wanted a child, and the accident was more than just a crushing blow. It was their sickest, saddest, deepest nightmare rolled into one.

But the final, crushing blow came when Kari's gynecologist informed her that she probably couldn't get pregnant again. He wasn't sure and it was too early to tell, but he was very frank when he told her that her chances were not good. *And if you do*, he had said, *there would probably be problems. Serious problems.*

The news was an uppercut that put her to the ropes. First a left, then a right, then—*pow!* The jab sent her reeling, dizzy and in shock.

It was terrible for Eric, too, who couldn't stand to see the woman he loved going through such brutal suffering. Sometimes, he would try to hold her, to comfort her, and she would turn away, crying in agony. He would leave her alone as she sobbed on the bed, falling deeper and deeper into a hell that Eric could not know. Other times, she fell into his arms, needing to be held tightly for hours and hours, and he did so lovingly, thankful to be near her, to be close to her and help her, to smell her hair and touch the softness of her skin. He loved her more than anything and the pain of seeing her in such turmoil tore at his very soul.

Sweet Kari. She had been eighteen when he met her, and he was nineteen. Kari had grown up in Indian River, and the two hadn't met until both had graduated from high school. Eric thought that it was ironic that, in a town where everyone knows everybody, he hadn't spotted the pretty girl with the brown hair. He had been working for his father's dive salvage company, diving Burt Lake to recover a stolen snowmobile that had fallen through the ice the previous winter. Someone had swiped the machine from the parking lot of a nearby bar. The thief had foolishly figured that his best and fastest route of escape would be across the lake. In *March.* The ice had already begun to melt and the Department of Natural Resources had posted thin ice warnings. The machine had broken through, but the thief was lucky enough to climb out of the frigid water and walk back to land. It had taken him nearly twenty grueling minutes to trudge the distance in his heavy clothing coated with solid ice. He nearly froze to death. Two months later, he was featured on the syndicated TV program *America's Dumbest Criminals.*

A sport diver located the machine later that June and called the Sheriff, who in turn called Eric's father, a well-known dive salver. He was the only one in the area with the know-how and equipment to bring the machine up from sixty feet of water. Eric's father, not excited about losing a day's fishing on an uninteresting retrieval mission, ordered Eric and three others on the crew to raise the sunken snowmobile. It was routine work, but it gave Eric yet another opportunity to dive, something he loved to do more than anything.

A cable had snapped while the machine was being hoisted onto the deck, and Eric cut his arm while grabbing the snowmobile to prevent it from falling overboard. It wasn't a serious injury, but the wound was going to need stitches. Driving himself to the hospital after they had successfully retrieved the Arctic Cat and dropped it off at the Sheriff's Department, Eric walked in through the emergency room doors of the hospital—and fell flat on his face. It had been nearly an hour between the time he had cut himself and the time he had arrived at the hospital and he had lost a lot of blood. Now, as he lay on the Gurney, he had another problem: a continuous nosebleed from kissing the linoleum floor. But the nurse was very nice. And *beautiful*. She was the first thing he saw when he came to in his hospital room.

They went out two nights later. Much to the dismay of both their parents, they were married only four months after their first date.

chapter 17

Not long after losing the baby, both began to lose interest in their high-paced jobs and the lives they were leading. Soon, every day spent gnarled in a traffic jam or dashing to airports was a tremendous waste of time and energy that was taking them farther away from their goals, their dreams, and each other. The opportunity for change finally came, but not in a very welcome fashion.

Eric's father had always said that he would die in the water. It was the fate of a man who tempted it often. "Yessirree Bob," he had said. "One day this old boy's gonna be the victim of somethin' stupid . . . really stupid . . . and that's gonna be the end of ol' Frederick J. Randall. Yessirree Bob, you watch."

He was half right.

One day while on his early morning walk to the grocery store for

a *Detroit Free Press* and a pack of cigarettes, he was hit by a
Chevrolet Impala whose driver had lost control, jumped the curb,
hit him square in the ass, and sent him head over Reeboks over the
guardrail of the Lincoln Bridge and into the Cheboygan River. The
car wasn't traveling at a high rate of speed, but the impact was
enough to crack the spine of the elder Randall. The coroner said
that he had drowned, fully conscious and aware, but paralyzed by
his damaged spinal cord. Frederick Randall had been powerless
to do anything but stare at the murky brown riverbed a few feet
below him. At that early hour, not many people were even awake
yet, so there was no one around to pull him out. The coffin lid
slammed shut for good when the driver of the Impala, who could
not swim, was forced to watch in stupefying horror as Randall's
limp body slowly floated downstream.

Eric had inherited the house, along with most of his father's
belongings. Most of his company's dive equipment, including two
boats, went to auction to pay off debts. Although the elder Randall
had run a highly successful business and was very respected around
the country and the world, he was very poor at managing his
money, and, for all practical purposes, was broke at the time of the
accident.

Eric's mother had moved to Atlanta after the divorce five years
ago and re-married. *("Yes, I'm certainly sorry to hear of
Frederick's death, that was terrible and all that, but no, I don't
think I'll be able to make it to the funeral and could you please
send down that wicker chair I love so much. Your father kept it in
the divorce and I really would like to have it . . . that is, of course,
if you don't have any use for it, which I'm sure you don't, do you,*

honey?") His mother had made a habit of gathering men, like a sixth-grader collecting bugs for a science project. She would've gotten an 'A' on her collection—except she was married to Frederick at the time. She divorced, and set out to complete her accumulation of the male species.

So Eric and Kari sold their furniture, packed up, and moved to the home his father had built on the Cheboygan River. It was a bit smaller than the apartment, but the view of the river, the fresh northern air, neighbors who actually waved to you as you walked to the mailbox, and the slower pace was appealing. Their savings would last four years, maybe five, if they lived frugally. Eric wasn't sure if he was going to continue in the dive salving business, even though the money was good. Kari had her degree in nursing, but she didn't think she wanted to continue in that field. No big deal. They would have plenty of time to decide.

After the last load had been dropped off at their new home in Cheboygan, the first night of the soft waves lapping the riverbank, the concerto of crickets outside their bedroom window, and the elderly woman next door who brought over a tray of brownies to welcome them to the neighborhood . . . *Well*, Kari had thought. *Whatever we're going to do, it's good to be home.* The wounds from the uppercut that had once landed her on the ropes finally began to heal.

chapter 18

After dropping off the tanks to be re-filled at the dive shop, Eric docked the *John Galt* at *The Boathouse* restaurant as Kari secured the boat. *The Boathouse* had been an actual, working boathouse in the 1950s. Over time it had become dilapidated, but several years ago it had been restored as a restaurant and lounge.

Eric sat down in a chair on the outside deck and watched Kari as she walked to the restroom. After a few minutes, she returned to the deck, and sat next to him.

"Hey, sexy," Eric said, grinning. "Missed ya. How about some night baseball a little later?" He kissed her cheek, and she smiled.

"If you're lucky," she replied playfully. Kari's brown hair, slightly bleached by the sun, covered her tanned, bare shoulders. A light breeze played with her bangs. She brushed away the hair from her face and again smiled at Eric. The tiny crow's feet around her green eyes appeared again, as they did nowadays when she grinned. Kari hadn't been the least bit put off when she awoke one morning to find the small intrusive lines that had begun their inevitable journey. She had the biggest, prettiest green eyes that Eric had ever seen, a great body that came with staying fit and in-shape, and more than once he had to reassure an inebriated patron at one of the local hang-outs that *no, she won't be going home with you tonight. Sorry about your luck.*

The sun was a brilliant, burning lemon-drop high in the hazy blue sky. Waves lapped at the dock, and agile seagulls swivelled above. Another boat pulled up to the dock, its occupants laughing, glistening with fresh tanning oil. Eric and Kari sat silently, taking in the sun, the air, the sounds of the river. A waiter came and took their orders, then hurried off. Eric speculated about the wreck. It had been on their minds constantly since the discovery, and both had been fascinated by the find.

"Maybe it's the *Nightingale*," Eric considered.

"Too far south," Kari replied, shaking her head. "My first guess would have been the *Newell Eddy*, but she was found two years ago." Years of diving with Eric and countless hours reading books had made her knowledgeable about shipwrecks and their individual histories. At least, more knowledgeable than Eric, who wouldn't waste his time doing something as tedious as, heaven forbid, actual *research*.

"What about the *Augustus Handy*?"

"No," Kari answered, again shaking her head. "The *Augustus Handy* foundered near Spectacle Reef and is completely broken up. What we found is in much too good of shape to be the *Handy*."

The waiter came with their drinks, and both took long, slow sips from their glasses. "My best guess," Kari reflected, "considering her size, and where she rests, is that she's the *Flight.*"

Eric was vaguely familiar with the legends regarding the *Flight.* She had been a one hundred-fourteen-foot schooner built in Cleveland in 1857. In November of 1865, she was caught in a storm and stranded on Bois Blanc Island for the winter. The following June she was set ablaze and entirely consumed by fire. In 1972, the burnt remains of a ship were found south of the island. For nearly a year, the wreck was thought to be that of the *Flight.* However, the vessel was about eighty feet in length, far too short to be the *Flight,* and its identity remained unknown. The *Flight* was just one of many yet-to-be discovered wrecks in the Great Lakes.

After finishing their drinks, Kari and Eric boarded the *John Galt* and started upriver to their home. Kari stood on the bow, hands lightly grasping the stainless-steel railing, hair gently tousled by the evening breeze. The sun was going down, and the warm air was filled with the chorus of thousands of crickets and the soft, distant murmur of traffic on Main Street. A few fishermen dotted the riverbank here and there, interspersed with an occasional empty lawn chair, its occupant behind the bushes taking a leak or visiting the next fisherman down the line. ("Ketchinenny?" "Naw." "You?" "Naw.") Eric recognized a few, and he nodded to them as the cabin cruiser plowed slowly upstream. Neither Eric nor Kari noticed the man in the Dodge truck parked in the lot adjacent to *The Boathouse,* nor would they have paid much attention if they had known he was there, anyway.

chapter 19

Air bubbles swarmed around him like a colony of crazed bees, unaffected by the desperate flailing of their helpless prey. Kicking and thrashing, entombed in a dungeon of water, he furiously searched for one precious breath of air amidst the churning bubbles.

Oh God, please . . . air . . . I need air!

That's how the nightmare always ended for Don Garrity. For years, he had been plagued by the same dream—sometimes twice a week, sometimes only once. Occasionally the dream would not come for months. Then, without warning, it would return to taunt him like a mischievous child poking at a dog through a fence with a stick.

The dream always started pleasantly enough. He'd be diving in the ocean amidst hundreds of brilliant, multi-colored fish. He would photograph a few and make his way along the coral reef. Four or five barracudas patrolled the outer perimeter like wary sentries. Occasionally, another barracuda would slowly glide in from the blue mist, seeming to materialize out of nothing. Don would watch the barracudas for a moment, and then return to photographing the various television sets and doorknobs scattered among the coral heads. At least, *this* time it was television sets and doorknobs. Sometimes it was radios. Or cars. Or books, or telescopes, or bubble gum machines. That was the crazy thing about dreams. While you're dreaming, the most bizarre things happen, and they seem perfectly normal at the time. But when you awoke, the dream seemed like two or three scenes from different movies, all edited together at random to create a single, phantasmagoric feature length film.

He was able to get some good shots on this particular dive. An old Zenith nineteen-inch black-and-white television was showing re-runs of the classic *The Three Stooges Meet Hercules*, and Garrity laughed though his regulator when Moe popped Curly a good one right in the eye. A Sears twenty-five-inch color set with a beautiful wood cabinet was playing an infomercial for another worthless piece of workout equipment. *("I use it every day,"* the Famous Athlete was saying. *"You too can look and feel great just like me!!! Just four EASY payments of $39.95! And you can trust me, because I'm a Famous Athlete!")* Garrity ignored the advertisement and continued along the reef. For him, being underwater was as natural as walking. He was happiest here, doing what he loved.

A giant brass doorknob, four feet in diameter, glistened brightly from its perch on a ledge of greenish-blue coral. He took a few pictures from various angles, confident that the *National Geographic* would certainly want a few for their next issue.

Then—

The same thing always happened. He would cruise a little farther along the barrier reef, and it would end. No tapering off, no fading away. It just ended. Don would turn around, and the reef would be gone. Below him—nothing. Above him, the hazy, aqua surface had also disappeared, replaced by an endless, police-light blue. The few barracudas that had been guarding the reef had deserted their posts, leaving Don floating in the barren, eternal depths of the sea.

Then the music would start. Dark, menacing classical music. Don *despised* classical music. As the music got louder, the blue of the ocean around him grew darker and darker. He couldn't swim for the surface because he had no idea which way was up or down. His camera and photo gear were gone. As his feeling of helplessness and terror began to grow, his mask was suddenly ripped from his face by some unseen force. The salt water burned his exposed eyes like hundreds of flaring matches, and he pawed at his face with his gloved hands, trying to douse the flames that scorched his corneas.

The classical music was replaced by a thrashing heavy metal tune. Just as bad as the classical music. The grinding guitars and painful wails roared inside his head. If there ever was a soundtrack for Book of Revelation, Don was sure this tune would fit in nicely. He placed both hands on his regulator, pressed it firmly into his mouth, and bit down on the rubbery silicone mouthpiece that was his only lifeline. Except, after he took one breath, the regulator began to wriggle and squirm in his hands and his mouth. The thundering, throbbing music smashed and pummeled his ears. He inhaled one last gasp of precious air. The regulator hose twisted and writhed in his hands as if possessed—it had been replaced by a slithering, arching snake that was attempting to force its way down his throat.

Recoiling in terror, he tried to pull the snake's head out of his mouth. He could feel its thin, sandpaper-like tongue caressing the roof of his mouth, licking from side to side, back and forth, over his teeth, tongue meeting tongue. It tickled his throat and lapped at his tonsils. Rough scales tore at his lips. The snake's body wrapped itself around Don's waist, crushing his torso and chest until he was sure his ribs were going to implode, snapping and cutting into his internal organs. In a frenzy, he pulled at the snake with all of his might and managed to wrench the reptile from his mouth. It was an insane madness, a terrible, maniacal event that seared his soul and cauterized his mind.

The snake reared its head back and opened its mouth, revealing two long, machete-like incisors. It struck at Don's face, missing by mere inches as Don turned away.

Riiiiinggggg . . . .

The sound was faint, as if coming from very far away, and Don was only vaguely aware of it. In an instant, his full attention had returned to the attacking demon. The snake was very strong. It twisted and turned in his hands, angrily trying to break free. Don struggled to hold his breath, his need for air becoming more and more demanding by the second.

Riiiiinggggg . . . .

Don's attention was distracted by the sound and the serpent broke free from his grasp, biting him squarely in the chest, penetrating through his wetsuit, its razor-sharp teeth spearing through muscle and bone, piercing his lungs. He could hear the crack of his ribs and the rip of ligaments and tendons as the snake's teeth ripped through his unprotected flesh. The snake gnawed and chewed, tearing pieces of tissue away to float freely, suspended in the surrounding waters like chunks of fresh ham.

Riiiiinggggg . . . .

Seawater rushed in to fill the open wounds. It burned at the exposed nerves and pumped into his bloodstream. Unable to hold his breath any longer, he gasped for the last time, expecting the water to rush in with hurricane force, expecting—

Riiiiinggggg . . . .

Air!! He could breathe! Don gasped and choked, taking in gulps of fresh, dry air. He opened his eyes.

He was in his bedroom. His hands clutched the twisted sheet that wrapped his body in a death grip. He was drenched in sweat.

Terrific, he thought. *If I'd sweated any more, I'd have drowned in my sleep.* His heart still pounded furiously.

Riiiiinggggg. He shook the grogginess from his head and rolled over. The sun was coming in through his bedroom window and he guessed it must be nine or ten in the morning. He reached for the phone.

"Hello? . . . Oh, hey!!! . . . Naw, that's all right. It was time to get up anyway . . . Sure, what's up? . . . No kidding? . . . Yeah, go ahead and overnight it and I'll take care of it and get 'em back to you the first of the week." And then the conversation turned to a lot of 'howya beens' and 'gotta get together one of these weekends,' and so on. Twenty minutes later, he bid good-bye, hung up the phone, and went downstairs to make some coffee.

chapter 20

Eric hung up the phone just as Kari came into the room. "I called Don. He said to send the film down, and he'd take care of it."

"Did you ask him to make enlargements?" Kari asked, rustling through the papers, bills, and other debris that littered the kitchen table. Usually she never allowed disarray on the kitchen table or anywhere else, but it was summertime. And not only was it summertime, but it was summertime in Michigan—far too short of a season to be overly concerned about household duties and chores. The minor ones, anyway. The lawn was beginning to look a little long, some bills needed to be paid, the Blazer needed an oil change, and the screen in the kitchen window needed repair. Maybe tomorrow.

"No," Eric answered. "But you know Don. I'm sure he'll send enlargements, duplicates . . . hell, he'll probably *frame* some of them for us."

Eric had met Don Garrity in Texas when both men were in their early twenties. Eric had been working for a big drilling operation that had contracted his father's company to do the dangerous dive work. Don was an underwater photographer struggling to make a living photographing anything that he could be hired to do, but without much success. He had written to Eric's father, asking if he could photograph some oil rig divers in action and conduct interviews with them. Don had wanted to do a feature story on the hazardous work of underwater construction.

At first, Frederick Randall had refused. But Eric persuaded his father to agree to it, saying that it could be good for advertising and public relations. Although the elder Randall was famous in his field, he was known as a difficult person to work for. His standards were ludicrously high, some thought. If a new diver could last two months, he usually lasted forever. Most of the men that worked for Frederick Randall had been with him at least ten years. Diving was a risky business under any condition, and his company had never had a serious accident. Frederick Randall meant to keep it that way.

So when Don showed up on the oil rig and offered his hand in greeting, all Frederick Randall could muster was a 'hrrmmmph' and something to the effect of 'stay out of the way.' Eric had been a little more cordial. The two were about the same age and hit it off pretty well. Don was fascinated with the underwater welding and construction that Eric was skilled at, and Eric was impressed with Don's experience as an underwater photographer. Until then, only a scant few of Don's photos had been published in newspapers and magazines . . . minor publications at that. What Don wanted to do on this particular job was a photo story. He admitted he had never actually written an article before, but he wanted to give it a try.

He stayed on the rig for two weeks, and three months later, the article and photographs appeared as a feature story in *Life* magazine. After that piece, things finally began to happen. The cork had finally popped, the can finally opened. Within a year, Don was ocean-hopping on a regular basis, photographing sharks in the Pacific or killer whales off the shores of Alaska. He'd photographed a shipwreck in the Atlantic, nearly a mile beneath the surface. A salvage company had built a small, unmanned remote controlled submarine. Don designed the camera housing and special lighting needed for video taping at that depth, and went along to assist in operations. The whole project had taken almost six months, and then Don was off again. He was making more money than he'd ever imagined, and, more importantly, he was doing it by working in the field he loved.

Quite often, he would meet up with Eric, who himself was flying off to here and there with his father, working various oil rigs or inspecting and repairing hulls of giant ocean-going freighters. Nevertheless, after awhile, Eric found the work boring. Oh, the danger was always exciting. And the *diving*—Eric had always loved the exhilaration of being underwater. For his fifth birthday, he'd received a cheap mask, snorkel, and fin set from his father. He'd filled the bathtub and spent hours diving among the dangerous coral reefs (two blue sponges) searching for the hidden treasure chest (a yellow bar of *Dial* soap) and fighting off the vicious, man-eating *Johnson's Baby Shampoo* shark. It was only natural that he would follow his father into the same line of work.

But now Eric wanted a little less time flying, more time diving, and more time with Kari, who was also becoming quite an experienced diver herself. He and Kari had logged an impressive total of nearly eight hundred hours underwater together since Kari had been certified to dive.

The turning point, and what would ultimately begin the end of Don's career, began when Eric was finishing a job off the coast of Galveston. Don was in Houston, visiting his parents, and flew to Galveston to spend a couple days diving with Eric. Eric picked him up at the airport and the two headed for the *Oyster Pub* where Don excitedly unfolded a map of the Arctic Circle and spread it across the table, pointing to a small 'X' that had been drawn haphazardly with a pencil. The location coordinates were scribbled below the mark.

"Right here!" Don's finger pressed the paper just below the mark. His eyes glowed, euphoric. "A ship was lost here in 1743! Imagine, Eric! That ship has been sitting there untouched for all that time!"

Eric looked, surprised at the man turned boy-in-a-candy-store that was seated opposite him. Don was usually more quiet and reserved. His bounding enthusiasm caught Eric off-guard. "Well, yeah," he began skeptically, "but so have a lot of *other* ships. There's a lot of wrecks a lot older than that in the ocean."

"But," Don emphasized, his eyebrows flaring up. "*This* ship supposedly went down with real treasure aboard—the Chair of the Nile. It's supposed to be made of solid gold!!" He tapped the spot on the map again with his finger.

Eric knew of the artifact. It was rumored to have been made for Cleopatra herself, it had been stolen in the 1600s, had popped up here and there, and then was stolen again—after which it disappeared entirely.

"So why hasn't anybody else salvaged it, if they know it's there?" Eric asked reasonably, spreading his hands in supplication.

"First off, until now, they only had a vague location of the shipwreck. I know a guy who works for the *National Geographic*. He's spent the last couple of years looking for this wreck. He believes he's finally found it."

"So why doesn't he dive it?" Eric sipped his beer.

"It's a little deep for his liking. And—" Don paused.

"And?" Eric prodded. Don blinked, drifting for a moment. His excitement seemed to fade, but he quickly picked it back up. But Eric noted the slight apprehension in his voice.

"—and because it's under the *ice*. The ship lies in two hundred feet of water under twelve feet of solid ice." Don let his words hang, and he searched Eric's face. There was only a slight raise of eyebrows, only faint lines creasing his brow, but Don knew that he'd got Eric's attention. Lights came on. An engine roared. A click here, an adjustment there . . . bingo. The bat smacked the ball squarely. *We have lift-off. She's all yours, Houston.*

Solid ice, Eric thought. He *loved* to ice dive. He actually enjoyed the extreme cold, the complete solitude, and the beauty. Under the surface, the ice formed spectacular stalactites and transparent, crystal mountain ranges. It was like diving in another world, on another planet.

Two more beers came, and among the loud music of a live classic rock band and chattering patrons, the two men discussed the logistics of such an adventure. Don was uncharacteristically being the more positive 'let's do it now' type, and Eric, in a complete reverse, was being a bit more analytical, weighing the pros and cons of such an expedition. *It would be exciting,* he thought. *And Kari could come. She might not want to dive, but she would love to be along for something like this.* And it might be dangerous, yes. But boring? Hell, no.

"Well, whaddya say?" Don said as he lifted the glass to his mouth. The waiter at the bar signaled last call, and the two men declined a final round.

"I say," Eric said as the two stood up and Eric dropped a twenty on the table. His eyes were aflame. *"I say, we go find ourselves a ship."*

It was to be the last time Don ever dived with Eric. In fact, it was to be the last time Don ever dived at all. Except in his nightmares.

chapter 21

Don sipped his coffee and read the morning paper. The nightmare was fresh in his memory, even though it had been interrupted by the phone call. For this he was thankful, but he knew the nightmares would come again. And again. And *again*. If he hadn't been awakened, it would have continued like it always had before. The snake would swim off, and Don would be left alone in the dark, deep waters of the ocean. Then a chilling cold would sweep through his body. He would look up and find himself staring at a beautiful mountain range of ice. The feeling of terror began to leave him, and in his dream he cruised effortlessly through the water, taking pictures of the ice regions with his camera that was now held in his hands. Only for a split second did he wonder how he had found the camera, for he remembered losing it while battling the snake. But then the thought passed quickly, as they do in all dreams, leaving him to take photo after photo.

Then would come the chilling realization. The rope connecting him to the hole in the ice was no longer around his waist. He began to pound on the thick, unforgiving ice, kicking, trying to cut the ice with his knife. Without warning, he began falling away from the ice, falling to God knows where.

This is where he usually woke up. Or at least, he *hoped* he would. There had been many nights when he didn't awake, and the dream would begin again, like he'd sat between movies at the theater. He imagined an usher walking up and down the aisles, sweeping his flashlight to and fro, making sure everyone was out of the theater. The usher would come to where he was sitting, flash a sinister smile, and shine the light in Don's face.

"Ahhhh, Mr. Garrity! Now, now, now! Is it a DOUBLE-FEATURE night, Mr. Garrity? Oh, I think it is, Don. I think tonight is a double-feature!! And do you know what? I think tonight is even BETTER!! Yes, I think tonight is a TRIPLE-FEATURE, Mr. Garrity!! In fact, this movie will be playing for as long as you live, Don Garrity . . . and probably even longer!!! Oh yesssss . . . Even longer . . . ."

Don poured another cup of coffee, and shook away thoughts of ice, snakes, ushers, and water. Eric Randall had called, for crying out loud. He hadn't spoken with Eric for two years. And even longer since the . . . .

Don couldn't think about it. Oh, he wanted to. How many therapists had he seen in the past couple years? Three? Four? *Four.* Four shrinks in three years. And they all told him the same thing: 'Repressed Memory Syndrome.' They said that he had tried so hard to forget that he had erased his memory banks. No, not erased. *Moved.* He had shifted part of his memory to an iron vault inside his head, locked the door and thrown away the key. Only he had the key, or at least that's what the Sigmund Freuds and Carl Jungs told him. *Hypnosis and psychotherapy will help,* they told him. *You need to re-live your experience and deal with the trauma. You didn't deal with it before, and that's why you locked it away in the First National Bank of the Cerebellum. Oh, and by the way, that'll be two-hundred bucks for the first hour.*

Screw that, Don thought. He already knew he suffered a trauma of some sort. He knew where the trauma had occurred and who he was with. He had a pretty good idea what he was doing, at least up to a point. But he knew that if he could force himself to deal with this, then maybe the nightmares would stop. Maybe he wouldn't close his eyes at night and see the devilish theater usher coming towards him.

Double-feature tonight, Mr. Garrity? Triple-feature?

Don had tried to remember what had happened, really tried. Maybe it was more than just locked away, maybe he would never recall what had happened.

But Eric knew. Eric must've dealt with it, somehow, some way. Maybe it just didn't affect Eric the same way it affected Don. Nevertheless, the two men never again spoke of what had occurred that day.

And Don Garrity was not about to ask.

chapter 22

Kari woke first and pulled back the curtains to reveal a dull, cast-iron gray morning. Marbled, cellulite clouds seemed to hang just over the trees, and a fine mist was falling. She closed the curtain and glanced at the bright red digital *7:58* glaring from the night table, then glanced at Eric who was still sound asleep.

She walked quietly to the kitchen, pausing only to swipe one of Eric's large flannel shirts and his maize-and-blue University of Michigan sweat pants. The sweats were slightly large on her, but she couldn't care less. She was walking to the kitchen, not down a runway.

She started the coffee and began going through the books in the bookshelf, looking for the one that listed all the ships lost on the Great Lakes. She remembered the book as being very thorough, providing intricate details of the ships, their cargo, their place of departure, their destination, why they were lost, and the locations of their foundering.

The coffee had finished brewing and she was still looking. She and Eric had collected hundreds of books, most of them on the three massive shelves downstairs in what Eric called his 'den.' Kari called it the 'Bottomless Pit of Hell,' and did not relish the thought of having to look for the book there. Downstairs overflowed with Eric's papers, magazines, and even dive equipment, and it was a wonder he could find *anything* down there.

But suddenly, there it was—*The Complete Guide to Great Lakes Shipwrecks* by Arthur J. Hibbler. She pulled the heavy text from the shelf. The book was filled with hundreds of photos, drawings, charts, and graphs. She flipped the pages, scanning them quickly for anything of interest. There were *thousands* of ships that had been lost in the Great Lakes. Schooners, barges, steamers, tugs, freighters—the list was endless. The Lakes were littered with the remains of vessels lost as far back as the 1700s.

If only we had a name to go on, she thought. Kari couldn't wait to dive on the wreck again, anticipating the rush of adrenaline, the mystery and intrigue of finding something that had lain hidden for decades, perhaps hundreds of years.

After flipping through the entire book and not finding anything of note, she placed the book on the table. She shook the image of the wreck from her mind, poured two cups of coffee and carried them to the bedroom. Eric was asleep, but he stirred as she sat on the bed next to him.

"You look tired. I'll let you sleep a little longer," she said.

"Nah," he said groggily. "I'm up." Eric sat up, and Kari handed him a mug. He sipped the hot liquid. "Raining?" he asked.

"Yeah," Kari replied. "Just started. It's a little colder, too." She peaked out the corner of the curtain. Then: "I've been looking in the books, but I didn't find anything about the wreck. I'm sure it's in there, but we don't have enough to go on."

"Do you really think it could be the *Flight*?" he asked.

"That's my best guess," Kari replied. "But there are so many wrecks that haven't been found. It could be any one of them. On the next dive do you think we could go inside?"

"You mean penetration?" he asked, after another sip of coffee.

"Yeah," Kari nodded. "Inside. It would give us—"

"Full penetration?" he interrupted, smirking.

"Yes. Or do you think—" She stopped speaking, noticing Eric's grin and his raised eyebrows.

"Right now, I've kind of got my own ideas on *full penetration*, Mrs. Randall. Wink, wink." He put one hand around her waist and one behind her neck and pulled her towards him.

"I hate wearing these damn clothes of yours anyway," she said playfully, wriggling out of Eric's sweats. The flannel shirt fell to the floor. Then they were together, their coffees cooling on the night stand.

Outside, thunder grumbled in the distance, and the wind picked up. It poured for most of the day.

chapter 23

The dark chords of Pink Floyd's *Comfortably Numb* echoed from the stereo in the cabin of the *John Galt*. It had rained for several days, but now the front had passed through, offering a reprieve from the heat. To the west, popcorn clouds hung in suspended animation like misty mobiles of the gods. Waves were less than a foot, and the afternoon was tranquil. Today would be the second dive on the shipwreck, and they were certain they would find a name and identify the vessel. Eric and Kari prepared their gear as the music filled the boat.

Hello . . . .

The slow, meditative voice of David Gilmour reverberated through the cabin.

. . . is there anybody in there . . .?

Kari stuffed her Nikon into her gear bag, along with her

flashlight. Eric looked down into the deep waters of Lake Huron. The waters were a sparkling denim blue, radiant beneath the sun and sky.

. . . just nod if you can hear me . . . .

The sun penetrated a few feet into the water, then the powerful darkness would not let the wavering curtains of light intrude any farther into the depths.

. . . is there anyone home . . . ?

Eric cut off the Pink Floyd tune in mid-song. The two helped each other with their gear and Eric jumped fins first, followed by Kari, into the cool waters of Lake Huron. They followed the anchor line down, and this time, they were in luck: the ship appeared in Kari's flashlight beam before they had even made it to the bottom.

The two made their way slowly along the port side of the ship, carefully looking for a name. They made a sweep around the wreck, closely examining the stern, searching unsuccessfully for any indication of an identity. Eric checked his air. *Three minutes.* He signaled to Kari with three fingers and then thumbs up, and she nodded.

Hell, Kari thought. *We're never going to find the name of this thing.* The two divers floated motionless alongside the massive wreck, pouring their lights over the deck. Dishes, silverware, the ship's wheel, and even an old whiskey bottle were visible in the beams.

She must have been some ship in her time, Kari thought, scanning a portion of the deck with her light. *I'll bet she was incredible looking under full sail.* She marveled at the condition of the ship, which, despite its apparent age, seemed remarkably intact, thanks mostly to the fact that no other divers had discovered her yet.

But Kari knew it was only a matter of time. Soon, the wreck would be discovered by other sport divers, many of whom wouldn't see any harm in taking just one souvenir. Problem was, if everyone decided to take just 'one' souvenir, the wreck would be plundered in no time at all. The wreck would become nothing more than a picked over pile of boards, a crushed carcass that would resemble a junkyard more than a shipwreck.

Kari continued on, sweeping the bright beam along the deck. She was agile underwater, even with over one hundred pounds of dive gear, and her movements were slow and sure.

There has got to be a name here somewhere, she thought again. *It's got to be—*

Wait a minute! She waved a hand in front of Eric's flashlight beam to get his attention. *This was a schooner, which means it had sails. Which means it had rigging, which means it must have had a capstan.* She motioned Eric to follow her as she glided over the wreck.

The ship's crew used the capstan for exerting the power required to heave on a rope to haul in or let out a sail or for pulling in or releasing an anchor chain. Many ships, especially the older ones, had their name engraved in the brass capstan cover.

Kari headed toward the ship's bow. Eric tapped her on the leg and she stopped, turning to look at him. He signaled with his hand, pointing to his gauge. Through their masks, her eyes caught his.

One minute.

She slowed as she reached the bow, scanning the deck with the flashlight. Silt and debris covered the deck, making it hard to discern discrete objects.

. . . and if there's a capstan, there must be . . .

A shiny glint reflected in the beam of the flashlight.

. . . a capstan cover. And if it has a capstan cover . . . .

The capstan was about twelve inches high and eight inches around and, barring some silt and stains, was in very good condition. It was caked with ruddy sediment, and Kari carefully brushed the debris from the cover by waving her hands a few inches over it. As the silt and debris floated away, Kari could make out fine lines and a design of some sort.

There has to be a name, she thought.

Eric took the flashlight from Kari's hand to give her both hands with which to work. She rubbed the capstan cover, and the smudge-like stains wiped away easily. She took one of the lights from Eric and brought it closer to the shiny brass cover.

A design.

Kari couldn't quite make out what it was, for debris had settled into the lines of the engraving. But there was no mistaking the letters below the muddled design. Big, clear letters nearly an inch-and-a-half high.

The Brittany.

Kari carefully cleared the cover of as much silt and debris as she could with her gloved hands. Totally absorbed in her task, she took one picture, then another, until a tap on her shoulder told her it was time to go.

chapter 24

The first prints were slowly appearing. In the darkroom, Don began to make out preliminary images on the sheets of light-sensitive paper. Kari had included a note saying that the photos were rushed and might not turn out at all and that she had snapped a few of them by placing the camera into some of the open spaces of the shipwreck and clicking away blindly. However, the first photo was quite clear. It was of the outside of the wreck and what looked like part of the mainmast and deck.

Don was struck by the apparent good condition of the wreck. After a short while underwater, most vessels deteriorated rapidly. This ship appeared to be old, yet it seemed almost untouched by time.

"Nice job, guys," he said quietly to himself. "Found yourself a good one."

The next photo *did* show some damage. It was a photo of the deck with a few boards and debris strewn about. Silt covered most of the rigging. Zebra mussels clustered about in various places. *My God*, thought Don. He whistled. *Rigging! There's still rigging on the masts.*

He looked down at the images forming on the paper. One was beginning to show the inside of a cabin. The flash had illuminated the entire space, and Don could make out an old chair and a few small crates.

And something else.

Oh my God, he thought, straining his eyes to make out the slowly-developing image. Don stared in disbelief at the all-too clear scene unfolding in the developer. He couldn't believe what he was seeing.

"*Holy shit,*" he whispered beneath his breath. The image appearing before him was disturbing, and Don stared, wide-eyed, watching the features emerge.

Good God. What the hell is this?

He developed the rest of the roll but didn't find anything out of the ordinary on the remaining film. He held up the single, still-wet photo in his hands. He made two prints and two enlargements. Leaving his materials and chemicals right where they were, he closed up the darkroom and headed for the phone.

chapter 25

Ed was probably right, thought Phillip, as the Bayliner plowed through the waters southeast of Bois Blanc island, scouring the area where the other boat had been. *The chances of anybody finding the ship by chance were . . . well . . . jack-daddy slim and none. Even if somebody knew what they were looking for.*

The rain had finally ended and Phillip was alone on the boat, criss-crossing the Channel. Often something would show up on the depthfinder that hadn't been visible the first time around. That's what made searching for a particular wreck so difficult. Phillip was beginning to think that their quarry could have been lost in Lake Michigan. The Laurentian Channel extended quite a distance past the bridge, turning south just below St. Helena Island, then running about fifty miles before it shallowed out and faded away.

Phillip glanced at the sonar again. Earlier in the summer near the Mackinac Bridge, he had charted the huge remains of the sunken freighter *Cedarville* and the *M. Stalker*, a one hundred thirty-five-foot schooner that had sunk in 1887. The *M. Stalker* was not in the Channel, nor was the *Cedarville*. But they were relatively close, and both were very popular dive sites. Often, Phillip had seen the bright red-and-white dive flags floating near boats anchored over these wrecks. This didn't worry Phillip in the least. Most of those divers were on a charter, paying a divemaster to take them to the wrecks, and most were not past the intermediate skill level. Divers of this caliber wouldn't be—or *shouldn't* be—diving anywhere near the Channel.

What bothered Phillip were the more skilled and dedicated searchers. Some *had* been successful. The *Newell Eddy* was proof of that, as well as the *Smith B. Cooperan* and the *North Hawk*, a wreck that created a big controversy not only in the diving community, but in the courts as well. The *North Hawk* was a schooner that had gone down during a violent storm in the early 1900s. She had been found by a search team from a university in 1990, and there had been a great deal of publicity about the find in the papers and on the radio and TV. Its cargo was rumored to include $60,000 in cash. In addition, there was jewelry said to be worth another $15,000, making the wreck of the *North Hawk* a very lucrative find indeed.

The *North Hawk* had foundered just outside the Laurentian Channel and rested fully upright in good condition in one hundred thirty feet of water. Although the researchers did not give an exact location, the news brought divers and wreck plunderers from everywhere, and prompted an immediate lawsuit from descendants of the deceased crew, who insisted that the wreck and its treasures belonged to them. Further, because it was located in the Straits Area Shipwreck Preserve, it was a federal crime to take anything from the wreck. The descendants won the rights to the ship in court, but when the wreck was finally penetrated, the divers were heartbroken and enraged to find that the ship had already been plundered and everything of any real value had been stolen.

Phillip, Ed, and Jimmy had charted and dived on the wreck a year before. When they found that it was not the object of their search they had initially left it alone without further exploration. After hearing the news about the potential monetary value of the discovery, the three men returned to the site and relieved her of her fortune in only two nights. Ed had the connections to unload just about anything, and the three men split the take. Ed had shipped much of the jewelry to a friend in Florida who wanted it for his private collection. The paper money had long since disintegrated, but the three recovered many silver dollars and other valuable items.

Adding insult to injury, Jimmy, using his dive knife, had carved a personal note in the decaying wooden hull for the next visitors:

YOU SNOOZ, YOU LOOZ!

Divers had photographed the desecration, and the story made the front page of the Detroit Free Press. Rewards were offered for information leading to the arrest of the perpetrators, but no responsible parties were ever found.

Later that morning, Phillip searched the waters north of Bois Bland Island. Nothing. He rounded the island to return to the channel and immediately cursed under his breath. The blue-and-white cabin cruiser had returned. The boat sat anchored, and a dive flag floated about twenty feet off the bow.

Shit! he thought. What in the hell are they doing in the Channel at the same spot they were in the other day, unless—

No. The chances are too small, he thought. But he knew that he would have to check it out. Maybe we missed something while we were farting around doing something else.

Making a note of the cruiser's location, Phillip headed for Bois Blanc Island to hang out at the Island Bar and have lunch. Two hours later, Phillip saw the blue-and-white cabin cruiser making its way slowly towards the mainland. He made sure they were well out-of-sight before he motored out to the location. To make it look good, he set up the downriggers for a little 'fishing.'

Who knows? Might even catch something today.

Phillip scoured the waters for the better part of the afternoon, but found nothing. Well, if they've found anything, they'll be back. Phillip turned the boat around, and headed the eight miles back to the marina.

chapter 26

Jimmy Durand pulled the needle from his arm as the Tetranobol rocketed into his bloodstream. He had no need for a tourniquet on his upper arm to help find an entry point, because he had veins that looked like a mole had burrowed under his skin. He took a deep breath, flexed, and tossed the needle into the garbage. He couldn't remember how long he had been on the steroids. Ten years? Twelve? When he first started on the 'roids, he was twenty-six—generally considered a little old to begin a competitive bodybuilding career. He had already been a pretty good size at the time. Just over six foot and one hundred ninety-five pounds. Years of pumping iron had given him size and definition, but he couldn't get quite big enough, couldn't get the bulk he wanted. He had trained hard, eaten right, did all the things the pros told him to do, but found he couldn't compete with the gigantic, inhuman monsters on the professional circuit.

So he hit the juice.

With Tetranobol, the 'Big T,' Jimmy's weight surged from one hundred ninety-five to an incredible two hundred thirty pounds in six months. His chest increased to gargantuan proportions, his thick back flared, and his shoulders were heaped and rounded like bowling balls. His quadriceps were the size of tree trunks and his calves the size of regulation footballs. And *nobody* messed with him. Not any more.

Growing up, Jimmy had been skinny. His older brothers had been larger, stronger, and faster than he. Whatever Jimmy did, his brothers could do better. A's and B's in school, while Jimmy settled for C's and D's. Jimmy got the shit beat out of him on a subscription basis. But the worst part of it was that when Jimmy wasn't being wailed on at school, he was being knocked into the next zip code by his old man.

Jimmy's father was what his neighbor called a 'Heritage Drinker.' *'I swear, when that so'ma bitch dies, his fambly's gonna get sympathy cards from them people what make Jack Daniels, Jim Beam, and Boone's Farm. 'Probly pay for the funeral, too.'* That astute assessment was courtesy of Earl Heddelsen, the Durand's neighbor and Jimmy's father's erstwhile drinking partner. But the elder Durand could drink him under the table, through the floorboards, and right into the ground. Nobody out drank Jimmy's dad. And when he came home, especially after the Whiskey, Ice, and Water Olympics, Jimmy's dad was in the mood for *sports*. Baseball was his favorite game. Jimmy had never forgotten the night his father came home thinking he was Mickey Mantle. His favorite bat was an oak lamp stand about four feet long.

"Jimmmeeeeee?" his father slurred, after stumbling through the front door.

No answer.

"JimmEEEE! DAMN it, son!!! Where'na hell arya?? Where ina . . . ina HELL are ya?!" Alcohol burned through his brain. Jimmy, then eight, remained in his bed, too afraid to speak, too terrified to run and hide, fearing even worse things if he tried to get away. He heard his father's heavy, drunken footsteps coming down the hall, heard the dull scraping of the lamp stand as his father dragged it against the wall.

"Jimmy!! Where you been, boy? What kinda . . . kinda trouble you been in, boy?" His father stopped at the doorway of Jimmy's bedroom, belched, then slouched against the doorjamb.

Tap tap.

The elder Durand knocked the lamp stand on the wood of the door frame. "I can . . . can see you there, right there, you little fu . . . fucker. You better answer me, boy. I says what kind of trouble you been in, you little shit-fer-brains screwup?"

Tap tap.

"I'm a gonna give you to the count of three to tell me where you was all day. I told you . . . you . . . to mow the lawn. I come home tonight and the FUCKIN' LAWNS NOT MOWED!!!" The liquor exploded like gasoline, and the shockwave pounded the dark room and echoed through the house. "What in the hell have you been doin' . . . doin' . . . all day?" He leaned back too far and almost fell down. "Shit. Fuck." He recovered and glared towards Jimmy's bed in the darkness. Jimmy could barely make out his father's bulging belly filling up the bedroom doorway.

"Are you laughin' at me, boy?"

No answer.

Tap tap.

"Now son . . . ." His father changed tactics. "I know there's a good reason why you didn't get the lawn mowed today. I jes . . . jes . . . know there is. I jes need ta hear it. Now, tell me what the problem was, and we'll get this settled, no . . . no problem." He leaned on the lamp stand.

Jimmy managed to whisper a weak voice. "There . . . there wasn't any gas in it," he whimpered. "And . . . and none in the can. I—"

Thud. Thud. Jimmy's father tapped the heavy lamp stand on the floor, heavier than before.

"I . . . I looked for gas. I did." Jimmy's voice trembled. "I looked but—"

"But you dinnet find none, didja?" Jimmy's dad sounded paternal . . . almost—*fatherly*.

"No."

"'No' what?" Hiccup. Cough. Grunt.

"No, sir." Jimmy was beginning to hope that his father might understand, that he would realize that his brother had forgotten to get the five-gallon can filled with gas like he was supposed to. He sat up a little in bed and pulled the covers down from his chin a tiny bit.

Thud. Thud.

"An I spose you jest couldn't . . . couldn't . . . walk down to the store and get some now could you?"

Jimmy was silent.

"Damn it, son. Ans . . . answer me." He belched again.

"You told me . . . not to . . . not to ever cross the highway . . . without—" Jimmy's voice was strained and shivering.

His father stopped leaning and did his best to stand up straight. "You know whatcher problem is? Huh? Do ya?" The elder Durand stepped through the doorway and stood at the foot of Jimmy's bed, leering at him. "Well, I'll tell ya. Yer a Goddamn loser. That bitch shoulda took you with her. That's why she left, you know. Couldn't take living with you no more. You hear me, you little shit-fer-brains? She shoulda took you with her, but nooooo. Filthy whore." Jimmy's mother had finally left after years of abuse and not Jimmy, nor anyone for that matter, knew where she was. The youngest Durand could barely remember her.

Thud. Thud.

Jimmy's father held the lamp stand in his right hand and raised it to his waist. "Son, you get out of that bed."

The seconds dragged by as Jimmy lay immobilized with fear. The stench of whiskey and cigarettes was sickening and Jimmy felt like he was going to puke.

Then Jimmy's dad stepped up to home plate.

The crowd began to cheer, and the sportscaster offered a play-by-play description. *"Now batting . . . Charles Durand. Chuck's had a good season so far this year, especially right here at home in his own stadium. He's been known to drill' em right into the rafters here at the ol' ball park. Let's see how he does tonight. Here's the wind-up and the pitch and . . . HOLY SMOKES!!! He put that one WAY into the upper deck!!! The crowd has gone mad as this fine ball player makes the rounds . . . but wait . . . he's . . . he's still carrying the bat . . . he's still swinging . . . he's still swinging as he rounds the bases!!!"*

Jimmy's father took a deep breath and exhaled, his lungs wheezing and sputtering from years of smoking. And he'd only recently given up smoking pot, saying that it was bad for his health and it wasn't grown as good as it used to be, anyway.

"You jes aren't never gonna learn, are ya." It was a statement, not a question. He raised the lamp stand above his head and brought it down full force on Jimmy's legs. Jimmy screamed, and his father placed his hand over Jimmy's mouth and pushed the back of his head into the headboard. *"And you can jes shut yer worthless trap, you little bastard."*

Crack!! He brought the lamp stand down square on Jimmy's knees. Jimmy's tiny body rocked in agony. He tried to scream, to get away, but his father was too strong. Every time Jimmy tried to move, his father tightened his grip on Jimmy's mouth. He felt like his jaw was going to break.

Well, not *yet*. That would be another moment or two.

"Now, I wouldn't be havin' to do this if you was . . . if you was a GOOD boy, now. But yer so damned stupid!!! If you was like yer brothers, now . . . ."

Crack!! The blow struck Jimmy in the stomach, knocking the wind from him and leaving him gasping for air. His father tightened his grip on Jimmy's mouth and moved his hands up on Jimmy's face, covering his nostrils. "If you was really worth a shit, I wouldn't hafta be doin' this alla time." As he released his grip on Jimmy's face, he swung the lamp stand one final time, catching

Jimmy smack-square in the jaw, knocking him off the bed and on the floor. "Now if you was . . . ." But Jimmy wasn't listening any more. His limp body lay unconscious on the floor. Blood trickled from his nose and mouth.

"Shit. Little bastard can't even stand to be diss . . . diss-a-plinned." He gave Jimmy one final kick in the ribs, dropped the lamp stand on the floor and walked out to the kitchen to get something to eat. Jimmy, in a daze, tried to lift his head as he lay on the floor. His face screamed in pain. His legs ached. His cheek was wet with something and blood had formed a pool in his mouth, which poured out onto the floor as he slowly moved his head. The images of what had happened slowly came back to him through a hazy fog. He heard the refrigerator door open in the kitchen, its dim light illuminating the hall.

"Jimmy!!!! Son of a bitch!! Did you eat all the fucking ice cream, you little bastard?!"

And the footsteps came again.

chapter 27

Jimmy was twelve when his father finally drank himself to death. He had come home from school to find his father dead on the floor, half-naked. His eyes were bulging, his skin was pale egg-white, and a bottle was still in his hand. Jimmy had left him there for nearly a week, and the smell had become horrendous, drifting outside and around the neighborhood. The thick, pungent odor had drawn thousands of flies and maggots. All the while, Jimmy had gone to school, eaten in the kitchen, and completed his homework while watching TV, stepping around his dear departed dad, seemingly not even noticing the caustic stench of rotting flesh in the California heat. A neighbor had finally peered through the window and discovered the body. The coroner estimated that Jimmy's father had consumed nearly a gallon of whiskey in a half-hour period.

California Social Services came and took Jimmy with them and for the next few years, he bounced around between orphanages and foster homes. Still skinny and meek, he was an easy target for school bullies and gangs alike, which were everywhere in the Los Angeles area. When he was seventeen, he ran away from foster care. Skirmishes with the law, a few B & E's here and there, and he was off again, to the next town up the road, the next opportunity.

Until he met Sharon.

He had been living in San Diego, sleeping on the beach and working part-time at a Coney Island hot dog shop. Sharon was a drifter herself, hitchhiking from Salt Lake City to the west coast. Like Jimmy, she too was sleeping on the beach, unable to afford housing. The two hitchhiked to Phoenix where Sharon's sister lived. There Jimmy got a job working construction, which paid reasonably well, and Sharon worked as a bartender at a nightclub.

It was Sharon's sister who got Jimmy interested in bodybuilding. She managed a gym, and Jimmy could work out free and use the sauna and whirlpool, if he helped out cleaning or doing odd jobs. He learned to enjoy the tight soreness of his muscles after pumping iron. His muscles ached and groaned but he kept at it, relishing the pain. He watched what the other bodybuilders were doing and imitated their workouts. This, combined with Sharon and his construction job, made Jimmy complete. He felt like he was *somebody*. He felt like he was going somewhere.

He and Sharon got married and they moved to Las Vegas with the construction company, for which Jimmy now worked as an assistant foreman. Sharon got a job managing a *Records Galore!* store. Both liked their jobs, made pretty good money, and could afford a reasonably nice apartment and a new car. He and Sharon were happy. They went out to the movies, dinner, and to parties. But not, of course, to the beach. They could never go there. No, no, no. Not the beach. Someone might see Sharon's bruises, and she would have to make up excuses. Again.

The phone woke Jimmy from his nap. It was late afternoon and he had nodded off on the couch. "Yeah? Hey what's up . . . no, just taking a snooze . . . uh-huh. Probably just screwin' around in the Channel . . . yeah . . . well, I was planning on heading up in a day or so anyway . . . look, handle it, will ya? I'll be up tomorrow afternoon."

The drive to Cheboygan from Detroit took Jimmy four hours. He had packed his clothes and left around ten in the morning, not bothering to tell Sharon or leave her a note. He rarely did. Sometimes he was gone for weeks on end and she'd have no idea where he'd gone. *She can just deal with it*, Jimmy reasoned.

He wasn't bothered too much by Phillip's call. Phillip had said that he and Ed had seen a couple divers diving in the Channel at the same location. Twice. *Big deal*, Jimmy thought. But a nagging thought kept popping up in the back of his mind. *What if . . .?* He pressed down harder on the gas pedal and the Trans Am responded, inching up to eighty-five miles per hour as he headed north on I-75.

chapter 28

Below deck, young Daniel Hawthorne lay in his bed, listening to the sounds of the schooner churning through the water. Every so often he can hear the Captain on deck, his occasional rumbling coughs drowned out by the gentle creaking and rocking of the ship.

After he is certain that the others are asleep, Daniel slowly swings his feet to the floor. He waits, listening for anything that would indicate that the other passengers might be awake.

Nothing.

He stands up quietly and walks out the open door of the tiny cabin he shares with the Captain and Jack Malloy, the only other crew member. Jack is already sawing logs—pretty loudly at that—and Daniel figures he will probably sleep through almost anything. He stumbles as he walks through the door, recovers, pauses to listen again for any indication anyone has heard, and walks down a dark corridor deeper into the ship. He isn't completely familiar with the inside of the ship and where everything is, but he is able to make his way without creating any further disturbance.

Slowly, his eyes adjust to the darkness and he identifies the outline of the cargo hold door. Quietly he pushes it open. It is totally dark, but he dares not risk lighting a candle or an oil lamp. He feels his way through the darkness, moving slowly, careful not to disturb any boxes or bags stored the previous day. Daniel searches with his hands through the piles of boxes, judging by feel more than anything.

There it is. Daniel puts his hands on the large wood-and-metal trunk. The cold steel of the locks and rivets that hold the box together glimmer faintly in the darkness. The chest itself is nearly seven feet long, over two feet high and two feet wide. There are brass handles on both ends that, for its current purpose, are perfectly useless for the task they were designed for. It would have taken eight or ten men to pick it up. In fact, the chest had been hoisted up and loaded by ropes tied to horses. The ceiling above had been removed to allow the chest entry into the hold. When it had successfully loaded, the planks had been replaced.

This is it, Daniel thinks. This is why the Captain seems nervous. Maybe he thinks that someone saw them loading the chest. Maybe he thinks that someone else knows what's inside.

He stares at the chest for a few more moments, then carefully creeps back to his bunk in the gloomy darkness below deck.

Christopher Knight

chapter 29

Phillip walked into *Goodtime Charlie's* where about a dozen patrons were busy on the fast track to a good buzz, shooting pool, laughing, and mouthing the words to an *AC/DC* song on the jukebox. The night was a scorcher, and the few run-down oscillating fans that sat on various tables didn't do much to quell the punky heat, as evident by the fine Saran-Wrap film of perspiration across arms and faces. Phillip nodded to a few people that he had casually met and walked past them and around the pool table.

Backwoods redneck hicks, he thought, as he smiled and nodded again. To Phillip, anyone who lived north of Bay City was a redneck hick. That's all there was to it. *There must be an imaginary line*, Phillip had always thought. He really had no reason to assert such a claim that anyone *north* of Bay City was in any way much different than anyone *south* of Bay City, but that wasn't the point. It was an ignorance that, despite its vastness, Phillip Keanan held without reservation. Northern Michigan lacked the modern conveniences of larger metropolitan areas, or so he believed. Everything was so small, and the pace was just so damned . . . *slow.*

Maybe if you guys sped things up a bit, we'd all be so much happier, he thought, as he smiled at a man he knew only well enough to acknowledge. He made his way to the bar where Ed sat feeding the very latest of his fishing fairy tales to Charlie Stachniack, the owner/manager/bartender/waiter.

"Here's the man right here, Charlie," Ed proudly boasted, slapping Phillip on the shoulder as he sat down. "If it wasn't for this brave soul right here, we wouldn't ever have got that fish on board!! Ain't that right, Phil?" He glanced sideways and winked at Phillip and then looked innocently back at the bartender.

"That's right, Cap'n Ed," Phillip replied, playing along with the game. Charlie Stachniack reached into a cooler under the bar and popped the top on a Budweiser, Phillip's usual, and handed it to him. He tipped and took a long sip. "One hell of a fish, that thing was."

"The biggest yet this year!" Ed chimed in, all six chins jiggling back and forth. "That fish got right up to the boat and went through the damn net. Ripped the nylon right from the aluminum. If it wasn't for the quick thinking of ol' Phil here—" He slapped Phillip again on the shoulder and took a sip of his own beer. "—if it wasn't for the quick thinking of Phil, that fish would be gone."

Charlie's eyes were as wide as dinner plates. He had known Ed and Phillip for a couple years, and didn't know much about either of them, but he knew they were pretty incredible fishermen, along with that crazy son of a bitch, Jimmy. Charlie didn't like him one bit, didn't like him in his bar because when that boy drank, he *drank*. But you didn't walk up to a guy his size and tell him not to come in here anymore, no sir. You'd have better luck pissin' on a pit bull. But the three of them came in with the most incredible fish stories that Charlie had ever heard and he fell for them all, hook, line, and sinker. Ed, Phillip, and even that monster, Jimmy, were damn near idols to Charlie. Of course, Charlie Stachniack wasn't known around town for his smarts or quick wit.

"So what did you do, Phil?" he asked, taking the bait.

"What did he do?! *What did he do?!*" Ed interrupted, exploding in an excited frenzy. "Why, he jumped into the water and battled that nasty bastard with his bare hands! He grabbed that bugger by the gills like this . . . ." Ed reached over the counter and grabbed one of Charlie's cheeks, twisting and pulling, pulling and twisting. ". . . and then he beat that fish on the head 'til it was so dizzy he couldn't swim no more. Just laid there with his belly up, barely alive."

"Barely alive," Phillip echoed, sipping his Bud and setting it back onto the table.

"Well, howdja get 'er in the boat?" Charlie was suckered. Again.

"Get her on the boat?!" Ed exclaimed. "Well, we never did. Tell him, Phil."

"That's right Charlie. We never did." Phillip sipped his beer again and looked at Ed, hoping to buy more time to figure out where in the hell this story was going. Then he smiled and looked at Charlie. "Well, you know Chuck," as Phillip sometimes called him, "I wouldn't blame you if you didn't believe me, but dammit, Ed saw the whole thing."

Ed put his right palm in the air as if he were being sworn into public office. "The whole thing," Ed repeated solemnly. He closed his eyes as he spoke, then opened them. Charlie stared, captivated.

"And you know Ed doesn't stretch the truth when it comes to these things," Phillip concluded.

"On my mother's grave" Ed added. He lowered his hand and placed it over his heart, closed his eyes again, and hung his head.

"But whad'ja do?" Charlie pleaded.

"I had Ed throw me a line—a *heavy* line—and I ran that line right through that fish's gills, out 'er mouth, tied 'er around that fish's head and we towed that beast to shore." Phillip sat back on the barstool, and picked up his beer like a champion.

"King Salmon," Ed said, matter-of-factly. "Went forty-nine pounds."

"Forty-nine pounds?! You still got' er?" Charlie had stopped drying the glass in his hand and looked at Ed, then Phillip, then Ed again.

"Hell yeah, we still got 'er." Ed raised his thumb and pumped it over his shoulder. "We shipped her in ice down to my taxidermist in the Keys. He's gonna mount that bitch, and I'm gonna keep her in my bungalow in Key West."

"Well, didja get a . . .?" Charlie was going to say 'picture,' but was interrupted by several patrons.

"Hey, Charlie!" the call rang out from somewhere near the pool table. " Four more Pabst drafts! And a shot of Tequila for Ray here!!" Charlie was gone in an instant, scurrying to fill the order. As the owner/manager/bartender/waiter, he usually kept pretty busy, even when the place was empty.

Phillip turned to Ed, addressing him in a quieter, serious tone. "That blue-and-white cabin cruiser was back again today. They were diving."

Ed raised his eyebrows. "Did you get a good look at the boat?" It was more of an order than a question. He shifted on his barstool, his enormous waistline bulging over his belt.

"Not really. Old boat. Maybe thirty feet long and in pretty good shape. The *John Glip* or *John Gump* or something like that." Phillip swallowed the last of his Budweiser. "After they left, I went over the area pretty good, but I didn't chart anything. But they could've found something that I missed. It's deep water there. Averages about two hundred feet. I wouldn't normally be concerned, but they were in the Channel, Ed. I'm sure of it. *Nobody* dives the Channel. Nobody. Unless—"

"Unless they're looking for something," Ed sneered. Both men were silent for a moment. Ed finished the last of his beer, and set the empty bottle down on the bar. The chattering crowd enveloped them, and Pearl Jam boomed from the corner jukebox. Glasses tinked, billiards collided, laughter echoed, fans whirred.

"Now, maybe I'm being a little paranoid and maybe I'm not," Phillip said. "But in all the years that we've been looking, we've never seen anybody else actually in the Channel. There's gotta be a reason." A long silence ensued before Ed spoke. "When's Jimmy gettin' up here?" He pulled a cigarette from the pack of

Camels on the bar and put it to his lips.

"Today. I called him and he said he was coming up right away."

"All right then." A match flared. Ed cupped his giant hand around the flame and lit the cigarette. He breathed a long cloud of smoke. "When Jimmy gets here, we'll go check out that area again. Then, if we need to dive, we'll. Meanwhile, we need to keep watch on that cruiser and see if she comes back. Did you check the marina to see if she's moored there?"

Phillip nodded. "Not there," he said. "I think it's somebody from upriver. I saw them stop at *The Boathouse* last week and then head farther upstream. I haven't seen the boat at the marina at all and I've been looking everyday."

"Well, we'll leave that whole thing alone for now. There's no reason to raise a fuss just yet. And if they did happen to find the ship . . . ." Ed paused as he reached into his pocket for some cash to pay for the beers. "Well then, we can deal with that if and when the time arrives."

The two men got up from their barstools and walked through the thickening group of patrons towards the door. A man in a dirty white baseball cap was trying to balance a beer on his chin, much to the delight of the other patrons. They cheered him on until the bottle slipped down his cheek, and his missed attempt at snatching the bottle sent it sailing to the wood floor, inciting a roar of cheers and laughter from the excited onlookers.

Rednecks, Phillip thought behind a concealing, pleasant smile. *Backwoods redneck hicks.*

The two men climbed into their respective vehicles and left.

chapter 30

Blink. Blink. Blink. The tiny red dot was flashing on the answering machine when Eric and Kari returned from their dive. They had stopped for dinner before returning, then by the market, and it was now late evening.

Blink. Blink. Blink.

"Got three messages," Kari said as she walked by the telephone on her way into the kitchen to put away a few basic groceries that they'd picked up from the party store. She looked at the kitchen table, littered with papers and bills. *The Complete Guide to Shipwrecks of the Great Lakes* lay open on the table.

"Probably more offers for dates," Eric mused from the other room.

"Well, I'll have to tell them I'm already taken," Kari replied.

"I didn't mean *you,*" Eric added, tacking on a lighthearted chuckle. Kari smiled and shook her head.

Blink. Blink. Blink.

She turned a few pages of the shipwreck book, then closed it and left it on the table. Eric came in with the last two sacks of groceries. "Ever heard of the *Brittany* before?" he asked, setting the brown bags on the counter.

"I'm sure I've come across it somewhere. It's probably in the book." She nodded towards the kitchen table, as Eric handed her the last sack.

Blink. Blink. Blink.

She was much more familiar with the names and fates of ships than he was. Mostly because she read more than Eric. Eric was intrigued with wrecks, but not so much as to make him drive the exhausting one mile to the Cheboygan Public Library and actually look something up. Most of the history of ships and shipwrecks Eric knew was from what his father had told him. That suited Eric just fine. If he needed to know something, he could always ask Kari.

Blink. Blink. Blink.

Kari surveyed the clutter on the table and decided it could wait until later. "I think I'm going to take a shower." She said this more to herself than to Eric, who was busy stirring a Captain Morgan and Coke as she walked by the answering machine and idly pressed the button. The machine sprang to life with a click, followed by a high-pitched garble of backwards voices until the tape stopped.

Click . . . Beeeeep! "Hi Kari, it's Amber. Hey, do you still have that red dress that you wore to . . .um . . . oh hell, I can't remember where you wore it . . . but could I borrow it this Friday night? Dan and I are spending the weekend at the *Grand* on Mackinac Island for our anniversary. Anyway, give me a call when you get in . . . and hi Eric!"

Beeeeep!! Click-bzzzzzz. A hang up.

Beeeeep!! Click. "Uh, Eric and Kari . . . this is Don. If you're there, pick up the phone." Pause. "Pick up the phone if you're there." His voice sounded strained, serious. Not at all like the usual mellow, go-with-the-flow Don Garrity. Even Kari, sensing the alarmed tone in his voice, came out of the bedroom, wrapping a towel around herself.

"Look, I developed those pictures you sent me, and you're not going to believe . . . well, you gotta call me tonight. You're not gonna . . ." Another pause. "You are NOT going to believe this. Call me when you get home. *Tonight. I'll be up.*" Before the message ended, Eric had already picked up the receiver and began to dial the number.

chapter 31

Don jumped, startled by the sudden electronic chirping of the cordless receiver that lay on the table in front of him. He had been reviewing the photographs of the shipwreck, examining the minute details in each. Except for the one photograph, the other pictures were surprisingly normal, showing what you'd expect from a schooner lost for years at the bottom of Lake Huron.

Except for that *one*. That one single picture.

He was holding the enlargement of the grisly photo in his hand when the phone rang.

"Hello?"

"Don? Eric."

"Yeah. Hey, I developed those photos that Kari took." Not even a cordial "What's up?" or *"How's it goin'?"* Don's voice was unnaturally tense and concerned.

"Yeah. Whadja find?" Eric replied.

"Where did you say you found this wreck?"

"Lake Huron. East of Bois Blanc Island near the Laurentian Channel. We charted her on a plain old depthfinder, if you can believe that. How did the shots turn out?"

"Well, most of them turned out pretty good. But there's one in particular that you gotta *see* to even believe, Eric. People. *Dead* people. Tell me that you didn't see them."

Eric was silent. He had seen a few dead bodies on wrecks, their lifeless forms gasping in terror, tormented prisoners locked in an underwater coffin. The sight of dead bodies didn't really unnerve Eric. *And it shouldn't be that out-of-the-ordinary for Don either,* he thought. *Don has seen corpses underwater before. So why all the drama?*

"No, we didn't see that," Eric replied in disbelief. "We were—"

"They were *murdered*, Eric," Don interrupted. "And I mean *butchered*. A long time ago, for sure, but these guys were *hacked*. It looks like the Manson family got to these people."

chapter 32

Kari slept silently next to him but Eric lay wide awake, thinking about how Don had described the photograph. One body lay in a corner. Its wrists, which were more like bones covered by grimy sediment, were bound by rope. Don said the body was in a supine position, legs apart, with its bony fingers resting on the floor. A large knife handle protruded from the side of the head. Like on the corpse's wrists, the skull was caked with silty residue and resembled more of a thick, brownish-gray texture.

The knife handle appeared to be four or five inches long. If the blade was the same length, it must have gone almost entirely through the brain. The mouth was open, exposing dirty brown teeth. Whoever this had been had certainly not been pleased by these unfortunate developments. The clothing, though also very rotted, was still on the body. Don couldn't tell for sure, but he said it looked to be the remains of a man.

To the left of the man was yet another corpse that had experienced the same fate. This body was facing away from the camera and its hands were tied. The body was on its knees, head thrown back and twisted at a grotesque angle, almost totally backward. Don said he could see the forehead and nose and a large hole right in the center of the top of the skull. Too small and not neat enough to be a bullet, Don had thought. More like a hammer hole. He couldn't be positive, but judging by the type of clothing, Don was pretty sure that this had been a woman.

Eric sat up in bed and looked out the window. A mercury vapor light glowed in the darkness, casting shadows on the slow moving currents of the Cheboygan River. He swung his legs to the floor and stood up. Kari shifted a tiny bit, but remained asleep. He walked into the living room that was faintly illuminated by the vapor light in the yard. He looked at *The Complete Guide to Great Lakes Shipwrecks* that lay open on the maple dining room table. The light from the mercury lamp outside was bright enough that he could read the small letters in the book and he flipped the pages, perplexed. *It's just not here*, he thought in frustration.

He and Kari had pored through the book and found nothing that would indicate that any ship called the *Brittany* ever sailed the Lakes. The *Guide* was the most authoritative book on the subject of ships and shipwrecks in the Great Lakes, and it wasn't there. *But it has to be,* Eric thought, as he turned the pages. He closed the book and walked to the sliding screen doors. The crickets sang as Eric walked out on the deck and sat in an old lawn chair. The aluminum and nylon creaked as he sat down, and he tilted his head and looked up at the stars.

Finding a schooner that had never been discovered was like finding a gold mine. Usually, when a shipwreck was discovered on the Great Lakes, it wasn't long before it was plundered and stripped clean. But he and Kari left things alone. The excitement of finding an untouched shipwreck was enough. But *murdered* people? And not just murdered, but *butchered.* Don's words spun in his head.

Like the Manson Family got to these people.

Why? Eric thought. *How many were there?* The questions kept coming, but Eric knew that there would be no answers tonight. *Hell, there might not be any answers tomorrow either.* Without knowing anything more about the ship, and not finding any record of her anywhere, answers were going to be elusive. Kari couldn't wait to re-visit the ship and wanted to penetrate the wreck tomorrow. She would have gone tonight if Eric suggested it.

A warm, light breeze rustled through the darkened trees, and Eric heard the familiar *sploosh* of a fish as it broke the surface, cutting short the life of a frog or mouse that had been unfortunate enough to have been spotted by the hungry fish. He watched the river for the rings of disturbed water that would indicate where the fish had risen, but found none. The fish was probably downstream a few yards in the shadows of the trees.

Sploosh. The fish rose again, and Eric got up from the lawn chair and wandered across the dew-covered lawn down to the water's edge. He stood at the edge of the river and contemplated a swim.

Sploosh. The fish rose again, eight or ten yards downstream from Eric. He decided against the swim because he was tired and he didn't want to have to take a shower before returning to bed. He gazed into the dark waters of the sleepy river, his mind wandering back to the shipwreck.

Butchered.

Don's words haunted him. Eric wasn't superstitious in the least, but the presence of bodies on board the ship added a morbid fascination. Years ago, as a teenager, he had taken a bottle from an old barge that he and his father had discovered in Lake Charlevoix. The barge's captain was still there, locked in the wheelhouse as he had been for nearly forty years, and Eric had figured that he certainly wouldn't miss one old bottle. Eerie nightmares of an old, rotting sea captain, returning to reclaim the piece of pirated property, had plagued him every night for weeks. The strange nightmares wouldn't go away. He and a few friends dived on the barge again later that month and he had taken the bottle back down and dropped it into one of the boat's cargo holds. He never had another old, rotting sea captain nightmare.

Sploosh. This time the fish sounded farther off, as if drifting downstream. Eric bent down on the grass at the river's edge and put his hand in the water. It was warm, and he reconsidered his swim. He glanced at his watch. 1:17. He looked down into the semi-distorted reflection of his face staring back up at him, strangely aglow in the black water. He extended his hand and swept the reflection of his face in the water, watching as his features contorted and shook.

The hand grasped the back of his neck and he turned sharply, losing his footing and almost falling in the river. The shadow behind him jumped back, first in fright, then laughing, then falling to the grass.

Kari.

Amidst her giggling, she told him that she hadn't meant to scare him, "but boy did you look funny when you jumped!! Like you'd seen a ghost!!" More giggling. Then: "Can't sleep?"

"Just thinking."

"About the ship?"

Eric sighed. "About the people. I mean . . . that's just too bizarre."

Sploosh. Farther away now. The fish was still feeding, but feigning back downstream. A bat swirled beneath the mercury vapor light, in swift pursuit of its next morsel. An unseen dog barked a warning on the other side of the river, several blocks over.

Kari took a few silent steps toward her husband and nuzzled his neck. In the darkness, she took his hand in hers.

"Come back to bed, baby."

The two walked silently across the cold damp lawn and back into the house.

chapter 33

It is late, but LaChance is still wide awake. He will steer the ship through the night and, come morning, when Jack awakens, he will turn the wheel over to him and get a few hours sleep himself. It is a routine he is used to, especially when he was sailing the ocean. A captain didn't get much sleep at sea. LaChance stares off into the night sky, lost in thought, his mind weaving in and out among thousands of flickering stars.

He had certainly been surprised to see Merman that night. The two men sat at LaChance's kitchen table, and, in the fading glow of an oil lamp, Merman told Nathan about the men who had been following him and how he feared for his possessions and for his life and family. When he told LaChance what that possession was, the captain didn't say a word. He was dumbstruck.

Merman told LaChance that he wanted to throw the thieves off by sailing his precious cargo to New York. He was sure that the thieves would think he would take the chest by rail, and had prepared a decoy to send by train. If the thieves robbed the train, all they would find would be a large crate full of rocks. By then the ship would be half way to New York. Merman could provide the ship and pay LaChance very handsomely for the job.

At first, Nathan was not inclined to accept the offer, but the fact that his friend feared for the safety of his family had changed his mind. He decided that he would help Richard, and sail his cargo to New York for him.

What concerned LaChance was that a few of Merman's family members wanted to sail instead of taking the coach with the rest of the family. None of Merman's family knew of the heavy wood-and-steel crate or what it contained, and Merman wanted to keep it that way for now. It would be better that he kept the secret to himself until they reached New York. At first, Merman had demanded that all of his family travel by stage. But his daughter and her husband, as well as Merman's son and his wife, had insisted on traveling by sea. Merman had made the mistake of telling them that he had purchased a ship to take their belongings to New York and this had excited them. They had never sailed before and wanted to ride along for the experience.

LaChance had spoken to them as well, telling them that the trip was to be for experienced sailors only. And the women . . . well, that was simply out of the question. In the end, the four had put up such a whiny fuss over the whole matter that both LaChance and Merman relented, deciding to allow the four to sail to New York aboard the ship. Better to let them go than to tell them the truth and risk more people knowing about the cargo than necessary. The four could assist with some of the simpler chores, and LaChance would be the only one who knew of the contents of the large, heavy chest in the cargo hold below deck.

chapter 34

A week before the ship was to depart, three men had followed Richard Merman to the shipyard and waited until he left. It was late at night and the offices of the shipyard were dark. The three men hid in the shadows and contemplated how to get past the night watchman. Besides a burly man sitting motionless and nearly invisible in the shadows at the front of the shipyard office, the docks were deserted. The three men might not have even seen him except for the man's lit cigarette. Alerted by the glowing ember, the men remained unseen and unheard in the darkness.

Jed Hollerand, the night watchman had been on the graveyard shift for nearly ten years and enjoyed it. It gave him time to think. He enjoyed being alone and listening to the waves lapping the shoreline and the wind whistling through the rigging and masts of the sleeping ships in the harbor. He would go home in the morning, sleep for awhile and then maybe do some fishing down *at the river. Heck, he might even hook up with that wary largemouth bass that had busted up his tackle and stole his bait the other day. He had the fish on the line for almost an hour before he lost him and he had roundly cursed himself, his tackle, the fish, and the river. And for good measure, he even cursed the small bottle from which he took a healthy swig now and then.*

He raised the cigarette to his lips and leaned out of the shadows, looking around. Nothing. He never saw anything. Oh sure, the usual kids playing games and goofing around, trying to scare him, or pulling juvenile pranks. But it was too late at night for that. The gaming hours were over.

He took a single, long, final drag on his cigarette and tossed it to the ground. Then, heeding the words of his boss to 'always make damn sure that those things were out,' he crushed the butt with the heel of his boot.

Jed had no warning before the heavy piece of lumber slammed into the side of his head. Hollerand groaned, and his body slumped to the ground. He was out.

Using the keys taken from the unconscious Hollerand, a lone man rifled through the office, searching drawers and scanning receipts, looking carefully at each one. Outside, the watchman lay on the ground, still and unresponsive. The dark shadow of a man stood watch at the door and another in the shadows next to a nearby building.

Papers shuffled in the weak glow of a small lantern. Finally, the man tucked a single sheet of paper in his pocket, then took his knife and pried open a locked drawer. He took a small amount of money that was in the drawer and left it open. He left the office door wide open as he exited, and the two men walked quickly toward the shadows where the third man waited. Then, as an afterthought, the man who had broken into the office returned to where Hollerand lay and took Jed's watch from his arm. He tried to pry off his gold wedding band as well, but it was too tight. No matter, the man thought. All they wanted to do was make it look like a simple burglary. A single thief, stealing cash and small valuables, and getting away as fast as he could.

He pulled the slip of paper out of his pocket. It was a receipt detailing the terms of the sale of a ship. The other two men took turns reading the paper and chatted quietly for a moment before disappearing into the shadows. Now it all made sense. Merman was trying to give them the slip. Presto-chango. He wasn't going to use the train, after all. He was going to ship his cargo by way of the Great Lakes to New York.

chapter 35

Jimmy pulled into Cheboygan exactly three hours and sixteen minutes after leaving Detroit. *Gotta be a new record,* he congratulated himself, as he wheeled into the motel and met up with Phillip at *Goodtime Charlie's.* Phillip called Ed from the pay phone, and Ed said he'd catch up with them at the bar.

Here we go again, thought Stachniack, glancing up as Phillip and Jimmy entered the bar. Charlie didn't mind Phillip or Ed, but *that sonofabitch Jimmy is a madman. You never know when he's gonna go off. Big Ed could have his mood swings now and then,* Charlie thought, *but that Jimmy character was out of his mind. Fruit Loops all the way.* However, there was one good thing about having Jimmy around. If any of the patrons started getting rowdy, Jimmy acted as part-time bouncer. Only once did someone stand up to Jimmy, and that guy got the shit beat out of him through his intestines and out his ears. Word got out pretty fast that you didn't mess with Jimmy Durand. And really, for the most part, Jimmy did seem to keep to himself.

Thank God for that, Charlie thought. *Thank God for that.*

"You guys are the most paranoid bastards I have ever seen," Jimmy said harshly, after Phillip told him about the divers they had seen in the Channel. Ed had shown up and the three sat at a small table in the corner. "One boat with divers in Lake Huron and you guys wig out." Jimmy laughed, shaking his head from side to side.

"It's not the fact that there are divers in Lake Huron," Phillip asserted, "but they're in or near the Channel, Jimmy. How often does anyone dive in or around the Channel?"

"And we're not *wigging out*, Jim," Ed insisted testily. He didn't care for Jimmy's smart-ass know-it-all attitude and it showed in his voice. "So far, we've been pretty damn fortunate that nobody else has been looking for the wreck. But we gotta start thinking about the possibility—"

"A *remote* possibility," Jimmy interrupted, rolling his eyes.

"Whatever." There was a certain terseness in Ed's reply, a certain *I'm-getting-pretty-tired-of-your-attitude* tone. He stared at his beer, then glared at Jimmy. "We've been looking for this thing for almost six years. And we are *not* going to take any chances of losing it to some stupid weekend bumblefuck divers who might have happened to come across it accidentally," he said angrily.

"I charted the place in the Channel where they've been diving. But I didn't find anything," Phillip added.

Bottoms up. Phillip's beer was empty, and Ed took the final swig of his own.

"Hey! Charlie! A couple more beers here!" Ed turned and hollered to the back room where Charlie was busy replenishing his stocks. He motioned with his hulking arm, and after a moment the beers came. Charlie walked away to finish his work, leaving the three men alone. The bar was nearly empty now, except for a few resident patients who sat on stools, nursing their medicine.

"Well, here's what we do," Jimmy announced. "We go out and check out the place where you saw that boat and those divers. We find what they've found, if anything. Chances are, it's nothing. If, by chance, it *is* what we're looking for, we'll deal with it then. There's no sense in getting bent to shit over nothing."

They agreed to head out at five the next morning, and the three men got up to leave. Ed went back to his cabin, and Jimmy headed to *Johnnie's Sports Bar* for a few more beers. Phillip went back to his motel room and lay in bed, listening to the occasional car traveling by on Main Street, and the sounds of a couple in the next room arguing about something on TV.

He could *feel* it. He knew that they were close. You can only search for so long and then it has to pay off. Ships don't disappear like all those books say they do. *It's out there,* he thought. *Somewhere in that damned Channel. And Ed, Jimmy, and I are going to find it. And—*

Jimmy.

God, how he'd changed. Physically and mentally. Everything about him. He hadn't always been the way he was now. Phillip and Jimmy had grown up together. It had been Phillip who protected Jimmy at school and around the neighborhood. Phillip wasn't much older than Jimmy, but back then he was big for his size, and Jimmy was so . . . so *tiny* and fragile. Plus, Jimmy's old man was always beating the tar out of him every other night—sometimes twice a night. Phillip felt sorry for Jimmy when he saw the fresh bruises on his arms, back, or legs. Jimmy did his best to cover them up, but most people knew that his old man was using Jimmy as his ninety-pound sparring partner.

After Jimmy's father died, Phillip saw Jimmy often throughout his teenage years, despite the fact that Jimmy bounced from foster home to foster home, always in some sort of trouble. Each one said that they couldn't handle him, that he wouldn't listen, he was disobedient, abusive, and too unpredictable. *Yeah, well, if your old man used you as a pinata, you'd be screwed up too*, Phillip wanted to tell them.

So he was shocked when he suddenly bumped into Jimmy in Detroit one afternoon years ago. More than shocked. *Stupefied.* Jimmy was *huge*. Muscular. Bigger than huge and muscular—he was a *monster*. This was not the Jimmy Durand he had grown up with. Jimmy had gone from Barney Fife to Conan the Barbarian. He was a walking, talking, true-to-life commercial for those Charles Atlas ads that were in the back of all those comic books. Phillip wouldn't have even recognized him if Jimmy had not said something first.

Jimmy? Jimmy *Durand?*

Then the two talked for hours and caught up on each other's lives.

Phillip, Jimmy, and Jimmy's wife, Sharon, began to hang out on weekends and hit the bars together. Jimmy rarely drank at the time but he seemed to always have some blow. Jimmy would exit the bar, leaving Sharon and Phillip together while he went to snort a few lines. Then he would come back in and Sharon would disappear for a few minutes. Then it was Phillip's turn. One night, the bar was closing and all three were so wired that they sat in the parking lot and snorted coke until almost six in the morning.

Phillip had wondered where Jimmy was getting the money to live this kind of lifestyle. Cocaine wasn't cheap, and Jimmy seemed to have it all the time.

"Where in the hell do you get all your money, man?" he asked him one day. He and Jimmy were cruising Telegraph Road, on their way to pick up Sharon from work and do some partying.

Jimmy laughed behind his dark sunglasses and tank top. "What are you talking about? What money?"

"Come on Jimmy. Cut the bullshit. You work part-time at a gym. *Part-time*, man. And Sharon works at a video store. You got two cars . . . *new* cars. And one *hell* of an apartment. Yet, I've never seen you short of cash. Not once."

Jimmy chuckled to himself and looked out at the streets. "You know what your problem is? When you want something, you don't do jack-shit about it."

"What's that supposed to mean?" Phillip didn't sound offended, and wasn't.

"Even when we were kids, you never had that 'go-get-em-no-matter-what attitude.' You missed a lot of opportunities cause you just screwed around."

"Well, maybe so, but I like to think my common sense took over."

"Your pansy-ass took over," Jimmy laughed.

Christopher Knight

"What's that got to do with your cars and your apartment?" Phillip asked.

"It's because I *wanted* that shit, man. I just found a way to get it. There's always a way to get what you want in this world if you're willing to do what it takes."

They drove a while in silence. "And just what *does* it take?" Phillip finally inquired skeptically.

"Whatever you gotta do," Jimmy replied with his best Tony Robbins motivational stroke. "That's it, man. You do whatever you gotta do. Don't let nothin' stop ya."

chapter 36

Phillip had told Jimmy that he had gone back to college at Wayne State, working on a degree in Business Management. He had become an avid scuba diver and worked at a dive shop in Sterling Heights. In fact, he was thinking of diving as a full-time occupation, having lost much of his interest in a Business Management career.

Phillip told Jimmy about a discovery he had made while doing research for his Michigan History class. Michigan History was a blow-off class, like woodshop or small engine repair in high school, and Phillip thought that if he could cruise through with a 2.0, that would be fine. He certainly wasn't going to put a lot of effort into it. One of the assignments for the class was to research a ship that had sailed the Great Lakes. Phillip, while looking through an old history book of the Lakes, opened it to the page that contained a complete listing of every sailing vessel that had sailed the Great Lakes in the 1800s. He closed his eyes and, extending one index finger and circling the page for a moment, stabbed at the book. His finger landed on the schooner *Aurora*.

He had worked haphazardly on the project for weeks. The *Aurora* had been privately owned, but was used extensively for shipping cargo up and down the Great Lakes. Her home port was Chicago, but she was not there very often. The *Aurora* carried grain, lumber, and other materials to many different ports and harbors of the Great Lakes.

Then the trail stopped. The *Aurora* had simply disappeared. No reports of foundering. All of her records just ended. It was impossible. There had to be some record somewhere of what happened to her. Phillip couldn't figure it out, and that pissed him off royally. *This is a blow-off class*, he reminded himself. *Of all the shit luck. I pick a ship that disappeared off the face of the earth. Not wrecked or destroyed, but* gone. *Into thin air.*

His professor suggested that Phillip look into the owner of the ship and proceed from there.

Great. Just what I need—more research.

He went to the county building and dug through file after file, cabinet after cabinet, looking for any reference to the *Aurora*. It took days.

And then, one afternoon, there it was.

The *Aurora* had been sold to W. H. Stockbridge, Inc. of Chicago, Illinois in 1850. She was used for various runs up and down the Great Lakes, mainly for the transfer of lumber. Then in eighteen hundred something—the ink had been smeared and Phillip couldn't read the writing on the old paper. But it looked like the ship had been sold to a Robert . . . no, Richard. Richard Merman.

The trail ended there. Finally, after days of fruitless searching at the county building, Phillip went to the library and asked for assistance in locating a specific family name. The librarian produced a genealogy of the Merman family. According to the records, one descendant of the Merman family was still living—a Mrs. Abigail Jewell in St. Clair Shores.

Phillip called directory assistance and got her number.

I can't believe I'm spending this much time on a stupid blow-off class.

The phone rang countless times, and he was about to hang up when a tiny, weak-sounding voice answered. He politely introduced himself and explained to Mrs. Jewell that he was a college student working on a research paper and asked if she knew anything of her relatives and of the ships they may have owned. *"Anything you may have would be most helpful, ma'am. I would really like to find out what happened to the ship so I can finish this research paper."*

Mrs. Jewell spoke very slowly and Phillip had a hard time understanding her on the phone. *For crying out loud,* Phillip thought. *Next time I research a ship, I'm gonna do something like the* Cedarville *or the* Fitzgerald *or some ship that somebody knows something about. None of these mystery ghost ships that don't even seem to exist.*

Mrs. Jewell did not know much about her relatives, at least that far back. However, she said that there was a lot of family memorabilia in a few boxes in the attic. "I'm not sure if the boxes are still there," she squeaked meekly in the phone, "but you seem like a nice enough young fellow. If you'd like to go through them, you're welcome to, if it might be of help to you."

Reluctantly, Phillip said thank you, and that he'd be over on Tuesday. *This is an awful lot of work for a blow-off class,* he thought, hanging up the phone, not realizing he was about to make the discovery of a lifetime.

chapter 37

Abigail Jewell, a sprightly seventy-four-year old, was waiting for Phillip with a tray of cookies and hot tea. She had fine, gray hair tied in a neat bun, and wore white slacks and an oversized pink sweater. She smiled sweetly, and Phillip was instantly reminded of the old woman from *Little Red Riding Hood*. It was like visiting his own grandmother . . . Except Abigail Jewell was *blind*.

He hadn't noticed it at first. She met him at the door, tray in hand. He *did* notice that she had appeared to look right through him, but she backed up and allowed him to enter, setting the cookies on the coffee table next to the couch. She walked into the kitchen and retrieved the teapot.

It was only when she set the stainless steel kettle down on the table that he noticed her visual impairment. The kettle clanked as she set it down and Mrs. Jewell reached out to feel the edge of the table as she sat down in the chair, as if she needed it for some sort of guidance. It was then that Phillip noticed that her eyes weren't moving, but appeared to be focused on something far away. It gave him an eerie feeling as she spoke, her head facing him, but her eyes looking somewhere to the left of him.

Sure is one trusting old biddy, Phillip thought. He ate a cookie, made small talk for a few minutes, and then requested that she show him the attic so he could begin his research. On the way down the hall and upstairs, she had said that Richard Merman had been her great-great-grandfather. She didn't know much about him, but a lot of the family history was upstairs in three or four boxes. Most of her relatives had passed on years ago, and she herself was widowed with no children. Again, Phillip was reminded of the grandmother in the old fairy tale.

She led him down the hall and to the door of the attic. He would need to get the stepladder out of the closet, she told him. He did, and standing on the third step, he pried away the square piece of wood that sealed off the attic. It was difficult to push away, as if it had been sealed up for many years. The muskiness of the attic drifted down to him, and the dry dustiness of the stale air filled his nostrils. The old woman said he could look through whatever he needed, that she had never been up in the attic and wouldn't even know where to begin. He pulled himself up through the square hole, and turned on the light.

"And if you need any more tea or cookies, just let me know, Mr. Keanan," Mrs. Jewell called up behind him.

My, what a big attic you have, grandmother.

Phillip went through the boxes. Dozens and dozens of old

photographs in picture albums were the bulk of what was stored. There were a few letters (many written to Mrs. Jewell herself, when she was young) and transcripts and legal papers that didn't make much sense to Phillip. But nothing on the *Aurora*. There were a few old yellowed photographs of Richard Merman, but he had yet to come across any mention of the schooner. He spent two hours going over old pictures, notes, and letters, but found nothing. Frustrated, he began to pile the papers, photographs, and letters back into the boxes. He was about to place the remaining contents into the last box when he stopped.

Wait a minute. What's this?

A leatherbound book, very old and tattered, lay under a pile of papers he had pushed aside. It was an inch thick and a few pages were falling out of the binding. Phillip must have set it aside with the papers without paying much attention to it. He carefully picked up the aged volume, flipped open the cover and started reading.

After skimming the journal, Phillip had found out all he needed to know.

And a *lot* more. A *shitload* more.

Now he knew why he had found nothing about the fate of the *Aurora*. He had been looking for the wrong name. Merman had changed the name of the vessel to the *Brittany*.

And with good reason.

He bade good-bye to Mrs. Jewell. "No, I wasn't able to find what I was looking for, but thank you. The cookies and tea were excellent." He could hardly contain his excitement, and was glad that Abigail Jewell couldn't see the gleam in his eye or the shine in his face.

What a fine young man, Abigail Jewell thought as she closed the door and listened to Phillip's fading footsteps on the concrete walk.

What a stupid, senile, blind old bat, thought Phillip, as he pulled the journal from beneath his shirt and placed it on the passenger seat of his Monte Carlo.

Phillip wasn't sure if he believed what he'd read. Although the prospect of more research didn't really thrill him, he certainly was going to check *this* out. Either this Merman character was one hell of a bullshitter or .... *No. Why would anybody lie in their own journal?* A journal that now sat in the passenger seat of Phillip's 1978 Monte Carlo.

chapter 38

Until he told Jimmy, Phillip had told no one else about his discovery, not even his professor. He didn't even bother to finish his report, and could have cared less about the grade he received. By the time he told Jimmy about it, his studies had taken a backseat joyride to nowhere fast, and his GPA reflected it. He showed Jimmy the research he'd done and Jimmy had seemed as excited about it as Phillip. Neither thought twice about whether they wanted to search for the wreck or not, they just started figuring out *how* they would go about it. Jimmy knew nothing about scuba diving, but certainly wasn't afraid to learn. Not considering what the payoff could be. Phillip had limited experience in wreck diving and knew nothing about trying to find something like this underwater. He knew nothing about depthfinders or bottom scanners and how they would go about searching for a lost shipwreck.

And that's how Ed Belmont had gotten involved.

Phillip was reluctant to tell anyone else about the discovery, but Jimmy said he knew a guy named Ed Belmont who could be a big help. Ed was cool, Jimmy had said. Kind of an asshole, but cool. He knew a lot about diving and treasure hunting. He knew how to find wrecks and dive for them, had been doing it for a long time, and would certainly be interested in a prize of *this* magnitude. *"We need this guy,"* Jimmy had insisted. *"He knows what the hell he's doing. Besides, he's so fat, he'll probably have a heart attack and die when we find the wreck and that'll just leave more for me an' you. And besides . . . he's Sharon's uncle."*

Phillip watched the news for a while in his hotel room (*"In other news tonight, a rash of cow thefts in the small community of Afton has put residents here on alert, and in Mackinaw City the debate rages regarding a possible new Native-American operated casino in northern Michigan. Turning to the weather . . ."*) then shut the TV off.

These people have no clue what the real world is like, Phillip thought scornfully. He shut off the light and went to sleep.

chapter 39

Young Daniel Hawthorne is in bed in the cabin below deck, very much awake. Jack Malloy is snoring loudly and has been for quite some time, and Daniel can hear the Captain shuffling around on deck.

How many more days? Three? Four? The men had said it would happen in the night, away from the few and far between small towns that dotted the shorelines of the big lakes.

He feels beneath his pillow and finds the gold coin the men had given him. One hundred dollars. He is almost rich. One hundred dollars in advance and another nineteen hundred —

Soon.

At twenty years old, Daniel is going to do fairly well for his first big business venture. He has been working the docks for five years, loading and unloading, sailing, even assisting with boat-building and repairing.

He fingers the smooth coin in the darkness. One hundred dollars. Last week, while loading crates on the schooner Annie B, three men had approached him. They described Nathan LaChance and asked him if he knew of him. Daniel said he didn't think LaChance sailed much anymore. Stuffing a ten dollar silver piece into Daniel's hand, one man asked if he would keep an eye out for them and let them know if LaChance appeared at the docks. Ten dollars was more than he earned in two weeks and he earnestly pocketed the coin and agreed to let them know if he saw LaChance.

Two days later, one of the men approached him again and extended his hand to Daniel. The two chatted for a moment and the man asked if he had seen Captain LaChance yet. Yes, as a matter of fact, Daniel had seen LaChance, working around the yard and preparing a ship for sailing. He didn't know the name of the ship, but in an odd turn of events, a man had approached Daniel on the docks yesterday. The man was expensively dressed, very city-like. Mr. Well-To-Do had asked Daniel if he would like to work aboard a ship going to New York. He'd be paid $25 in New York, and another $25 when the schooner returned. The ship's captain was Nathan LaChance. Daniel happily told Mr. Well-To-Do that he would take on the job.

The man asked Daniel a little about Mr. Well-To-Do, as well as LaChance, and when the ship would be leaving. Daniel liked the man and the two agreed to meet at a local tavern after Daniel was done working that day.

The bar wasn't very full as Daniel stepped inside. The man he had spoken with earlier in the day was sitting in a corner booth, along with the other two men that had approached him earlier in the week. They waved him over and hollered to the bartender for another round.

Later in the evening they revealed their plan to Daniel. They were going to hold up the ship that Daniel would be working aboard and steal some very special cargo. If Daniel agreed to help, he would be paid $2,000. That was more than he could make in over two years. He asked the men what the cargo was and why they wanted it so badly. They were elusive, and told him only that it was something that belonged to them anyway.

Two thousand dollars.

Daniel was wary and unsure at first, but the prospect of $2,000 was irresistible. He asked them specifically what he would have to do, uncomfortably aware that this would make him a thief and a mutineer. They told him that it would be very simple—just help them to load the cargo onto their own ship. The cargo, he was told, was very heavy, and they would need an extra hand. Someone they could trust. Daniel would then board the other ship with the men and they would make their get-away. Simple. The only thing Daniel would have to worry about, they said, was getting back home. They would drop him off at a nearby port, pay him, and he would be on his own. Daniel figured that would be easy enough. He could take a train back home for about $5, a small price to pay for such an enormous take.

He had mulled it over. Two thousand dollars. He would be set for life. Still, he'd never stolen anything before, unless you counted that bottle of liquor he had taken from the back of a wagon years ago. Assisting in the pirating of a ship would make him a wanted man, but there were lots of places he could go and hide out for a long time. He really had no ties here and the thought of moving somewhere else, of experiencing the sights and sounds of another city enticed him. Along with $2,000.

So Daniel agreed, and told the men that he would help them get *whatever it was that they wanted so badly. Daniel guessed that it was probably money. How else would they be able to afford to pay him $2,000?*

The day before they set sail, Daniel loaded the last of the cargo and baggage on the ship. He had gone over a list of provisions again with Captain LaChance and Jack, the first mate, and they sent him to town to get some last minute supplies. The men met Daniel as he left the shipyard, quizzing him about the contents of the ship.

Yes, he told them, there is a large crate or chest of some sort below deck. Yes, it's way too heavy for one man to lift. The men told him to keep an eye on that cargo. It was going to help pay his salary.

Two thousand dollars.

The men gave him a $100 coin in advance and Daniel hastily stuffed it into his pants pocket. He had never before had so much money in his possession at one time. He was rich—and he was going to be richer. Two thousand dollars' richer. Not bad for a couple week's work.

Clutching the coin beneath his pillow, Daniel finally drifts off to sleep to the gentle rocking of the ship as it sails on through the night.

chapter 40

Kari looked at the pile of books that lay stacked on the desk. It was early in the day, and, except for two librarians, she was the only person in the library. She glanced at some of the titles: *Ships of the Great Lakes* by Robert Turnbull; *Gone, But Not Forgotten* by Nancy and Howard Mealader; and *Great Lakes, Great Ships* by J. Matthew Clarkston. There were eight more books, all about either ships or shipping on the Great Lakes. She pulled the top one from the pile and flipped to the index in the back. *The Belle Isle, Arthur Benton, Eleanor Bevious, Carl Bradley, The Roderick Bunting* . . . but no *Brittany.*

Kari checked through the indexes of the remaining books but found no mention of the *Brittany* in any of them. She returned to the first book and flipped through the pages. *It's got to be here. Ships don't disappear without any record. Nor do people disappear without their loved ones looking for them,* she thought in frustration.

The photos had arrived yesterday from Don Garrity via Federal Express. Kari's initial fascination with the discovery of the wreck had rapidly turned to shock, then to a sickening sadness. *How could somebody do that?* she wondered. Don's description over the phone, although graphic, did not match the true impact of the photo itself.

She returned the books to the shelf and sat down in front of the microfiche. Every issue of the *Cheboygan Tribune* since they had first started publishing had been microfiched. Kari didn't really know exactly *what* to look for but she assumed that if a ship and people went missing, *someone* would have reported it to the police and it would have been in the paper.

Maybe when Don gets here, she thought, *he'll have some clues.* Don had called them last night, wanting to come up and video the shipwreck—from the surface, of course. Don still didn't dive. But he would bring his underwater cameras and recorders and could watch on the monitor from the *John Galt* while Eric and Kari dived on the wreck. For Don, it would be *almost* like diving—or the closest he would ever get to it again. Kari was certain of that.

She placed the sheet of microfiche film in the tray and watched as hundreds of newspaper pages flashed by on the screen in front of her. She slowed the tray and the pages stopped. She read the headlines of one page briefly and then returned to the fiche for the year 1843. *Might as well start at the beginning,* she thought.

chapter 41

It was cloudy, but the rain had stopped and the temperature had started to rise. Eric stepped from the porch, carried two bright yellow air tanks down to the dock, and loaded them aboard the *John Galt*. Now that the weather had broken they were anxious to return to the dive site. The clouds were starting to disperse, and slivers of sunshine sliced through the sky.

Eric went back up to the house, pulled a root beer from the refrigerator and walked back down to the boat. Kari should be back from the library soon and there were still a couple things that needed attention on the boat. *There's always something that needs attention*, Eric thought. The *John Galt* was a fine boat, but she was not without her quirks. There was always some minor engine work that needed to be done, a couple paint chips here and there—the usual stuff. He climbed aboard, root beer in hand. High above a cloud swept by, exposing a puzzle-piece of blue sky. Sun beamed down.

"Hey, man! You gettin' any fish?" Eric turned in the direction of the voice. A boat was heading slowly upstream and a man was at the helm smiling, looking at Eric. He was young, maybe late twenties. Jet-black hair. Dark, Jack Nicholson sunglasses and a Hawaiian-print tropical shirt. A pair of binoculars hung on his chest. The twin of every vacationing tourist on the face of the planet.

"Not fishing," Eric replied, shaking his head. He figured the conversation was over, and he moved to step below deck to look at the engine.

"I thought I saw you out fishin' the other day. Out in the Channel. You got a secret spot you're hiding?" The man seemed a bit too chummy, and Eric glanced back over at him.

"Oh yeah, that." Eric thought for a second. "Been doing some diving. Seeing a few fish at about sixty feet, though."

"You're diving way out *there?* " the man asked incredulously, raising his thumb and swinging his arm back towards the lake. Eric nodded.

"We're practicing," he explained. "My wife and I are going diving in Cozumel this fall. Wall diving. The Channel is good practice because of the currents." It was only a *bit* of a stretch. After all, Kari and he *were* planning on a dive trip to Cozumel in November.

The man in the boat, apparently satisfied, nodded and bade Eric a good day. Eric waved. The boat sped up and soon was rounding a bend upstream. He'd seen that boat before and recognized Mr.

Smiley-Chummy, at least by sight. *Probably just a summer resident,* he thought.

Not long after Mr. Smiley-Chummy had disappeared upstream, Eric heard the Blazer pull into the driveway. Doors opened and closed, and moments later Kari walked down the sloping lawn to the river. "Sorry I'm late. I went through every book I could find in the library and didn't find *anything.* Not a single thing. The only other place I could think to look was in the microfiche. They've got every issue of the *Cheboygan Tribune* on microfilm. But it's almost impossible, Eric. I have no idea what to look for other than reports of wrecks or missing persons. All the wrecks I came across in the paper were ships that were in the books anyway. I spent two hours in front of that machine and only got through a few month's worth of papers."

"What about the historical society?" Eric asked.

"I haven't checked there yet. But here's what I'm wondering. If this ship sailed from, say, Detroit, would it be reported in the local paper? If it went down and no one knew about it, how could they publish it? And if there was nothing ever published about it in the local paper, do you think that they would know anything about it at the historical society?" It was a rhetorical question and Eric shrugged his shoulders.

"Yeah, but remember that ship sank a long time ago," he reminded her. "We're talking a different time here. There was no radio, no telephone . . . a lot of things happened to boats on the lake and no one ever knew."

"But they don't just disappear, Eric," Kari insisted. She raised her hand to her forehead in salute, shading her eyes from the sun.

"There has got to be some record somewhere," she insisted.

"Somewhere there is," Eric agreed. "But we need more to go on, that's all." He took a sip of root beer, and set the bottle back down. He flashed his best All-American grin. "So . . . let's go find it."

chapter 42

Phillip guided the Bayliner upstream to the *Pier 33* party store, docked, and used the pay phone. The phone rang endlessly at the other end before it was answered.

"Hey. I'm down here at *Pier 33*. I found our mystery boat. She's called the *John Galt* . . . Nope. Just one guy, but it looked like he was getting the boat ready to head out . . . Yeah. False alarm." There was relief in his voice. "Says he and his wife are divers and they're practicing for some vacation or something. I don't think it's anything, after all. Meet me down at the marina in about an hour. I'll go back and hang out upstream from them to see if they leave, but I'm sure it's nothing. They're just getting ready for a vacation." Pause. "Cool. See you then."

He returned the receiver to its hook and looked around. The *Pier 33* sat on a hill overlooking the water. It had a large docking facility with enough slips for thirty or forty boats. Dozens of seagulls sat on pilings and on the docks, undisturbed by the handful of boaters venturing out. Phillip was sure more people would be out today. The sky was clearing and the wind was dying down a bit. When the weather was nice, it brought the boaters out in droves. The Cheboygan River could sometimes be worse than a traffic jam on the highway.

He walked back to where the big Bayliner was docked. A few other boats had filled the slips along the river, and Phillip grabbed the line for an old man who tossed it to him. He tied the line to the dock and raised his hand in response to the man's gesture of thanks. Phillip turned back to his own boat.

"You from 'round here?". The man was now standing on the dock and he leaned forward and extended a hand to Phillip.

"Nope, just for the summer. Here for the fishing," Phillip answered.

"Well, you're in a great spot. Big fish in these waters. *Big fish.*" The man spread his arms as he spoke.

"How about you? Where you from?" Phillip replied, eager to draw the conversation away from himself.

"Here. All my life. Retired now," the old man replied. Phillip tuned him out as he rambled on about his family for what seemed like an eternity. Phillip nodded in agreement, careful to add in a courteous *'no kidding?'* and *'how 'bout that'* where they were needed. He was sorry now that he'd tied the line for the guy. He didn't know he would be roped into a conversation with a local would-be talk show host. *Shit, the guy's lived here forever,* Phillip thought, still grinning and listening to the old man. *Probably start tellin' me about the winter of '44 or something.*

Two kids, probably no more than thirteen or fourteen, walked towards them carrying flourescent-colored snorkeling gear. They were laughing and jiving one another and the one on the right almost pushed the other kid off the dock with a playful shove.

"There's some fun there," the old man said, nodding toward the kids as they slipped on their fins and jumped into the water. Soon the two snorkelers were floating in the current, taking a breath and diving for a few seconds, returning to the surface with a hollow *blhooooogh!* as water exploded out of their snorkels.

"Used to do a little a that twenty or so years ago," the old man prattled on, flashing a toothy grin. "Even scuba dived a little. Boy, that was fun. Seein' them fish underwater. You ever dive?"

"Well, not really," Phillip lied. "I'd like to learn more, if I knew—" Phillip said, starting to edge away from the man.

"You need to talk to that Randall kid," the old man interrupted with a wave of his thumb. "Now *he's* a diver. Some say he's the best there is, now that his pap's gone. Been divin' all over the world. His wife dives, too, and from what I understand, she's pretty good herself. Nice folks. You oughtta talk to 'em if you're thinkin' about learning to dive."

"Yeah, maybe I will. If I ever get around to—"

"They live right down there," the old man interrupted again, pointing downstream. "You've probably seen his boat around from time to time. Old, but a nice one. He and his wife restored it themselves. Blue and white. They call 'er the *John Galt*. Don't know who *that* is."

Phillip had only been half paying attention until he heard that.

Christopher Knight

John Galt. Don't know who that is.

The image of the blue-and-white cabin cruiser played through his head, and he saw the gold lettering in his mind's eye. *That was the name of the boat that belonged to the guy I just talked to downstream.*

The *John Galt.*

"Yeah, maybe I will look him up," Phillip said slowly. He turned to face the old man, looking him in the eyes. "Pretty good diver?"

"Oh, yeah. Been diving all his life. Oceans, oil rigs, you name it. Like I said, they say he's the best."

"What did you say his name was?" Phillip asked, as if he'd taken a genuine interest. And indeed, he had. But his newfound interest had nothing to do with learning how to dive.

"Eric Randall's the name. Lives right downstream there a ways." The old man motioned with his hand again.

In the river, the two young snorkelers were following the edge of a lily pad bed, every so often taking deep breaths and diving to the river bottom. A half-dozen black cormorants sat on a log like a row of sea crows, still full of fish from the days' hunting. Boats of all sizes churned slowly along, heading north toward Lake Huron, or south to continue through the snaking inland waterway.

"Thanks," Phillip said distantly. "I think I *will* look him up." Phillip bid the man good-bye, shook his hand again, and boarded the Bayliner.

Practicing, huh? For Cozumel? Not if you're the hot-shot diver that old geezer says you are. Cozumel would be a walk in the park. You're practicing, all right. You're practicing lying through your teeth.

He started the boat and headed down river. *Should have figured. Should have known.*

A silent alarm slithered through his bloodstream. Randall had lied to him.

Why? Why . . . unless he had something to hide?

chapter 43

The Bayliner approached the final bend before the Randall's home. Phillip slowed down. Here, there wasn't a lot of boat traffic, just one small aluminum fishing boat a hundred yards or so behind him. The *John Galt* was just pulling away from the dock, and a woman on deck was busy coiling a line. She finished the task and disappeared below deck. Randall was at the helm of the *John Galt*. The boat turned and headed downstream, towards the deep, open water of Lake Huron.

Phillip followed the *John Galt* at a distance, until the boat was at the mouth of the lake, and then he eased the Bayliner into the marina. He guided the big boat into its slip just as Jimmy drove in to the parking lot. Judas Priest blasted from the Trans Am, and Phillip could hear Rob Halford and the guys belting out *Living after Midnight*. More than once, Phillip had reminded Jimmy that, by golly, you may not know it, but Judas Priest *had* recorded more than just *British Steel,* the cassette Jimmy played repeatedly, over and over again. And more than once the harbormaster had asked Jimmy to turn it down a little bit when he got near the marina and Jimmy *said* he would, but that was as far as he ever went. Jimmy Durand pretty much did whatever the hell he pleased—especially when it came to Judas Priest.

The Trans Am screeched to a stop, and Jimmy jumped out, wearing gray bicycle shorts and a black T-shirt that he'd ripped the sleeves from. It was a 2X, and it barely fit him. He stalked down to the slip, the wood planks squeaking under his weight.

"I found out a little more about our friends in the boat," Phillip sneered as Jimmy climbed aboard. "First of all, the boat is the *John Galt.* Second of all, they *did* find something. I *know* they did." He filled Jimmy in on how he had followed Eric upstream after he had filled up the *John Galt* with gas. He told Jimmy of the brief conversation he'd had with him, and how Randall had said that he and his wife were 'practicing for Cozumel.'

Jimmy seemed unfazed. "So, the guy lied. That doesn't mean he's found the *Aurora.* The chances of anybody finding it are small. We're the only ones who know it's there. Christ, Phillip. We've been looking for this thing for six years, and we haven't found jack shit. Chances are this guy and his wife have found something else. Another wreck entirely, if it even *is* a wreck."

Phillip thought a moment, and looked out at the *John Galt,* now a mere speck on the lake. He looked back at Jimmy.

"Is that a chance you want to take?"

Jimmy turned and looked out over the water, watching the *John*

Galt slowly make its way across the quartz-blue expanse of Lake Huron. His stony silence answered Phillip's question.

Whoomp, there it is, Phillip thought, staring at Jimmy. It was just a hint, just a tiny spark, but Jimmy couldn't hide it. Not from Phillip, who had known him for so long. *No, no, no. I can spot that a mile away. Ten miles.* He could smell it on Jimmy, could watch it envelop his herculean body like a black aura.

Rage.

It welled up beneath Jimmy's skin, rearing just a bit of its ugly head. It rose and fell with every breath, it beat at the door with every thundering heartbeat. There was madness in his pores, a dark mania in his blood.

Rage. It wasn't detectable by anything that Jimmy had said, or even the way he had said it. It was his *actions.* His countenance. There was something in his features, a certain fire in his movements that displayed a hidden, secret fury, and Phillip knew that Jimmy was doing everything he could to keep it inside, everything he could to keep the beast harnessed. Rage was a caged animal, tormented and teased and whipped into a frenzy of gnashing teeth and claws.

Whoomp, there it is. Whoomp, there it is. Whoomp, there it is. Whoomp . . . .

Phillip started the motor while Jimmy untied the boat, and the Bayliner glided out of the marina, out the mouth of the Cheboygan river, and headed north toward the Laurentian Channel.

Toward the *John Galt.*

chapter 44

The water in the Channel was a bit rough, but not bad enough to call off the dive. The sun was shining, the wind had diminished to maybe five knots or so, and waves welled up to a moderate three feet. The *John Galt* rocked and swayed as Eric killed the engine and dropped anchor. Eric and Kari suited up and soon were following the white nylon line down into the depths to where *The Brittany* rested, one hundred sixty feet below the surface.

Both Kari and Eric were uneasy. They had tried not to think too much about the images in the photograph that were burned in their minds. They had tried not to think about the woman, her hands tied above her, her head flung back, a gaping hole in the top of her skull. They had tried not to think about the man in the corner, his hands tied and resting on the deck, the knife blade protruding from the side of his skull, with a look of stupefying horror frozen on his badly decomposed face. Even Eric, Kari noticed, was quieter, almost somber. Both knew that the wreck was not simply just some object that lay at the bottom of the lake, but it was also the final resting place of people—people who had once lived and breathed and laughed and worked. Yes, the dives were exciting, yes, the exhilaration was addictive. But here, in the sacristy of the deep, a certain reverence and respect was commanded. As a result, they had decided not to penetrate the wreck on this dive, but wait until Don arrived with his equipment. Until then, they would concentrate their efforts on gathering what information they could from outside the ship.

In the grainy haze of sixty feet, their eyes met, giving each other a telepathic *A-okay*. Eric produced his flashlight and clicked it on. With slow flutter kicks, almost trance-like movements, the two divers descended into darkness.

chapter 45

"There they go."

Jimmy lowered the binoculars to his chest after he spoke, and they hung free from the strap around his neck. Phillip, at the helm, slowed the Bayliner and it chugged to a stop. Water lapped at the hull as the boat bobbed in the waves, some half-mile from where the *John Galt* was moored.

"What's up?" Phillip asked, joining Jimmy at the stern. He raised his hand to shield his eyes from the afternoon glare. Far off to the west, a line of bruised storm clouds was slowly swallowing up the horizon.

"They just hit the water," Jimmy continued, pointing in the direction of the trawler moored in the distance. "Both of them."

"You wanna just hang and check out their site later?" Phillip asked.

Jimmy turned and shot Phillip a *what?-are-you-crazy?* look. "Fuck no," he replied sharply, shaking his head. "I wanna go find out what they're diving for. *Now.*" He raised the binoculars up and he could just barely make out the dark forms of the two divers bobbing at the surface. In seconds, they had disappeared beneath the waves.

"Maybe we should just sit here for a while and see what they're up to. I mean . . . it might just be better to keep a low profile."

Jimmy lowered the binoculars and crossed his python-sized arms. *"Maybe* we should go and find out why they've been diving the same spot for the last few days. And *maybe* we should find out why that guy lied to you." Jimmy stared at Phillip. The remark brought a tinge of anger and resentment, and Phillip decided that, yes, indeed, they needed to find out what the hell was going on. He returned to the helm, turned the key, and the big Bayliner rumbled to life. The engine slipped into gear and the boat pressed on toward the Channel.

chapter 46

In the inky darkness, Eric reached the wreck first. Diving here, in the Great Lakes, especially this close to the channel, was completely different than ocean diving. In many of his dives, he had descended far deeper than the one hundred sixty-foot depth of the *Brittany* and hadn't needed to use a light. This was a completely different story, and he was thankful for the two lights that he carried.

Close behind him, Kari pulled the camera from her bag and took a few photos near the bow. The flash exploded, illuminating the surrounding area like chain lightning.

Eric, wary of disturbing the layers of residue that covered the vessel, shined his light into every small crack or nook he could find, but he didn't see much. Kari moved along the hull, shining her light into the ship as well, looking, searching, for—

—*the bodies.* She couldn't remember the exact place where she had taken that particular picture.

Eric shined his light through a space in the hull where the planking had fallen off. Even in the glow of the flashlight, the room was dark, tomb-like. Fine particles of debris wafted through the beam. Items were scattered haphazardly about: broken boards were strewn on the floor, coated with years of settled silt; a bottle lay on its side, covered with the same; a hobbled chair with only three legs tilted sideways in a corner; a small wooden crate, smashed open and empty, lay crumpled next to the chair. Everything was coated with a film of the same layer of green-brown sediment.

And just to the right of the chair—

Eric gasped unexpectedly in his mouthpiece. He knew that he'd come across the remains again, was prepared for it. But somehow, in the lonely, darkness of the depths, the scene had come alive. The bones, the decaying carcasses—all that was left of what had been real, living people—seemed so much more actual, more *legitimate,* than the picture that Kari had snapped. It was a feeling that left him a bit sad, yet, at the same time, excited, anxious, and *dizzy.* He felt like he was in limbo, and his mind spun slowly.

Shit. It's the nitrogen.

He immediately ascended several feet, and the symptoms left him.

Wow. Haven't felt that in a while.

Kari appeared next to him. She flashed the 'okay' sign with her gloved hand, raising her eyebrows behind her facemask.

You okay?

Eric responded by flashing her the same sign.

Okay. He pointed at the opening in the hull several feet below him, and both divers descended to the split. The dizzying narcosis did not return.

Kari peered through the small opening. Eric could sense her sudden apprehension as she surveyed the horrific scene through her mask. Shadows swayed as the beam swept through the hold, displaying a grisly scene that had remained frozen in time for so many years.

Eric trained the light on one of the disfigured skeletons. *So, it is a woman,* he thought. He had been certain before, when he saw the photograph, but somehow actually *seeing* the lurid spectacle made the crumbling skeleton even more appalling. The scene in the hold had a theater-like quality, as if the events that had taken place so long ago had never really happened at all, but rather the display was the work of some skilled special-effects artist with a penchant for disturbed graphic imagery.

And the photograph Kari had taken certainly did not do the horror any justice.

Good God, she thought, gazing into the hold. *What went on here?*

The woman's hands, what remained of them, were bound to rafters above. The hole in her skull was the size of a quarter, most certainly a gunshot wound. Her clothing was slowly falling apart, but the photo hadn't revealed the puncture holes that reality so vividly displayed. Eight or ten abrasions punctured the rotting clothing, piercing the woman's back. Her torso, mostly decayed and rotting and nearly resting on her knees, swayed ever so slightly in some mystical, unseen current. Her skull was turned and flung backwards, resting on her shoulder blades. Her eyes were gone, and cold, dark sockets stared emptily at the two divers.

Kari directed her light to the right of the woman and the skeletal scaffolding of the man appeared, just like in the picture. His bony, emaciated fingers rested on the floor, his legs apart. His features were less decomposed than the woman's, and the look of terror on his face caused Kari to inadvertently look away. Again, the photograph alone had not revealed what they were now seeing. In the depths of the Laurentian Channel, Don's words echoed.

Like the Manson Family got to these people.

The man appeared to have been stabbed repeatedly in the chest. Holes punctured his clothing, and as the delicate cloth wavered in the water, ribs could be seen. The knife handle stuck out from the side of his skull, yet it was impossible to tell if that had been the blow that had killed him. He had been stabbed so many times in the chest that it was surprising the clothing hadn't fallen apart from the holes alone. His rigid jaw hung down to what would have been his neck, screaming an eternal, silent scream. And his tongue, even after all these years, was—

Wait a minute, Eric thought. *That's not his tongue.* He shined his flashlight directly into the man's mouth. Shadows shrieked and skirted away.

That's no tongue. That's . . . that's a . . . knife!

The weapon had been forced so far back into the man's mouth that it was not visible in the photograph, being obscured by the shadow of the upper teeth.

Jesus. That thing probably went right out the back of the guy's neck. Eric paused as the reality struck him. Saliva gurgled in his throat and he swallowed, then took a long, deep breath. He exhaled, and a hundred translucent bubbles broke apart and rose. *My God. They stuck him to the wall with a knife.*

Kari had arrived at the same conclusion as Eric and she recoiled at the very idea. *What would make somebody—*

Her thoughts were interrupted by Eric pointing to the side of his head and then pointing up. She looked at him quizzically, trying to read his eyes behind his mask. Again, more insistently this time, Eric pointed to the side of his head, then pointed upward.

Then she heard it. A distinct buzzing, a humming. Like high-tension electrical wires. Grasshoppers singing in an August meadow.

A boat. A boat was coming.

chapter 47

The sun was shining on and off, the wind was light, but the waves were rolling in pretty heavy. The storm was coming. Slowly, but it was on its way for sure. Foamy crowns wrestled in the swirling sea, and alabaster gray clouds were sweeping in from the southwest. Jimmy was at the front of the Bayliner, drinking his second Budweiser and gazing out over the waters toward Bois Blanc Island. The island ferry had just departed with its fifty-foot plume of water arcing up behind the boat. All other boats had headed inland, back to their slips, their marinas, their docks, to wait out the coming storm.

Except, of course, for the *John Galt*. It sat moored in the channel like a blue and white loon, swelling up and down in the increasing waves.

The Bayliner motored farther into the lake, toward the anchored trawler. It wouldn't be long now.

Jimmy reached into his leather duffel bag and pulled out a nylon case. He fiddled around for a moment, then extended his arm towards Phillip. Phillip didn't notice the gun until it was pointed directly at his forehead, just inches away.

"BANG!!" he exclaimed, raising the gun barrel in a feigned recoil. "You're *DEAD!!!*" Seeing Phillip's expression, Jimmy lowered the gun and almost fell off his chair, laughing hysterically.

Phillip's heart slammed his rib cage like a pile driving woodpecker. *Ba-bam, ba-bam, ba-bam.*

"You son of a bitch!! Don't you EVER do that again!! Ever!" Phillip shouted. His heart was racing and his pulse pounded in his head. He shook his head and took a couple of deep breaths.

"You should have seen your face!!" Jimmy's huge frame was doubled over and he was laughing hysterically. "I mean, did you ever *shit!!!* You better go to the head and clean your drawers, man!!" Jimmy continued laughing, while Phillip worked at regaining his composure.

"When did you get that, anyway?" he asked nervously, still shook up.

"Oh, a while back," Jimmy said, waving the gun in front of him. "Just in case. I got another one, too. Just like this one. I keep it under the seat of my car for emergency purposes. You can never be too sure." Jimmy popped open the cylinder of the .38 Smith & Wesson and pulled out a bullet as if he were inspecting it. He replaced the shell and snapped the cylinder back into place. "You never know when you may need one of these babies," he continued, holding the gun proudly with one hand, his testosterone near boiling as he felt the blue steel on his skin. "Sometimes your best friends will be the ones that will try to do you in. Sorry I scared the shit outta ya." Then he rolled back in his chair, laughing even harder. "But *man*, you shoulda seen your face!! Man, were you freaked."

"Hold it," Phillip interrupted, as he raised his binoculars. "Hold on a minute. I can see Randall's boat, but—" He eased off the throttle and slowed the boat to a standstill. The waves were four feet now and the wind was still increasing. The sun had disappeared for good, as evidenced by the dark clouds that had shifted in from the west.

"Well, *I'll be damned*," Phillip said as he lowered the binoculars and handed them to Jimmy. "Check that out."

chapter 48

Bzzzzzzzzzzzzzzzzzzzz . . . .

Sound travels great distances underwater and comes from all directions, so there was no way of knowing exactly where it was coming from, but Eric guessed that it had to be pretty close. Above them, anyway, and not too far from the *John Galt*. The sound grew louder until, quite suddenly, it lowered in pitch. The engine rumble was less defined but still very much present, evidence that the boat must have slowed.

The engine noise suddenly stopped. Someone had killed the engine.

Eric motioned to Kari and reluctantly they went back to the anchor line and began their ascent. They didn't have much air left in their tanks anyway, and would only be cutting the dive short by a minute or so.

Who's brought their boat way out here? Eric wondered. He racked his brain trying to think of who might have recognized the *John Galt* and had decided to pay a visit. They stopped at scheduled intervals to allow the nitrogen bubbles in their blood to thin, and Eric listened intently for the motor.

Nothing.

At seventy-five feet, the dim light of the surface began to appear, but Eric could see only distorted gray contours when he looked up. A brown trout suddenly appeared from nowhere, again giving both divers a start. This was almost certainly the trout that had surprised them on their initial first dive to the wreck.

Oh. Just you guys again.

They ignored the large brown and the fish did the same, slowly slinking off and vanishing.

Seventy feet.

Sixty-five feet.

On the surface, high above, Eric could now make out the dark shape of the *John Galt.*

And the dark shape of another boat right next to her.

chapter 49

Eric and Kari looked up at the two large shapes floating in the water sixty feet above them. The boat next to the *John Galt* was larger, but that's all the two divers could tell. Just two fuzzy, fat whales, lounging on the surface.

Twenty feet.

This was their final decompression stop. *Waves are picking up,* Eric thought, gazing up at the tumbling, leaden surface. He hadn't noticed it until now, but the sun had vanished, and the sky appeared to be overcast again.

They waited in place, holding the anchor line for five minutes, to finish their final decompression stop. Then Eric signaled thumbs up to Kari and they drifted anxiously up the last twenty feet. They surfaced on the starboard side of the *John Galt*, opposite the port side where the larger boat sat. Kari broke the surface first, followed immediately by Eric.

In a split instant, Eric saw that someone had boarded the *John Galt.* In the next instant, he recognized the blue uniforms, orange vests, and flashing blue lights of the Coast Guard. A uniformed man motioned with his arm, commanding the divers toward the boat.

Yeah, Eric thought, *like we're going somewhere else.*

The waves had increased to four feet, and the *John Galt* and the Coast Guard trawler rose and fell in the swelling waters. Eric took his fins off and handed them to a uniformed guardsman, then took off his vest and tanks in the water. He handed the heavy apparatus to another man, who pulled the two tanks on board. Eric helped Kari do the same with her gear and the two climbed the short aluminum ladder.

"There's a big storm moving in," one of the men told Eric. "We need all small crafts off the lake." Eric looked out over Lake Huron. Smudges of dark, ugly clouds reared off to the west, and the wind was picking up by the minute. Both boats, the Coast Guard trawler and the *John Galt,* were heaving in the waves that were slamming into their hulls.

"We saw you heading out here and tried the radio, and we were on our way out when we saw you suit up and jump in. And by the way—" he pointed to the dive flag that was tied upright to an inner tube, "—that goes in the water when you dive, not up here on deck. You, of all people know that." Eric did not recognize the uniformed man, but apparently he had recognized Eric. Frederick Randall had a reputation for being a maverick diver, one who bent the rules. But his reputation had also earned him respect, and it was also widely known that Eric had indeed followed in his fathers' footsteps . . . and probably a bit too well. "When I saw you diving without a flag I was going to write you a ticket, but I'll just give you a warning this time."

Eric nodded a dutiful 'thanks' and apologized for not placing the flag out. Kari stood by, drying herself with a towel, silent.

"What are you diving for way out here? You know you're awfully close to the Channel." The question had been followed by a statement, as the guardsman knew that the divers were aware of their location.

After all, it *is* Eric Randall.

"Well, nothing really," Eric replied, glancing at the frothing, dark waters. "Something popped up on our bottom scanner. Only a rock formation, though."

The conversation ended with the Coast Guard officer again warning them about the weather conditions. The trawler left, followed shortly by the John Galt.

chapter 50

A light rain began to fall and the temperature had dropped five degrees while they had been diving. Kari stripped off her wetsuit and put on a pair of sweats and manned the helm while Eric found his jeans and a gray pullover. Angry white manes rolled atop the waves, climbing and receding, then climbing again. The lake was absent of watercraft, except for the Coast Guard trawler which was a few hundred yards in front of the *John Galt* and another boat which had been heading north a few minutes ago, toward them, but now had turned back as well and was heading back to the mouth of the Cheboygan River.

The rain fell harder, and sprinkles dotted Kari's face as she put on a rain poncho over her sweats. Eric returned from below deck, wearing his University of Michigan sweats and a heavy blue turtle neck sweater. He relieved Kari at the helm and she stood next to him as the *John Galt* rode the steadily rising waves.

"It was probably a good thing we left when we did," Eric said loudly, his eyes scanning the sky. "This front came out of nowhere."

Kari's mind turned back to the dive and the wreck. "What do you think happened?" she asked, raising her voice above the howling wind. "Those people weren't just *killed*, Eric. They didn't just go down with the ship. I mean . . . ." She shuddered. "God . . . that was awful. And that poor woman . . . ." She shuddered again.

"It's hard to say," Eric answered. "It's not like the Lakes were known for pirates. In fact, I've never heard of anything of the sort. Not in Lake Huron."

The waves decreased in strength and size when the *John Galt* made it to the shelter of the break wall that extended north from the western shore of the Cheboygan River. It was raining even harder now, and Eric pulled on his rain gear.

"Killing somebody is bad enough, but those poor people were tortured. Did you see the holes in the shirt of the one in the corner?" Kari put her hand under Eric's rain gear and sweater, pressing her hands against his skin to warm them.

"Stab wounds, I think. They looked more like slices. And the knife down that guy's throat . . ." He didn't finish. They were both silent for a moment. The heavy patter of rain was now a continuous drone as the raindrops bounced off the *John Galt*.

Kari went below deck to get out of the weather and finish storing the dive gear. She called to Eric from the cabin. "What time did Don say he was going to be here?"

"He didn't. He just said sometime this evening. I figured we'd go and have a few drinks and dinner at the *Hack-Ma Tack*." The *Hack-Ma-Tack Inn* was located farther up the Cheboygan River. Like *The Boathouse*, it too was popular among boaters who frequented the inland waterway.

"That's fine, but I don't think we'll be taking the boat there. Not tonight anyway." His eyes scanned the pallid, overcast sky. "This front looks like it's here for a while."

They were in the shelter of the river now and the waves had abated, but the wind and the rain continued. Eric docked the *John Galt* in front of their home and secured the boat while Kari bagged up the uneaten sandwiches and trotted up the wet, grassy slope and into the house. When Eric finished, he, too, bounded up the squishy wet grass and through the sliding glass doors. A Captain Morgan and Coke waited for him on the counter.

Kari was examining the picture of the capstan cover, turning it around in her hands as if a different perspective would reveal its secrets. She handed it to Eric. "Do you think we should have told the Coast Guard about the ship?" she asked.

Eric took it and shook his head. "They'll find out soon enough. If we tell them now, we might as well be broadcasting it on the six o'clock news. Somebody somehow would find it and that would be that. There'd be divers all over her in no time. I guess it's kind of selfish, but I want to find out what happened on that ship and why. Before anyone else discovers her. We're not even sure how old the schooner is or how long it's been there. If anything, I may call up Mike Felsing and tell him about it. I'm sure he'd really want to see this." He waved the photo in his hand as he spoke. "If anyone can track where the *Brittany* came from, it will be him. And, he's someone we can trust."

Eric set the photo on the table. Mike Felsing had been a friend of his father's. Frederick Randall had met Felsing in Detroit, where he was a Detroit police officer. The elder Randall had been called in to help locate a possible murder victim in the Detroit River. He'd found the guy, all right—sort of. They just never found his *head.* The body had been decapitated, probably by a boat propeller. The victim most certainly was dead before he had been dumped into the water, as evidenced by the numerous .32 caliber holes in the man's torso. The police divers could probably have found the guy on their own, but they weren't having much luck and time was crucial. Frederick Randall found the corpse, the man was charged, and Mike Felsing got his man, just like in the movies. He was deeply thankful to Randall, and was surprised to meet up with him again at *Leggs Inn*, a restaurant in Cross Village where Felsing and his wife, Evelyn, had a cottage. This had been back in the sixties, and the two men became friends. After Felsing's career was cut short by a gunshot wound, he had retired to Cross Village full-time.

But Mike Felsing was known as a dogged investigator. He had more successes, more cases solved in his years on the force than anyone in recent history. Not because he was lucky, not because he had a knack, not because he had some 'sixth sense' like cops on TV. No, Felsing was successful for a single reason: hard work. He wore out all leads until they were bones. All that was left was the truth.

Eric was certain that, if he could get Mike Felsing to assist in the research of the *Brittany*, they would get some answers.

chapter 51

Phillip and Jimmy watched from the cabin of the Bayliner as the *John Galt* chugged passed the marina and up the river. They had spotted the Coast Guard trawler heading toward the *John Galt* and had slowed to watch from the safety of a good distance. They watched as guardsman boarded their boat, watched the Randall's returning from the dive. When Phillip saw the Coast Guard trawler pulling away from Randall's boat and heading back towards Cheboygan, he too had turned around and headed for the marina. The Bayliner now bobbed gently in its slip.

"When is Ed supposed to be back?" Jimmy asked. Ed had set off for Traverse City to get some dive equipment. One of their regulators had developed a problem, and two of the spares weren't operating properly, either. Ed wanted a new hands-free dive light, and a few other things he said might come in handy. What those things were he didn't say.

"Probably later this evening," Phillip answered. "That's a long haul. And he took US-31, which means he had to go through Petoskey. It takes forty-five minutes just to get through that mess alone." A virtual bottleneck had made traveling US-31 through Petoskey and Bay View a nightmare. Three miles could sometimes take nearly an hour.

"Well, let's follow Randall," Jimmy recommended, stretching his telephone pole-sized arms. "Let's find out what the hell he's doing."

"Not yet," Phillip suggested, shaking his head. "We gotta be careful. But, on the other hand," he continued, reconsidering his own stance, "there's a chance that if he *did* find the ship, he could go shooting his mouth off and then everyone would know. That would blow things all to hell. And I haven't spent six years to let some local-yokel redneck screw this up for us."

"No shit," Jimmy agreed in a scalding tone. He popped open another beer and handed it to Phillip. Neither spoke for a few minutes until Jimmy downed the last of his Budweiser and told Phillip that he'd *better go and call the bitch. She's probably wondering where I am. No, scratch that. She knows I'm up here fishing with you and Ed.*

"Why don't you meet me at *Johnnie's* tonight around nine," Phillip suggested. He twisted his wrist and glanced at his watch. "Ed should be back by then. I'll leave a message on his machine." Jimmy said that'd be great, and all two hundred thirty pounds of him strutted down the dock and to his car.

Good grief, Phillip thought, watching Jimmy open the door to the Trans Am and tuck himself inside. *He's so beefed up he can't even walk like a normal human being. He can just barely fit in his car.*

Phillip secured the boat, locked everything up, and jogged through the rain to his truck.

chapter 52

Eric lay on top of Kari, kissing her chin. The rain had stopped, but the mid-afternoon sky was still dark and threatening, as if waiting to unleash another pounding fury of wind and rain. It had even hailed, and the tiny ice balls bounced in the grass and made a terrible racket as they battered the roof and the deck, melting and disappearing almost as quickly as they had come. The steady *drip drip drip drip drip* as the rain rolled off the roof ticked away like a metronome outside the bedroom window, keeping time throughout Eric and Kari's afternoon waltz.

"I think I need a cigarette after that," Eric said, his face close to hers.

Kari slapped his butt, laughed, and smiled a perfect smile. "Like you've even touched a cigarette in ten years."

"Well, I figure now's the perfect time to start if there ever was one," he grinned.

Kari raised her head off the pillow and kissed him lightly on the forehead. "Is Don staying here tonight?"

"I don't think so," Eric replied. "Says he's going to rent a cabin on Mullett Lake for a few weeks. I told him he's welcome to stay here, but you know *Don*. Doesn't want to impose. He'll probably keep most of his equipment in our garage, though. Those cabins don't have much storage area. Says he's got a camera mounted on a mini-sub. It's two feet long and weighs about thirty pounds and he says it's easy to operate. Cost him a fortune. But he'll be able to video the entire ship. You and I will attach high-powered lights on the masts and deck. He thinks that if we don't stir up much silt and debris, we can illuminate the entire outside of the ship. When we do actually penetrate it, though, we'll have a different video camera. A smaller one that we'll carry with us."

They showered together and got dressed. Kari picked up the house, slightly annoyed that Eric, once again, had suddenly disappeared when there was some cleaning to do. *Funny how he has a knack for being invisible when the dishes need to be washed or the bathroom needs to be cleaned,* she thought. Eric had indeed disappeared, to the garage, where he moved around the mountain bikes and some other boxes so Don would have a place to store the equipment.

chapter 53

Don Garrity pulled the black Dodge Caravan into the mini-mart in West Branch and wheeled up next to an open pump. The rain had begun, and it looked like it was going to stay. As he re-fueled, he checked the map to approximate a time of arrival at Eric and Kari's.

Two hours. Maybe two-and-a-half, if this rain keeps up.

He called them from the pay phone but got no answer, hanging up as soon as the machine clicked on. *Well, Eric had said that they were going to dive again today. Weather must be better there than it is here.*

The mini-mart was filled with travelers and tourists. A heavy man in a rumpled T-shirt stood in line in front of Don, smelling of beer and motor oil. On the back of his shirt, the profound statement *'Lead, Follow, or Get Out of the Way'* was printed in bold cursive letters, beneath a long-haired, helmet-less motorcycle rider. The large man couldn't decide if he wanted the Marlboro Reds or Lights, saying that they were for his wife's sister, and he was holding each pack up to the window as if showing someone outside the choices, talking to his reflection in the window. He finally opted for the Lights, and handed the Reds back to the girl behind the counter.

Don grabbed a bag of Jolly Ranchers, a bag of pretzels, paid the cashier, and left. Deciding that maybe candy and pretzels may not be enough after all, he swung through the Burger King drive-through and then jumped back on to I-75, heading north.

Won't be eating dinner until later, he thought. *No harm in a burger or two.*

The rain came down harder and it became difficult to see. Don had the wipers on high, but he could barely make out the headlights of the car behind him or the taillights of the car in front of him. He tapped his brakes to alert the driver behind him that he was slowing down. Suddenly, a loud rumble shook the Caravan as hail began drilling the mini-van, drowning out the radio. Traffic was now moving at only thirty miles per hour, and a few cars had pulled off to the side and stopped altogether. Don glanced up as he drove under the sign signaling '*ST. HELEN - THIS EXIT.*' He turned onto the off ramp and slowed, stopped at the stop sign, and turned right. The tympani of hail on the mini-van was deafening. *If this gets any worse, my windshield's going to cave in*, Don thought.

Then he found what he was looking for—a bridge over the road. Don pulled under it and stopped. He watched the hail and heavy rain from the shelter of the bridge, relieved to have found a retreat from the pounding storm. He scanned the radio dial, but most of the signals were fuzzy and weak under the concrete-and-steel of the overpass. He turned the radio off, reclined his seat, and closed his eyes.

Might as well wait it out.

The van was filled with Don's underwater photography gear. He hadn't been sure what he would need, so he had brought it all, along with much of his developing materials. He wanted to develop any still photos right away and couldn't risk taking the film to someone else to be developed and run the chance of somebody else finding out about the wreck.

He turned his head and glanced back at the mass of electronic equipment piled in the back of the van, placed his glasses on the dash, and nodded off to sleep.

And the nightmare came again.

chapter 54

Don awoke, swimming in sweat. His knuckles were white from gripping the steering wheel. Large, plate-sized stains ringed his armpits and darkened his shirt. A long trail of wet blotches began at his collar and ran down his chest. His brown hair was drenched, and perspiration was running down his face and through his beard and mustache. He was soaked.

Cripes, he thought, looking around himself in an astonished, sleepy haze. *Might as well have been sleeping outside in the rain.*

He unzipped the bag that sat on the passenger seat and pulled out a fresh pair of jeans and a T-shirt. After he was sure that no one was coming, he hopped out of the van, hastily stripped, and put on the dry clothing. As he looked out from under the bridge, he could see that the rain had given way to a light, continuous drizzle. The wind had stopped altogether and it felt like it might be getting warmer. Crazy Michigan weather.

Back on I-75. His nap had lasted almost two hours, but he could still make it to Eric and Kari's by seven or so. It was drizzling, but traffic was back to its normal ten miles per hour above the posted speed limit, and within an hour he had passed though Grayling and was twenty miles south of Gaylord. He checked the rear-view mirror and saw the equipment piled high in the van. Much of it hadn't even been used since . . . well, since—

He was looking at an underwater camera and the shock wave hit him like a truck. A tremendous rush of fear struck him and shook his body. He had a vision of being underwater, of millions of bubbles, the camera hitting his body then falling away from him. His body convulsed as if struck by a gunshot. But as quickly as the feeling had hit him, it flashed away.

He slowed to pull off the freeway, shaken, then decided to pull himself together and keep traveling. He shook his head from side-to-side, beads of sweat again rolling from his brow down his face, trickling through his beard. His heart pounded in his chest, and he was on the verge of hyper-ventilating. He took a long, deep breath, slowly exhaled, and repeated the process again and again. *Where in the hell did that come from?*

But he knew. Somewhere, deep inside, it was there, hiding in the shadows, lurking in the darkest corners.

Now it wanted out.

It had been chained for much too long, tucked away and out of sight for far too long. It was time for the grand re-entry, the homecoming, the Great Return. *Hey Donny Boy, remember me? I'll bet you do.* It was his own voice from the past, long forgotten, and discarded. Don tried to ignore it, to tell himself that it was his mind playing tricks, that it wasn't there. But it *was* there, a haunting whisper in the shadows of his mind, mocking him. *Gather the clowns and horses and floats and candy and get ready, Donny Boy,* it said. *The Parade is comin' to town.*

chapter 55

The night was warm and sticky. Thick. The menacing licks of Ted Nugent's *Stranglehold* drifted through the open door of *Johnnie's Sports Bar*. Phillip parked on Main Street and looked around. Judging by the number of other parked cars, there wasn't a lot going on at *Johnnie's* tonight, which was fine with him. Phillip waited outside in the truck for a few minutes. It wasn't that he didn't want to go into the bar alone, it's just that, well . . . he didn't want to go into the bar alone. Phillip wasn't from around here, wasn't one of them, and didn't want to be.

A burly kid, who couldn't have been much more than twenty-two, stepped out of the doorway and stared up into the night sky. Tilting his head back and spreading his arms he sucked in a deep breath and gave an animal-like howl, much to the delight of some of the patrons inside. He howled again, the crowd inside cheered, and he turned and went back through the open door.

To hell with it, Phillip thought and stepped out of the Dakota. He wanted a beer; he'd have one. He locked the doors and walked across the street and into the bar.

Two dozen people were milling around and two girls were shooting pool. Near the back, a small cluster of people had successfully created a smoke screen with their cigarettes, each person lighting another as soon as they finished the last one. Phillip chose a table in the front corner, away from most of the crowd. The waitress came over and he ordered a Budweiser.

Phillip was always a little early and Jimmy was always a little late. He sipped on his beer and watched the people in the bar. A loud group at the end of the bar leaned on the stools and bragged about the deer they had shot the previous year. The two girls laughed and joked while they attempted to play pool and one of them, a dark-haired woman, bent over lazily to shoot. As she did, her boyfriend pinched her.

"Dammit Tone-EEEE!! Don't dooooooo that!" She fell into his arms giggling.

Phillip shook his head slightly as he took another sip of his beer. It wasn't that the people were any different than those in any small town. They were hard-working, hard-playing people. But Phillip himself had an air about him that many people, especially around here, didn't like. Phillip walked, talked, and acted like he was better or smarter than anyone. He didn't even have to say anything. In fact, if someone *did* strike up a conversation with him, Phillip, beyond the usual uh-huhs and occasional nods, didn't respond with the same friendly warmth.

He had just taken another sip of his beer when a man came over to his table, smiling. Phillip half smiled back and made no effort to speak. It was the man that Phillip saw step outside and let out the Howl from Hell.

The Howler belched and took a deep breath. "Watch this," he said, addressing Phillip. He took another breath, turned his head to the ceiling and let out a piercing yell that curled Phillip's hair. The howl lasted a good five seconds and Phillip didn't move. The crowd cheered and laughed and the Howler grinned from ear to ear. His blue jeans didn't quite make it up and over his gut, nor did the front of his black *Insane Clown Posse* T-shirt quite reach the top of his jeans. From behind the bar, the bartender repeated a warning to him, telling the Howler that, *once more, and you're outta here*. Howler, if he even heard the bartender, did not respond. He stood his ground, smiling at Phillip.

"How 'bout that?" the Howler exclaimed proudly. "Pretty good, eh?"

Phillip sipped on his beer slowly, and set it back on the table. "Yeah. Real good."

Things would have turned out a lot different if Phillip had left it at that. But now he was *pissed*. No, he was more than just *pissed*. He was *livid*.

The Howler turned to walk away and Phillip addressed him. The comment wasn't very loud, but it was loud enough.

The Howler stopped and turned around, facing Phillip. He was no longer smiling. "What did you say?" His cheeks were flushed and his nostrils flared. He'd heard what Phillip said the first time, but his testosterone needed the added boost of hearing it again.

There was something about those words. *What did you say?* There was power in those words. If you spoke them just right, you could almost feel blood beginning to boil. Take two parts idiot to one pint alcohol, speak loudly, stir. A recipe for instant power. Call it the 'Idiot's Delight'. Even Martha Stewart couldn't pull that one off.

Phillip took a slow sip of his beer. "I said *'yeah, real good. Sounds like you've been practicing on a few sheep'.*" He spoke slowly, quietly, as if talking to a child, staring directly into the Howler's intoxicated eyes.

The bartender had already started to move, but he had to walk down to the end of the bar to come around. In the meantime, the Howler had kicked a chair out of his way and Phillip had stood up.

Guess I probably should have expected this.

He was able to block the Howler's first punch but the second caught him flat in the temple, and he fell back over a table behind him. The Howler backed him into the corner and hit Phillip in the stomach. Phillip wasn't sure what was worse—being punched or having to smell the Howler's dirty shirt. He reeked of chewing tobacco, cigarettes, beer, and sweat all rolled into one. *Not only a howler*, he thought, *but a smelly one at that.*

Phillip was not a veteran of bar fights and he was barely able to hold his own—mainly by hanging onto the Howler's shirt. Over Smelly Howler's shoulder, the bartender's face came into view as he tried to restrain the swinging madman who had cornered Phillip. Phillip hoped the bartender would do something pretty quick, as his stomach wasn't feeling all that well now, and he had only been able to get a few good licks in of his own.

Suddenly, the bartender's face disappeared.

Oh shit. Now I am in trouble, Phillip thought desperately.

Smelly Howler backed off for a moment, drew his right arm back, and was about to let it fly when another face came into view over his shoulder.

Jimmy.

chapter 56

How about that, you smelly son of a bitch? Phillip thought. *Turn around. Turn around and let's see you really howl, you hay-chewin' redneck.*

But Smelly Howler didn't have the time. The arm that he had been preparing to unleash was now behind his back. Jimmy grabbed the back of his head, and with one giant effort, slammed Smelly Howler's face into the table. He hit so hard one of the table legs broke. Jimmy let go of his arm and let him tumble to the floor. The bartender, who Jimmy had pulled off and literally thrown to the floor, got up. Jimmy didn't say a word, he just pointed to him as if to say 'just stay out of this.' But neither the bartender, nor any of the other patrons in the bar, looked extremely anxious to come to the rescue of Smelly Howler, who was now on his feet, facing two hundred thirty pounds of death in a tanktop. But for some crazy reason, Smelly Howler had decided that yes, indeed, there was enough testosterone in his system and *by golly, I am going to whup this guy's ass and teach him a lesson or two. Go ahead, set me up, Joe. Set me up with another round of Idiot's Delight.*

Smelly Howler threw a punch and Jimmy easily deflected it. It swung off to the side and he threw another one, this one a bit slower and aimed poorly. Jimmy instantly seized Howler's wrist, held it for a split-moment, gave it a twist and a jerk, and everyone cringed and gasped as the bone audibly snapped like a dead branch.

Snap. Crackle. Pop. It's the Rice Krispie treatment, Mr. Howler. Smelly Howler screamed in pain and leaned over, favoring his newly-broken arm. He looked like he was going to cry.

But it was far from finished. There was still a good swig or two left in that bottle of Idiot's Delight, certainly enough to give Smelly Howler the advantage over Mr. Universe. He took a breath and let the surge of pain and adrenaline convulse through his flesh. Anxious patrons looked on, content to wonder what was going to happen next. No one wanted to get involved in this one, no sir.

The bartender shouted something. Smelly Howler's friends shouted out encouragement, happy to share some of their own Idiot's Delight. Ted Nugent's maniacal guitar fanned the flames in a blistering crescendo of napalm and battery acid.

Suddenly Smelly Howler lunged, forcing his good arm out in front of him . . . with a knife in his hand.

Jimmy bobbed sideways and easily missed the onslaught. He spun, and with a powerful roundhouse kick with his right leg, knocked the knife from Smelly Howler's hand. The weapon arced up, then clattered to the floor.

A look of stunning realization came over Smelly Howler's face, like he just realized that, indeed, the bottle was empty. Bone dry. *You can all go home, fellas, we're all out of Idiot's Delight. The tap's run dry.*

Jimmy snared the back of Smelly Howler's pants with one hand, and with the other, his neck. With one powerful heave, he threw him clean up and out the window. The glass exploded outward, and deadly shrapnel filled the air. The ensuing *ooohs* swept through the patrons like a shockwave. Smelly Howler landed on the sidewalk amidst a thousand shards of shattered glass. He was cut all over and blood poured onto the sidewalk, forming crimson rivulets that began to drain over the curb and onto the street. He *did* begin to cry now, and a few people streamed out of the bar to help him. Nobody even looked at Jimmy as he stood by the broken table, ready for more if anybody wanted to partake. He posed stiff, rigid, his chest heaving, muscles bulging, stone-like. His head snapped around.

Anybody else? Anybody else care for a little swig of Idiot's Delight? Or is the keg dry?

A city police car was sitting at the light less than a block away and the sound of breaking glass alerted the driver. The cops responded with an audience-grabbing, tire-squealing, *Adam-12* U-turn, screeching to a halt in front of *Johnnie's*. Sirens blaring and lights flashing, two cops bolted from the car. One attended to the babbling Smelly Howler, while the other went inside. Surprisingly—and much to Phillip's relief—Jimmy put up no fuss at all, and even apologized to the bartender for the mess. The cop handcuffed Jimmy, sat him in the back of the patrol car and drove away. Phillip had been questioned, but not arrested. After all, he hadn't taken the first swing and the cop couldn't find the rule where suggesting that someone had been engaging in intimate relations with a sheep was against the law. The cop *did* recommend to Phillip that it was probably a good idea if he didn't show his face around *Johnnie's* for a while. "Like, maybe a couple years," the cop had said. And he meant it.

Phillip walked out of the bar and got into his truck to wait for Ed, who would be showing up any minute. *Rednecks,* he thought. *Local-yokel rednecks.*

chapter 57

Ed made the one hundred ten-mile trek to Traverse City, getting to the dive shop at four in the afternoon.

The place was empty except for a single employee who was cleaning the inside of the windows when Ed walked in. "Hey there. How are ya?" The clerk recognized Ed, but couldn't remember his name. Maybe he didn't know his name. But the huge man had been in the shop before. He remembered that he came in about once a month in the summer, sometimes spending well over $1,000 in cash during each visit, always buying top-of-the-line gear. And he seemed to know what he was doing, shunning any offers of assistance from the employees.

Ed handed him the regulator, explained that it was not working properly and that he wanted another just like it.

"You want me to have a look at it? Maybe I could fix it."

Ed shook his head and his cheeks shuddered. "Naw. If you can get it working, keep it. I just want another one." The clerk pointed to a section with dozens of regulators and Ed found the one he needed. Then he browsed around, picking up a few other things. Two new, high-powered dive lights and a new mask that was supposed to be fog-free. Ed piled all the gear on the counter and paid the man nearly $900, all in cash.

"Going shark diving?" the man at the counter asked.

Ed looked up at him puzzled. He looked at the items on the counter. "Oh yeah. Australia. It's a freakin' zoo. Can't be too careful, ya know."

"Sure thing. Well, good luck . . . oh . . . and send us a postcard. We'll stick it up in the store."

"Will do." Ed made two trips to load his purchases into the bed of the Ranger and covered everything with a heavy canvas. The clerk waved to Ed as he drove off and Ed waved back and honked his horn.

Quite a sale, the clerk thought. *The guy spent a whole five minutes in the shop and spent nine hundred bucks. And I've never sold three spearguns in one day, let alone to one person.* He picked up his rag and went back to the business of cleaning his windows.

chapter 58

The black mini-van pulled into the Randall's driveway at 7:20 p.m.
Eric was doing some work on the *John Galt* and Kari was the first
to greet Don. She gave him a hug, chatted with him for a moment,
went through the usual *'gosh, you look great's'* and *'geez, it's good
to see you's,'* and then they walked arm-in-arm around the house
and down to the river. Eric had heard them talking and was now on
deck. His old jeans had big, black, oil stains, and his torn flannel
shirt looked more like an old kitchen rag that had been thrown over
his shoulders.

"Lord, you are still uglier than sin!" Eric exclaimed, smiling
good-naturedly. The two men shook hands and embraced. "And
what's this?" Eric continued, pulling at Don's full but closely-cut
beard.

"Ah, just a little dirt," Don grinned, and reached his hand behind
Eric's head. "And what's *this*?" Eric's hair wasn't very long, but

he usually kept it short. Now the back of it actually touched his collar.

"Ah, you know how women are," Eric replied, nodding toward his wife. "She likes to grab it in the heat of the moment." He winked.

Kari laughed, rolling her eyes. "He hasn't got his hair cut 'cause he's too lazy to go all the way downtown to the barber shop," she said. "And he won't let me do it."

The three talked for a few minutes, mostly about old friends, who was doing what and where they were doing it. Eric and Don had made a lot of mutual friends in many parts of the country, mostly in the dive business, and Eric hadn't been in touch with very many since they'd moved to Cheboygan.

Don showered and the three decided upon *The Boathouse* for dinner. *The Boathouse* was downtown and since the rain had stopped, they decided that it would be a nice evening for a walk and to show Don a little of Cheboygan. They chatted away the short drive and parked on a side street, near the city park, adjacent to *The Boathouse*. It was growing dark as they strolled through the park. Eric had just finished telling Don that not a lot of excitement ever happens in Cheboygan, when the three heard the loud crash of breaking glass, followed by sobbing. As they turned and walked up to Main Street, they saw that a man lay on the sidewalk amid a sparkling, deadly carpet of broken glass. People were crowding around him, and a cop car, its lights flashing like a pinball machine, sat in front of the whole scene.

"It looks like he went through the front window of *Johnnie's*," Kari said.

"That'll be a first," Eric replied. "That window is almost six feet above the ground. He must've been fighting Hulk Hogan or something." He turned to Don. "Looks like the excitement of the city has followed you to Cheboygan, Don." Eric elbowed him, and smiled. Don shook his head and laughed, and the three proceeded through the park and to the restaurant.

chapter 59

After returning from Traverse City, Ed went to his cabin and napped. When he awoke he was hungry. He drove to *Subway* and then stopped at Phillip's motel room. It was just after eleven p.m.

He was not the least bit happy when Phillip told him that Jimmy had been arrested. Belmont exploded into a tirade about how Jimmy was going to blow it for all three of them if he kept it up.

"That son of a bitch is going to fuck everything up," Ed said in disgust. "The last thing we need is attention, and Jimmy goes out and beats the shit out of some punk and winds up in jail." He crushed out his cigarette and immediately lit another one. "Fucking asshole," he breathed, shaking his head and exhaling smoke.

"I called the jail," Phillip said. "He stays the night. Can't bail him out until morning."

"Serves the bastard right," Ed sneered.

Phillip filled Ed in about what they had seen earlier in the day. He told him about his conversation with Randall and about what the old man had told him at *Pier 33*. Ed agreed that Randall had fed him a line—a big line—and had indeed probably found something in the Channel. He took a drag from his cigarette.

"If Eric Randall is the kind of diver this guy says he is," Phillip speculated, "you can bet that there is something out there. He's not diving to look at rock formations."

"Well, that means we go look again. The sooner the better. You got those coordinates?"

Phillip nodded. "Down on the boat. They're not exact, but we were close enough to estimate an approximate site. I marked them on the chart."

"Good. Let's go. Let's go see what the hot shot diver and his wife have found."

"Tonight?" Phillip replied apprehensively. "Right now?"

"Why not?" Ed replied. "You afraid of the dark or something?"

Both men rode in silence in the very late Paul Sprague's Ranger down to the Cheboygan marina.

chapter 60

The Boathouse wasn't crowded—the rain had put a damper on the boating activities for the day. Eric and Kari ordered their usual drinks, but Don had to think about it for a minute.

"Bring him a Captain Morgan and Coke," Eric said to the server. "That works for everybody."

Within minutes the drinks came. Don sipped his cocktail gingerly. "So, you went diving today?" His eyes glanced from Kari to Eric.

"Yeah. We found those two . . ." Eric hesitated a moment to make sure he was out of earshot of other diners. "Those two bodies that are in the photograph. There's a plank missing from the hull. That's how Kari took the picture and missed seeing them the first time. She held the camera up to the hole, which is only a few inches high and about two feet wide. It's a deep wreck, Don. One hundred and sixty feet."

"Are you using mix?" Don asked. 'Mix' was a different blend of compressed gas used for deep dives. Nitrogen was replaced with helium of some other inert gas, eliminating the queasy and euphoric effects of compressed nitrogen.

"No," Eric replied. "Nowhere around here to get the stuff. We're using plain old air. Two tanks each. That gives us a good twenty minutes bottom time and about an hour of decompression on the way back up. On that first dive, we spent most of our air searching for the wreck."

"By the time we found it," Kari interjected, "I only had time to snap a few shots. Fifteen to twenty minutes really isn't much bottom time."

"Well, that'll change with the camera I brought. Do you have enough time to rig up the lights?" Don asked.

"What kind of time will we need?"

"Six, maybe seven minutes?"

"Yes. But not much more," Kari replied, nodding.

"Great. They're easy to rig and we might be able to light the entire ship. That way, the three of us can stay aboard the boat and send down the mini-sub with the camera to explore the outside of the whole ship. The lights will last about three hours, and they'll be brighter than the single light that is mounted in the housing of the mini-sub."

"Will we have to make another dive to retrieve the lights?" Kari asked.

"Ultimately, yes," Don admitted. "However, the lights could stay there for a day, a week, or more if necessary. But the retrieval is easy. You'll use small lift bags and let them rise to the surface themselves. Any exploring done within the wreck will be done the old fashioned way with your dive lights."

"One more thing," Kari said, "about the bodies in the photograph." She explained the stab wounds and the knife that was shoved through the man's mouth. It was a grisly feature that was not discerned in the photograph.

Don was silent for a moment, sipping his drink. He stirred the ice with a straw. "Well, one thing's for sure. Somebody wanted those people dead awful bad. Whoever they are and for whatever reason, I'd really like to know."

"But here's the weird thing," Kari continued. "I've been looking in all of my books and at the library and I can't find one thing on the *Brittany*. I've started searching through old copies of the *Cheboygan Tribune* on microfiche, but that's going to take awhile. Not to mention I have no idea what to look for."

"Well, there's no telling where the ship might have come from," Don said. "But I'm sure there has to be a record somewhere of her loss."

"We haven't told anyone about the wreck, except you," Eric said. "I've been thinking of talking to a guy in Cross Village. Mike Felsing was a good friend of my dad's. He's a retired Detroit cop. Kind of an amateur Michigan historian-slash-author-slash-mystery enthusiast. Mike would eat this up, and he'd keep quiet about it."

"Well then, we should talk to him," Don agreed. He paused, sipped his drink, and made sure once again that no one was within listening distance. He leaned closer, and his eyes flashed from Eric to Kari. "I think you guys have found something pretty damned special. Somebody wanted those people on that ship dead for a reason. Or they wanted what was on the ship. Frankly, I think it's the latter. They wanted something so bad they went through a lot to cover their tracks . . . and to hide their actions from history. I think you've found a lot more than just a shipwreck."

Eric and Kari didn't say anything.

"However," Don warned, "if there were any valuables aboard I'm sure they're gone."

"Somebody did that to people for *money?*" Kari asked, bewildered. "Don . . . it had to have been a bloodbath."

"All I'm saying is that it's a possibility," Don replied. "There aren't many wrecks in the Great Lakes that are known to have been carrying much in the way of valuables. Eric, you've dived on a lot of wrecks in these lakes. Have you ever found anything of real value?"

Eric and Kari both shook their heads. "The laws in the great Lakes are quite a bit different than the oceans," Eric answered. "Even if we *did* find something, it's illegal to remove it from the wreck. And in the Straits Shipwreck Preserve, we're talking *felony.*"

"What's on the agenda for tomorrow?" Don asked, raising his glass to his lips.

"Depends on the weather," Eric answered, lowering his gaze and swirling the ice in his empty glass. "It's supposed to be nice, but I thought you might want to take the day to get settled at the cabin on Mullett Lake. We can store your gear in our garage."

"Yeah, thanks. That'll help. But it won't take the entire day to get settled. And I'm kind of eager to get going."

"How about in the afternoon tomorrow?" Kari said. "You could meet us at the house after you got settled." She was as anxious as Don was to get started.

"Great. Probably two or three then."

Eric and Don argued about the tab, with Eric winning out. He paid the bill and the three walked back through the park and onto Main Street, then across the street to the waiting Blazer.

"Wanna see our marina?" Eric asked, swinging the truck into traffic.

"Sure," Don replied.

"It's two minutes from here. Right near the mouth of Huron."

It was nearing midnight, but as they passed the marina they noticed that a few late nighters still sat on the dock in lawn chairs, smoking, sharing a drink with their neighbors and relaxing. Crickets and cicadas droned from nearby bushes, and occasional laughter rose up from a few small groups of people. Cyclones of mayflies boiled beneath glowing lights like mad confetti caught in the vortex of whirring fan blades. A boat, a good-sized Bayliner, was leaving one of the slips. A giant beach-ball of a man was fiddling with the downriggers. But instead of turning to the right and heading upriver, the boat made a left and headed out onto Lake Huron.

Strange, Eric thought. *Most people around here don't fish Huron at night.* After a moment, he forgot about the boat entirely and he turned the Blazer around, drove back through town, and back to the house.

chapter 61

The night was dark, the moon hidden behind a thick blanket of clouds. Ed carefully steered the Bayliner through the marina, out of the mouth of the river, and into the lake. The waves had calmed considerably, it was no longer raining, and the night air had warmed. He turned off all of the boat's running lights except for a tiny light inside the cabin. *No sense in tellin' everybody we're out here.* An unlit Camel dangled from his lips, and, after a few moments, he struck a match and inhaled deeply. He held his breath for a moment, then exhaled with a long sigh.

Phillip sat in the chair opposite the captain's seat. He checked the GPS coordinates in the low light, leaned over to make an adjustment, and sat back. "Okay, slow down. We're pretty close."

Ed slowed the boat. Phillip reached over and made an adjustment to the bottom scanner. Ed had purchased the unit last winter in the Keys. It was a newer scanner, and it made searching for underwater structures and objects much easier than it had been even a few years ago.

The bottom scanner sprang to life, and in seconds Phillip and Ed were looking at a computer-drawn image of their own boat and the bottom of Lake Huron which, at present, was sixty-five feet below them.

"This'll do fine, just fine," Ed said. He took a long drag from the Camel and left the cigarette perched in his mouth. He squinted as the smoke rolled up his puffy cheeks and into his eyes.

"Seventy feet," Phillip reported. "Not in the Channel yet, but I think we're close." After a few minutes the monitor blinked and a new image formed on the screen. Now, the boat's depiction was smaller on the monitor, and the gap between its shape and the bottom of the screen was much wider. "Here we go," he announced. "We're in the Channel."

On the screen, the Laurentian Channel dropped into emptiness, going from seventy feet straight down to almost four hundred feet in some places. Falling off the ledge into the Channel would be like falling off a cliff. If there *was* anything there, the bottom scanner would show it as a hump. However, although the floor of the Channel was fairly flat, underwater formations were common. It would be impossible to tell exactly what it was they had charted until they had dived on it. But Ed knew all about that.

And way down in Weeezeanna, Paul Sprague did too.

chapter 62

The Bayliner moved at a snail's pace, back and forth across the width of the Channel. The scanner showed nothing of interest, only a few small objects and some slight changes in depth. Phillip was almost nodding off, an untouched beer in the holder on a small table.

The bottom scanner blinked and changed scales, indicating a move to more shallow water. Then it blinked again, back to the deeper scale. *There's something*, he thought, his mind snapping to attention. "All right, here we go. Here we go." He emerged from his drowsy state and stared into the small monitor. "Okay, turn around," he told Ed. "There's something back there. Something big."

Ed turned the boat around and went back over the area that they had just covered, but the bottom scanner charted nothing. "Go back again. There's something there," Phillip insisted. "I saw it. There is something *there.*" His adrenaline was pumping and his heart pounded. He could *taste* shipwreck. He could feel the old, wet planks on his tongue, the silt grinding in his teeth.

It's here. There's something here. I know it.

He locked the finder to its smaller scale so it wouldn't skip to a shallow mode if they charted the object again. *Come on, come on,* he thought in frustration. *I know you're down there.* The line at the bottom shot up nearly an inch at the bottom of the screen, continued with a few sharp, jagged movements—

Right—

and then returned to its normal, flat pulse as it followed the bottom.

—there.

"Son of a bitch!!" Phillip shouted excitedly. "Mark that!! There she is!! *Mark that!"*

Ed cut the motor and scribbled down the coordinates. "I'll bet you a hundred bucks that this is what Randall and his ol' lady have been diving," Phillip crowed. "I know it is."

"Well then," Ed said, as he crumpled his empty cigarette pack and tossed it into the garbage. "Let's dive 'er. Let's find out once and for all."

Phillip froze.

"Both of us? Leave the boat alone? What if . . .?"

"You're right, Phillip" Ed said agreeably, picking up a dive mask and holding it in front of him. "You win. I'll stay up here while *you* dive. Just in case any boats come. Smart thinkin' boy, smart thinkin'." He smiled a crooked grin and Phillip stared at him. His frown finally turned to a grin, and he shook his head. "You've got an angle around everything, don't ya?"

Ed nodded, and Phillip stared at the small jagged mountain at the bottom of the screen.

Shit. That thing is deep.

It was 2:15 a.m.

He took the mask from Ed's outstretched hand, walked below deck, and suited up.

chapter 63

Phillip followed the anchor line into dark nothingness. The beam of his flashlight penetrated the water for only about fifteen feet. He concentrated it on the anchor line and slowly descended into the depths.

One hundred feet.

Total blackness. Of course, it was totally black on the surface, too, since he was diving at night. It was an eerie feeling, and Phillip was glad for the security of the white anchor line. Sure, he'd dived at night before. But not *alone.* He'd never dived alone. That was breaking rule number one. There were many divers who disobeyed this rule on a regular basis, but Phillip wasn't one of them.

Until now, anyway.

He stopped suddenly, alarmed. There was something there. Something had moved close by. He could sense it, feel it, hear it. The somesthesia only heightened as he flashed the light about.

What the hell was that?

He shined the light back and forth. Something had moved, he was sure of it. He clung to the rope, moving the light in nervous circles. *Nothing there*, he reassured himself. *Must've—*

OH SHIT!!

The trout had circled Phillip from behind. Now the twenty-pound fish was directly in his face, and when he suddenly appeared in the beam of white light, Phillip nearly jumped out of his wetsuit. Bubbles flocked and whirled, sirens screamed in his head. His heart thundered, and he caught himself.

Oh shit, he breathed through his regulator. *Oh shit. Man. Oh shit*. Adrenalin flushed his bloodstream. His heart continued to hammer, but he breathed easier.

The curious trout, unaware he had caused such a commotion, floated motionless for a moment before slinking casually away into the darkness. Phillip followed the monster with his light, keeping it trained on the big brown as it faded slowly off into the deep. Phillip held the anchor line, calming himself, angry that he had allowed himself to get scared to death by a fish. A big fish, yes, but nonetheless, a fish.

He checked his gauges. The little thrill had taken up a lot of air. He hoped he would have enough air to find the wreck, if it indeed *was* a wreck, and identify it. According to Richard Merman's journal, there was only one thing on the ship that would hold the secret to its identity . . . the capstan cover.

chapter 64

Daniel awakes before dawn. He is still tired, so he stays in bed for a few more minutes. Finally, he dresses in the darkness and carefully climbs the short stairway to the deck where Captain LaChance stands at the helm. Off to the east, the sky has started to lighten, and a hazy, burnt pink band stretches across the horizon. Beneath the glowing sky, a long, dark strip spreads horizontally, outlining the western Michigan shoreline some twenty miles away. The morning is clear and cool, with a light breeze from the northwest.

Thousands of stars blanket the heavens, slowly fading with the coming day. Daniel remembers how, when he was a boy, his mother had told him that there was a star for every single person in the world and that as soon as someone was born, a new star lit up. Whenever somebody died, somewhere a star went out.

"You have a star, too," she had said. "Tonight, I'll show you

your star.   And I think you will like him.   I know he likes you."

After it had gotten dark that night, his mother had taken him out into the field and pointed to the sky.   "There.   There is your star.   Daniel Hawthorne's own star.   That star will be with you always, until you one day grow old and die."   He had shivered at that thought, yet he understood even at that young age, that he and everyone grew old and passed on.   Or 'croaked' as his sister had called it.   He didn't like that.   He didn't want to 'croak.'   Tears had come to his eyes, and his sister, sensing his fright, had chased him around the barn, taunting and teasing him.

"Croak!! Croak!! Croak!! Danny's gonna croak!! Just like a big ol' fat frog!! You are, you are!! Danny's gonna croak!! Croak!! Croak!! CROAK!!!" He ran screaming and crying to his mother, who had scolded his sister for being so mean to her little brother. But even then he knew. He knew everybody was going to croak someday.

Now, standing on the deck of the Brittany, he gazes into the sky looking for his star. His star is the brightest in the sky. The North Star, as others call it, is part of the Big Dipper. Years ago, he had rejected the story his mother had told him and now knew that stars were just stars. Nevertheless, he looks at the northern sky and there, like a tiny fireball millions and millions of miles away, 'his' star burns brightly. He walks quietly to the helm where LaChance holds the wheel of the ship. The Captain smiles a tiny bit, something Daniel hasn't seen him do since the ship had left the harbor yesterday morning. "Little early, isn't it, boy?"

Daniel cringes inside. He hates to be called 'boy.' He is an adult, a grown man, and has earned the right to be called by his first name, Daniel, or certainly his last, Hawthorne, when properly preceded by a 'Mister.' But he doesn't feel comfortable telling the

Captain that.

"Yes sir."

"Everyone else still asleep?"

"Yes, sir."

"Well, Jack should be gettin' up soon and it'll be my turn to get a few winks for a little while." Jack Malloy is thirty-two years old, but he looks closer to fifty. He'd chosen the tough life of a sailor and loves every moment of it. Jack has sailed all over the world, and says that as soon as they reach New York, he will be heading out across the ocean to Italy and from there to Spain.

Daniel likes Jack. Jack seems happiest when he is hard at work, and he tells stories that in one moment can make you die of fright and in the next be laughing 'til your stomach hurt. Jack Malloy is an interesting fellow, all right.

"Is there anything I can help with, Captain?" Daniel asks.

"Yes, there is, matter of fact. You can steer for a minute while I use the head."

Daniel takes a firm grip on the wheel while LaChance stands at the ship's rail and relieves himself. "Gotta keep old Michigame full somehow," he says, as he adjusts his trousers and takes the wheel again. He turns and gives a knowing grin to Daniel, like he has done something illegal. His face is nearly totally obscured by hair. His long, bushy mustache covers his mouth and his beard creeps high up on his cheekbones. Even his eyebrows are bushy. "You sail much, boy?"

There it is again. 'Boy.' But his tone is easy and not at all patronizing and Daniel likes that.

"A little bit, sir. Mainly I work the docks, loading and unloading but I know my way around a ship or two," Daniel replies with a touch of pride.

"That's good. We need experienced sailors. And if we can't get

experienced sailors, we need men that are willin' to learn. You seem willin' to learn."

"Yes, sir. I'd be glad to help with anything, sir."

"Well, there's lots to do. But right now it's easy time. At sunrise the work begins." He dips into his coat and finds his pipe and tobacco and offers Daniel a smoke. Not wanting to seem innocent and naive, Daniel accepts the pipe. He touches the match to the pipe and inhales and within an instant has coughed the thick smoke back out. He spits the pipe to the deck where it spills its contents. Orange embers dance on the hardwood planking. LaChance laughs, steps on the smoldering tobacco, and picks up the pipe. Daniel is still coughing, and LaChance puts his hand on his shoulder.

"If I ever seen somebody spit out a pipe faster, I don't remember it. But boy, you sure spit it out with honor."

This causes even Daniel to laugh, and the two chuckle a few moments more. The burnt pink has become a fiery orange in the east, and the stars, one by one, are quickly fading and disappearing altogether as the blanket of night gradually lifts.

Jack Malloy appears on deck. "Well, looks like it's nap time," says LaChance. "Jack is the Captain while I sleep, and you, Mr. Hawthorne, are the first mate."

"Yes, sir," Daniel says. He tries not to show it, but he smiles a tiny bit anyway. Mister Hawthorne, First Mate.

Jack takes the helm, and the Captain retires to his quarters for a much-needed nap.

LaChance can't sleep, although he's tried, despite the fact that he had been up for twenty-four hours and is dog-tired. There had been a few moments during the night that he could have napped, but he didn't dare. He had taken a deep breath of cool air, stretched, and had continued to watch the horizon. It had been a clear night and the sailing was easy. He had stayed close enough to shore to see the few lighthouses that speckled the shoreline of Lake Michigan. LaChance knows the waters well and is confident that Jack will do fine. He has only one worry. And it has to do with a certain cargo that is being carried below deck.

In the darkness, he opens his eyes and tells himself that he doesn't need to go check, that all is well and will continue to go well. The trip will be over in a few days and he will be on his way home to Margo and the kids. In a matter of days.

chapter 65

Daniel is certain that Jack Malloy has no idea of the valuable cargo that was on board. For Jack, this is a routine sail. When this voyage is done, he'll be off on his next sailing commission.

"Nice morning. Good sailing today. How long you been up with the Cap'n?" Jack asks.

"Just a few minutes," Daniel answers.

"Gonna be a nice day," Jack says again, drawing a deep breath of fresh, morning air. The sun has crept up over the horizon and the ship seems to be coming alive: the wood, the billowing sails overhead, and the deck below Daniel's feet.

Jack Malloy has dark hair, piercing brown eyes and a greasy handlebar mustache. He is thin and his face is rugged, his cheekbones and jaw gaunt-looking—but not in an unhealthy way. He moves easily, confidently, and precisely. Just being in the presence of Jack Malloy had a calming effect on most people.

Captain LaChance had put it best: "If Jack Malloy doesn't like you, you could pretty much bet you weren't worth being liked." Thankfully, Jack seemed to take a liking to Daniel and the two have become instant friends from the moment they met on the docks. Jack likes how hard and how long Daniel is willing to work. It was Jack Malloy who had recommended Daniel to LaChance, saying that he'd seen him on the docks, and he was one of the hardest workers around.

"Well, whaddya think? A storm comin' up?" Jack stares straight ahead as he posed the question.

"A storm? The weather's perfect," Daniel answers, surprised.

"Well, hold on a minute. First of all, the weather's always perfect. God didn't make nothing that wasn't perfect."

"Well, what I meant to say was although it was cloudy and rainy for the past coupla days, it cleared up yesterday, and today looks even better." Daniel looks at the sky, searches for clouds and finds not a single one. They have all drifted far to the east, and the sky is a fresh, newly-born blue. The wind is moderate, about eight knots out of the northwest. Jack glances up, scans the sky, and then returns his gaze to the waters in front of him.

"It doesn't matter what it looks like. Doesn't matter at all. What matters is what it feels like. What's it feel like to you?" He looks at Daniel, who must have had a questioning look on his face, because Jack smiles and speakes before Daniel has a chance to respond. "It's what some call a 'premonition.'"

"Preno . . . pre . . ." Daniel stumbles awkwardly over the word.

"Premonition," Jack corrects. "A sixth sense. Do you know what the five senses are?" Daniel nods and Jack continues. "Well, they say that there is a sixth sense—one we don't know much about. Like when the animals start gettin' wild and actin' strange and then a day later, BOOM! a tornado comes. That's a

sixth sense, Daniel. A lot of animals have it. Some people have it. A feeling of things to come. Have you ever had a feeling and you knew that something was about to happen?"

Daniel thinks about this for a moment. "Well, once a few years ago, I was sleeping and I dreamed that Jasper, one of our horses, was in trouble. I couldn't sleep and I kept feeling that something was wrong. So I went out to the stable to check on the horses and found out that the barn was on fire. I started yelling for Ma and Pa and I opened the barn and let all the animals loose. The barn burned to the ground but we didn't lose a single animal. Not one."

"Well, there you go," Jack says, nodding his head. "You had yerself a premonition. Problem is, not many people pay attention to their premonitions. And it's too bad because if they did, they could avoid an awful lot a trouble." He looks over his left shoulder to the west. "Nope. There's a storm comin'. I can feel it. I can feel it like I can feel the wheel under my skin. I can see it like I see the waves on the water. I know when a storm is coming. It's comin'. I don't know when, but it's comin'." Jack smiles and looks at Daniel.

Daniel smiles back and glances nervously over the waters. The day is bright and beautiful without a hint of storm clouds, but Daniel knows that at a moment's notice, furious winds can whip up, the skies can darken, and God help you if you are on one of the Lakes when that happens. If you worked the docks, you knew somebody who had lost their life to the thrashing seas. Only a few weeks ago, a ship had went missing with one of Daniel's childhood friends aboard.

"But where does a premonition come from?"

Jack gazes intently towards the north and Daniel follows his stare. In the far distance, a ship is approaching.

Daniel squinted in the morning sun. "Know 'em?" he asks.

"Too far away to tell," Jack answers. "Prob'ly I do." He watches the ship in the distance for another moment or two and then remembers Daniel's question.

"Well, all I know is what my daddy told me. Only he didn't call 'em premonitions. He called 'em 'messages.' Messages from the other side."

"What's the other side?" Daniel asks.

"The only other side there is. Messages from the dead. See, my daddy believed that only the spirits knew what was going to happen in the future. And sometimes, these spirits tried to warn you about certain things. Like the weather. My daddy sailed for years and years and could guess the weather better than anybody. He always told me that it was his papa lookin' out for him. His father died when my daddy was a boy. Since he couldn't talk to his daddy, he liked to believe that his daddy could talk to him through the wind and the trees and the clouds."

The other ship has gotten closer and Jack recognizes it. "That's Earvin Mayfield's ship, the Sea Gull. Recognize them sails anywhere." The schooner will pass about a mile away on their port side.

"Where do you get your messages from, Jack?" Daniel asks.

Jack pauses, as if not sure what to say or how to answer. "Well, I'm not superstitious and I'm not sure I believe all what my daddy told me. But I do know that since he passed on, I have these messages about the weather almost everyday. I know what day it's gonna rain, how much rain we're gonna get, and when the sun's coming back. Right now, I ain't sure exactly when the storm will hit. But she's on her way, all right. It's just a . . . a knowing. Sometimes I think it is my daddy, maybe lookin' out for me."

"So you think a storm is coming? For sure?"

"Daniel, I know a storm is coming. And so does Captain

Christopher Knight

LaChance," Jack replies firmly.

"When's it gonna be here?"

"Don't know. Soon. Real soon. Maybe in a day or so. That's the problem with messages. Sometimes, they ain't all that clear. No, that ain't it. They're clear, all right, but sometimes folks don't read 'em right or they don't pay attention at all. Yep. And sometimes when a storm comes, well, it ain't got nothin' to do with the weather."

There it is again. That grin that lasted a little too long. But Daniel hadn't noticed. He picks up a line in his hand and starts about his daily duties as the Brittany pressed further north.

chapter 66

The Blazer pulled into the driveway, and its three occupants climbed out. The warm night air was filled with the steady chant of crickets as Eric, Kari, and Don walked up the driveway to the house. Don retrieved a small bag of clothing from the van and locked up the vehicle for the night. They would unload the heavier gear in the morning before Don went to the tiny cabin on Mullett Lake.

Inside, Kari opened a bottle of merlot, poured three glasses and took them out to the table on the deck facing the river. The *John Galt* sat motionless, rocking slightly in the current. It was late, but none of the three were tired. They sat and talked for an hour, until Eric finally announced that the day had caught up with him. He kissed Kari, opened the sliding screen door, bid Don good night, and headed off to bed.

Kari poured Don another glass of wine, then one for herself. "Cheers." She raised her glass, and Don met her glass with his. "We're glad you came."

"Thanks for the invite, Don replied, "although I don't think I could've stayed away after what I saw in those pictures. Man, when I saw that one with . . ."

Sploosh. A fish rose to the surface of the river behind the *John Galt.* Don turned his head.

"Eric has been hearing a big fish feeding the past couple nights," Kari said. "He thinks it's a bass or a pike." They listened in silence for moment, but did not hear the fish again.

"So, you haven't been diving?" she asked tentatively. Although the question was quite simple, it was a difficult one to ask. It was, as they say, *difficult water to tread.*

Don slowly shook his head, looking away. Kari was immediately sorry she had brought it up. "I'm sorry, Don. Forget I said anything."

"No, no. It's all right. It's just . . ." His voice trailed off, and he took another sip of his wine. "It's just that I can't come to grips with what happened. I know I need to but I just can't."

"But Don," Kari reassured him. "Everything turned out fine. Really, it did."

Yeah. It turned out fine, all right, he thought. *I'm having nightmares about diving for television sets and doorknobs and regulators that turn into snakes. Sure, everything turned out fine, all right.*

"I'm not comfortable diving anymore," he said. "I tried once. Couldn't get five feet below the surface. And I was in a *pool*, for

God sakes." He didn't tell her that he had been to almost a half-dozen shrinks and they all told him he was on the fast track to Bonkersville if he didn't get this whole thing straightened out and dealt with pronto.

"Eric misses diving with you," Kari said. "He had—" she paused, and then corrected herself. "—*we* had a lot of fun. Eric talks about you a lot. He has always said you're the best."

"Kari, I can't. I don't know why. I just can't."

Sploosh. They both turned their heads and in the moonlight saw the rings dissipating in the water a few yards behind the *John Galt.* There was a long, uncomfortable silence.

"Kari, I can't remember *anything.* Not one thing. Or to be more precise, I remember everything up until a certain point. Then the rest is gone. No matter how hard I try, I can't remember what happened."

"Have you talked to anybody about it?" Kari asked.

Oh, yeah. Sure, I've seen 'anybody' about it. Matter of fact, I've seen four *'anybodys' about it. And they all think I'm a bowl of Fruit Loops with no spoon.* "Yeah, I've talked to a couple of doctors about it," Don answered, looking down at his shoes. "They call it 'Suppressed Memory Syndrome.' But you know how doctors are. There's so many of them, I think they have to invent 'syndromes' or 'disorders' for everybody, so they can keep the cash coming in. They think I need to work it through with plenty of therapy at a hundred bucks an hour. But I'm not sure if I'm ready to do that yet. Besides, I could think of a lot better ways to spend a hundred bucks."

Kari chuckled quietly, then the two sat in silence for a few moments.   Then the conversation turned to Cheboygan and summers in northern Michigan.   Overhead, the loud crank of an occasional nighthawk rang out through the warm night air.

"I'm going to bed," Kari said finally. "Do you need—"

Don stopped her in mid-sentence, showing the palms of his hands. "I'm fine. I'm going to sit out here for a few more minutes and then hit the sack. I'll see you in the morning."

"Good night, Don." Kari kissed him lightly on the cheek, turned, and slipped through the screen door, leaving Don alone on the porch.

chapter 67

Sploosh. Don watched the glowing rings in the water as they widened and smoothed, finally disappearing in the slow moving currents of the Cheboygan River. He sat quietly on the deck under the canopy of brilliant stars and reviewed the events that had preceded . . . *preceded what?* He remembered that he had flown to Chicago and stayed with Eric and Kari for a few days to make final preparations before heading off to the dive site in the North Atlantic. For the next three weeks, they would be living with a crew of explorers in tents and crude shelters. The temperatures would average about ten degrees Fahrenheit during the day with the possibility of dipping to twenty below overnight. The wind chill factor could reach fifty to sixty degrees below zero. It was not going to be a Caribbean vacation by any stroke of the imagination. Part of the crew was already at the dive site cutting holes in the ice and determining the exact location of the wreck which lay in one hundred fifty feet of water. Not an extreme depth, but deep enough to require special precautions . . . especially beneath the ice.

Don, Eric, and Kari flew in by helicopter a week later. The bitter cold was a shock even with all their cold weather gear. The snow was falling when they arrived and a storm rolled through that evening, giving them a chance to meet with the researchers. Eric and Don would be diving the wreck. Don would be diving with an underwater camera, wired to the surface where an eighteen-inch monitor would send vivid pictures back from the depths. The monitoring apparatus was set up in one of the bigger tent-shelters which was heated by a small gas stove.

Don also remembered setting up the gear the next day. Their spirits had been high and they had laughed and joked while Don double-checked the camera and underwater equipment. When everything was ready the hole was widened. The divers would be connected to each other by a line that would in turn would be held by two men on the surface. One tug meant that they needed more line, two tugs meant to pull up the slack. If there was trouble, Don or Eric would give three sharp tugs on the line and the men would pull them back to the surface.

Although Eric was accustomed to diving under the ice, this was to be Don's first time and his anticipation was overflowing. He had heard Eric talk about it excitedly and now he was finally doing it himself. He and Eric sat on the edge of the hole, comfortably warm in their drysuits. Unlike wetsuits, which allowed water inside, the drysuits were sealed and the two divers wore a layer of warm clothing for extra comfort. Eric was the first in the water, followed by Don. The surface team handed Don the camera and—

That was it. That was all Don remembered. It was like someone had taken a large eraser and removed the memory from his brain. He remembered when he had accidentally recorded over Santana's *Abraxas* tape. The next time he had tried to play it, there was nothing. He had re-wound the tape and fast forwarded, searching for any music at all, but it was gone. Carlos and his buddies had hit the road.

Like my brain. I accidentally recorded over my brain. Shoulda popped the tabs and this wouldn't have happened. Rewind. Fast forward. *Nope. Nothing. Somewhere, my memories and Carlos Santana are sittin' in a Mexican cantina, sippin' on a Margarita and doin' shots of Jose Cuervo.*

After a while, he rose from his chair, went into the house, and went to bed.

chapter 68

Well, that son of a bitch won't be taking any swings at anybody for awhile. Jimmy lay on the bunk in his jail cell, wide awake. He would have to stay here for the night and then, if any charges were filed, he would probably be able to get out on bail shortly thereafter. *God, was it funny when that poor bastard started crying! What a baby! I should have broke both of his arms.*

He stretched and tried to get comfortable. The small bunks in the cells weren't made for the likes of Jimmy, or anyone his size, for that matter. Not only was the bed stiff and cold, it was just too damn small. He wondered if he should ask for an upgrade. Maybe he could find something with a king-size bed and a Jacuzzi.

This brought a smile, and he decided that, yes indeed, it *was* worth it. It was worth a night in jail to see old Smelly Howler crying like a baby.

Yep. Two broken arms. Next time, two broken arms, and maybe a leg or two. He smiled again. Jimmy loved inflicting pain. He loved everything about it. He loved the control he had over his victim, whomever it may have been. People didn't like pain, were afraid of pain. Most people would do anything to escape it. But, if you were the deliverer and not the receiver, well then, that *changed* things. The deliverer called the shots. The deliverer wielded the *power*. The deliverer was a *god*.

Like father, like son.

He remembered every beating his father had ever given him. Every single one. He remembered an oil dipstick that his father had used on his back when he had come home from school late. In reality, Jimmy hadn't come home from school late . . . but rather, his father had gotten home from the bar early, and had expected Jimmy to be there.

His father relished the improper distribution of pain. Years of drinking had destroyed his ability to think clearly and act responsibly. For Charles Durand it began in his teenage years; it ended in a disgusting heap on the living room floor. In between there had been three marriages, all ending in divorce. It was amazing that all three women even escaped with their lives. And growing up, Jimmy saw all of it. The beatings, the screaming, the blood, the bruises. Broken bones, busted chops, lost teeth. This was normal. This was life. This was how you dealt with situations beyond your control. You take charge, you take action. You take mental hostages with the threat of overwhelming force. Jimmy watched.

Jimmy *learned.*

When you need to get something from someone, you just beat it out of them. It seemed so simple. Something bothering you? Hey . . . ain't your fault. Gotta be the fault of someone else. Didn't matter who, just pick the nearest target.

So when Jimmy, all of ten years old, had cornered a chipmunk in the garage and caught it in a box, he knew what he had to do. The chipmunk needed to be *punished*. It shouldn't have been in the garage. Chipmunks belong outdoors.

Gonna have to teach you a lesson. Yep. This is gonna hurt me more than it is you, Mr. Chipmunk. I don't want to have to do this, you know, but you've got it coming.

He caught the chipmunk in a shoebox and put a board over the top so it couldn't jump out. He searched the garage for his father's leather gloves. He found them, and although they were way too big for young Jimmy's hands, they would have to do.

He slowly inched the board over the edge of the box and peered into the tiny cubicle. The chipmunk was hunched in the corner, eyes flashing. He made a lightning-quick move for the opening and Jimmy quickly brought the board back over the box, thwarting the animal's escape. This was going to be trickier than he thought. Slowly sliding the board back again, he covered the opening with his gloved hand. The chipmunk made a dash for it, but Jimmy was faster and he pressed its tiny body to the bottom of the box. He removed the board and forced the chipmunk firmly into his fist, squeezing it hard to prevent the animal from getting away. The chipmunk bit wildly at the leather gloves, but Jimmy's fingers were safe inside. Jimmy squeezed tighter, not wanting to give the rodent enough room to wriggle free.

Bad Mr. Chipmunk. You've been a bad, bad boy. Do you know what we do to bad chipmunks?

He held the chipmunk in a death-grip with his left hand and searched the garage again. Not finding what he was looking for, he went into the house, chipmunk in hand, and rattled single-handedly through the kitchen drawer. He kept checking over his shoulder to make sure his father had not come home yet, knowing that he would not take too kindly to having a live chipmunk brought into the house. It was the kind of thing that would bring another ball game on.

Jimmy finally found what he was looking for: a sewing needle about three inches long. He carried the chipmunk into the backyard. Holding it tightly with his left hand, he slid the needle through the space between two of his fingers until he felt resistance. *Sorry about this, Mr. Chipmunk. But we gotta teach you a lesson.*

He held the end of the needle between his right thumb and forefinger, paused a moment, then forced it into the animal. The chipmunk let out a shrill, high-pitched squeal as the needle pierced its body. Jimmy held it there for a moment, slowly working it up and down, each movement causing the chipmunk terrible anguish. He struggled to break away, but Jimmy just forced the needle in deeper. A droplet of dark, reddish-brown blood oozed between the leather fingers, and Jimmy slowly pulled the needle out. He could feel the rapid heartbeat of the chipmunk. Its mouth was open, gasping for air. Jimmy picked yet another spot between his fingers and forced the needle into the chipmunk again, causing the tiny animal to writhe and squeal in burning pain. Jimmy squeezed tighter to make sure it wouldn't get away. He poked the needle in further and more blood dripped between his fingers. The animal tried to bite him, but was only able to get a piece of the leather gloves. He jerked the needle sideways, feeling it tear at soft flesh and brittle bones. With each swath, the chipmunk cried out in pain, but now it wasn't struggling as hard to get away. Jimmy pulled the needle back out and the chipmunk convulsed violently, and then stopped, its tiny mouth open, panting rapidly.

Oh, no, not yet, Mr. Chipmunk. We're not through with you yet.

Jimmy walked back into the garage and searched the shelves until he found a mayonnaise jar with a lid. The jar contained nails, and it was a little tricky to hold the squirming chipmunk and unscrew the lid, but Jimmy managed. He dumped the nails out on the workbench and stuffed the chipmunk inside the jar, quickly replacing the lid to prevent an escape. The chipmunk, too weak and in pain to even try, sat panting in the mayonnaise jar. Jimmy watched the rapid quivers of the small animal's fragile ribcage. Its tiny heart was beating very, very fast. Blood oozed from the needle holes and ran down the chipmunk's fur, staining the glass jar.

Guess what, Mr. Munk? In some countries they have firewalkers. Do you know what firewalkers are, little Chippy? They walk across white-hot coals. Have you ever wanted to do that, Mr. Chipmunk?

Jimmy ran back inside the house and found an emergency candle in the kitchen drawer. It was a dirty yellow and had been used several times, but it would work perfectly. He told himself that he didn't *want to do this*, didn't *like to do this*, but it *had to be done*. After all, the chipmunk *had* been in the garage, hadn't it?

Yes, it *had.* It needed to be punished; it needed to be *disciplined.*

He returned to the garage and looked at the chipmunk through the glass. This really was what the chipmunk deserved. He had it coming to him.

Jimmy placed the candle on the table and lit it with the pea-green *Cricket* lighter he had also found in the kitchen drawer. He picked up the jar and the chipmunk instantly came back to life, scrambling to get out, its tiny toenails going a mile a minute on the slick glass.

Scrit-scrit-scrit-scrit-scrit. Scrit-scrit-scrit.

Bad chipmunk. Bad, bad chipmunk.

Then, as an afterthought, Jimmy placed the jar back on the table and put a leather glove on his right hand as well. No sense burning himself. He picked up the jar.

The chipmunk, as if sensing what was about to happen, stared at the lit candle for a moment, then his tiny legs went into overdrive once again, going nowhere fast on the slick glass, trapped inside the mayonnaise jar, inside a Miracle Whip furnace.

Like father, like son.

Jimmy stood up in his jail cell and stretched, and then lay back down. *Yeah, that son of a bitch at the bar had it coming all right. In fact the bastard was lucky. Damn lucky.*

Finally, after an hour, he fell asleep.

chapter 69

Phillip checked his dive computer on his wrist. The tiny dials, numbers, and letters glowed brightly in the dark, unaided by the flashlight. *One hundred feet.* He checked his air as well and found that he had used up nearly a third of his air already. That surprise run-in with the trout hadn't helped, elevating his heartbeat and causing him to breathe much faster. *Gotta watch that crap.* He continued his dive, gliding along the anchor line, following the beam from the flashlight deeper and deeper.

Suddenly, a shadow caught in the beam. Phillip stopped moving and held his breath. He swung the light back several feet, looking . . . .

An ancient mast, covered with slime, came into view. Phillip's heart banged inside his chest.

Well, well, well. I knew it.

Phillip had come down directly on top of the wreck. The anchor had hit bottom ten feet from where the ship lay in her watery grave, and Phillip had come down right on the edge of her deck. He shined his light along the deck of the ship, and whistled in his silicone mouthpiece. *So, this is what you and your old lady have been diving, eh, Randall? 'Practicing for Cozumel'? I don't think so.* He shined the light up along the massive masts that towered above the wreck. *She's in such good shape there's still some rigging on the masts.*

He checked his gauges again. He had two minutes before he had to head back up to the surface. He swam along the hull towards the bow. The ship was listing towards her starboard side and was partially buried in the sand.

Jesus. There he is again. The large trout had returned and hovered motionless in the beam of his flashlight just ahead of Phillip. *Hey, man. Are you that same fish that scared the hell out of me back there? I'll bet you are.*

Holding the light in his left hand, he reached down to his right thigh and pulled his dive knife from the sheath. He had moved closer to the unmoving fish, which stared back in curious amusement. Phillip brought the knife up slowly and held it out, his arm fully extended. He brought it closer to the fish. *You know how easily you could be filleted right now? I could gut you with one quick twist of this here knife, Mr. King of the Deep.* The fish was only inches from Phillip's mask and filled his entire field of vision. *Boy, you don't know how close you are to death right now.* His knife was a foot away from the side of the trout. One quick jab to the head and it would swim wildly about, sideways and upside down, like the time he had poured a half bottle of Bayer aspirin in his aquarium when he was a boy. The tiny goldfish had flipped out, swimming erratically and bumping into the glass until they finally went belly up and floated on the surface.

Nah. I'll let you live. Let somebody else catch you for dinner. Then, just to show the fish how easy it would have been to kill him, he barely touched him with the long shiny blade.

There was a sudden explosion, a hand grenade going off, and it was as if Phillip had been kicked by a horse. The fish bolted off, and the backwash from its huge tail knocked Phillip backward like he had been hit with a baseball bat. He dropped his light and it tumbled twenty feet to the bottom of the lake. His mask and regulator were knocked off his face and his mask drifted slowly to the bottom.

chapter 70

Phillip was frantic. He swept the left side of his body with his arm, groping in the dark for his mouthpiece. He swung his arm once, twice. He couldn't find it. He could feel the tightness beginning in his lungs, telling him he needed air. The flashlight beam glowed in the depths below him, but he had no time to retrieve it. He had a more serious problem at hand at the moment.

He was going to need air, and *soon*. Within *seconds*.

He swept frantically in the darkness for his regulator hose. The tightening in his lungs had become a twisting pain. Fifteen seconds clicked by and now he was thrashing with both arms, trying to find the regulator hose, trying to find the mouthpiece, which could only be a few inches out of reach.

He flung his left arm wildly backwards, feeling the steel tank, his vest, and ... *there! God, it's there*!! He grabbed the hose and plunged the regulator into his mouth, exhaling to clear the water in the mouthpiece. He felt an incredible wave of relief when he inhaled and could feel the air rushing to his lungs. But he still had no mask, and his face hurt from being exposed to the extreme cold water.

He took a few breaths to calm himself and regain his composure.

Okay, okay. Got it. You're alright. Gonna be fine.

He looked down. Without his mask, he could only see the fuzzy image of the flashlight beam below him, and he carefully descended to the glowing bar of light. He retrieved it, all the while taking steady, even breaths. He stood on the bottom, trying hard to remain motionless and not kick up any silt or debris while looking for his mask. It was going to be hard enough already. He squinted as he swept the flashlight beam back and forth, and finally . . . *finally* located his mask not far from where the flashlight had fallen. Holding the light under his arm, he pulled the mask over his hooded head and fit it to his face. He exhaled through his nose to expel the water from the mask, giving him a clear vision of the icy depths. Phillip took a long breath and rested for a moment, one hundred sixty feet below the surface.

Holy shit. That was too close. Way too close. He grabbed his dive gauge and brought the glow-in-the-dark dials in front of his mask. *Shit.* Nine hundred pounds psi left. *This is gonna be close.*

He wouldn't have time to search for the capstan on this dive. He would have to begin his ascent *now.*

He swept his light around, found the anchor and began his climb. He would have to shorten his decompression stops by a minute or two at each one and he would have to stop every twenty feet instead of every fifteen. *That will have to do. As it is, I might not have enough air to make it all the way.*

He decided that this had been a bad idea, diving alone, diving so deep. He told himself that he was going to let Ed know just that, when he reached the surface. *If* he reached the surface.

He stopped every twenty feet for four minutes to allow the minuscule nitrogen bubbles in his bloodstream to become accustomed to the pressure change. The last thing he wanted to do was to get the bends and have to be flown to the decompression chamber in Ann Arbor. Nope, that would mess everything up. There would be awkward questions from the authorities. Questions that could expose their activities.

One hundred feet.

A quick glance at his gauges told him that he had less than two hundreds pounds psi. *Gonna make it-but just barely. It's gonna be close, but I'm gonna make it.*

He made his final stop at twenty feet beneath the surface. *Ed probably couldn't give a rat's ass if anything happened to me. But this is his new mask, and man, would he be pissed if I drowned and he never got it back.*

The time at his last decompression stop was almost up. He held the anchor line with his right hand, and shined the light straight down, watching the white rope fade off and disappear into the dark waters of Lake Huron. *Damned fish. One little knife-prick and he* . . . Phillip stopped in mid-thought.

The knife. I had the knife when that fish—

He shined the light on his right thigh, knowing that he would not see the shiny handle of the knife sticking out from the sheath, knowing it wouldn't be there.

Gone.

Somewhere, directly below him at the bottom of Lake Huron, lying not too far from the wreck, was Phillip's shiny, stainless-steel knife, partially buried in the sand.

Phillip didn't tell Ed about the fish or dropping the knife. Nor did he mention that he was royally pissed off because he had had to make the dive alone. All he told Ed was that he didn't have enough air to reach the capstan cover at the foremast. *I should have went right for the capstan in the first place. If I hadn't dicked around with that fish, we'd know for sure right now whether it was the* Aurora *or not*, Phillip thought.

They decided to wait until morning, bail Jimmy out of jail, and come back for another dive. This time both Ed and Phillip would descend to the ship while Jimmy stayed with the boat on the surface. Phillip sincerely hoped he would be able to find his knife before Ed did, otherwise he'd get one of Ed's '*I can't believe you're so careless-you're gonna screw this whole thing up*' speeches. If Randall showed up they'd deal with that then. Besides, nobody *owned* the ship. Phillip, Ed, and Jimmy had as much right to be diving the wreck as Randall.

chapter 71

Eric made omelets, bacon, and toast while Don showered. Kari was still asleep and he would wake her when breakfast was ready. He walked out to the blue-purple mailbox and retreived the day's *Cheboygan Tribune*. Back inside, he poured a cup of coffee and spread the paper on the table in front of him.

'*County Fair Draws Thousands*,' the headline read. Underneath, an aerial photo showed a birds-eye view of the fair, its rides and midways and people milling about. Eric flipped the top half of the paper underneath the bottom half, and continued to scan the headlines as he sipped his coffee. '*Incident At Local Bar Sends One To Jail, One To Hospital*.' Eric pulled the paper closer, remembering the man lying in splinters of glass outside *Johnnie's* last night. He scanned the article, and images replayed in his head as he read.

A fight at a local bar last night sent one man to the hospital with a broken arm and multiple cuts after the man was thrown through the window of Johnnie's Sports Bar. Witnesses say that Andrew Keith Jacobs, 21, of Mackinaw City, began fighting with one of the patrons. The bartender, while attempting to break up the quarrel, was interrupted by James Ronald Durand, of Detroit, who began fighting with Jacobs. During the ensuing scuffle, Jacobs received a broken arm. Witnesses say that Durand picked up Jacobs and threw him through the window of the bar. Jacobs is in stable condition today at Community Memorial Hospital. In addition to the broken arm, Jacobs received over one hundred stitches to various cuts and lacerations sustained from broken glass. Durand was not injured, and was taken to Cheboygan County Jail, where he is expected to be released after a bond hearing this morning.

Don walked into the kitchen, fresh from his shower. Eric pointed to the article in the *Tribune*. "See what you brought up here with ya?" he joked.

Don scanned the article and placed the paper on the table. "Hell, this happens on every block every night in Detroit," he said. "You guys have a bar fight and it makes the front page," Don replied.

Kari walked in groggily and sat down at the dining room table. She too read the article, but set the paper back down without saying anything. Eric brought the plates of omelets, bacon, and toast to the table and the three ate hungrily.

The conversation turned to planning the events of the day, and it was decided (without discussion) that Eric and Kari would dive and set up the lights. Then the lights would be turned on from the boat and Don would send down the mini-sub camera as they watched from the deck.

Kari cleaned off the table while Eric and Don examined the photograph of the capstan cover. The *Brittany*, Don said, running his fingers over the lettering on the photograph as if he could feel them, and, in doing so, divine more information. "And you say you can't find this name in any of your books?"

"Nope, not one mention," Kari answered, wiping off the counter. She pulled out *The Complete Guide to Great Lakes Shipwrecks* from the bookshelf and placed it on the table in front of Don. "This is the 'bible' of Great Lakes shipwrecks. You'd think that there would have to be a record of her in there somewhere."

"You know," Eric said, "Ships often had several names over the course of their working life. Maybe she's listed in there under another name. It's too bad we can't quite make out what's engraved on the cover above the name *Brittany*." He turned the picture around in his hands and then placed it back on the table.

"Did you say you had a friend that could help us with this?" Don asked Eric.

"Mike Felsing. He's an old friend of the family. Mike knew my father real well and I knew him well myself, years ago. I haven't spoken to him in a while, though, but I'm sure he and his wife are still around. He's got relatives all over Cheboygan county, for that fact." The three agreed that Eric should call Felsing, tell him what they'd found, and see if he had any ideas. "Better yet," Eric said, "I could probably drive over and pay a visit. I haven't seen Mike or Evelyn in a while and it would be good to spend some time together again. Hell, Felsing's like my grandfather and I haven't even called in a couple years."

The three finished their coffees and Eric and Don carefully unloaded the lights, depthfinders, scanners, cables, wires, and the mini-sub camera from the van. Don thanked Eric for breakfast, then hopped into the van and headed for Mullet Lake. He would return at two-thirty. Eric watched the van drive off. *Same old Don,* he thought.

Well, *almost* the same old Don.

Eric shut the garage door and went back inside. He fetched his telephone book, found Mike Felsing's number and picked up the receiver.

chapter 72

Alone in his motel room, Phillip's mind whirled, ablaze with anxiety. Everything could fall apart if somebody else knew about the cargo of the *Aurora*. They had spent six years searching the Channel for the vessel and although he hadn't made a positive identification that this ship was indeed the *Aurora*, he *knew* it was. He just *knew* it. But more importantly, what did *Randall* know? They couldn't possibly know what was aboard it until they had penetrated it.

Either way, we'll find out more about the wreck tomorrow . . . or later today, he reminded himself. It was nearly 4:00 a.m. when he had reached the motel. He plopped down onto the bed and fell into a troubled sleep, awakening every few minutes to worry. *Soon*, he consoled himself. *We'll get this whole thing wrapped up soon. Then I'll be set for a long, long time. Probably never have to work another day in my life.*

The phone rang all too soon, jolting Phillip awake. He reached for the receiver and grabbed it before the second ring. It was Ed. He had bailed Jimmy out of jail to the tune of $300 and the two were waiting for Phillip at the marina.

"All right. Yeah. I'll be there in a few minutes. What? Okay. Whaddya want?" Ed gave him the order and Phillip dressed and jumped into the Dakota and headed for McDonald's. *They drive right past the place, now they want me to run in and grab Egg McMuffins. Lazy bastards.* He ordered the food at the drive-through window and the teenage girl stared at him as she quickly handed him his change without speaking. *Kids these days. They don't have any manners.*

At the pick-up window, a kid handed him his bag of food and like the girl at the first window, also stared at him. "Rough night, eh?" he smirked. Phillip looked at himself in the rear-view mirror. He had not combed his hair, and it stuck out every which way. His eyes were bloodshot, and oblong purple sacks hung like hammocks below them. Phillip rolled up the window as he sped away. *Smartass kid.*

It was 8:30 when he pulled into the marina. Ed and Jimmy had readied the boat and were standing on the dock waiting for Phillip. The sun had risen, and the light fog that had crept in during the early hours had already burned off. A few fishing charters were leaving the marina, heading out for a little fishing, a little drinking, a little more drinking, and then maybe a little more drinking. *Fishing isn't a sport,* Phillip thought. *Fishing is what you do to hide an alcohol problem.*

Phillip waited while Ed gulped his four Egg McMuffins and Jimmy inhaled all three of his and three hash browns. "Jail food sucks," he proclaimed, "and the coffee wasn't much better." Phillip thanked Jimmy for coming to his rescue the night before, but Jimmy waved it off. Surprisingly, Ed didn't say much about the incident. Phillip thought that maybe Ed had noticed Jimmy's see-sawing tempers lately, and was watching his own toes a little more. Sure, Ed had his own temper tantrums, but for the most part, Phillip thought Ed was reasonably harmless, for the most part. All talk, no action. A three hundred seventy pound bag of certified, Grade-A, American hot air.

Of course, the late Paul Sprague, now residing somewhere in the depths of his beloved *Weeezeanna*, would offer up a slight difference of opinion.

chapter 73

They reached the Channel shortly after 9:30. Ed and Phillip had put on their wetsuits while *en route* and when they reached the dive site, both were ready to hit the water. Ed was first, and his body hit the water feet-first with the force of a 10-megaton nuclear bomb. The ensuing shockwave expanded like a tsunami doughnut. Phillip jumped in after the churning wave rolled off. They decided against putting out the dive flag, but if Jimmy saw the Coast Guard or Sheriff's Marine Patrol boat approaching, he would toss out the black innertube carrying the red-and white flag. Just to be legal and all that. Getting a ticket was of no concern to the three, but secrecy was. They didn't want any unwarranted attention.

In the water, Ed began to descend and Phillip struggled to keep up with him. *Geez, for a fat boy, he moves pretty well under water.*
Eighty-five feet.

At this pace, they would reach the bottom in no time at all.
Darkness encroached.

One hundred twenty feet.

The darkness ate them alive.

One hundred sixty feet.

They were at bottom, in the belly of the Great Freshwater
Whale. Both shined their lights around in the darkness, but the
shipwreck was nowhere in sight. Ed glanced at his compass and
headed north, cruising about six feet above the bottom. Phillip
moved fifteen feet to the east, then moved parallel to Ed so they
could cover the ground more quickly. Even fifteen feet away,
Phillip could barely see the beam from Ed's flashlight. They went
forty feet north, then they headed back south to the anchor. Ed
headed west now, and Phillip followed on his right this time, once
again about six feet from the bottom and about fifteen feet from
Ed.

Phillip saw it first, and signaled Ed by clicking his light on and
off. Ed joined him, and the two aimed their beams along the hull
and surveyed the massive wooden hulk of the ship. Ed wasted no
time. He ascended to the deck of the ship and, after a quick sweep
with his light, headed towards the bow. Phillip followed, mentally
calculating where he might find his knife. When he passed the spot
where he thought he had been when he dropped it, he feigned back
and let Ed go on ahead. He hovered at the edge of the deck,
shining his light down, trying to see, but he was too far from the
bottom. He followed the hull down to the sand and shined his light
back and forth. The shiny blade and handle should make the knife
easy to find. When he didn't have any luck there, he glided a few

feet further up the hull, towards the bow. Nothing.

Son of a bitch. It's got to be here.

He *had* to find the knife. He couldn't take a chance of Randall finding it first. He moved along the hull towards the bow, stopping every few feet to survey the bottom. *It has to be here somewhere,* he told himself. *It's got to stick out like a sore thumb.*

A light from above shined down on him and Phillip looked up. Ed clicked his light a few times, and reluctantly Phillip gave up the search. Ed motioned for Phillip to follow him, and the two glided towards the bow, stopping at the foremast. Ed pointed at the capstan. The cover was there but the covering of silt and debris had been disturbed. The word '*Brittany*' was clearly exposed in the beam of the flashlight.

Ed was visibly filled with rage. His eyes bulged behind his mask, his nostrils flared. His breathing became deep and hoarse. *Randall knows!* his mind screamed. *That son of a bitch and his wife know what they've got! They knew exactly what to look for! They've fucking figured it out. Son of a bitch!* It took everything he had to keep himself from flying into a demonic rage. He felt like breaking something, like ripping something apart. But—

No. Not here. Not on the bottom of the damn lake. Jesus Christ! They know what they've got. They probably have known all along.

Phillip hovered in the water next to Ed, glaring at the capstan cover. It had been wiped clean of its residue. There was no guesswork needed anymore. Randall had been looking for the *Aurora* all along . . . and he'd *found* it. He could sense Ed's monstrous rage. It seemed to darken the water even more, darken it with a toxic poison. Phillip's anger was also flaring, and the more he thought about Randall, the more he wanted to bash in his skull.

That'd serve him right, he thought. *That'd give him what he's got coming to him, the lying sack of shit.*

Ed took out his knife and pried angrily at the capstan cover. Maybe Randall had found the wreck and knew what he'd found, but Ed would be damned if he was going to make it any easier for someone else to identify the ship. In less than a minute, he had loosened the capstan cover enough to wrench it off, raising a violent cloud of silt in the process. But it no longer mattered; they could do no more on this dive. Disgusted, he threw his hand into Phillip's flashlight beam and signaled with his thumb to head for the surface. The search for the *Aurora* was over . . . and the salvage of her incredible cargo was about to become a race.

chapter 74

An idea. That's all I need. Just an idea to get started. Mike Felsing stared at the computer monitor and the cursor blinked back at him, taunting him from the empty screen. He had been sitting at the small desk for nearly an hour and hadn't written a single word. Every three minutes the glowing white field was replaced by the darkness of the starfield screensaver.

Sure as hell won't be buying one of these kinds of computers again, Mike thought. The mouse hadn't worked from day one and after waiting for a replacement from the factory for over a month, he finally went to Radio Shack and bought one. The diskette drive was defective as well, and now the monitor was going bad. Mike Felsing was not having a good 'first experience' with the new age of information. Maybe computers weren't all they were cracked up to be, after all.

After several minutes of inactivity the starfield screensaver returned again. He shut down the computer and stared out the window of his second floor workroom. Lake Michigan was calm, and the morning was bright and beautiful. He idly watched a freighter come into view, partially hidden by the light fog that hung over the water. Mike and his wife, Evelyn, had been coming to the cottage on Lake Michigan since the fifties. After he had retired from the Detroit City police force a few years ago, they had moved up north to live full-time.

At the moment, he was trying desperately to write another mystery novel. The first one had been so easy—easy, compared to this one, that is. Of course, he had written it while he had been laid up in the hospital from a gunshot wound that had nearly taken his life. He had been on routine patrol with his partner when they had stopped a beat-up rusty Ford Elite for speeding. As both officers approached the car, a youth in the back seat had fired a sawed-off shotgun through the rear window. No warning, no nothing. No reason. Just *BAM!* and a softball-sized hole ripped open Mike's gut. The Ford Elite sped off, and its three occupants were killed in a storm of gunfire at a roadblock later that night. Mike Felsing was not expected to live. Evelyn remained by his side that night, the next day, and throughout the following night. She didn't sleep or eat and a doctor finally told her that if she didn't take care of herself, that she would be the next patient to check in at William Beaumont Hospital. She managed to eat part of a doughnut and drink a little water and fell asleep at her husband's bedside. When she awoke, Mike, still unconscious, was holding onto her wrist. Later that evening, he had opened his eyes and smiled a tiny bit.

Evelyn burst into tears.

While Mike was recuperating in the hospital, the insanity and the total boredom of lying in bed all day, channel hopping on the TV and reading nearly drove him out of his mind. He requested a pad of paper, a clipboard, and a box of pencils. He had always wanted to write a genuine old-fashioned whodunnit murder mystery. He wrote every day, sometimes as much as two thousand words. After he got out of the hospital he was confined to bed at home and continued to write. Much to his surprise, a friend of Evelyn's who was a literary agent accepted his manuscript, and within a year, the hardcover rights had been sold to a publisher. Eventually titled 'Subtle Misgivings,' the book had sold almost fifteen thousand copies. Not an incredible amount, but nonetheless, a successful printing. Enough to give Mike the confidence he needed to write another one.

But now, try as he might, he couldn't seem to get started on a second book. He had finished one chapter, decided it was trash, and scrapped the idea entirely. With the new computer, he had figured it was going to be a cinch. It wasn't. And he was becoming more frustrated by the week.

He took his binoculars out and was focusing in on the ore carrier when the phone rang. He picked up the portable walk-around unit, fumbling with the antenna that he had bent in the screen door earlier in the spring. "Hello? . . . Who? Eric Randall? Hey! How in the heck are ya? . . . Back in *Cheboygan!?* Well, I'll be." They chatted for a few minutes and caught up with one another's lives. When the conversation finished, he shut the phone off and went downstairs. Evelyn was potting a plant on the kitchen counter. She was a thin graceful woman, always smiling, never in a rush, always taking time out to talk with neighbors or chase a frog with a few of the neighborhood children.

"Who was that, dear?" She looked up, smiled at Mike, and continued working with the plant. Potting soil clumped on the counter top.

"Would you believe it was Eric Randall?" Mike replied, wiping up some of the dirt with his hand and re-depositing it into the planter.

Evelyn stopped, her hands frozen at the current task. "Eric? My gosh, how is he? Is he—"

"He says he's doing great. And Kari too. They've moved back to Cheboygan."

"They have?" She turned her attention back to her project as she spoke. "Well, we are going to have to get together soon," she said firmly.

"Sooner than you think. He and Kari will be here in about an hour."

"Here? In an hour?" She wiped her hands on her apron and began to clean up the kitchen. The plant could wait a few minutes.

"Eric says he and Kari found something. A shipwreck. He says he wants to show me something and says maybe I can help. I hope so."

"Well, maybe this will lead to your next idea," Evelyn suggested, already busying herself in the kitchen.

"I hope so," Mike breathed in exasperation. "I think I'm going to go nuts if I don't get something written soon."

"Me too," Evelyn smiled, and gave him an innocent peck on the cheek. She hated to see her husband in such turmoil over his writer's block.

Maybe Subtle Misgivings *was all that there was,* Mike thought. *Maybe there was only one mystery novel in ol' Michael Felsing, aspiring author, and shot-up ex-Detroit cop. Maybe there never will be a second novel from these tired old bones. Maybe the well has dried up, leaving nothing but a hollow pit-empty and used up long ago.*

He heaved a sigh and helped Evelyn clean up the kitchen.

chapter 75

Don parked the Caravan at the office and sat for a moment, looking at the tiny resort. The cabins were small and not very far apart, but they had a spectacular view of Mullett Lake. Towering, arthritic oak trees with long, crippled branches reached skyward, shading the tiny cabins. At the lakeshore, giant weeping willows hung lazily out over the water. Their long slender branches twitched gently in the light breeze. An old wooden rowboat was turned upside down on a small sandy beach, and a hand-painted sign nailed to a tree warned that there was no lifeguard on duty.

Don stepped out of the van just as the manager strode out of the office and towards him. He was short, heavy and maybe seventy-five years old. His hair was cast-iron gray and messy, and Don was certain that he had probably been sleeping. He wore old coveralls that at one time had probably been deep blue, but which had long since faded to a creamy aqua. A hole in the left knee had yet to be repaired, and the white T-shirt he wore under the coveralls sported three or four built-in air conditioners.

"Must be Garrity. I'm Duane. Yours is the one down there on the end." He pointed. "Don't allow no pets. You don't have any pets, do ya? Can't allow no pets. Used to, but had a cat nearly rip one of the cabins all to hell. Can't stand cats anyway. Too selfish, all of'em are. You don't have much stuff for stayin' two weeks. You are stayin' two weeks now, aren'tcha? That's what I gotcha booked for. Two weeks."

Don seized the opportunity when Duane paused and assured him that he would be staying the entire two weeks, and no, he didn't have any pets. He picked up his two bags and the two men walked under the shade of the oak trees, down the slight embankment to the tiny two-room rustic lodge. The newly-painted brown cabin had a small bathroom with a shower stall, a mini-refrigerator, a stove and a sink, but not much else. That was okay. Don wouldn't be needing much more.

"Oh. And before I forget, come here and let me show you somethin'." The two walked towards the lake and Duane stopped at an old hand-pump well. "This here is the best water you'll ever taste. Lots better than the water you'll get in the cabin. Don't know why. They both draw from the same well. But that's the way it is. Go ahead, taste it." Duane reached down and pumped the arm a few times and a stream of cold water ran from the chute. Don cupped his hands and captured some water, lifting the makeshift cup to his lips. It was very, very cold. And, he had to admit, it *was* very good.

"Bet you bein' from Chicago an' all, that probably tastes like heaven, eh? None a them city chemicals to mess it up. Just pure water. Oh . . . how did ya wanna pay? Cash or credit card. First week in advance. Checks are okay, too, I guess, 'cept if I find out that it's no good, you'll be outta here like the Democrats in the last election. Old Gee-Dubya really showed them bastards, huh?" Duane snickered and Don laughed politely as he opened his wallet and paid him in cash for the first week.

"That's great. I'll be back around next week to collect for the second week. Other than that, you probably won't see too mucha me or the wife. We tend to leave our guests alone most of the time, except I do all the lawn work myself, so I'm sure I'll see you from time to time, but other than that, you probably won't see hide nor hair of me. Oh. One more word about the cabins . . ."

Man, this guy sure can talk, Don thought. He followed Duane back up to the cabin and waited by the doorway as he stepped into the bathroom and looked in the shower stall. "Yep. This is the one. Take a look inside there yourself." He stepped back out of the bathroom because it was too small to permit both men in it at the same time. "You see the handles? One marked 'hot' and one marked 'cold'? Well, they're reversed. The hot one is cold and the cold one is hot. Haven't got around to fixin' that yet. Had one guy here last summer, he turned the handle that said 'hot' to let the water run and get warm for a minute. He stepped in the shower and you could hear him holler all the way to the office. Damn near froze his balls off. Folks in the next cabin thought he'd been murdered. Can you believe that son of a pup tried to sue me for that? Judge thrown it outta court. How do you like the walls?" Duane had successfully run one topic right into the other, and now he lifted his thick, gray-haired arm and was pointing. Don was beginning to look for a means of escape. "Did the walls myself," Duane continued. "In fact, just re-did the inside of all the cabins. Put lots a money in 'em, me an' the wife did. These are brand new curtains. Wife put 'em up yesterday for ya." He reached over a tiny counter and drew them aside. The window, though small, allowed a nice view of the lake.

"What's that?" Don asked, pointing to an object hanging from a thin monofilament line above the window. It was a tree branch, bent all the way around to form a circle, about four inches in diameter. Inside the circle, a black thread had been woven into a spider web pattern. Directly in the center was a small opening, about a half-inch wide. Dangling inside the center hole was a small feather, hanging delicately from the web.

"Dreamcatcher. Wife's got 'em hangin' in all the cabins. You can buy 'em in town at gift shops. Some are bigger, some are smaller. Course, the size prob'ly don't have nothin' to do with how well they work. If they work at all that is. Humbo jumbo, that's what I call it."

Don reached up and held the dreamcatcher carefully in his hand. "What's it supposed to do?"

"Well, I'll tell ya. The Indians make 'em. Or 'Native Americans' for them politically correct folks. You one of them?"

Don shrugged, which seemed to satisfy Duane. "That's good. Anyway . . . Indians say that you put one of these up over the door or window in your house. At night, when you go to sleep, the dreams filter through the dreamcatcher and that web there catches the bad ones, the real scary ones, and don't let 'em through. The bad dreams get caught in the web and stay there 'til morning when the sun is supposed to burn 'em up. That way, you're only supposed to have good dreams. Isn't that the craziest thing you ever heard? Sell like hotcakes at the stores, though. Somebody's heapin' in the cash off these little buggers. Hey! I got a collection of shotguns that you gotta see. I got—"

"I'd love to, Duane, but I'm kind of tired. I could use a little nap."

"Oh sure, fine. When you wake up, come over to the office. I got me an old Remington twelve-gauge pump that you're gonna love." He went on for another few minutes before finally leaving Don alone.

Garrity left the door open and let the fresh, clean air in. He looked out the window, and the strange, web-like ornament caught his attention.

A dreamcatcher. It did resemble a spider web with its intricate lines woven in between and around each other. A light breeze moved the tiny feather ever so slightly. *What did old Duane call it? Oh yeah. 'Humbo jumbo.'* "I'll be the judge of that, Duane," Don said aloud, as if talking to the dreamcatcher. Don was not superstitious, but decided that if the dreamcatcher worked he'd buy a dozen.

Hell, I'll buy a hundred.

Christopher Knight

chapter 76

Don Garrity turned his attention to the two leather bags that sat on the bed, and began the very short task of hanging up and putting away the few clothes he had brought. He changed into a pair of shorts, as the day was already warm. *Noon,* he acknowledged, looking at his watch. *Still got awhile before I head to Eric and Kari's.* He left the cabin, after being careful to remain inside and out of sight for his thirty-minute 'nap', and walked down to the lakeshore. He took his shoes off and stepped into the water that lapped on the beach. Actually, it wasn't much of a beach at all. It was a strip of sand about six feet wide, the entire length of which could be walked in about twelve seconds.

The water was warm and Don stepped out a little further. The bottom was soft and sandy with dozens of fresh-water mussels scattered about. And zebra mussels, the damned things. They were no bigger than a thumb nail and affixed themselves to everything—stones, sunken pieces of wood, other mussels, whatever. They might be good for filtering the water and cleaning it up, but right now they were tearing the shit out of Don Garrity's feet.

A crayfish skittered away as Don approached, then turned to challenge him from a safe distance, its oversized claws reared and ready for battle. As Don stepped closer, the crayfish darted away again, and turned again in its fighting stance, preparing for war.

He waded easily through the ankle deep water and headed south along the lakeshore, and the soothing water lapped at his shins as he walked. His feet sank into the soft sand, and Don was careful to watch where he was walking, mindful of the razor-sharp zebra mussels.

Farther out on the lake the water teemed with activity: small and medium-sized boats, day sailers, two catamarans, and a half-dozen jet skis. A billion tiny suns sprinkled the surface, and the appearance was tranquil and calm. Several ducks flew by, all mallards, skidding to a stop on a watery runway not far from the shore, a flurry of flapping wings and quacks announcing their arrival. Within minutes Don was out of sight of the resort, walking in front of summer cabins and large homes. He walked slowly, his hands in his pockets, soaking up the glorious mid-day sun and looking at the houses that lined the shore. There were people in yards, some sitting in lawn chairs, others barbecuing, laughing, talking to one another and enjoying the hot summer day. Some waved and Don waved back.

Just about every home had a dock protruding from the shore of

Mullett Lake. Some were nearly fifty feet long. Don walked around a few of the shorter ones until he came to a long one. He tried to walk around the end of that one as well, but when the water was about to reach his shorts and he was still only half way, he decided that nobody would get too pissed off if he climbed over the dock and continued his walk.

A bead of sweat ran down his cheek. *Man, it gets hot out here even on the water*, he thought. There wasn't much of a breeze and he bent over, cupped his hands and splashed his face with the cool, refreshing water.

As he brought his hands to his face, the image struck violently, without warning. Bubbles, thousands of bubbles, and freezing cold water. He couldn't breathe. He thrashed wildly about, not knowing what had happened or where he was. The icy water burned at his face and he rolled over and over in the water. He was trapped. Don Garrity was drowning.

chapter 77

Eric . . . my God . . . where is Eric?

A torrent of water rushed into his mouth and down his throat. He flailed wildly and his arm struck something. He turned and faced a jagged wall of ice. He frantically searched with his hands to find an opening, a way out. It was no use. Garrity whirled to face the depths and saw a form in the murky waters below him. *Eric!! Eric!!* he screamed. *Gotta reach Eric. I've got to—*

"Hey Mister!! *Mister!!*"

Don coughed and sputtered and he discovered that he could breathe again. The ice had vanished and he found that he was laying face down in Mullett Lake in eight inches of water. He coughed again and vomited. He propped himself up shakily on his hands and knees. Like the incident in the van yesterday, the paroxysm had departed as quickly and mysteriously as it had arrived.

"Hey Mister!! Are you all right?!"

Don, kneeling in the water, turned to see a small boy on the shore. A man was running from the house and he passed the boy and rushed into the water. Don began to stand up and the man helped him. He held Don's arm as he spoke. His voice was alarmed, concerned.

"Hey, are you okay? We saw you from the house. Are you all right?" The man gripped Don's arm tightly to prevent him from falling again. Don's glasses had fallen off in the water and he groped for them and picked them up. He wiped his face with one hand, squeezing water out of his beard.

"Yeah, I think so. Yeah," Don answered without much conviction.

"What happened?" the man asked. "It looked like you were having a seizure or something."

"I must've started choking. I had a, uh, sandwich not long ago. I guess it didn't agree with me. How long was I in the water?"

"Didn't look like too long, course I just saw you when my boy started yelling. Must've got quite a scare, huh?"

You don't know how much, pal. Don looked over at the boy, standing on the shore.

"Thank you," he told the boy, who nodded his head up and down without speaking. Don turned again to the man. "And thank you, too. Sorry to cause a disturbance."

"No problem. You want a glass of water? You need to sit down for a minute or something?"

"No, thanks. I'm fine, really. I'm staying over at Everett's

Resort, down there." He motioned with his thumb. "I'll be fine."
He thanked the man again and turned to walk the short distance
back to the cabin.

He lay on the bed, resting. The entire episode in the lake had
probably lasted no more than two or three seconds, yet Don felt
drained, as if he had just finished running a marathon. He glanced
at his wristwatch. *12:45. Well, I guess I have time for that nap.
Eric and Kari aren't expecting me until 2:30.* He closed his eyes
and was almost immediately fast asleep. In the window, the
dreamcatcher dangled, the tiny feather in the center of the web
shivering in the gentle air currents that danced through the small
room.

chapter 78

The four of them were sitting comfortably on the deck of Mike and Evelyn's cottage that overlooked the lake. Frosted iced teas and a tray of cookies sat on a small table. They had chatted endlessly about 'old times', although Eric had a hard time remembering most of them. After all, Mike had been a friend of his father's. Much of Felsing's recollections were only vague memories for Eric, who had been quite young.

"Well now," Mike said, sipping on his tea. "What was it you said you found out in the Channel? A shipwreck?"

"Yeah. With a few surprises." Eric explained how they had literally stumbled upon the sunken ship. He showed them the photos Kari had taken. Both Mike and Evelyn were horrified when they saw the blown-up photo of the tortured, decaying bodies.

"One hundred and sixty feet!!" Mike exclaimed, his brows

furrowing with concern. "Good Lord, is it safe to dive that deep?"

Eric assured him that it was with the proper precautions. "But there's something else. Something I wanted you to see." He handed Mike the photo of the capstan cover.

"The *Brittany*," Mike read aloud.

"Have you ever heard of her?" Kari asked.

Mike paused, and squinted at the photo. "Well, not off the top of my head, no. But that doesn't mean anything. Let me go see what I've got." He placed the iced tea on the table beside his chair and went indoors and upstairs to his workroom, returning after a few minutes with a half dozen books. All four searched each of the books, first through the indexes in the back, and then page by page, looking for any mention of the *Brittany*.

"That's really odd," Mike said, after they had gone through them. "I thought for sure that we'd find her in one of these."

"I said the same thing," Kari responded. "And I didn't have any luck either. I started going through old copies of the *Cheboygan Tribune* on microfiche at the library but I haven't found anything yet. I'm planning on going back later this week."

"I'd love to do that for you, if you wouldn't mind," Mike offered eagerly.

"That would be great," Kari said gratefully. "In fact, it would be a big help."

"How many people know about the wreck?" Mike asked.

"Well, we've told Don Garrity, the guy I told you about on the phone. He's here right now, staying over on Mullett Lake. And that's it. We're trying to keep it as quiet as possible. Don wants to put together an hour-long feature on the wreck. In fact, we're going out today to set up some lights. The fewer people that know about her, the better."

"Lights?" Mike inquired. "What lights?"

Eric told him about the special lights and Don's mini-sub camera. Mike was fascinated. He picked up the grainy photo of the capstan cover. "Why don't you leave this with me for a day or so. I bought every possible bell-and-whistle with my computer, for all the good it does me. I can scan it into the computer and tweak it. Maybe I can bring out the rest of the design or words on the cover."

Eric agreed and he and Kari took their leave. It was almost 1:30 p.m. and Don was due back at the house shortly.

"I knew he wouldn't be able to resist it. I just knew it," Eric crowed to Kari, as they waved good-bye and backed out of the two-track dirt driveway.

"I hope we haven't sent him on a wild goose chase," Kari answered.

"That man lives for wild goose chases. If anybody can figure out where the *Brittany* came from, it's Mike. And besides . . . with Mike spending all that time at the library in front of the microfiche, that'll give you and that body of yours more time to be in bed with me. It's night baseball season, you know."

"Ooh, batter up," Kari replied, slipping closer to him in the front seat of the Blazer.

Don snapped awake just after 2:30. *Cripes. I'm going to be late.* He glanced at his wristwatch and groaned. *No, scratch that. I'm late already.*

He hastily threw on a T-shirt, grabbed a sweatshirt in the event that it may be cooler on the lake and closed the door behind him, walking swiftly across the lawn towards his van.

As he approached the Dodge, Duane spotted him. "C'mere and see them shotguns!" he shouted, getting up from his lawn chair and motioning Don inside.

"I'm afraid I'm going to have to take another raincheck, Duane," Don shouted from across the lawn. "I'm a little late as it is. Tomorrow. I'll be over in the morning."

Looking not the least put off, Duane returned to his chair and picked up his beer. "I'll put some coffee on, then." He waved as Don wheeled the Caravan out of the drive and sped away.

chapter 79

The three men sat gloomily on the deck of the Bayliner. They had argued all the way back from the dive site about what to do, how, and when. The bickering continued in the slip. The capstan cover lay accusing at their feet, a visible reminder of their problem. The sun blinked from above, blotted out by an occasional offending cloud.

"Well, at least no one else can identify her," Phillip said weakly, nudging the cover with his foot, trying to lighten the atmosphere. Jimmy shot him a look that made Phillip's blood freeze and made him shift uncomfortably in his seat.

Ed made a disgusted noise and tossed his still-lit Camel overboard, then promptly lit another. "Chances are," Ed said, "that Randall has no idea what's on board the ship. I'll bet he accidentally found her in the Channel."

"You guys are forgetting the obvious," Phillip said. "So what if Randall's found her? The important thing is that *we* found her, too. We can start salvaging right now. We just have to be very careful. If we act fast enough, we can be done, gone, and outta here before he even knows. We can pull this off right under his nose."

"And if he finds out about what we're doing, then what?" Jimmy snapped with angry sarcasm. "They got laws about taking shit from wrecks. We'll be *fucked*. And I'll tell you right now . . . this boy does not get fucked. Not this time."

Neither Phillip nor Ed responded, and the three fell silent. "Speak of the friggin' devil," Ed said. He placed the cigarette to his lips and inhaled. Phillip and Jimmy followed his gaze. Chugging past the marina and heading out into the lake was the *John Galt*. And this time there were *three* people aboard.

"Now, who do you suppose *he* is?" Phillip wondered aloud.

"I don't give a rat's ass if it's Thurston Howell the fuckin' Third," Jimmy snapped. "We gotta get movin'. It's going to take us long enough to salvage the treasure. Now we gotta do it without somebody finding it before us."

"Well, the first thing we've got to do is get our salvage gear ready," Ed ordered, tossing the small, lit cigarette into the water. "The lift bags are down below in one of the lower compartments. And I got a couple more at the cabin, if we need 'em. And we need to get that portable air compressor from my cabin, too."

"Ed, we don't have time for that," Phillip interrupted. "Randall's diving today. We might not have 'til tomorrow."

"Oh, we'll have 'til tomorrow, all right," Ed said, in a self-satisfied tone. "I'll take care of that." He found a book of matches in the pocket of his shorts, lit another cigarette, and continued speaking as he exhaled the smoke. "Matter of fact," he sneered, "I think that this will be Randall's last dive for a while."

The three watched as the *John Galt* entered the ice blue waters of Lake Huron, heading for the Channel.

chapter 80

The conditions on the lake were perfect for diving. The waves were under a foot and the mild wind was just enough to keep the afternoon heat at bay. Eric filled Don in on their meeting with Mike Felsing and his offer to do research. "I left the photo of the capstan cover with him. He thinks he might be able to scan it into his computer and clean it up some . . . see if he can make out the rest of the design or words," Eric said.

Don went over the lights with them as they neared the Channel. There were four of them, with lenses the size of dinner plates and housings about a foot square. "They really are simple," Don explained. "These are the clamps," he said, demonstrating how they worked. "You should have no problem attaching them to the masts. Make sure that wherever you clamp one, you clamp one on another mast at the same depth. It's best to have the lights uniform."

"They aren't very big," Kari observed.

"They don't need to be," Don assured her. "They're pretty powerful. Intense. If you place the lights in the right spots they should be able to illuminate the entire ship for several hours. I would advise you not to stare directly at them after you turn them on. When you get one clamped, turn it on by pressing this button." Don turned the bulky light over in his hands and showed her a large orange button. "It's big and easy to find," he continued. "Even with your gloves on."

A few gulls dipped in the sky and Eric slowed the boat. "Just about there," he said. Kari started readying the gear below deck and within a few minutes Eric had brought the *John Galt* to a halt and let out the anchor. "We should be about fifty feet west of the *Brittany*. I charted her just before we stopped."

The three spent an hour fiddling around with the camera and its housing. Don would control the tiny sub from the surface by watching the video monitor. The two hundred feet of cable that was the mini-sub and camera's power line took up a large portion of the boat's deck.

"If you can guide me to the location where you took the photograph, we might be able to get a glimpse of the interior of that room with the camera," Don said.

Sunken ship. Deep water. Dead bodies. This is gonna be like a Jacques Cousteau movie produced by Wes Craven, Eric thought.

Eric and Kari suited up.

chapter 81

Jesus, I sure hope Ed knows what the hell he's doing, Phillip thought. He was sitting in his truck at the end of Highbanks Road. With his binoculars he could see Randall's boat in the distance and could just make out what was going on. So far, that wasn't much. The three people on the boat seemed pretty occupied, but with what, Phillip couldn't quite see.

What did Ed mean, anyway? 'I think this will be Randall's last dive for a few days'? Phillip wondered uneasily for the umpteenth time. The whole thing was beginning to piss him off. Ed always kept things to himself, forgetting that there were three of them in this. He and Jimmy had a right to know what was going on. Especially now that things had speeded up with the Randall's discovery of the shipwreck. *What in the hell was he going to do?*

He had said to leave it up to him, he knew how to handle these kinds of situations. "You go keep an eye on what Randall's doing," he had said, "and Jimmy and I will take care of a few things later tonight." He had laughed that stupid wheezing laugh, the two all-weather radials heaving up and down. Even Jimmy had looked at Ed with concern. *Well, whatever it is,* Phillip thought, *don't screw up, Ed. Jimmy says the jail food sucks.*

Through the binoculars he could see that the three were moving about on the boat. *What in the hell is that?* Phillip leaned against the truck to steady his vision. The two men were lifting a fairly large object and setting it slowly on the deck.

Son of a bitch.

He lowered the binoculars slowly, squinting out over the lake. With a simple naked eye, it was impossible to discern much of anything. All he could see was a tiny, blue and white shape bobbing far out into the lake. But with the binoculars—

He raised them to his face again in disbelief.

It's a camera! They're gonna video the wreck!

Phillip watched as the man and the woman slid into their wetsuits, and the second man emerged from the cabin carrying what appeared to be a light. He went back below deck a number of times, each time bringing one of the lights with him. Then they tossed a black innertube with a dive flag overboard.

They're gonna dive and they're gonna video the wreck with a camera. They know what they've found, all right. You don't go through the trouble of underwater video for nothing, Phillip thought worriedly. He cursed himself for taking six years to find the wreck, he cursed himself for allowing someone else to find it first. And, he cursed himself for his own stupidity—because he knew that somewhere, lying half buried in the sand near the shipwreck, was his shiny stainless-steel dive knife.

Christopher Knight

chapter 82

Eric had been right on target. The anchor fell only forty-five feet from the *Brittany* and within moments of reaching the bottom themselves, Eric and Kari were on the wreck. The cumbersome lights made movement difficult. They weren't very heavy underwater, but their size made moving them strenuous. Kari could not hold the flashlight and carry a light at the same time, so she followed Eric's beam of light until they reached the ship. Kari let one of the lights rest at the foot of the foremast. Eric set his down as well and inflated his vest, allowing him to gradually glide up along the mast with little effort. Kari removed her flashlight from her small bag and shined it over the deck, casting eerie shadows and creating hidden darkened corners. *How weird*, she thought. *Lost for so many years, and now, like a ghost from the past, it's showing its face again.*

A brilliant light caught her by surprise. *My God! It's almost like daylight!* Eric had clamped his light to the mast about twenty feet above the deck and turned it on. The area below was lit up in murky sunshine. She looked up directly into the light and then, remembering what Don had said, turned her eyes away. Small purple spots clouded her vision. It was like looking into the headlights of a car, only much brighter. She could see Eric returning to the deck to get another light and she slowly kicked her fins and rose up the main mast. She positioned her light carefully, making sure it was level with the one Eric had attached to the foremast. She clamped it to the mast and turned it on. *This is incredible*, she thought.

Beneath her, history was unfolding. Darkness had enveloped the *Brittany* for over a hundred years and now she came alive in the first light she had seen since the sun had last set on her. Kari was mesmerized as she got her first good look at the wreck. It was in incredible shape. A few boards were scattered about here and there and a few planks lay on the bottom around the hull, but all in all, the *Brittany* was intact. Her once proud masts stood solemn and lonely, jutting up and leaning to the side with the list of the ship. A few curious fish weaved slowly in and out of open holes and hatchways. The *Brittany* didn't appear to be underwater, but looked more like a showpiece in a museum.

Eric retrieved another light and cruised slowly along the deck beneath Kari. He looked up at her, gave her the 'all okay' sign, and continued on. Kari returned to the foremast and picked up the last light, following Eric towards the stern of the ship. She passed over the forward hatch, its rectangular black hole beckoning like a candy store to a child. She paused briefly to shine her light down into the bowels of the ship. Wooden boxes, crates, and tools were scattered below. A film of silt and debris, an inch thick in some places, covered everything. She struggled to restrain the urge to enter the hatch, to plunge headlong into the depths of the ship and uncover the secrets she had held for so long.

She clicked her flashlight off, no longer needing it in the glare of the powerful lights. Eric had finished attaching the third light and turned it on, chasing more of the darkness away from the ship. She glided up the mizzenmast and lined up the light evenly with Eric's, pulled the clamps tight, and turned it on. Eric hovered just above the mainmast and stared down at the breathtaking scene. One hundred sixty feet below the surface, the *Brittany* now showed herself again. Lit up as bright as the day, she lay silent and serene.

Eric checked his air gauge and gave Kari the 'thumbs up' signal. Although they had spent only four minutes on the wreck, they'd used up more air than normal dealing with the bulky lights, and they would need to leave now to give them time to decompress while they ascended to the surface. They hovered for a moment and took another look at the brightly-lit wreck. It was a breathtaking sight and neither wanted to leave, but they pressed on towards the anchor line and began the slow process of returning to the surface.

chapter 83

Don stared into the depths of Lake Huron, watching Eric and Kari fade away down the anchor line. Within moments they were gone and as soon as they disappeared completely he shifted his gaze to Bois Blanc Island, floating in the hazy distance. Shards of glass carved razor-thin dreams into a green-blue sea. It was hot, and Don doubted he was going to need the sweatshirt today.

He spent the next ten minutes checking the monitor cables and connections and making sure the details were in order. Not far from the boat, he could see the intermittent air bubbles from Eric and Kari as they boiled to the surface. He could watch where the bubbles traveled and trace where Eric and Kari had just been. Twenty minutes later the divers returned to the surface and Kari was removing her regulator from her mouth almost before her head was out of the water. "It's spectacular!" she shouted as she bobbed in the water. She raised her mask from her face to her forehead. "Don, it is unbelievable! The lights lit up everything! I didn't want to come back up. It's terrific!"

"It really is incredible," Eric said, as he removed his fins in the water and handed them up to Don. He took off his vest and the two tanks in the water as well and Don pulled the heavy equipment aboard. Kari did the same as Eric climbed up the ladder and he helped her with her gear.

"We've got the lights set up on the masts," Eric said. "The entire wreck is visible. God, Don . . . wait 'till you see her."

"Well, the camera is all set," Don assured. "Let's get it going." After they stowed the dive gear below deck, Eric and Don lifted the camera over the side and placed it in the water, where it dangled from the heavy cable just beneath the surface. "Hold it there for a moment," Don requested, and he walked into the cabin and turned the monitor on. He made several adjustments. "Okay, you can let 'er go!"

Eric and Kari came into the cabin and sat down, and the three watched the monitor intently as the mini-sub and camera sank slowly to the bottom of the Laurentian Channel.

chapter 84

One hundred feet above the wreck a tiny, murky image began to appear on the screen. Using the control pad, Don guided the camera towards the fuzzy white dot the size of a dime on the monitor. The image grew stronger and brighter, closer, and soon they could make out the details of the hull.

"Look at *that*. That is *amazing,*" Don whispered in awe. All three were enthralled as Don guided the mini-sub slowly towards the *Brittany*. He lowered the camera a bit and swept in from the starboard side. As Don moved the small sub and its camera housing closer, more details of the ship came into view. Don spoke, his face locked on the screen in front of him. "Man, you were right. She's pristine. Nobody has touched her since the day she sank!"

Kari reached forward, her finger touching the screen. "Look at the wheel. And over there . . ." she moved her finger to the left, pointing to an object on the bow, "is the windlass. And there's some of her hardware scattered on the deck."

Don brought the mini-sub to within twenty feet of the wreck. He dove the sub to the bottom and surveyed portions of the hull. The motion of the motor stirred up some of the silt on the bottom, temporarily clouding the image on the screen and Don carefully backed off. "That's just what we *don't* want to do," he said. "I didn't think that there would be so much silt on everything. Stirring up that shit will really obfuscate our field of view."

"Yeah. It'll probably make it hard to see, too," Eric chided.

Don shot him a quick, sarcastic glance and a smile. "Smartass."

"Head up to the main hatch." Kari directed, sweeping her finger across the screen. "It's open, and there's a large entry way. We might be able to get the camera inside a little without stirring up too much debris."

Don maneuvered the mini-sub until the dark hole of the main hatch came into view. The area around the hatch was coated with the greenish feather-light silt. "I think we'll be all right, if we don't go in more than a foot or two. That may not allow us to see too much except the entryway." He inched the sub closer down and in the shadows a stairway came into view.

"Hold it! What was that!?" Eric exclaimed. "Go back a little to the right. Okay . . . can you go in a little more?"

Don gently pushed his right hand an eighth-of-an-inch forward and the mini-sub crept into the main hatch. The sub was now completely inside and the light beam penetrated the darkness, shining a plate-sized circle on the floor.

"Over . . . just a bit," Eric guided. The bright circle moved on the wood planking as Don carefully guided the controls. "There."

Kari gasped, and Don raised his eyebrows. "Check that out." The skeleton was broken up and deteriorating but, like the other two bodies, shreds of clothing covered portions of its frame. "There's number three, guys," Don said. He turned the sub a tiny bit, trying to get a clearer view and the eerie vision disappeared, enveloped in an exploding cloud of silt and debris.

"Shit," Don exclaimed beneath his breath, cursing his carelessness. He maneuvered the mini-sub carefully in the small space but it was no use. The churning silt filled the monitor, and Don finally backed the sub out of the hatch. As he backed the sub away from the *Brittany,* the dusty silt billowed out of the main hatch. "Well, we won't be seeing much more in there today," Don said. "That's going to take awhile to settle. Sorry about that. But we did get that all on video. We'll be able to freeze the frame and get a better look."

Don piloted the mini-sub around the mainmast and then re-approached the deck, being careful to remain a good distance from the ship to keep the silt from becoming stirred up. As it glided toward the gunwale Don froze the controls and suddenly backed the mini-sub up. "Hey, look at that. One of you must have dropped something."

Kari and Eric glanced at each other as if to say 'hey, it wasn't me.' They peered over Don's shoulder at the bright metallic object getting larger and larger on the screen.

"It's a knife. One of you dropped your knife," Don said, matter-of-factly.

"Get closer if you can," Eric said, his voice serious.

"Okay, but we might stir up some of the bottom." He inched the mini-cam to a few feet above the knife. It was centered in the middle of the screen and a small portion of it was buried in the sand. The handle was gray and black, the blade a shiny silver.

"That's not *my* knife," Eric and Kari said at the same time.

The three were silent for a moment, staring at the gleaming stainless-steel blade, partially covered with silt.

"That's an IDI Titanium." He fingered the screen, tracing the knife on the monitor. "Nice knife, but it isn't mine."

"Could you have knocked it off the boat?" Don asked.

"We don't even *own* a knife like that, Don. That's not one of our knives." Eric insisted flatly. "I've never seen it before. That's somebody else's knife. Someone else has been diving here."

Eric, Kari, and Don sat in silence, not speaking and hardly breathing. The mere presence of the knife didn't create any major problems because anyone had the right to dive the wreck. Judging by the amount of undisturbed silt that covered the wreck, no one had yet penetrated her. *But if others were diving here, it won't be long before they get inside of her*, Eric thought. *If they haven't already.*

"Oh, well," Kari finally said. "So we aren't the first to find her. I guess we're going to have to share."

"There's no telling how long that knife has been there, either," Don said. "It's stainless steel so it's not going to rust. That thing could have been dropped earlier this summer. Or it could have been dropped by someone who was attempting to make it to the wreck, but gave up because it was too deep."

"No," Eric said. "Look at it. There's no silt on it. Hell, if somebody dropped it last week there would be at least a fine layer of silt. This thing is totally clean. Somebody dropped this thing yesterday."

Kari looked out the windows of the cabin, half expecting to see a boat approaching, filled with divers, all wondering who it was in the blue-and-white cabin cruiser. But the lake was empty of boats, except for a few sailboats off in the distance toward the Mackinac Bridge. She turned her attention back to the knife, which sat accusingly in the center of the video monitor.

"Well," Don began, "the knife isn't going anywhere. Might as well keep going and see what else there is on the wreck."

chapter 85

Sharon Durand hung up the phone angrily. *Damn him.* She knew there was no point in getting upset, but she couldn't help it. She fought back tears and busied herself around the house, putting away the dishes that had been drying in the sink, wiping off the counter and the table, and sweeping the kitchen floor although it really didn't need it.

She was used to being left alone, especially in the summer when Jimmy headed up north with Phillip and Ed to go fishing of all things. She didn't mind him being gone that much, except that she never knew when he was taking off or when he would be coming back. Often, he would disappear for a day or two and then she would come home from work to find a message on the machine. *Hi, I'm up here fishing. Sorry I forgot to tell ya, but I guess I got busy and all that. I'll be home in a few days. I love you, you know that.* Bye. He returned home when he felt like it with no explanation. He didn't talk about what he had done while he had been gone and Sharon had given up asking. She had asked to come along only once. *Absolutely not,* Jimmy had said flatly. *This is a 'guy' thing. Suppose I went to the bathroom with you and your girlfriends? You wouldn't like that, would ya?*

Sharon stared out the window at the cars passing on the street. *He never used to be this way. When we met he was so kind, caring, and concerned.* Sharon banished that thought brusquely. If she didn't, she might have to comprehend the truth—she was married to a monster. A man whose emotions could change in an instant and whose demeanor would change in a flash without warning. And he was taking steroids again which didn't help. He got off them for a while, but lost too much bulk—or so he thought—and had started back up again. She had tried talking to him about it, but he had lit into her about everything she had done from alcohol to pot to cocaine. *Besides,* he had said, *it's none of your damn business.* So she went on getting the living hell beat out of her like clockwork when Jimmy's raging ego and insecurity took control of him and he lashed out the only way he knew how.

And what in the hell got him interested in fishing anyway? He had never fished before we met, never even so much as talked about it. Now, for the last few years, that's all he does in the summertime. He and Phillip and that sleazeball Ed Belmont. I can't believe he's related to me. Sharon hadn't met her Uncle Ed until her family attended a reunion in New Orleans when she was twelve. He smoked too much, drank too much, and was the biggest slob on the face of the earth. *You'd think he'd lay off the food a little while, for crying out loud. He's getting fatter and fatter every year.* Thankfully, she only saw him about once a summer, when he would drive from Key West up to his summer home near Cheboygan. He always stopped and stayed the night with her and Jimmy, but usually Ed and Jimmy would take off until the wee hours of the morning, leaving Sharon by herself. The two would return well past 2:00 a.m. and the house would reek of Ed's cigarettes for days after he left.

One morning she made breakfast for herself, Ed, and Jimmy. She sat down at the table, but the pungent stench of rotting nicotine was overwhelming. *And he's not even smoking,* she thought. She felt like she was going to get sick. It wasn't that she minded the cigarette smell; she smoked once in a while herself when she and Jimmy went to the bars. *But I'm not choking down two packs a day,* she thought.

And she hated the fact that Jimmy and Ed seemed to get along so well, despite the fact that Ed was the type of person that Jimmy usually hated. Of course, you never could really tell exactly who Jimmy would hate, it all depended on the mood he was in at the time he met them. When Jimmy first met Ed, he didn't want to have anything to do with him. Jimmy couldn't believe that all Ed did was hang out on a boat looking for treasure of all things. "He's a low-life bum, that's all he is," Jimmy had said. Until one day she came home from work and Jimmy had asked her for Ed's phone number.

"Ed? Uncle Ed? Belmont?" Sharon said, surprised.

"Yeah. Phillip wants to do some fishing and I told him that Ed knows a lot about that shit."

"Why does Phillip want to go fishing all of a sudden?" she asked.

"Aw, you know Phillip. Wants to get away up north. Do some vacationing, some fishing, you know. You got his number?" Jimmy asked again.

Sharon found the number in her address book and gave it to him.

"Phillip is in for a big surprise if he wants to go fishing for tarpon or barracuda up north," she said.

Jimmy had called Ed the next day when Sharon wasn't home.

Now, Jimmy and his Freewheeling Fishing Friends were at it again, which meant that she wouldn't be seeing Jimmy until God knows when. On the phone she had tried to explain to him that they needed to talk. He had told her that she was free to talk. *In fact, you're talking now, Sharon. That's what telephones are for. Talking.*

Vacation or no vacation, Sharon thought, *I need to talk to him. Face-to-face.*

Then:

To hell with him, she decided. *If he doesn't want to listen to me on the phone, he can listen to me in person, whether he likes it or not.* She packed a few things in the car, jumped on I-75, and headed north to Cheboygan.

chapter 86

Jimmy lay on his back on the bench and grasped the bar positioned above him. The three men had split up earlier. Phillip had headed out to Highbanks Road to keep an eye on Randall's boat and Ed headed to his cabin to start preparing some of the salvage equipment. Jimmy had gone to the Cheboygan Health and Fitness Club for a workout. The free-weight room had a small portable stereo, but Jimmy brought his own portable CD player, cranking up Black Sabbath's *Heaven and Hell*. A few other people who were also using the weights soon left, either done with their exercises or sick of Jimmy's blaring music. Jimmy couldn't have cared less.

I dare 'em to ask me to turn it down. I dare 'em to even talk to me.

He held the bar above him, slowly lowering 300 pounds to his chest. Ronnie James Dio lashed out with powerful, threatening vocals.

. . . Sing me a song, you're a singer; Do me a wrong, you're a bringer of evil . . .

One. He pressed the bar high above his chest and then lowered the weight slowly back down.

. . . The devil is never a maker; The less that you give, you're a taker . . .

Two. Three hundred pounds raised easily back up and back down to Jimmy's chest.

. . . So it's on, and on, and on; It's Heaven and Hell.

Three. He set the weight back onto the rack and added two twenty-five pound plates, slamming them against the others on the bar. His anger boiled just beneath the surface as his thoughts jumped from Randall to the wreck to Sharon. *That stupid bitch*, he thought as he lay back on the bench and grabbed the bar. He had called her from the pay phone at the marina earlier in the day and she had given him an earful. *Yeah, she's really tough when I'm almost three hundred miles away. We'll see how tough she is when I get back.* He had hung up on her, went back to his motel room to retrieve his work-out clothes, and then headed for the gym.

Jimmy pushed up the weight off the rack bringing the three hundred fifty pounds slowly down to his chest. *And that Randall. Who the hell does he think he is?* In a rage, he pressed the bar high above his chest, lowered it back down, and thrust it violently back up. Geezer Butler and Tony Iommi wielded a throbbing, thundering manifesto, creating a dark, menacing symphony.

. . . The lover of life's not a sinner; The ending is just a beginner . . .

The weight came down and back up again and back down again to Jimmy's chest.

. . . The closer you get to the meaning; The sooner you'll know that you're dreaming . . .

He drove the weight to his arms' full extension and placed it back on the rack, taking off the two twenty-five pound plates and adding two forty-fives. Three hundred-ninety pounds.

. . . So it's on, and on, and on . . .

We are so close, he thought. *We are so close and nobody is going to mess it up. Not Randall, not Sharon, not nobody. The bitch even had the nerve to ask if she could come up here when she knows better.*

. . .Wo it's on, and on and on . . .

Jimmy lay back on the bench, gripped the bar and took a series of deep breaths.

. . . It goes on, and on, and ON; Heaven and Hell!!

He grabbed the bar and brought it down, the cold iron touching his chest. He pushed it up a couple of inches, then lowered it again.

Well, nobody is going to stop us, he thought. *Not nobody. 'Cause they'll be dead. They'll be so dead they'll be cold before they hit the ground.*

Jimmy continued to press the bar up and down, never higher than a few inches from his chest, pumping faster and faster to the beat of the unearthly overture. *And we'll fix Randall tonight. He and his bitch and whoever else won't be doing any diving for a few days. And that'll be all we need. A few days.*

After Phillip had left, Ed told Jimmy to meet him back at the marina at 1:00 a.m.

Yep. We're gonna slow that bastard down for a few days.

Jimmy exploded in a frenzy and thrust three hundred ninety pounds to a full extension, paused for only an instant, inhaled deeply and lowered the bar back to his chest. Bill Ward kept time, pounding rhythmically as the haunting dirge stormed on, picking up tempo for the final wicked crescendo. Ronnie James Dio screamed menacingly from the CD player.

. . . They say that life's a carousel; Spinning fast you've got to ride it well . . .

Jimmy's strength was failing and he struggled to complete the next repetition. He lowered the bar again, forcing another rep with some difficulty.

. . . The world is full of Kings and Queens, who blind your eyes and steal your dreams; IT'S HEAVEN AND HELL . . .

Jimmy forced the weight up with all his might. He struggled, and the bar trembled. *Shit. I'm losing it.* He held the bar inches above his chest, pressing with everything he had. *One more inch. If I can get it one more inch, I'll get it up the rest of the way. Come on, you—*

. . . They'll tell you black is really white; The moon is just the sun at night . . .

His strength gave out and the bar came crashing down to his chest, knocking the wind from him. He gasped for a breath and tilted the bar to the left, working to keep the entire weight from resting on his ribcage. One side of the weights slid off the bar and crashed to the floor, causing the other side of the bar to drop and snapping the lighter end into the air. Again, weights pounded and

314 The Laurentian Channel

clanged to the floor and Jimmy lay on the bench for a moment, holding the empty bar to his chest, inhaling deeply. Black plates scattered the floor like dishes. The noise brought a few people up from downstairs to ask if Jimmy was okay. He nodded and said nothing. After a few moments he stood up and replaced the weights on the rack, moving to another bench to work his shoulders.

... And when you walk in golden halls, you get to keep the gold that falls; It's Heaven and Hell ...

He flexed in the mirror, the veins in his arms and neck exploding from beneath his skin. He picked up two eighty-pound dumbbells, listening to the fading aftershocks of the song.

"You're right, Ronnie," he whispered aloud, pressing the two weights above his head. *"You are absolutely right."*

chapter 87

Sharon turned off I-75 at the Sea Shell City exit. The billboards had announced its presence from miles back. *'SEE THE GIANT, MAN-EATING CLAM!!'* the billboard screamed in six-foot letters. *'THOUSANDS OF SHELLS FROM ALL OVER THE WORLD!!'* Adjacent to Sea Shell City was a Marathon station, and she stopped to get a Diet Coke and fill up the Grand Prix. Cheboygan was about twelve miles east of here and if she had read the road map right, this exit would take her right into town. She'd never been to Cheboygan before. Hell, she'd never been north of Flint before and she was enchanted by the forests, beautiful hills, and farmlands. Jimmy had discouraged her from coming up here. "It ain't for you," he'd said. "You're a city girl. Always will be. Lotta bugs and shit up here." If they went anywhere together, which they occasionally did in the winter, it was usually to Florida. But never to northern Michigan. Trees lined the two-lane paved highway and she looked around in fascination. *So much prettier than glass, concrete, and steel,* she thought. She felt oddly out of place, yet at home at the same time. She felt relaxed and comfortable as the Pontiac wound through the peaceful country setting.

I wonder if I can even find Jimmy. She had no idea where he stayed when he came up here. Sometimes it was a motel, but a few times when she'd called before, the motel clerk had told her they didn't have anybody registered there by that name. Jimmy said it was because he used an alias and when she asked him why, he said it was all in fun. He'd sign in with names like Claude Bawles, or Stu Pedasso. *Funny, Jimmy. You're a regular Howie Mandel.*

As she drove, the trees thinned and the houses began closing in on one another. She passed a sign announcing the city limits of Cheboygan. She turned right at the stoplight and drove down Main Street and in five minutes she had driven right through town. She kept an eye on the motels as she passed, looking for Jimmy's black Trans Am, but didn't see it. She slowed when she passed by the Lincoln Bridge Plaza, thinking she saw his car parked in front of a *Little Caesars* restaurant. But the car was a Camaro.

After going all the way through town and not seeing the Trans Am, she turned around and stopped at a gas station to ask for directions to the marina. She figured if Jimmy was fishing, he might be there. *If* Jimmy was fishing. Actually, she wasn't concerned about him sleeping with another woman. He'd done that enough already, and a few more points in a small northern Michigan town weren't going to matter much. What pissed her off was that he kept lying to her about it. Actually, it was more like he taunted her, the way he smiled and said he'd "never ever do that sort of thing, baby doll, you know I love you."

She cruised back through town again until she located the marina. She drove up and down the parking spaces adjacent to the slips. No Trans Am. Nor did she see Phillip's truck or Ed's Ford Ranger. *Hell, Jimmy might not even be here. Probably lied to me about that, too,* she thought bitterly. It was a thought that had crossed her mind several times on the long trip north.

She left the marina and instead of driving back through town again, she turned right and followed US-23 as it wound through the outskirts of town. There were a few motels along either side and she watched carefully for the sports car. The town quickly began to taper off. No Trans Am.

She turned into the first driveway she found to turn around and head back in to town. *I'll find him. If he's here, I'll find him.* She braked quickly when she found her herself staring directly at the large billboard on the front. *Cheboygan Health and Fitness Club*, the big sign advertised. *Public Welcome.* Jimmy's Trans Am was parked directly beneath it.

chapter 88

Daniel keeps a wary eye on the sky as he goes about his duties. There is a lot to do on the Brittany, and no sooner had he finished one task than Captain LaChance set him to work on another one. It is hard work, but the sunshine and the continuous laughter makes it seem easy. Jack Malloy is a real jokester and always has a riddle or anecdote to keep both he and the Captain in stitches. LaChance seems to have a good sense of humor as well, occasionally countering one of Jack's jokes with one of his own.

Daniel is actually having a good time. He likes this kind of work. Sailing is much better than working the docks—more exciting and not at all monotonous. But every once in a while, a sick feeling rises from deep inside him. He keeps telling himself . . . two thousand dollars. Two thousand dollars. Over and over. It had worked for awhile, but the uncomfortable feeling is getting stronger.

He stops his work for a moment and stares across the serene

blue waters. The day is a scorcher, and he is sweating profusely. The sun reflects off the shiny brass capstan cover on which the scripted letters stand out clearly. The Brittany. He wonders why they have changed the name and why all references to its previous name, the Aurora, have been stripped away. Many people were superstitious about changing the name of a vessel; they said it was bad luck.

No one is going to get hurt, he thinks. That's what they had said, hadn't they? A robbery. A simple, no-nonsense holdup. He hears Jack and the Captain laughing behind him and the sick feeling comes back stronger. I sold them out, he thinks. Captain LaChance and Jack Malloy are hard-workers, making an honest living, and I sold them out. They are paying me well to sail to New York and I betrayed them.

No. He banishes the thought, pushes it away. He must.

Two thousand dollars. He repeats it over and over, and mentally pictures the money in his hands, until he is able to temporarily block out his feelings of guilt.

Christopher Knight

chapter 89

Evelyn Felsing had gone into Petoskey to go shopping and Mike was tinkering around with the crippled computer, trying to get the scanner to work. *Why are all these damned instruction manuals written in Japanese?* he fumed. *Actually, a Samurai sword might come in useful right now*, he thought in disgust. And the toll-free technical assistance number that he'd called did nothing but waste an hour of his time. He hadn't even been able to speak with a live human being, for crying out loud. He hung up the phone and decided he'd try his luck on the infernal machine himself. So far he'd only scanned beautiful images of pure black squares. Well, to be fair, one image had had a fat white streak across it, so maybe he *was* catching on.

He had just pressed another mysterious button in pure frustration, departing from the manual instructions entirely, when he heard a car enter the dirt drive. It was Evelyn. She honked to let him know to come down and help her unload the groceries. After he had carried the sacks into the house, they retired to the deck with chilled iced teas.

"How's the scanning coming?" Evelyn asked him, setting her glass of tea on the deck railing. The sun glowed on her face.

"About as well as my book," he replied, smiling a frustrated, but good-natured smile. The two sat in companionable silence in the afternoon sun, sipping tea and listening to the waves lap on the shore below. Sandpipers bobbed and weaved behind the tongues of receding water in their run-run-*stop* fashion. A half-dozen seagulls fought over the remains of a small, dead fish that had washed ashore. A westerly breeze, gentle as a baby's breath, slipped in and out of the surrounding trees. Evelyn finally excused herself to go make supper and Mike reluctantly returned to his computer for another bout of scanning fun.

Again he punched another button randomly. *Well, I'll be damned,* he thought, staring at the monitor in amazement. *I did it. I don't know how, but I did it.* The photo of the capstan cover filled the entire screen, sharp and clear. Mike sat down in front of the computer, full of excitement now. But he still couldn't read what was etched above the *Brittany's* name. He carefully saved the image, afraid he might accidentally push the wrong button and the miracle would disappear, never to be recovered.

Consulting the manual repeatedly, he experimented with enhancing the contrast and tweaking the brightness in a thousand different combinations. He reversed the colors, creating a black-and-white negative of the cover.

He accidentally tapped the wrong key and the photo suddenly flipped upside down.

Aw, hell. How did I do that? He surveyed the keypad to try and remember what key he'd just hit. Something in the photo on the screen caused him to pause.

Hold on a minute, he thought. *What's that?*

The reversed colors brought out lines and details not previously noticed. Again, he adjusted the contrast, and suddenly the obscured image emerged with startling clarity. He could no longer read the words '*Brittany*'—but that didn't matter anymore.

"*Well, I'll be damned,*" Mike whispered to himself. He stared at the result for a long moment, savoring the feeling of accomplishment. The strange design on the capstan wasn't a design, after all—it was *lettering*. Upside down, it became discernable and clearer. A word in big, crisp letters that stood out bold and clean. It read: *Aurora*.

chapter 90

You gotta get what you can while you can as soon as you can. Ed had picked up that life lesson from a skipper in southern Florida while he worked for him on his charter fishing boat. Ed had been in his early twenties and liked the hustling chance-taking attitude of the skipper. He explained to Ed how he hid money from the IRS so his fish chartering business didn't show much of a profit, if any. He said the chances of getting caught were slim and none. "Besides," the skipper said, "you gotta get what you can while you can as soon as you can." Not exactly Ralph Waldo Emerson or Henry David Thoreau, but fitting nonetheless. And it sounded good to Ed Belmont.

You gotta get what you can while you can as soon as you can.

In addition to his fishing charter business, the skipper also supplemented his income by doing a little bit of recreational pharmaceutical distribution. This impressed Ed. It wasn't anything that he was interested in; alcohol was Ed's only drug of choice. Alcohol and nicotine. But it proved that the skipper was a mover when it came to getting what he wanted, proved that he lived by his words. And if it happened to be a little illegal, well, so what? The skipper had been running dope through Miami for years, and made a ton of money. When the feds started closing in, the skipper disappeared one day without a trace. Ed heard that he had taken off for the Virgin Islands and was relaxing in luxurious comfort until things cooled down a bit.

Ed sat at the table in his small cabin, smoking a cigarette. *We'll slow that son of a bitch down, all right. We didn't come this far to get dicked over by anyone. Me and Jimmy, we'll take care of it tonight.* He exhaled and let out with a disbelieving *hrrrmmph.*

Jimmy. That crazy idiot. He's gonna kill himself with that crap he pumps in his veins all the time. Jimmy had never actually told Ed that he was using juice, but it wasn't hard to tell. *Your legs don't look like damned steel logs with veins, no matter how much you work out,* Ed thought. *Not without a little added anabolic enhancement.* Ed stopped to consider that by eating over ten thousand calories a day, mostly fat and junk food, he was doing the same thing to his heart that Jimmy was doing to his. *Hell, I'm a bodybuilder, too,* Ed snickered to himself. *You build your body your way and I'll build mine my way.*

Ed barely tolerated Jimmy, and if it weren't for the wreck they wouldn't be hanging out together. Of all the luck—having a relative who's married to a guy who happens to be close friends with a guy who had stumbled upon a hidden fortune. At first, Ed thought the whole story was just a bunch of hogwash bullshit made up by some wanna-be treasure hunter looking for fast riches. After a few days of his own research, though, he was convinced that Phillip had really latched on to a big one at that old bag's place. The treasure was well-known among divers and seekers. There had been rumors and stories about the missing *Montoya* fortune. The ship had washed ashore during a storm off the coast of Florida in the 1800s. Two thirds of the enormous treasure had been accounted for, but the rest had seemingly disappeared.

Until Phillip Keanan found Richard Merman's journal.

Phillip himself didn't completely understand the magnitude of his discovery until Ed had confirmed his findings.

Of all the shit luck, Ed had thought. *Finding the lost fortune while doing your college homework.* Still, it was enough for Ed to change any plans that he had made, drop everything, and begin searching for the ill-fated *Aurora.* Or *Brittany,* or whatever the hell you wanted to call it. Ed couldn't care. What he cared about was the fact that hundreds of divers had been looking for this treasure for years. And a snot-nosed college kid had figured out where it was. Phillip wasn't incredibly brilliant, but he *could* keep his mouth shut. That was fifty percent of the battle, right there, and the first rule of plunderers was: shut your mouth.

And Jimmy was, well . . . *Jimmy.* He could be a valuable asset or a curse, depending on the day and hour. Phillip had taught him to dive. No special class, no certificate. No dive manuals or guidebooks. One afternoon, Phillip outfitted Jimmy with some rental equipment from the dive shop, gave him a few pointers, a lot of do this and do thats, but whatever you do, don't do this—and that was it. Jimmy had descended to one hundred twenty feet on his first dive. He was fearless.

They had spent an enormous amount of time and money in the last six years looking for the *Aurora*. Fortunately, Ed had the financial comfort to afford such a lifestyle. Phillip managed, having inherited a small amount of money from some relative, and Jimmy . . . *hell, who knows where he gets his money from*, Ed thought. So far, the search had been funded mostly by Ed, and he would receive a full half of the take—plus expenses—of what they found in the wreck. Jimmy and Phillip would split the remainder. Ed had bought the boat and considered the modest $300 a month for the dinky cabin as an expense. Not to mention his meals, cigarettes, and beer. At least for the five months that he spent in Cheboygan every year.

A mosquito bit Mickey Mouse on the ear and Ed smacked it. The bug balled up and rolled underneath his hand as he swept it away, leaving a fine red bloodstain two inches long. *Damn thing woulda sucked me dry.* Ed crushed out the cigarette, stood up, and shuffled through a few old boxes that were piled in the corner until he found the small black toolbox. He opened it and, after surveying its contents thoughtfully, closed it and placed it on the counter.

That'll do.

He pulled another Camel from the pack and placed it to his lips. *Yep. We'll show that bastard Randall, and whoever else is with him. He ain't gonna be diving for a few days.* Ed lit the cigarette and inhaled deeply. *Not with that boat he won't. No fucking way.*

chapter 91

Sharon had decided not to confront Jimmy at the Fitness Club.
Instead, she waited across the street in the parking lot of the
Cheboygan Motor Lodge until she saw his car pull out and head
towards town. She followed him and watched as he pulled in to the
River Terrace Motel. Instead of pulling in behind him, she pulled
into the *Big Boy* parking lot across the street and watched as he got
out of the Trans Am. She felt foolish, following him around like
a spy or something, but then again, you never knew with Jimmy.
If he saw her here in Cheboygan after he had told her he didn't
want her around, he might go ballistic and beat the living shit right
out of her then and there. *Which wouldn't be much different than
getting the shit beat out of me at home*, she thought. *Just in a more
pleasant, wooded surrounding.*

Her heart was beating rapidly and her hands were shaking. *I'm not nervous,* she told herself, *just too much caffeine in those Diet Cokes. Getcha every time.* It wasn't that she was afraid of confronting Jimmy; she'd certainly done that enough in the past—and paid for it when she did. But this time it was different. What was he going to say? What would he do? She sat in the car in the *Big Boy* parking lot, nervously tapping the steering wheel. She had driven all the way up here and hadn't given much thought to how she was going to approach Jimmy.

A motel. That's what I need. I'll check in to that motel out towards the fitness center. I'll get my shit together and relax for a while. I'll talk to him tomorrow, she decided at last.

After checking in to the *Cheboygan Motor Lodge,* she relaxed for a while in the bathtub and after lying sleepless on the bed for several hours, she decided to go for a walk.

Although it was almost midnight, she had a couple nervous moments when cars appeared. She had walked a mile or so from the motel and now stood in a park at the edge of Lake Huron, staring out over the water. The lake was calm, and the gentle lapping of water on rocks was soothing. The Mackinac Bridge was brilliantly illuminated about fifteen miles to the northwest, and the flickering, Christmas-tree lights of a large freighter wavered in the night heat as the vessel slowly chugged along in the shipping lane. Sharon could hear the low drone of its engine as the massive steel boat churned through the water.

Only a few other people were in the park. A man and a woman, probably in their mid-fifties, walked hand in hand along the shoreline. A car cruised by slowly, making its way around the small circle drive of the park, its radio blaring an obscure rap tune. Once in a while, she heard the boisterous laughter from a late night reveler from the adjacent marina. It was almost one a.m.

Walking towards the marina, she could see the masts of the sailboats in their slips. There were still quite a few cars parked in the lot, but not many people up and about at this late hour. She hesitated for a moment, and then turned to walk the docks of the marina.

Jimmy awoke angrily. Not for any reason, in particular. He just wanted to be pissed. That was reason enough. He was groggy and realized that he probably shouldn't have taken a nap before going to meet Ed at the marina. But he had been tired and he figured that if he didn't get at least a little sleep, he'd really be bushed later that night. And he had no idea how long this was going to take. The only thing Ed had told him was that they were going to 'take care' of Randall. Whatever the hell he meant by that. He looked at the lighted dial of the clock on the table. *12:47 a.m.*

He stretched, and threw on a pair of black sweats and a light brown tank top. Within minutes of waking, he was behind the wheel of the Trans Am, heading through the sleeping town, on his way to the marina.

Shit, I gotta pee, Sharon thought and began to look around for a restroom. The ladies' restroom was in the small building that housed the harbormaster's office but, to her dismay, the door was locked. '*Boat owners and their guests only,*' read the sign on the door. '*Key required for entry.*' As she turned away from the door, she saw a large man walking directly towards her.

No. It can't be.

His head was down, and Sharon didn't think he had spotted her. She ducked around the side of the building and hid in the darkness of the trees. In that fraction of an instant she had recognized him.

Ed Belmont. She could pick out that behemoth frame anywhere. He passed her not ten feet away and turned to walk out on the docks. *Well, how about that,* Sharon marveled, *maybe they really are fishing.* She stayed hidden in the shadows and watched Ed as he boarded a boat and lit a cigarette.

The minutes ticked by. Sharon watched the silhouette of the big man on the boat, and the orange glow of the cigarette that periodically was raised and lowered. Muffled laughter came from one of the boats in the slips. Other than that, the marina was quiet.

Ed Belmont finished his cigarette, and the glowing butt arced out and down like a falling star. Sharon heard the muffled *pfffffittt* as it hit the water. Then Ed turned and went into the boat's cabin.

Now's my chance, Sharon thought. She peered around the edge of the building. Just as she was about to slip from the concealment of the shadows, she heard a car approaching. Although she was hidden from Ed, she was in full view of any car that pulled into the marina. She froze, not sure what to do, then decided that if she just walked and acted normal she would probably not be noticed.

The car was coming fast, and she could see the headlights breaking through the trees. She started walking as if she were just out for a leisurely stroll (*which I am,* she reminded herself) and told herself just to play it cool, that it was just somebody who had run up to the store to get some food or beer. The headlights slowed and the car approached the marina.

At the last moment, Sharon panicked and made a giant leap for the safety of the trees. Kneeling down and staying close to the bushes, she watched Jimmy's Trans Am as it whipped past and parked at the first space in the lot, right in front of where she had been standing thirty seconds ago.

chapter 92

Don honked the horn as he pulled out of the driveway and Kari waved as she was closing the drapes. It was just after one in the morning; he hadn't planned to stay this late. The three had spent the late afternoon and evening watching the video of the shipwreck over and over, finding places where Kari and Eric could penetrate the *Brittany* with the least amount of danger to themselves, or damaging the fragile ship.

The short drive to his cottage was uneventful except for when he had surprised two men as he came around the corner of Eric and Kari's street. His headlights caught them just as he rounded the turn and the two men immediately ducked off the road and into the shadows. *Must've thought I was drunk*, Garrity thought. *Good thing I wasn't going any faster. That heavy guy would've been road kill.*

In five minutes Don was through town and heading out M-33. In another five minutes he pulled into Everett's Resort. The huge oak trees blocked out the moonlight, and the walk across the grass was totally dark. Twice he almost smacked into a tree trunk as he maneuvered cautiously in the dark. When he reached the cabin, he flipped the lights on. As he crossed the floor something crunched under his foot. A muffled, potato-chip crack. He lifted his heel and turned and looked down. *Nice going, Don,* he mentally scolded himself.

The dreamcatcher had fallen from the window and lay on the floor, the outer ring broken in two pieces, held together only by the web. The tiny thread in the middle had snapped as well, and the feather was nowhere to be found.

Well, I'll bet ol' Duane will be happy about that. He picked up the broken dreamcatcher and surveyed the damage. It was beyond repair. Don decided that he'd run into town first thing in the morning and get a replacement before Duane noticed. He set the damaged pieces on the counter, laid down in the small steel-framed bed, and fell instantly asleep.

Knives. Hundreds of shiny, stainless steel dive knives of all sizes. Don photographed them from several angles. The water felt good and there were hundreds of colorful fish dancing about him in the rich light-blue sea. And dreamcatchers. The coral reef was full of them and he photographed nearly a dozen of them as they hung lazily from the coral, their fragile feathers swaying to the movements of the current. Suddenly, Don was alone. No fish, no reef, no dreamcatchers. Just the never-ending depths below, above, and around him. *We're back, Donny boy. We'll always be back. Cause you know what, Donny boy? We never leave. Never ever.*

He awoke from the nightmare bathed in sweat. His heart was racing and he was gasping for air. He lay in bed another moment before getting up, fumbling for a towel in the dark to dry himself off. The sheets were wet so he stripped the bed and hung one sheet over the bathroom door and the other over the shower curtain rod. He lay back down on the bed although the mattress was still damp.

Moonlight was streaming in through the small window over the tiny sink and Don could see the outline of the broken dreamcatcher on the counter. *Right there is the whole problem. The dreamcatcher is busted.* He sat up in bed and looked at the mangled dreamcatcher on the counter. *Nah, that's bullshit. Like Duane said: it's humbo jumbo. A gimmick to sell to tourists.* He lay back down on the bed and fell asleep once again, but not before he had scotch-taped the broken dreamcatcher to the window.

chapter 93

Heavy knocking on the cottage door woke Garrity. He had a slight headache and was groggy from his nap. "Just a second," he shouted groggily. The knocking stopped and Don got up and hastily threw on yesterday's khaki shorts and a shirt. He opened the door.

"Mary, Mother of God!!" Duane said heartily. "You look like this *every* morning?" Don managed a weak smile and Duane laughed. "Got in a little late, eh? Yep, I sawed yer car comin' in last night. I see everybody when they come in. That's my job. Just in case somebody comes here that ain't supposed to be here. Hey, I got that coffee goin'. Why doncha c'mon over and meet the boss. I'll show ya them shotguns, too." As usual, Don hadn't yet been able to get a word in edgewise, which was fine. It was a bit early to be conversational.

"Yeah, okay. Let me get my shoes on," Don finally said, and backed away from the door to look for his leather deck shoes. Duane followed him inside. "Weatherman says we're gonna get some rain today, so I hope you don't have no plans for bein' outdoors," he said, his eyes scanning the small cabin. "Course, if the rain don't bother ya none then yer all set, but most people just hang indoors up here when it's rainin' out. Or go shoppin' or sumpthin.' Me, I go fishin' sometimes. Caught the biggest fish of my life in a downpour. Nineteen sixty-six. That son of a . . . "

Don wondered when Duane took time out to breathe. But then Duane abruptly stopped talking as he looked out the window above the kitchen counter. *Whoops*, Don thought. *I'm busted.*

"Dreamcatcher broke, eh?" Duane said, eying the window cautiously.

"Yeah. I'm really sorry, Duane," Don replied sincerely. "It must have fallen off the window sometime yesterday and I stepped on it last night. I'll get into town today and get another."

"No rush," Duane said, as he turned away and walked out the door. "You're the one that's gonna have the nightmares, not me."

Don blinked, suddenly struck by the simple truthfulness of Duane's words.

Well, you've certainly got that right, Duane, he thought.

"Come on. Coffee's a-waitin'."

Don followed Duane out of the cabin and the two walked across the dew-covered grass to the office, or the 'Main Lodge' as Duane called it. True to Duane's word, the sky was a hazy gray and looked like it could open up at any moment. Birds flitted about in the trees, and the air was gloriously fresh and clean. An unseen

mourning dove cooed from somewhere, and several ducks were
sleeping on the grass near the small beach, their bills tucked
comfortably beneath their wings.

Duane opened the door and ushered Don inside. The office was
tiny, and littered with papers. The walls were tongue-in-groove
pine, and the wood had faded over time to a gaudy yellow. Several
copies of *Field & Stream* and *Outdoor Life,* all dating back to the
early 90s, were piled on a small table next to a dilapidated old
chair. A large calendar, open to the month of June, hung on the
east wall, with the word 'booked' scribbled on every single day of
the month. A door on the back wall led to the Everett's home, and
Duane stepped around a desk, glanced down at a skyscraper of
papers, then opened the back door. Don followed wordlessly.

"I got me some beauties. Lemme get ya a cuppa coffee. And
I'll find the boss for ya, too." He lowered his voice a little, glanced
warily around, and continued. "Lissen, I gotta warn ya—don't
swear in front of her. Boy, if there's one thing she hates, it's
cussin'. She don't like that shit one bit." Duane returned a
moment later with two cups of coffee.

"Hope ya like yers black. Forgot to ask. You want anything in
there?"

"No. Black's fine." Don sipped the coffee.

"Good. Drink coffee like a man."

Don spent the next half hour in silence as Duane showed him
the numerous shotguns displayed on the walls, stopping to talk
about each one, where he got it, how much it was worth, and so on.
Don listened with only half his attention, thankful that was all he
needed to do. His head was still throbbing a little.

Christopher Knight

He tuned back in as Duane was saying ". . . and this one here is my favorite. Remington side-by-side double barrel twelve-gauge. Got 'er at a garage sale. Never been shot, even once. The guy that bought 'er died just a few days after he got it home. Heart attack. Guess he was just walking through the living room and boom! All over. I bought it from his widow. Nice piece a work, ain't she?" Don nodded. "Most folks keep their guns in a locked case, but not me," Duane continued. "I like 'em on the wall. Prettier that way. And I clean every single gun once a week. They never get dusty or rusty. And I always keep one of 'em loaded. I'm the only one who knows which. In case someone decides that he'd like a few of ol' Duane's goodies, if ya know what I mean."

"What if you forget which gun is loaded?" Don asked.

"I never forget which one is loaded. Lessee . . ." Duane leaned over and pulled a shotgun off the wall, a single shot H & R twenty-gauge. Without warning, he swung the gun around, aiming at Don's chest. Duane pulled the hammer back and brought the gun to his cheek, and squeezed the trigger.

Click.

Don stood frozen in place, the victim of an instant heart attack. His face flushed and his cheeks felt hot. His skin tingled. Then he actually felt his chest with his hands, searching for a hole, wondering why he was still standing.

"Nope. Guess it ain't that one," chuckled Duane. He smiled a Cheshire cat grin, then broke out into laughter as he lowered the gun.

Don tried to manage a weak smile. *He's nuts. The guy has lost his mind.*

"Hoo—woo! That gets everyone!! Ooooh, boy! Wuzzat funny! I gotta hand it to ya. You didn't even flinch. Lotta folks I do that to run as soon as I point the gun at 'em. You stared 'er down like a man. Here, lemmee show ya sumpthin'." He cracked the barrel open and handed the gun to Don. "Look down there."

Don looked down the barrel. Or tried to. He was still shaking.

"Filled with lead. Can't even get a shell in there. My brother and I did that at his shop years ago, just to have a little fun with folks like you."

"What if you grab the wrong gun?" Don asked. His voice trembled a tiny bit.

"It's the only H & R I own. No mistakin' it. I'd know it in the dark. Just like this one." Don handed the gun back to Duane, who returned it to the wall and pulled another gun down. He racked the pump once and a shell ejected from the gun.

"Gen-yoo-wine buckshot. Blow the balls off a charging bull elephant from fifty paces. Hold on a sec." He loaded the shell back into the shotgun and placed it back on the wall, then tiptoed to a door and peeked inside. He closed the door again, lowering his voice. "Nappin' again. Looks like you'll have to meet the boss some other time. She hasn't been feelin' too good lately. Been sleepin' a lot. Doctor says that's okay, if she feels like sleepin', let 'er sleep. Problem is, she wakes up at three in the morning and can't fall back to sleep. If we didn't have that satellite dish with all them TV shows, I don't know what she'd do. Drive me nuts, prob'ly."

Don was finally able to thank him for the coffee and to bid him good-bye after the twentieth shotgun story. He walked with some relief across the grass to his cabin. Whitecaps had formed on Mullett Lake. The sky was still gray and overcast and it looked like it was going to rain any minute. He showered, put on a fresh pair of shorts, and threw on his sweatshirt. The three had agreed to play it by ear today and dive if the weather stayed good. It looked like it was going to be a tough call. He locked up the cabin and headed into town for some breakfast, and then on over to Eric and Kari's.

chapter 94

The *Aurora*, Mike Felsing thought, rubbing his hands together in anticipation. *Now we're getting somewhere.* Mike had moved his computer table to give him more room to spread out his books. The monitor, terminal, and keypad sat on the floor near the wastebasket. He flipped open *Great Lakes Ships and Shipping*, going right to the index in the back. *Alaskan. Archangel, Ariel, Armenia . . .*

Aurora.

A wave of euphoria swept through Felsing. *It's here,* he thought. *The darned thing is actually here.* He stared at the page, and read the listing silently.

The *Aurora;* page 276. Mike flipped to that page and moved his index finger down the columns of print. Halfway down, he found the entry.

Aurora, the: One hundred-ten foot schooner, built by G. Michaels and Sons in Milwaukee, Wisconsin, 1842. Owned by Greiner, Inc. until 1849. Moderately damaged in a storm in 1850, repaired and placed back into service 1851. Transferred to private ownership in 1859; Richard P. Merman, purchaser. Thought to have been decommissioned shortly after private purchase.

Felsing marked the page with a slip of paper and closed the book. *Strange. Why would someone change the name of the ship from the Aurora to the Brittany and make no record of it?* And to just hastily engrave the new name on the capstan cover was even more odd.

He placed the book aside and selected the *Illustrated Guide to Ships of the Great Lakes: Photos and Drawings* by Melvin Skaggs. It was filled with hundreds of old photographs and sketches of schooners, steamers, props, and freighters. Not much written detail was given for the sailing vessels, just the basics of where the ship was built, who owned her, and what became of her.

Again, he flipped to the back of the book and scanned the index. The *Aurora*, pg. 10. An old black-and-white photograph showed a schooner in full sail, leaving harbor. She was truly magnificent with her sails filled with wind. In the bottom right corner of the photo, scribbled white letters were barely legible. *"The Aurora. Aug 2, 1850—Chicago."* His excitement grew as he realized he was looking at the same ship that Eric and Kari had found. He closed the book after slipping a piece of paper between the pages.

He turned to *Great Ships: The Definitive Directory* by Neil Compton. It was a very large, heavy book and he slid the book out with both hands and laid it on the table in front of him. He turned to the back and perused the index. *Aurora*, the, page 74. Mike was heartened to find that there was an entire page on the *Aurora*. *All right! Now we've got something.* But despite the amount of text devoted to the ship, the book held no new information on what had become of her. *Well, it's pretty obvious that she wasn't decommissioned. Not if she's sitting at the bottom of the lake with the bodies of murdered people aboard, she wasn't.* He turned out the light and walked downstairs to relax on the deck for a while before retiring to bed.

chapter 95

Don arrived shortly before 10:30 a.m. Eric was in the front yard, pushing a very old, oily lawnmower. He saw the black Dodge Caravan and killed the motor. The old engine chugged and sighed to a stop.

"Well, what do you think?" he asked Eric, as he stepped out of the van. "Weather going to hold out?" The two men shook hands, and they walked from the van to the house.

"I think it'll be fine," Eric replied, glancing up at the veil of gray sky, a single sheet of creamy, gray clouds. "Supposed to be like this all day, maybe some rain, but all in all, it doesn't look like it'll get worse. Might be a little bouncy out there, but nothing to keep us from diving," Eric replied. "Besides, I want to retrieve that knife and maybe poke my head into that hatch and get a closer look at that other body."

"We also need to retrieve the lights," Don reminded him. "Batteries are bound to be low."

Eric opened the front door, and the two men walked inside.

"Don, you look terrible today," Kari chided playfully, and greeted him with a hug and a gentle kiss on the cheek.

"Didn't get a lot of sleep last night," Don replied. "The bed in the cabin is kind of uncomfortable." He didn't bring up the nightmare, had no reason to.

"I thought of a way to retrieve the lights more quickly than using lift bags," Eric offered. "We can clamp the lights to the anchor rope, maybe eight or ten feet apart. That way, we'll get them back when we pull up anchor. You won't have to fiddle around with any lift bags. That will give us a minute or two more of bottom time to find that knife and check out the hatch."

Don agreed, and they boarded the *John Galt* and headed downriver to collect the tanks from the dive shop. The trio loaded the six large canisters of air and stored them belowdecks.

The overcast sky hung like a thick blanket overhead, and the winds licked out of the southwest at about fifteen knots. The *John Galt* bobbed up and down as she plowed through the three-foot waves. It was slower going than usual and was going to take a little longer to reach the dive site.

"We should be just about—" Eric was interrupted in mid-sentence by a red light on the control panel and a high-pitched pulsating alarm. He squinted, puzzled by the sudden noise. "What the hell?"

"I'll go check it out," Kari said, as she hurriedly scrambled below deck.

"What's that?" Don asked, pointing to the red light.

"High water alarm. But don't worry—it's probably nothing. We've had a short in that alarm panel before. The boat is pretty old, and I've had to replace a lot of her wiring. I think that—"

"Eric!! We're taking in water!! Lots of it and fast!!" Kari shouted frantically from below. No sooner had she spoken than he noticed that the boat had slowed in the water. Eric cut the engine and jumped below. He was horrified to see that water was pouring into the engine room.

"Kari!! Radio the Coast Guard!! Send out a Mayday!! We're going down if we don't get this plugged!!"

"What's happening?" Don asked. His face hung, white and anxious, in the center of the engine compartment hatch.

"We lost the propeller shaft!" Eric shouted. "It must've gotten loose and backed out of the stuffing box, and there's water coming in through the hole. We've got to get it plugged now!!" Eric started searching the boat, opening compartments and pulling out anything that he might be able to use to plug the hole.

"Mayday! Mayday! This is the *John Galt*," Kari spoke into the microphone. "We have a Mayday. Location approximately one mile southeast of Bois Blanc Island. We're taking on water. Calling the Coast Guard, this is the *John Galt*. We have a Mayday!" The radio crackled and came to life as the Coast Guard dispatcher acknowledged the distress call. Kari continued to speak with the dispatcher while Don and Eric searched for something to plug the hole in the engine room.

"The Coast Guard wants to know what's wrong!!" Kari shouted down to Eric.

"Tell 'em we're fucking sinking and if they don't get their asses out here *now*, there's gonna be three people swimming awfully goddamn fast!!" he shouted back.

Kari hesitated only an instant, then keyed the microphone. "We're taking on water rapidly and the captain requests immediate assistance and the strength of many mules to prevent a water evacuation." Don laughed and even Eric managed a grin as he shook his head.

"She has a way with words sometimes," Eric said, reaching for a blue life preserver.

"Better her on the radio than you," Don answered. "I don't think the Coast Guard would take too kindly to your language."

Eric found his dive knife and plunged it through the blue cushion. It made a subtle *pop!* as the steel tip punctured the vinyl. He slashed forcefully, cutting the preserver in half, and folding it over. "Let's hope this works," he said, as he waded through the knee-deep water and pushed the torn and folded cushion under water and into the gaping hole. "That will at least slow it down a bit. Don, tell Kari to turn on the bilge pump." Don disappeared and an instant later the pump's motor whirred to life.

"I'm not sure if that cushion is going to hold," Eric said, taking a deep breath, "but it might slow down the water flow a little and the bilge pump will buy us some extra time."

"They're on their way," Kari said, appearing beside him. "A boat from Cheboygan and a helicopter from St. Ignace. Boat should be here in just a few minutes. Did you get the hole plugged?"

"I think so. Don, give me a hand—" Eric started to say, but Don wasn't listening. His face was a mask of horror, his eyes stared blankly, unseeing and unmoving. "Don?"

Don's hands began to shake and soon his entire body was wracked by a violent spasm of choking. Veins exploded beneath his skin as his body tightened in the throes of the seizure. As if struck with a high voltage shock, Don gave one final turbulent convulsion before he collapsed, and fell to the deck, unconscious.

chapter 96

Don had been watching the water that was pouring in through the hole and filling the engine room. Then time slowed down. Eric's words became barely audible, like a tape player low on batteries. He felt himself begin to shake uncontrollably and swayed between reality and unconsciousness. *Oh God. Not now, please not now!*

Air bubbles seemed to fill the entire cabin in front of his eyes and he found himself trapped in an ice-water coffin. It was cold. *So* cold. Frigid water filled his nostrils and mouth and he fought to force it back out, but it was no use and water rushed down his throat and filled his lungs. His frantic kicking slowed, and he began to give in to the inevitable force of what was certain to come. He could see Eric in the waters below him, trapped and helpless.

"Don?" The voice came to him from a long way off, as if it was echoing down a long tunnel. At first, he wasn't even sure he'd heard it, but there it was again, more insistent.

"*Don . . .*"

His vision faded, the murky waters became dark, and all sounds ceased. Then Don heard and saw nothing at all. He felt no pain or fear. And then, as quickly as he had been enveloped in the darkness, Don felt it pulling away and even the inky black faded from his vision, leaving . . .*nothing.* There was no darkness, no water, no bubbles, no ice, no Eric. In the confines of his mind, in the dark alleys that he feared most, Don simply ceased to exist.

We're back, Donny boy. And you may think you're dead, but you're not. Because as long as you live, Donny, we do too. As long as you live, we'll be here, hiding in the places you don't dare go. You're like a child afraid of the cellar, Donny. And we'll always be here, like shadows from the street lamp outside your window at night. Remember that, Donny boy. Remember that.

Then shapes and forms started to reappear and he could hear muffled voices. He realized he was lying on his back. Two large shapes loomed over him like wavering clouds.

"*Don, can you hear me?*" one of the clouds said. "*Don?*" It sounded like a woman. Don concentrated and tried to bring the hazy objects into focus. Kari and Eric. They were kneeling above him and Kari's hand was behind his head as she waved her hand over his face.

"I . . . I'm okay...." Don whispered shakily. He was able to lift his head now and with the help of Eric and Kari, he held himself up, resting on his elbows. "My head hurts," he said, rubbing the back of his head with one arm, supporting himself with the other. "What happened?" he asked. But he already knew.

"You smacked your head on the deck," Eric said. "I couldn't catch you in time. You kind of zonked out."

"Sorry about that. I've been having dizzy spells lately," Don explained evasively. "My doctor thinks it's low blood sugar." An evasion that bordered a full-blown lie. He suddenly remembered the water rushing into the *John Galt*. "The boat—"

"It's fine," Eric reassured him, nodding. "Water's still coming in, but not as fast as before. We'll be able to be towed in."

"Are you sure that was from low blood sugar?" Kari asked, her voice full of concern. "I mean, your eyes rolled back in your head. You had more of a convulsion or a seizure. It wasn't an ordinary black out. At least, it didn't look that way."

"Yeah, I'm sure. Help me up." Eric grabbed Don around the waist and he rose shakily to his feet. He rubbed the back of his head again.

"Might want to get that lump checked out," Eric said. "You hit the deck hard."

"Nah. I think I'm all right." His hands lowered and he stroked his neck. "Really. I'm pretty hungry though."

"Here." Eric reached into a nearby cooler and pulled out a Snickers bar and an apple.

"Thanks," Don said, taking both. The sound of a helicopter caused them all to look up and scan the horizon, making Don wince and put his hand to the back of his head. The chopper was rapidly drawing near, and a Coast Guard trawler was moving swiftly towards the *John Galt*. A few other boats that had heard Kari's plea for help had also joined in, mostly out of curiosity.

"Why don't you sit down and take it easy for awhile. I can

handle it with the Coast Guard," Eric said.

Don sat down, pulling the wrapper from a candy bar. *Low blood sugar. Yeah, right. How long am I gonna be able to get away with that one?*

chapter 97

As night fell on the second day at sea Daniel is tired. No, more than tired—he is exhausted. Jack said the ship has traveled more than two hundred fifty miles since leaving the harbor. They are making good time.

When is it going to happen? he wonders. No one is going to get hurt. It is just a simple theft, he reassures himself. He pushes off his feelings of guilt with thoughts of riches. Daniel dreams of the things he'll buy with two thousand dollars. Nice clothes, a horse . . . whatever his heart desires. He drifts off into a deep, but troubled, sleep.

On deck, Captain LaChance is uneasily watching the night sky as one by one the stars disappear behind an advancing line of clouds. He notes that the wind has shifted, and the air has grown noticeably cooler in just a matter of minutes. Soon the entire night sky is darkened by the ominous clouds.

Jack joins the Captain on deck. "Storm's movin' in. Felt this one comin'," he says.

"She's movin' in fast all right, but it doesn't feel like rain though. At least, not for a while, anyway." The Captain takes a drag of his pipe and the two men fall silent.

"Well, I'm going to finish up a few things and hit the hay," Jack says. "Anything you need help with?"

"No, thanks. We're set for the night."

"I'll be up around five to relieve you."

"That'll be fine, Jack. Good night." In a moment, Jack is gone and the Captain is alone at the ship's wheel, sailing the Brittany on through the night.

When Daniel awakens, he is alarmed to find that he has overslept and he dresses hurriedly and runs up onto the deck. "You were right, Jack," he says, as he joins him at the helm. Jack looks at him questioningly. Daniel pokes his finger towards the sky and spoke. "The weather. Storm's comin'."

"Yeah," Jack affirms, "this afternoon. Maybe tonight."

The two men grow silent, content to watch the waves, the weather, the sky. The water has grown rougher in the coming storm, creating white-crested waves and troughs.

"Do you have a family, Jack?" Daniel asked.

The question catches Malloy by surprise. "Yes, my mother and father. And I have a sister."

"No. I mean a wife and children."

" Nope. Never married. Ain't no woman in the world that would put up with the life of a sailor. 'Specially this sailor. How 'bout you?" Jack grins, turning the question around. "You got yourself a girl?"

Daniel blushes and turns away. Cool mist beads on his face, and he wipes it away with his coat sleeve. "No. Well, yeah, sort of. Not really."

Jack laughs. "Which is it, boy? Do ya or don't ya?"

"Well, I guess I don't really. There's a girl I been thinkin' of askin' to the Cornhusker Fair. I see her every day. Her father works over at a mill on Cooper Street."

"I know the one," Jack interjects.

"I used to work there. That was my first job. She helps her daddy out once in a while with the paperwork. She sure is pretty. But I don't talk to her much. I want to ask her to the dance."

"Well? What's stoppin' ya?"

"I dunno," Daniel says, hanging his head and looking at the ground, mildly embarrassed. "I was thinkin' maybe when I get back. Then I might ask her."

Jack turns to look at him. "Well, looks like you got some thinkin' to do on this trip, don't ya?" Jack smiles at him and Daniel turns away.

"Yeah. I guess I do." And with that, Daniel leaves Jack alone at the helm and begins his chores for the day.

Christopher Knight

chapter 98

The late night activity had taken only an hour. Jimmy and Ed had encountered no problems, with the exception of one minor scare when they were surprised by someone driving a mini-van. They hadn't seen or heard it until the last minute, and they had been walking near the middle of the road when it rounded the corner. But it wasn't unusual for people to be out for a walk in the summer, even at that time of the night. If they had been seen, Ed and Jimmy would have looked like two guys walking home from the bar. When they had reached the Randalls' house, Jimmy stood guard while Ed slipped aboard the *John Galt* and did his work. Five minutes later the two men left as silently and quickly as they had come.

The following day, Phillip and Ed sat in the Bayliner in the marina, waiting for Jimmy. They had agreed to meet at noon and head out to the dive site. Ed told Phillip what he and Jimmy had done the night before.

"He's in for a lot of fun next time he takes that boat out, that's for friggin' sure," Ed boasted, spewing a cloud of smoke. "That boat's going down like a fifty-dollar whore."

"Isn't Randall going to know that someone was messing with his boat?" Phillip asked.

"I doubt it," Ed said, shaking his head. He place the Camel to his lips and inhaled. His whole body seemed to swell and fill with smoke. "He's going to think that it was a problem that went unnoticed for a long time." Smoke fluted from his nostrils like an obese dragon. "Besides, even if he does figure it out, by that time we'll be gone and outta here."

Jimmy arrived and the three men were preparing the boat when Phillip called to Ed who was below deck. "I don't mean to bust your bubble or anything," he said smartly, "but you-know-who is passing the marina right now and the boat looks like it's in fine working order. They're headed out to the lake."

Jimmy turned to look and Ed poked his head up from below. "Not for long it isn't. Give 'em twenty minutes. Turn on the radio. They'll be callin' for help in no time." He nodded his head smugly. "This'll give that bastard something to think about besides a shipwreck."

Sure enough, only a few minutes later the radio sputtered to life with Kari's Mayday call. The three men gathered in the cabin of the Bayliner, listening to the buzzing banter on the ship's radio. "What did I tell you?" Ed bragged with arrogant satisfaction. His voice hissed like a snake. "Those sons-a-bitches are sinkin'. They won't be doing any diving for a little while. Let's go."

The Bayliner lumbered out of the marina and headed out into Lake Huron. They could see quite a bit of activity on the water: a Coast Guard helicopter on its way from St. Ignace and a Coast Guard boat from Cheboygan which was ahead of them. About a half-dozen other boats had heard the commotion and were checking things out, too. *Like a bunch of rubberneckers on the freeway,* thought Phillip. *Gotta know what's goin' on so they can talk about it to everyone else. They got so little goin' on in their own lives that this is probably the most excitement they'll have all year.*

"Let's go find us a fortune," Ed said, as he dropped anchor on the now deserted dive site. Phillip and Ed suited up and plunged into the dark waters of Lake Huron.

Jimmy pulled a bottle of orange juice from the cooler, flipped open the June issue of *Playboy* and waited. He was content to be the answer man for other fishing boats as they plodded by. One hundred sixty feet below him, Phillip and Ed were just reaching the wreck.

chapter 99

The two divers descended near the bowsprit. As they glided back towards the stern, ghostly shadows jumped in the two flashlight beams. Phillip broke away from Ed and followed the starboard hull to the bottom, sweeping his light back and forth.

Come on. I know you're here somewhere, he thought impatiently. *I'm not leaving an eighty-dollar knife at the bottom of the lake.* He was about to give up when something reflected his flashlight beam. A tiny spark, a glimmer of silver, a wave of relief.

Hey! I been looking for you.

Phillip swam over and picked up the knife, returning it to the sheath strapped to his leg. He glided back up the massive hull of the ship and found Ed, who was hovering over the main hatchway, shining his light down into the confines of the ship. Ed looked at Phillip, waved for him to come over, and pointed into the hatch.

Phillip shined his light down into the ship and instantly drew back in shock. A small cloud of silt mushroomed around his fins. *A body! It's a body!*

The human remains were just a pile of bones, but they lent an eerie presence to the dark gloomy area below deck. Ed pointed to Phillip and motioned him inside the hatch. Ed was so big that it would be impossible for him to maneuver in the tiny rooms and corridors within the ship. With some trepidation, Phillip slipped through the hatch. For the first time in over one hundred years, there was life moving about inside the *Brittany*.

Even though Phillip took pains to move cautiously and slowly, his slight motion immediately kicked up the fine silt and thoroughly clouded the hatchway area. *Got to be more careful,* he warned himself. If he kicked up too much silt, visibility would be cut to nothing. Inside a shipwreck, not being able to see the way out, was a diver's worst nightmare.

He moved forward a bit, slowly, swept the light from side to side and found a doorway that had not yet been obscured by the explosion of sediment. Slowly he proceeded farther into the darkened ship.

For the first time in a long while Phillip felt real excitement. It was always enthralling to find a wreck, but he knew that *this* ship held a fortune. His heart was racing with anticipation and his adrenaline surged. *It's in one of these rooms!* A closed door beckoned to his right. He placed his hand on it and slowly pushed on it. The wood felt like it was going to crumble beneath his gloved hands, but the door opened without much effort and a small amount of silt fell away and spun in the still waters.

His light probed the inky blackness of a small cabin. Wooden crates, boxes, and debris—all covered with an inch of ruddy sediment—lay strewn about the floor. Phillip drifted over the threshold and played the light over the tumbled objects. A chair lay sideways in a corner and a few bottles and dishes were smashed into broken shards on the floor.

Phillip checked his air nervously. He only had about one minute before he had to meet up with Ed to begin their ascent to the surface. He glided carefully over to one of the crates and examined it with his light. It was about a foot square and looked like it would fall apart in his hands. His heart pounded. *This is it,* he thought. He exhaled, and a cloud of swirling bubbles rose in front of his mask and whirled upward. He unsheathed his knife and gently tried to pry open the top. Suddenly the wooden crate crumbled, spewing its contents to the floor. A boiling tornado of fine dust filled the small area, exploding up and around and making it impossible to see more than an inch front of his face.

Phillip turned to look for the door but it was hidden by the roiling sediment storm that filled the room. He felt a tiny flash of panic. *Steady. Steady. Take it easy.* He moved quickly towards where he thought the door was, no longer concerned about ruining the visibility, as he was already swimming in a glass of chocolate milk.

He reached out his arm and found a wall. Phillip took a smooth, deep breath, and exhaled. There was so much silt that he could not see the bubbles rise. *No problem,* he thought, remaining calm. *I'll just follow the wall until I find the door.* To his great relief, he found the passageway on the next wall without further incident and moved through it. As he did so he breathed a mental sigh of consolation. *See? Just gotta be cool. Next time I'll bring a guideline.*

The corridor was also filling rapidly with the silt that was boiling out of the cabin door. He was close enough to the hatch area that he was able to find his way back without difficulty. Ed's light was shining down through the hatchway. He was looking at Phillip questioningly through his mask. Phillip shook his head. *Nothing yet.* Ed motioned with his thumb and the two divers headed back to the surface.

While the Bayliner was being re-fueled at the marina, Phillip, Ed, and Jimmy discussed the possibility of diving again that day. If the weather held, and it appeared that it would, the three agreed that they would make another dive after the nitrogen levels in their bodies had returned to a safe level.

Ed paid the dockhand for the fuel, and maneuvered the boat into its slip in the marina. Just as the engine fell silent, Phillip grabbed Jimmy's shoulder and pointed.

"You got company."

Jimmy turned and looked towards the parking lot. A hot flush suddenly crawled across his skin. In the lot, next to his black Trans Am, was a red Pontiac Grand Prix. And leaning against the Grand Prix was . . . *Sharon.*

chapter 100

The brief reunion was not what Sharon had expected. She had gone to his motel first and, not finding his car there, had gone to the marina, where she had waited for three hours. She had gotten out of the car when she saw Jimmy's huge frame and trademark baggy shirt aboard a white boat that was gliding into the marina. He was looking straight at her. *Well, at least I won't get knocked into next week. At least not here. Not with people all around.* Nevertheless, she expected Jimmy to be furious that she had done exactly what he had said *not* to do. Instead, he walked up to her, gave her a big hug and a kiss and smiled. She almost fell over in surprise.

"Well, well, fancy meeting you here," Jimmy said mildly. He put his hands on her shoulders, smiling. Sharon tried not to act surprised.

"You're . . . not mad?" she asked, searching his eyes.

"Mad, no. Surprised? *Yes.*" She continued gazing into his eyes, looking for a hint of deception. If he was acting, she thought, he sure was doing a good job. "I'm *glad,* he continued. "I wanted to apologize for yesterday on the phone."

Now that was *not* Jimmy. She felt like asking him 'who are you . . . and what have you done with my husband?' but decided not to push her luck.

Sharon followed Jimmy through Cheboygan to the *River Terrace.* "For crying out loud, don't they have a maid in this place?" Sharon said, upon entering Jimmy's room. His clothes were haphazardly tossed in a pile at the end of the bed, which wasn't made. Empty orange juice containers and empty *Subway* carry-out bags littered the tables, chairs, and floor.

"Yeah, but I told them I didn't want anybody coming around and making up the room until I said so. If I'm sleeping at 10:30 in the morning, I don't want some housekeeper waking me up," Jimmy explained in a reasonable tone.

An hour later they lay in bed, their passions exhausted. The phone rang, and Jimmy reached over Sharon and picked up the receiver. "Yeah. Hey, what's up? . . . Yeah. All right. See ya then." He reached back over Sharon and replaced the phone to its cradle. "That was Ed and Phillip. We're going fishing tonight. You wanna go?" he asked, knowing full well that Sharon hated to fish. Still, it was a risky question.

"No, thanks," Sharon replied. "But what time will you be getting back?"

Jimmy breathed a mental sigh of relief: if she had said yes, he would have been forced to come up with an excuse why she *couldn't* go, and that might have been tough.

"Probably before dark. You wanna have some dinner before I go?"

Sharon was caught totally off guard once again, but she didn't let it show. *Is this* really *Jimmy?* she thought. *He just seems so . . . agreeable.* "Yeah, that would be nice," she answered. "I'm staying over at the *Cheyboygan Motor Lodge.*"

"Screw that," Jimmy said cheerfully. "No sense in wasting money. Go get your shit and bring it back over here." He reached over to the table and handed her a plastic key card. "I'll get another from the front desk. Oh, hey, you wouldn't mind maybe runnin' over to the laundromat and doing a load of clothes, would ya? I'm getting kind of low."

chapter 101

Mike Felsing hunched over the microfiche machine at the library. The images sped by on the screen in front of him and he slowed down, studying a page of the *Cheboygan Tribune* for a moment, and then sliding the tray once more, causing the images to fly by once again.

He had decided not to call Eric and Kari until he had more information on the *Aurora*. Since none of the books in the library had revealed anything that he didn't already know, he had decided to look through some old editions of the *Tribune* to see if he could find anything. He knew that the *Aurora* had been sold to Richard Merman in 1859, after which her name had been changed to the *Brittany*. The capstan cover had been re-etched with her new name. Therefore, he reasoned, it followed that somewhere during or after 1859 the *Aurora* had foundered in the Channel.

Mike decided to begin with January of the target year. He stopped the microfiche and checked the date of the newspaper. *1857. Couple more years to go yet.* He shifted the tray, likening the images on the screen to his life, the days and years that had flashed by so quickly. He wished he could slow it all down like he could do so easily with the microfiche.

Felsing stopped the tray and looked up at the screen. *A little more—there. 'January 2, 1859.'* The masthead said *'Happy New Year, First Edition of the New Year.'*

He scanned the entire front page, looking for anything that might have to do with a ship or shipwreck in Lake Huron. Finding nothing, he scanned the next page, which was shown on the same screen. Nothing. He sighed. *This is obviously going to take awhile. But what the hell—it's not like it's taking my time away from writing.*

After two hours of searching, he had been through all of 1859 and had acquired a mild headache but he had not come across any mention of the *Aurora/Brittany*. There had been plenty other shipwrecks—sometimes five or six in one week—but no *Aurora/Brittany. Oh, well. Another day. I'll find 'er sooner or later. I may have to go through every single paper until 1950, but I'll find 'er.*

He removed the fiche, stood up, and shut off the power to the machine. He waved goodbye to the librarian and within a few minutes he was on his way to see Eric and Kari.

Christopher Knight

chapter 102

The *John Galt* had been towed to a dry dock where it was pulled from the water, and the three walked home from there. "I don't understand how that could have happened," Eric said. "I checked everything a month ago and it was fine."

"How long do you think it'll take to get the *John Galt* fixed?" Kari asked, as they sat at the kitchen table, eating the packed lunch that, as it turned out, had not been needed. Outside, the light mist had become a steady drizzle, only adding to the gloom.

"I have no idea," Eric responded. "Dave Shandler said he'd call sometime this afternoon or this evening. We were pretty lucky he'll be able to take a look at it so fast."

"More importantly, right now, how are *you*, Don?" Kari asked.

"Fine," Don replied, "except I think I am going to need some aspirin after all. My head still hurts."

"You should really go and get that checked out at the hospital," Kari said. "You banged it pretty hard." She got up, went to the medicine cabinet in the bathroom, and returned with a bottle of Bayer aspirin. Don popped open the lid and swallowed three of the little white tablets, washing them down with a sip of water.

"Are you saying that I should go have my head examined?" Don replied, smiling. "I'll be fine. Really. Now that I got some food, I'll be all right. Just got to watch that blood sugar." He wondered if they were buying the blood sugar story. He *was* getting more concerned, though. Although he didn't like the nightmares that came and went, he could *handle* them—he couldn't hurt anybody in his bed. But he'd had these flashbacks, or whatever they were, three times in the last three days—one of them while driving the van when he could have done some serious damage to himself or others.

His worried thoughts were interrupted by the sound of a car pulling into the driveway. A horn honked twice. Eric turned his head and leaned back, looking out the front window.

"Who's here?" Kari asked.

"It's Mike." Eric got up and opened the front door. Mike Felsing took large heron-steps around some puddles that had already started to form in the driveway. He held a large envelope over his head to shield himself from the rain. Eric held the door as Felsing strode inside. Hands clasped, and Kari and Mike hugged briefly.

"Mike Felsing, Don Garrity," Eric announced, introducing the two men. Don stood up and shook hands with Mike.

Turning to Eric, Mike spoke. "I wanted to show you this instead of telling you about it over the phone," he said, with a broad smile. Triumphantly he opened up the manilla envelope and laid the printout of the capstan cover photograph on the table.

"Hey, you got it cleaned up!" Eric exclaimed, picking it up. Kari and Don hovered over his shoulder.

"I think you'll find that the 'design' isn't a design after all," Mike said, lacing his fingers together over his stomach and leaning back in his chair, smiling contentedly.

Kari, reading over Eric's shoulder, almost shouted, "The *Aurora*!" And then a moment later, she repeated it, puzzled, "The *Aurora*?"

"That's your ship, right there," Mike said, leaning forward and tapping the picture in Eric's hands. "The *Aurora.*"

"But why would the capstan cover have two names? And what happened to the *Brittany's* name?" Kari asked.

"In order to bring out the *Aurora's* name I had to change the settings on the computer to bring it into focus and in the process the Brittany's name faded into the background," Mike explained. "She was purchased by a Richard Merman in 1859, but I wasn't able to find out much more than that. There's no record of her foundering or being destroyed. My theory is that somebody wanted to save money and not buy a new capstan cover after they changed the name. They half-heartedly tried to scribble out the *Aurora* and wrote the *Brittany* below it."

"You want to see it?" Eric asked.

"What? The wreck? Yeah, but . . ."

Eric put his hand up, silencing him in mid-sentence. "We got two hours of footage yesterday." Eric got up from the table and turned on the VCR and TV and Mike's eyes lit up. When Eric pushed the 'play' button, the snow on the screen disappeared and Mike got his first glimpse at the long-lost *Aurora*.

"Wait 'til you see this," Eric said, as they neared the part where Don had sent the camera into the hatch. "This is something else." Mike watched intently, spellbound by the images on the TV screen. The shadowy, decaying skeleton appeared.

"That's not one of the bodies in the picture you showed me," he said.

"No," Kari said. "Those were photographed farther up along the bow in a cabin. This is right below the main hatch."

Kari gathered her shipwreck books and each of them selected one and began to go through it. "Here it is," Kari said, pointing to a page in her book. "Purchased by Richard Merman, decommission unknown. That's all it says."

"I didn't have any luck at the library, either," Mike explained. "I started to go through old copies of the *Cheboygan Tribune* on the microfiche beginning in 1859, the year that Merman bought the ship, but I didn't see any mention of the *Aurora* or the *Brittany* sinking. 'Course, I only was able to look through one year of papers. I'll keep looking, but it makes it hard when I'm not sure what to look for. And there sure were a lot of shipwrecks in those days."

Eric focused his attention on the television screen again. "Check this out, Mike." They all turned back to the TV as the shiny knife came into view. Mike looked puzzled. "That's not one of our knives," Eric explained. "Somebody else has been diving on her, and fairly recently, judging by the fact that no sand or silt has settled on the knife. We're kind of disappointed because we thought that we were the first ones to find it, but whoever they are they don't seem to have disturbed much of the wreck. I mean, it doesn't look like anybody's yanking off planks to make tables to sell in gift shops. Not yet, anyway."

"When are you going to dive on her again?" Mike asked. The three exchanged glances. Up until now, no mention of the afternoon's near disaster had been made.

"Well, we had a little problem today, Mike," Kari began, and explained how they had given the Coast Guard and some other boaters a little excitement.

"So, we're kind of at the mercy of the boat shop," Eric explained. "But a friend of mine, Dave Shandler, is looking at her today. He says it didn't look like there was too much damage done and we might be able to have her back in a day or so, provided he can get another prop shaft."

"Well, if you find out that your boat is going to be laid up for a while, let me know," Mike offered. "I've got an old Chris-Craft in the garage. She's a little weathered, and not the prettiest thing to look at, but she's seaworthy. She'd do fine in a pinch."

Eric thanked him, and turned his attention to the books that Kari had spread over the table. An examination of them produced no new information about her loss.

"The ship is in too good of shape to have foundered in a gale," Eric pointed. "Take a look at the masts . . ." He pointed to the screen, pressed the rewind on the remote, watched the images move in high-speed reverse for a moment, then stopped it. "The masts are in almost *perfect* shape. And up here. The bowsprit is intact. Even the bulwark is in relatively good shape. If she went down during a storm, there'd be more damage to the masts and rigging."

"But remember there's a large part of the ship that we weren't able to video," Kari said. "A major portion of the ship's starboard hull is buried in sand."

The phone rang and Kari answered it. She looked at Eric. "For you. It's Dave," she said, handing the phone to him.

"Hey. What's up, Dave?"

"Well, good news and some more good news," Dave's gravelly voice boomed through the wireless phone.

"That's what I wanna hear," Eric said, holding his thumb in the air for the other three in the living room to see.

"First of all, I was able to locate a shaft for you today," Dave said, and then paused. "I found two of the original bolts that you left on the floor. Man, you must've really been crankin' on 'em."

Eric paused before answering. "What do you mean?"

"Well, the bolts were completely stripped on the outside. You must've really been reefin' on 'em."

"I haven't touched any bolts or the shaft or the stuffing box. Not since early May."

"Well, somebody has," Dave replied. "I got two bolts here and both of them look like they been turned by a pair of pliers that didn't quite fit right. They didn't just fall off. No problem, though. I'll be able to put 'em back on and they'll be fine. But I guarantee you one thing: They didn't come off by themselves."

chapter 103

Daniel awakens and sits upright. It is dark. He thinks he has heard something, but now, as the sleep fades from his mind, he isn't sure what it is that had woke him.

There. There it is again. It is a banging sound, coming from somewhere deep in the ship. Daniel creeps out of bed, pulls on his coat, and stands at his bedside, listening. But the only sounds are the normal creaks and groans of a ship at sea.

Thud. This time the sound is very clear and Daniel jumps. He knows he has to check it out. After all, that is his job, isn't it? That is one of the things the men want him to do . . . make sure that nothing happens to the large heavy chest that sits locked in the bowels of the ship.

Thud. His eyes are adjusting to the dark now, and he can see the faint outline of the door against the darker corridor. Quietly, he leaves the cabin and stalks toward the hold where the chest is stored.

Thud.

His mind races. What if one of the passengers is trying to get into it?

The door to the hold is closed. Daniel hasn't heard anything in a minute or two and he puts his ear to the door. Silence. The seconds tick by. Then:

Thud.

This time there is no mistaking it. The noise came from behind the door; it sounds as if someone is banging on wood. He stands motionless, wondering what to do.

My knife, he thinks. I'll go get my knife, and a candle.

Daniel tiptoes silently back to his cabin and retrieves his knife, lights the candle, and creeps warily back to the door of the hold. His adrenaline is pumping furiously and his mind is spinning. He stands by the door and listens again.

Silence. But he is sure that whoever was making the noise is still there. He hadn't been gone long enough for someone to leave without hearing them. He grasps the door handle and pushes. The door squeaks and then floats easily open. The flickering candle illuminates the small cargo hold. Daniel's heart pounds like a drum, and he looks cautiously about the small room. Boxes and crates are piled on top of one another in a semi-uniform fashion. Daniel had helped load and stack them himself—except, of course, the massive wooden trunk hidden beneath the smaller crates. That had been loaded by Captain LaChance, Jack, and the horses.

Daniel squints, his eyes darting from side to side, alert. Dancing shadows frolic in the flickering candlelight.

"Who's here?" His voice quivers and wavers.

No response.

He waves the candle back and forth, the shadows grow larger, then smaller, then larger again. "Hello?" he says, and waits.

Silence. He steps inside the hold.

Thud. He jumps and the candle almost goes out. The noise is close . . . very close. He holds the knife out with one hand and the candle in the other. Something moves in the shadows and he swings the candle in its direction.

Thud.

Then he sees it. An empty whiskey bottle. As the ship rocks gently, the bottle is rolling between two crates. Relief wells up inside him and he bends to pick up the bottle, setting it tightly between the large chest and a smaller crate so that the bottle can no longer move. Standing before the chest, he reaches forward and takes one of the locks in his hand. It is cold in his fingers, and he feels the solid strength of the steel as he holds it in his palm. Someone really wants to keep people out of this thing. He releases his grip on the lock and knocks on the crate with his fist. It sounds solid.

Gold, Daniel thinks in awe. It's probably full of solid gold!

A cold hand on his neck stops his thoughts in mid-stride, and he lets out a yell—an instant before another large cold hand covers his mouth, silencing his scream.

chapter 104

Eric awoke before dawn and plodded to the kitchen without turning on a light. He had gone over and over the sabotage of the *John Galt* in his head all night, long after Kari had fallen asleep. *Someone is trying to stop us from diving*, he thought. *But why?*

He fumbled in the cupboard for a glass and ran the faucet for a moment, waiting for the water to get cold. He drank, rinsed out the glass, and placed it in the sink. He checked the living room and found Don's dark shadow slumbering on the couch. He had dozed off while watching the video, and hadn't protested when Kari insisted that he spend the night in the guest room. He hadn't even made it that far though, instead falling asleep on the couch, where Eric and Kari had left him. He didn't even wake up when Kari propped a pillow beneath his head and covered him with an afghan.

Eric opened the screen door and stepped onto the porch. Only a few lonely crickets chirped. The river gurgled and babbled quietly as if it knew the hour was late. The lights of the city glowed, reflecting off the low overhanging clouds. The air was heavy and humid.

He stepped off the porch and his feet sank into the wet grass. He walked down the sloping lawn and stepped onto the dock, staring at the place where the *John Galt* would have been moored.

One, maybe two days at the most, Dave Shandler had said. He'd probably have the *John Galt* back in operation by Thursday. *In the meantime,* Eric thought, *we've got to figure out who messed with the boat.* He didn't want to go to the police. Not just yet, anyway. That would draw too much unnecessary attention. *Not until we find out what the hell is going on around here. And that knife. I'll bet that if we find the owner of that dive knife we'll find out who vandalized the Galt. We've got to get our hands on that knife.* He crept silently back to the bedroom and climbed into bed. Kari murmured groggily and placed her arm around him as he lay down next to her, and soon he was fast asleep.

chapter 105

The sun had just gone down when the black Trans Am pulled into the marina parking lot. Jimmy could see Ed and Phillip standing on the bow of the Bayliner and he could tell by their impatient looks that they had been waiting for him for some time. *"Screw 'em,"* Jimmy said aloud to no one. He locked the car and walked casually onto the dock and leapt onto the Bayliner, which Ed had already started to back out of the slip.

"Hope you don't mind me bein' a little early," Jimmy sneered sarcastically. "I just really wanted to get a head start." Ed shook his head disgustedly and Phillip grinned. In a way, Phillip admired the way Jimmy lived—that 'devil-may-care' attitude, the haughty, arrogant confidence, and how he seemed to relish pissing other people off, knowing that they could not or would not do anything about it. Most people would kill to have the confidence that Jimmy had. But Phillip knew that somewhere inside of Jimmy Durand, there was a coward—someone who needed to control and be in control at all times and needed to be bigger, stronger, and smarter than everyone else. Control was a weapon that Jimmy used in every battle. Control was power, and Jimmy had proved it to himself over and over. Phillip wished he had that kind of control but he wasn't willing to do the kinds of things that were necessary for that kind of false security, no matter how real it seemed.

Besides, he thought, *I'm not very good at beating women to within an inch of their lives.*

The boat left the marina, made the short jaunt downstream along the breakwall, and headed out into the lake. A small fishing charter was just coming in, and its captain smiled and waved. Ed, ever the smiling ambassador, called to the captain.

"How'dja do?" he asked, without removing the cigarette from his lips.

"One Laker. Good one, too. Maybe fifteen pounds. You fellas just headin' out?" the other captain shouted.

"Best time for them lunkers, I say," Ed responded, nodding and taking a drag from the Camel. The boat was soon out of earshot and the captain's shout of "good luck" was drowned out by the engine noise and the waves that slapped against the hull of the Bayliner. The wind blew off the lake from the north and the late evening was rapidly giving way to night. The steely-gray cloud cover from the day remained, but the rain had tapered off, at least for now.

They reached the dive site in an hour, and in another twenty minutes Ed and Phillip had plunged beneath the surface, descending for the second time that day to the wreck that lay in the depths below. A mast had appeared directly under the two divers and they followed it down into the darkness until their flashlight beam reflected something that definitely was not wood and was certainly no part of the mast or its rigging.

Ed trained his flashlight beam on the object.

What the hell? A light? Some sort of spotlight has been mounted on the mast. The two divers stopped and hovered in the water, shining their beams at the large black object clamped to the barren pole. Ed shook his head and waved it off. It didn't matter now. They already knew that the Randalls had found the wreck but now, thanks to that terribly unfortunate accident aboard the Randalls' boat, time was on their side.

They battled the mild current of the Channel until they came to the main hatch. Phillip was about to re-enter the hatch when Ed grabbed his arm and shook his head. Phillip followed Ed as he glided slowly over to the port side and down along the hull. Ed pointed to a spot where the wood was rotting away, leaving a gaping hole in the hull a few inches wide and three feet long. He pulled out his knife and began poking at the wood. It gave away easily and he grabbed at a plank and pulled. The waterlogged board tore away from the side of the ship, and small chunks of debris tumbled away. He and Phillip grasped the next plank and pulled. That board also gave way easily in an explosion of silt and flotsam which was slowly dissipated and carried away by the gentle current.

Phillip shined his light inside the enlarged hole. Once again, he was shocked by the sight of contorted forms in the corner of the tiny cabin and he shuddered. The torment and pain were still visible in the decomposing skeletons, bound and tied as they had been for over one hundred years. Richard Merman had written in his journal that he wasn't sure what had become of the crew and passengers.

But Phillip knew. *Jesus,* he thought in horror. *This wasn't your ordinary run-of-the-mill heist. Somebody must've actually enjoyed doing this.* Even Ed paused as he scanned the corpses with his flashlight, but if he was any more than just mildly startled, it didn't show in his eyes. He swept the flashlight about the cabin and turned to Phillip, shaking his head. Phillip understood. The cabin held only a few small boxes and a couple chairs but no chest. No sense in wasting precious air looking at a couple soggy stiffs.

Phillip followed Ed as he moved along the hull. He stopped and slid his knife between two planks and a chunk of wood fell away immediately. Ed pried at the small opening he had created and soon the entire plank tumbled end over end into the darkness below. When he was able to get his entire massive hand in the hole, he reached in and pulled away the boards on either side. They gave way with low, slow splintering sounds. Phillip shined his light into the room through the hole. Unlike the other cabin, this room was filled with crates and boxes. Phillip looked at Ed who returned his glance with a nod of his head. Both grasped the plank below the hole and pulled. It gave way easily, as did the three below that. The hole in the hull was now large enough for both of them to penetrate the small cargo hold. They maneuvered carefully through the hold amid the thick, floating silt that had been stirred up.

Hearts thundered. Six years of searching was about to pay off. Merry Christmas and Happy Birthday, all rolled into one huge present.

Ed picked up a wooden box, which promptly disintegrated in his hands. A cloud of sediment filled the hold as heavy ceramic dishes tumbled to the floor. The thick cloud made it difficult to see and Ed backed out of the room. Phillip remained inside, fumbling around in the murky storm. He found a pile of boxes by feel and inserted his knife blade carefully under the edge of the lid of the top one. The edge of the lid literally crumbled. They would have to be careful. If the crates and the planking gave way that easily, then the entire ship wreck might be on the edge of collapse.

He picked up the box and, with gentle, easy fin-strokes, slowly propelled himself backwards out of the ship. Outside, he held the box gently as Ed pried the lid open.

Coffee cups? Phillip thought disgustedly. *What was this, a U-Haul Rent-a-Ship?* Ed pulled out a mug and tossed it aside. It vanished, tumbling down into darkness. He checked his gauges, finding that they had already exceeded the amount of time they should have been down. He tapped his watch and angrily shot his thumb up. Phillip took one of the coffee mugs and dropped the rest, crate and all. It disappeared below them, bouncing off the hull and shattering, the cups bounding along the hull and falling into the black below.

Back on the boat, Phillip handed the mug to Jimmy. He held it up, spun it around in his hand and cocked his eyebrow. "I hope we have a little more to show than a coffee cup for six years of work," he said cynically. "I'm not doing this so I can fill my cupboards." Phillip took the mug back and ignored the comment.

Ed pulled off his hood and slipped a cigarette into his mouth even before he was finished taking his suit off. As Ed was stripping off his wetsuit, Jimmy turned his gaze away. He couldn't stand the sight of Ed's huge belly flopping out as he unzipped it. *A heart attack waiting to happen,* Jimmy thought. *And it'll happen. You bet it will. I'll bet he's got arteries filled with Play-Doh.*

"Well, we didn't find it, and times a-wastin'," Ed said.

"So?" Jimmy replied, with more than a hint of defiance in his voice.

"So," Ed sneered, taking a long drag of his cigarette and stepping out of his suit, "we got two more full tanks on board. Suit up, Jimmy, 'cause you're gonna find us that fortune."

Jimmy stared at him in disbelief. "You're out of your mind. Me? Alone? Get *fucked.*" He began to turn away but Ed reared up and stormed up to his face. Jimmy could smell the stale odor of tobacco on his breath and the pungent odor of his body. Eyes met eyes, and fury collided head-on. It was a train wreck of rage and anger.

"Listen here, you goddamn holier-than-thou shit-for-brains jackass," Ed growled. "We've been lookin' for this thing for six years. Six goddamn years, you sonofabitch. I will not let you fuck it up because your candy-ass doesn't want to make a deep dive alone." He pointed to the water. "Randall's got lights strung up all over the fucking ship. We bought ourselves a little bit of time, but not much. He's gonna be back out here, and soon. We can't mess around anymore, damn it, and if *you* want to, well let me know, cause we don't need to be dragged down by your sorry ass anymore." Ed inched forward, eyes afire. He gritted his teeth and lowered his voice. "We are closer than we have ever been and if you fuck this up because you don't want to dive by yourself I will kill you. *I swear to God I will.*"

At the helm, Phillip stood rooted to the spot, expecting the worst. He had never seen anyone stand up to Jimmy like that, but if anyone was going to, he figured it would be Ed. Lately, Ed had been rather even-tempered, but the strain of someone else finding the wreck first had taken its toll. Ed's nostrils flared in the glow of the cabin light and Phillip could see the veins near his temples throbbing beneath his skin. Phillip believed that, at that moment, Ed *could* have killed Jimmy. Even Jimmy looked a little wary, taken aback by Belmont's explosive tirade.

Ed stood his ground, waiting for an answer. Tense seconds ticked by. Ed took a drag from his cigarette, then tossed it into the lake. Jimmy stared at him, frozen. His arms were crossed in defiance. Eyes locked like headlights in a dangerous game of chicken.

"Fine," Jimmy spat, backing away. "Where's my fucking wetsuit?"

chapter 106

They were right, Jimmy thought. *It's pitch black down here.* He continued along the anchor line until he found the wreck. The mast appeared suddenly in the flashlight beam, thrusting out of the murky blackness, and the sight jolted him, seeing it appear so quickly in front of him after seeing nothing but the anchor line on the journey to the bottom of the lake. He followed the mast to the deck, and swung the light around. Jimmy couldn't care less about the history of the ship, nor was he impressed even by the sight of the old vessel. There was only one reason why this ship was important to him and it didn't have anything to do with historical value.

It has to do with getting what the hell you deserve out of this life, he thought, *and I deserve a shitload more than what I've already got. All I had to do was find that crate. That's all. Just find that damn crate and get out of here.*

Ed had given him a small crowbar and he carried it and the flashlight in the same hand, gliding just above the deck. He found the place that Ed and Phillip had described where they had torn away the planking and looked inside. The sight of the decomposing remains gave him a start. Ed and Phillip hadn't mentioned the bodies and he stared at the figures for a moment, their silhouetted shadows cast on the wall behind them. *Wow. Look at you, bud. Got a knife stuck in your throat. Now that's creative. Shoulda used that idea on my old man. I'm sure he would've really got off on your knife swallowing trick.*

He swung the beam to the left and the shadows on the wall moved in the opposite direction. *Well, you're not in much better shape*, he thought, staring at the remains of the woman. *You got yourself a bad case of hole-in-the-skull. Gonna have to get that looked at pretty soon or it's gonna kill you.* Jimmy had seen all kinds of pain and torture and had felt more than his share before he was ten years old than most would ever feel in a lifetime. Two dead bodies in a shipwreck were just another fact of life to him. Or fact of death, depending on how you wanted to look at it. *You're either the beater or the beaten in this world*, he reminded himself. *The strong survive; the strongest thrive.*

Jimmy left the corpses slumbering in their watery tomb and moved along the hull to the next gaping hole that Ed and Phillip had made. Shining his light into the cabin, he entered the room slowly. On the far wall a small door stood partially open, beckoning him into the bowels of the wreck.

Gotta be careful now, he reminded himself. After passing

through the door, he found himself in a corridor. Directly across from the door he had just come through was yet another door, also partially opened. He was leery of traveling into the wreck without a line, but there was nothing he could do on this trip: he'd left the spool of guideline on the boat. He turned around and saw that he wasn't far from where he'd entered the ship, and decided to press on, deeper into the wreck.

He pushed the door gently but it was so warped that it wouldn't move. He shined the light inside and gazed about the room. Again, only a few small crates and boxes, not much to indicate—

Hold it! He stopped the beam of light on the corner of a large wooden crate that was half hidden by a jumble of smaller boxes around and on top of it. It was hard to determine its exact size. But it looked large—or at least larger—than the others, and his excitement revved.

He pushed the door harder. It still didn't budge and the opening was too small for him to slip through. *Screw this*, he thought. He put the light and the crowbar under his arm, placed both hands on the door and heaved. The door ripped away from its hinges, the warped wood snapping easily. It crashed to the floor, creating a muddled storm of silt. He swam through the enveloping cloud, intent on reaching the large box that lay against the wall in the corner of the cabin.

Disregarding the billowing sediment, he brushed the smaller boxes from around the large crate. Debris swirled around him. He moved to within six inches of the chest and confirmed its dimensions with his gloved hands. It had been well made and, judging by the steel straps and the locks, was still intact and felt like it was going to stay that way.

Holy shit! We found the thing! We actually found it! There had been a time, a couple years ago, when he had pondered bailing out and leaving the search to Ed and Phillip. But his ego wouldn't let him, especially after they'd plundered the *North Hawk*. A pretty lucrative find, indeed, but only a mere drop in the bucket compared to what the *Aurora* was carrying. His ego told him that he needed this, he had to have this. He was due.

And Sharon. Well, to hell with her. If she's still around, fine. If not . . . .

Jimmy checked his gauges and was surprised at the rapid rate at which he was using up his air. He only had two minutes before he would have to head back to the surface.

A low rumbling sound took him by surprise. At first, he thought that a wooden box was falling, but it was too loud and too sustained. In a split instant, he knew what it was.

Oh shit.

He left the crowbar sitting on the box, grabbed the flashlight, and headed for the doorway. The rumbling and creaking pounded all around him. He had never been in this situation before, but he had a pretty good guess about what was happening.

He reached the door and was half way through it when the first timber struck him, pinning him down. His regulator was knocked from his mouth, but he grabbed it quickly and replaced it. He turned to push the heavy beam off of him but the bulkiness of the two tanks and the rest of his equipment made it difficult to move himself, much less maneuver the large timber off him.

Silt and debris obscured his flashlight beam. Rubble was falling all around now and Jimmy could no longer even see the door that led to the cabin right across from him. *Stupid!! Stupid!!* he thought. He had already figured out where he had gone wrong. He had torn the warped door off of its hinges and that had been just enough to weaken the supports above. Now the rotting beams and decaying trusses came down on him, one on top of the other, pinning him inside the wreck of the ship, one hundred sixty feet below the surface of Lake Huron.

chapter 107

Daniel struggles ferociously against the hand clamped tightly around his mouth. He swings his free arm wildly, only to have it pinned to his side by another large hand. He is helpless and cannot move.

"Hold on, hold on . . . you're gonna wake the dead makin' noises like that."

Jack. Daniel stops struggling and he feels the grip on his mouth loosen.

"Stay quiet and I'll let you go," Jack growls. Daniel relaxes and Malloy pulls his hand away and releases his arm. Daniel had dropped the candle and it had gone out. He picks it up, re-lights it with shaking hands, and turns to face a smiling Jack, his face hauntingly different in the lambent glow of the candle. His sharp facial features are carved into planes of shadow and light. The shimmering reflection of the candle flame dances in the wet, glossy *mirror of his eyes.*

"What are you doing down here?" Daniel asks, half-relieved, half-angry. Jack shouldn't have scared him like that.

"The question," Jack replies, grinning strangely, "is what are you doing here?" He is still smiling, not a wicked smile, but then again, not at all a kind smile. A suspicious smile.

"I heard a noise. A thumping noise. I was just looking to see what it was," Daniel says defensively.

"I heard it too," Jack says. He is still staring at Daniel, with that strange smile on his face.

"Did you find out what it was?" Jack asks carefully.

"Yes. Yes, I did. Right here." Daniel slowly swings the candle towards the large crate and the stacks of smaller wooden boxes. "Right there," he says, pointing to the empty whiskey bottle. The transparent glass wedged between two crates reflected the candle and the bottle cast tiny, fluttering shadows of its own. Daniel turns to face Jack again. Malloy is still looking at Daniel.

Had he even looked at the whiskey bottle? Daniel wonders. Jack is not smiling now.

"Well, good," Jack says, in a falsely hearty voice. "That means we can both get some sleep. Come on." He stands motionless, waiting for Daniel to move. Daniel leads the way out of the small room in the dim light of the flickering candle. The two men walk in silence through the darkened ship. Daniel creeps into his bunk and blows out the candle.

Jack stands near the door, enshrouded in darkness. "Daniel?" Daniel raises his head and sits up on his elbows. "Sorry about that back there in the hold," Jack apologizes. "I didn't mean to scare you, but I didn't want to surprise you and have you shout or scream and wake everybody up."

"It's all right," Daniel mumbles. "I wasn't that scared anyway."

Jack stumbles off to his bunk and within minutes Daniel can hear him snoring.

What did Jack know? Daniel wonders, not for the first time since he had been discovered in the hold. He has never seen that look in Jack's face before—a cynical, untrusting glare that never wavered. Daniel is certain that Malloy had never even looked at the whiskey bottle and that his eyes had never moved from Daniel's back. It was as if Jack were guarding the cargo as well. Did Jack know what was in the chest?

Daniel got little sleep that night.

Christopher Knight

chapter 108

He was trapped. The water gnawed and chewed, and he knew it would only be mere moments before it came pouring in, filling his mouth, his nostrils, his lungs. He was completely helpless. He struggled in vain to look for help, but of course, that was ridiculous. There was no one. If he could only—

His chest tightened, his need for air greater and greater with every passing second. He had no idea how long he had been under water. Time had stopped, and an hour could have been only a second, or maybe an entire day. Or a lifetime.

He had heard somewhere that drowning was supposed to be a peaceful occurrence. That it really wasn't at all painful, that once your lungs burst, it was pretty much all over, and in the final moments of your life, things became very calm. He'd even read somewhere that many people reach orgasm at the split instant before death, and he'd wondered if it was true or not.

Dandy. Coming and going. Well, it sure looks like I'm about to find out.

Still, he was not yet at the point of giving up. As long as he remained conscious and able to control his movements, however frantic they may be, he was going to go out kicking and screaming, regardless if anyone could hear or see him. His air was gone, and he remained alive only by the oxygen that was circulating but now rapidly depleting in his bloodstream. He expelled a small amount, the tiny bubbles rising above him and fading from sight. If he could only find—

But that was impossible. It was too late.

He looked in the waters around him. His vision blurred, and he couldn't make out shapes or objects, whether they were far away or two feet in front of his face. Colors faded, and everything took on a bluish gray hue. The pain twisting in his lungs was unbearable. There was nothing more he could do. There was no one around, no help, no escape. He needed to expel the ever increasing level of toxic carbon dioxide that his own body had created, but he knew. He knew the moment that he did, it would be over. The moment he exhaled, his body would force himself to inhale, and the water would come, swiftly and painfully. And then it would be over.

His vision was now completely distorted, his head still turning frantically from side to side in vain attempts to quell the terrible need for air.

It sure doesn't feel very peaceful.

It was his last thought before the water took over, forcing itself into him and causing him to convulse violently. It rocketed through his nasal passages and forced its way into his lungs. His body stiffened, became rigid, and he froze. The pain was gone.

My God . . . I'm going to make it after all. I am. Everything was okay now, and he relaxed in the calm, quiet tranquility of the depths. He no longer felt pain, and he no longer struggled. He was going to be—

I can't move. Holy shit . . . I can't move . . . I'm—

And those were his last thoughts as the darkness came upon him, like a fast moving cloud blotting out the sun on a summer day. The waters became darker and darker, dimmer and dimmer, and then—

Nothing. Complete darkness.

And in the final instant before he slipped away for good, forever, into the eternal beyond, Don Garrity woke up.

chapter 109

Garrity opened his eyes, and the blue light from the mercury vapor enveloped him, streaming through the dining room window. For a moment he was disoriented, unsure of exactly where he was. Then it came to him. He was on the couch, at Eric and Kari's. He had grown tired and must have nodded off. The nightmare must have woke him.

He was warm. Thankfully, he hadn't turned into a raging sweat factory, as his clothes were still on and he didn't want to have to sleep the rest of the night in soaked clothing. Nor would he want to explain to Eric and Kari why his sweats and T-shirt looked like he had just pulled them out of the river.

The nightmare, he thought. It was different. Well, different, but—

The same.

And it began to worry him again.   The nightmares were becoming increasingly more frequent, and the weird flashbacks, or visions, or whatever the hell they were . . . they were causing a problem.   When you pass out on a boat for no reason at all, and have to lie about it to your friends . . . well, something is screwed up.

Like my head. My head is messed up, and probably has been for a long time. At least, ever since—

His thought was interrupted by a shadow moving quietly in the darkness. He could hear the figure moving about in the kitchen, the cupboard door open, and the water running in the sink. Eric. Or Kari. He couldn't tell. He heard the water shut off, and heard the water being gulped even from the couch in the living room, some twenty feet away.

Eric.

Don heard the glass tink against the sink, and Eric's shadow paused briefly as it passed the living room, then continued on down the hall. Don almost said something, but didn't. The shadow was gone instantly, and he was alone again in the living room.

He closed his eyes, but sleep would not come. He wasn't tired, or, at least, didn't feel tired. In fact, he was wired. The nightmare had sent his pulse skyrocketing and adrenaline pumping through his body, and he felt ready to get up, ready to start the day. He opened his eyes and squinted in the darkness towards the kitchen. The glowing blue digital numerals of the microwave gave off enough light itself to nearly illuminate the kitchen, but it was difficult to read.

Two twenty . . . no. Three. Three twenty-six. Too early to get up.

He sat up, and looked out at the lights across river, slightly indistinct and fuzzy from looking through the screen door. A few crickets chirped here and there, and the soft murmur of the river drifted through the early morning air. He could see the outline of a small fishing boat moored across the river, and saw the empty space where the John Galt would have been moored. His thoughts returned again to the near disaster in the Atlantic, and of him fading, falling, falling . . . .

And then he remembered the nightmare from just a few minutes ago. Or, at least some of it. He couldn't be sure if he remembered it all, because if he'd forgotten some part, well, he didn't remember it. He remembered the pain of the water rushing into his lungs, the fear and terror. And he remembered the feeling of easiness, the comfort. He had relaxed, letting the waters enshroud him, and it had been all right. It had felt good. His pain had gone away, the fright and the horror, and he had called a truce with the seas. He was at harmony, at one with the cold waters that were to become his grave. He felt the comforting closeness, the smooth caress of the waters, the loving arms of the deep holding him passionately, gently, refusing to let go. He had squirmed and twisted in her grasp, and finally gave in to her, allowing himself to be at ease, relaxed and at peace as the darkness came upon him.

The hushed rippling of the Cheboygan river called to him, singing a soft lullaby. After a few minutes, he had finally fallen asleep.

chapter 110

One hundred sixty feet below the surface of Lake Huron, in utter blackness save for a single flashlight beam, Jimmy Durand was in a watery hell.

Now you've done it, he thought. Luckily, he found that he could still move his arms. One large timber lay on his back over his two tanks, but by making a slight rolling motion, he was able to tumble it off of him and push it over his head. This freed him up a bit more and he swung the flashlight beam behind him to examine his legs. The pile of boards was not large, but each timber was big. And *heavy.* He strained to break free, and found he could move one leg a little. The other leg wouldn't budge.

He checked his air gauge. At this very moment, he should have just been starting his ascent to the surface. *Great. This is just what I needed. If that son of a bitch Ed hadn't decided to make another dive tonight, this wouldn't have happened. I swear to God I'm going to —*

He stopped in mid-thought, cursed through his regulator, and told himself to start thinking about the immediate problem at hand. He realized that he was taking deep, heavy gulps of air and he corrected this with longer, slower, more controlled breaths. It wasn't like Jimmy to panic and he wasn't about to start now. *Not if I want to live to wring that fat bastard's neck.*

But now he had another problem: he was getting narced. The nitrogen buzz began to cloud his thinking, and his vision blurred.

Focus, he thought, trying to clear the dizzying euphoria from his mind. *Stay focused. Stay focused.*

He turned sideways again to look at the timbers that lay on his legs. He set his flashlight down and aimed the beam towards the pile of boards that held him prisoner. With both hands free, he grabbed a piece of wood and heaved. He worked it up and down and as he did, he felt the pressure on his left leg ease. Working the beam back and forth, he wrestled it loose and freed the leg.

Alright. Halfway there now.

He checked his air gauge. He was rapidly running out of air. The toxic nitrogen slithered through his brain, fuzzing his thoughts. He was aware of his vision tunneling, like he was swimming in a long, dark tube. He shook his head to try to lessen the effects, but it did no good. The only solution would be to ascend and allow the narcosis to fade away.

He slipped the fin off his newly-freed left foot and used that leg, along with his hands, to pull and push at the other pieces of broken timbers. Some were incredibly heavy, compounded by the weight of other boards that lay heaped on top of them. Slowly, he was able to work a few of the smaller ones free and cast them aside. Some simply crumbled and broke and were easily swept away. But he still wasn't able to get his leg free, and he knew he was running out of time. He didn't bother to check his gauges because he didn't want to waste even one precious second. Frustrated, he placed his good leg on one of the heavy timbers and pushed with all his might. As he strained, he felt his pinned leg give way a tiny bit. He pressed harder with his good leg, straining and grunting through his regulator.

He heard a creak above him and the entire ship seemed to shudder. *Oh shit. Not again.* The nitrogen buzz was screaming in his mind, and his vision blurred even more. He feared blacking out.

Despite the creaking he continued to push. Unless he got out of here in the next few minutes anyway it hardly mattered if the entire ship caved in on him. He was sure he was peeling the flesh right off his leg and half-expected to see a bloody stump of gristle and bone emerge from under the beam when—and if—he was finally able to release it.

Creeeeaaakk . . . kk . . . kkkkk . . . .

The trusses and timbers above him thundered in his head, and the effects of the nitrogen made it seem as if his whole body was frozen. Soon, the narcosis would eat him alive.

He pressed harder, and although the pain grew increasingly more intense he was no longer aware of it. Pain was no longer an issue. Living long enough to strangle that fat asshole was the issue.

Jimmy focused, made one last desperate heave—and was free.

Christopher Knight

The skin on his ankle and foot was ripped open, but Jimmy barely noticed. He was *free.*

The creaking above his head grew louder and more weighted, and in the flashlight beam he could see a wavering curtain of silt that rained down from above. He grabbed the fin that he had removed from his left leg. The right one was lost behind the pile of timbers. It was awkward maneuvering without fins and he half-walked half-swam through the door of the tiny cabin and out the hole in the side of the hull. The narcosis had caused his vision to blur even more, and he felt drunk and disoriented. Just as he cleared the hole, another portion of the ship gave way with a thundering roar, and Jimmy was struck by a burst of exploding silt and fine debris that blasted from the crumbling ship.

Ignoring the collapse and the debris in the water around him, he slipped the single fin on his good leg and swam up the hull and to the anchor line. Immediately, the effects of the narcosis began to leave him, and clear thoughts began to return. His tunnel vision faded, and fuzzy images cleared. He checked his gauges and decided that he would decompress every thirty feet for one minute. That was all he would be able to do even though it probably would not be enough. He had never had decompression sickness, but he'd heard stories and knew it wasn't pleasant. He figured that he would probably have to go to the hospital. *At least it's better than dying.*

At one hundred feet, Jimmy realized he had another problem. Although the effects of being narced had left him, he felt light-headed. He looked down. His right leg was bleeding profusely. He shined the light on the torn shredded portion of his wetsuit. His leg was scraped and cut and thick, crimson fluid swarmed and swirled in the beam of the flashlight. His leg was a mangled bloody mess. One of the gashes on his foot looked as if it might extend right down to the bone.

At forty feet his air was almost gone and it was getting harder to breathe as he dragged the last of it from his tanks. Ed and Phillip were probably having a beer, playing cards, or flipping through Jimmy's June issue of *Playboy*—oblivious to the catastrophe deep below. He decided that he'd have to skip his last decompression stop entirely. He felt faint, and he'd be damned if he was going to make it this far only to pass out just below the boat and drown. If he got bent and suffered decompression sickness, he'd deal with that when he was on the surface. He wasn't looking forward to the nauseating pain and cramping, but it sure was a lot better than spending eternity stuck in the muck at the bottom of the Lake Huron.

He surfaced twenty feet from the boat. It was a dark night and the air was cool, but it felt gloriously warm to Jimmy. He gasped, sucking in deep gulps of air for several seconds as he floated, savoring its sweetness.

Swimming to the boat was clumsy with the heavy tanks and only one fin. He reached the ladder and slipped out off his buoyancy vest and tanks. Phillip pulled the apparatus out of the water without saying anything and Jimmy stayed in the water a moment longer, holding the ladder, resting.

Alive.

Ed leaned over the side, the shape of his huge head looming against the night sky, and the red ember of a cigarette twitching from the side of his mouth as he spoke. "Took you long enough," he hissed. "Whadja do . . . *get lost?*"

chapter 111

Mike Felsing got up early the next morning, eager to start writing again.

Now there's a switch, he thought, rubbing the sleep from his eyes. His mind was spinning with the excitement of finding the real name of the ship and the fact that someone was possibly trying to thwart the Randalls' attempts at diving. When he awoke, he felt the ideas coming in waves. He needed to write. He *could* write. Not about the mystery ship, but a novel. *His* novel. Another mystery. He knew that when he sat down in front of that piece-of-junk computer, his fingers would begin flying over the keypad. He didn't have any specific plot in mind: maybe an off-duty cop finds a dead body washed ashore, or he finds a boat floating in the water, its occupants murdered, or . . . .

But now, as mysteriously as the urge to write had come, it had departed as he sat in his small workroom overlooking Lake Michigan. The ideas were silent and his fingers unmoving. Every three minutes, the starfield screen saver appeared on the monitor and he would tap the mouse to bring back the white void, empty except for the tiny black cursor blinking methodically in the upper left corner. The problem was that his mental attention was completely consumed by the mystery of the *Aurora/Brittany*, its change of name, its last voyage, and its murdered occupants.

Finally, he succumbed to the lure of the mystery ship, shut the computer off, and drove to the library. An hour later, the pages of the *Cheboygan Tribune* were once again streaking before his eyes on the screen of the microfiche machine. When he found where he had left off yesterday, he stopped, and began scanning the pages slowly and carefully. After a half hour of concentration, he became frustrated, reminded of the practical impossibility of this mode of attack, especially when he didn't know what he was looking for.

I have no idea what to look for, he thought.

The murders on the vessel would have been a scandal, especially in those days. They would have been talked about for years and written about extensively. If they had been known about at the time, it would be unthinkable that it would not have been in the newspaper. *Maybe it was Merman,* Mike thought. *Maybe he killed those people on the ship to collect the insurance money. Money is a powerful motivator. Maybe Merman hired somebody to kill the crew and blow a hole in the hull with dynamite. Far-fetched, but possible.*

But Mike's cop instinct told him that that wasn't it. Whoever had killed those people had taken *pleasure* in it. If they had been murdered for insurance money, they would have been killed in the quickest means possible, but not tortured.

Not tortured, he thought. *Good God . . . not like that.*

Mike considered the possibility that there had been something aboard the ship that the killers wanted. That was more likely. *But what would it have been?* The Great Lakes were never known as a thoroughfare for treasure ships, and Mike had heard of only one such incident, that of the *Gunilda*. When she went down in Lake Superior she was rumored to have been carrying precious jewels and gold worth one million dollars. However, the usual cargo on the Lakes were commodities like lumber, grain, or ore.

Mike looked up and caught the librarian's eye. He nodded and she waved and walked around the desk towards him. "Is there anything I can help you find?" she asked pleasantly.

"Well, maybe." Mike leaned back in his chair. "I'm trying to find out more about a shipwreck that occurred in 1859. I'm wondering if there might be an old article about it in the *Cheboygan Tribune*." He hoped she wouldn't press for further information about the ship. The librarian thought only a moment before answering.

"We have something new that might help. Over here."

Mike followed her to a desk where a lone computer sat. "The Historical Society made a list of all articles and features in the *Cheboygan Tribune* all the way back to when it was first published. They've been working on it for over a year and they just finished it last month. Most people don't even know we have it yet. There are over four hundred topics, and thousands of articles listed." She sat down, tapped the keypad, and instantly the directory glowed on the screen. "For instance, if you're looking for an article about a shipwreck—"

Pause. Tap-tap. Ta-tap-tap.

"—you go to the 'shipwrecks' topic on the menu." She clicked the mouse and the screen changed, filling with another directory. *Amazing*, Mike thought. Technology had grown so rapidly in just the last couple years that it was scary. Not like *Psycho* scary. Not like IRS audit scary. But *scary* scary. "And from here," the librarian continued, "you can search for individual ships by name or even by year, if you wish." She slid out of the chair and offered it to Mike. "Let me know if there is anything else you may need." Mike thanked her and she walked back to the front desk.

Mike seated himself in front of the computer and stared at the long list of articles that filled the screen. He pressed the 'down' arrow key and held it and the file spun upward. He was both dismayed and relieved to find that there were hundreds of articles on either shipwrecks or related stories all the way back to the first year of the *Tribune's* printing.

He heard the soft scrunch of approaching footsteps and turned to see the librarian at his side again. "One more thing," she offered. "We don't have the text of the articles on the computer. It just lists the date, page, and column in which you'll find the story. You'll need to go back to the microfiche to read the text. But it will save a lot of time searching on that old machine."

"Can I print a list of the articles from the subject menu and take it over to the microfiche?" Mike asked.

"Certainly," she replied. She tapped the keypad and in a moment, the printer awoke, buzzing as the inkjet cartridge printed the information on the paper. Five minutes later, Mike had four pages that listed the title and location of nearly four hundred articles. Mike thanked her again and took the pages from the printing tray. A quick scan revealed that there was no listing under *Aurora* or *Brittany*, but then he hadn't really expected to find any. Papers in hand, he returned to his chair in front of the microfiche. He was thankful that the library was nearly empty that day and there was no competition for the microfiche, for he felt a renewed excitement at the possibility of finding out more about the newly-discovered wreck and didn't want to have to share the microfiche with another researcher.

The work was laborious. At first, he scanned the pages, looking for headers that sounded like they could have involved the wreck that the Randalls had found. Mike found that he could eliminate most of the entries from the header alone. He put a check next to all those that indicated a specific location near where the ship rested, regardless of date.

Mike's stomach rumbled and, when he glanced at his watch, he knew why. It was nearly noon. *A few more headers, then I'll go to lunch*, he promised himself.

Just as he was about to quit, a header caught his eye . **"Strange fire seen over water" (July 29, 1859, third page, fourth column).** Mike glanced at the year again. *Didn't I go through that entire year yesterday?* But he had been looking for words like 'shipwreck,' 'sinking,' or 'ship missing' not 'strange fire.'

He found the fiche he needed and placed it in the tray. He found the story quickly. It was just a small article, almost a footnote.

CHEBOYGAN-A fire in the water? That's what more than a few Cheboygan residents say they saw, south east of Bois Blanc Island two nights ago. Over a dozen people reported seeing the flames shortly after dusk. Witnesses say the fire burned very brightly for nearly ten minutes before disappearing. As of this printing, no ships have been reported missing, and no trace of any wreck could be found, either washed ashore or floating in the water. "It's possible," says town constable Henry Richer, "that the persons witnessed a large bonfire on Bois Blanc Island itself." Most of the witnesses dispute this, saying that the flames, although a distance away, were quite visible and very large, and definitely over the water. One witness, Theodore Howard of Cheboygan, reported seeing two ships in that same area at dusk, and it was within that very hour, Mr. Howard says, that he too witnessed the flames. However, local authorities have no reports of missing ships, and say the investigation of the strange sighting is closed unless further information becomes available.

Mike tilted his chair back and thought for a moment. He had seen the video and there wasn't any evidence of fire. But a good portion of the wreck was buried in sand. Was it possible that the ship sank because of fire, possibly in one of the holds?

He printed the article, folded it, and put the list into his pocket.

A few minutes later, he was seated at *Big Boy*, trying to decide between lunch or breakfast. After opting for an omelet, he took out the list and article and spread the five pages on the table. The article was interesting but more than likely it had nothing to do with the wreck. *It's too bad none of these people are alive today*, he reflected. *Then it might be easier to . . . .*

A sudden inspiration struck him and he looked up from the papers. He shook his head, mentally slapping himself. *Geez, retire for a few years and apparently you forget everything you ever learned!* As he waited for his omelet, he went to use the pay phone in the lobby. His fingers couldn't dial the number fast enough.

chapter 112

Kari awoke before Eric, as she usually did, and went to start coffee in the kitchen for the three of them. But as she tiptoed silently to the kitchen, she realized that it was not necessary to be so quiet. Nor would it be necessary to make coffee for *three*. The couch was empty and there was a slip of paper on the armrest.

Eric and Kari—Thanks for the couch! Headed back to the cottage. I'll call— Don.

She placed the note on the counter and started the coffee. Eric would probably sleep for another hour or so. Through the sliding glass doors she could see that the wind was bending and tossing the maples and spruces that lined the water. Even the river was agitated, although it was sheltered by the homes and trees along the banks. The hand of the *Vernors* thermometer nailed to the tree near the deck was pointing at the upper left corner of the man's smiling face as he tipped his head back, sipping the soft drink. She couldn't make out the temperature, but anything between the man's lower ear and his forehead was in the lower sixty-degree range.

She crept back into the bedroom and put on her sweats and Nikes. She didn't need to leave Eric a note. He would see that her running shoes were missing and know she had gone for a jog.

Waves lashed at the shore, and Sharon Durand shivered in the cool wind. She shoved her hand in her pockets and hunched her shoulders for warmth, pressing her breasts together, absently watching the turbulent waves scrub the waterfront, mopping the jagged rocks with soapy seafoam. Jimmy hadn't come home until nearly five that morning. There had been an accident, and he had gone to the emergency room at the hospital. He told her that while they were docking at the marina, he had gotten his leg caught between the boat and the dock. It had cut it up pretty good. He had come home limping, his leg below the knee almost entirely wrapped in bandages. He took four Percodans before crashing.

Well, maybe we can talk later today, Sharon thought. *When he's feeling better*. Although Jimmy would sleep most of the morning she was wide awake, so she slipped into her blue jeans, threw on one of his sweatshirts, and went for a walk.

The wind tangled her black hair. A few ring-billed seagulls wheeled and cried in the skies above her, seeking scraps of food left by yesterday's picnickers. Many other gulls just sat in the sand, on picnic tables, the pavement, and the large rocks in the water just west of the beach area. They looked chilled, their bodies plump and fluffed up as the wind toyed and played with their feathers.

She shivered again, maybe from the cold, maybe from the thought of telling Jimmy. *What would he do? God, I wish he wasn't so damn unpredictable.*

But Jimmy needed to know. He needed to know that he was going to be a . . . *daddy.* Toddlers played in the parks of her mind, playing with their loving and devoted *daddies.* Smiles. Laughter. Tickles and giggles. *Swing, Daddy, swing! I wanna ride on da swing!* More giggles, more laughter. A hug and kiss from Mommy, ice-cream cones, hot dogs, fireflies in a jar. The images kept coming and coming. Roasting marshmallows on a stick, watching the stars at night. *Good night, Mommy . . . don't let the bed-bugs bite . . . .*

Sharon suddenly felt very alone. Gordon Turner Park was empty, except for the gulls. The marina was lifeless at this early hour, the cruisers and sailboats sleeping in their slips, sheltered from the restless wind and waves. The only human being in sight was a jogger—a woman—who was running in the gravel down Huron Street, toward the park.

chapter 113

Eric awoke to the sweetness of fresh coffee swirling through his
nostrils. Kari was gone and when he sat up, he saw that her
running shoes which she religiously placed next to the dresser were
gone. He hadn't heard her leave. He ran his hand through his hair
and over his face, feeling sandpapery grizzle on his cheeks. He
hadn't shaved since the day before yesterday.

And what day was that, anyway? he thought. *Friday? Monday?*
Since the move from Chicago, time had stopped. Days were
endless; nights were just pauses.

He got up, found Don's note, poured a cup of coffee, then
shaved and dressed. If he hurried, he would have time to go look
at the *John Galt* over at Dave's. He wanted to take a look at the
stuffing box and the bolts that Dave had found. The bolts that were
stripped on the *outside*.

Like someone was really reefin' on 'em.

He poured another cup of coffee, this time into his thermal travel coffee mug. He pushed the lid on and then jotted a quick note to Kari in case she came home before he got back. Almost as an afterthought, he searched the closet by the front door for his rain parka. It wasn't raining just yet, but it looked like it might.

The *John Galt* hung suspended in the air at Shandler's dry dock. Dave had left the bolts in plain view in the engine room. The replacement shaft lay on the floor, ready to be installed. Eric picked up one of the bolts. It was old, and the bright steel color had faded away long ago, giving way to a darker black-slate hue. Around the edges, on each of the six sides, the head had been stripped, displaying rows of silver teeth. It was just as Dave had said. Someone had loosened the bolts on purpose.

But who? He knew of no one who held a grudge against him. Vandals? No, vandals would have spray-painted obscenities or juvenile slogans on the boat. Like last year when some kids had spray painted '*EmiNeM fucKing RulEs!*' on the Bois Blanc Island ferry. No, whoever had done this had known exactly what to do and what the result would be—and had wanted it to happen. *And what's more, they must have done it right in front of our house,* he thought angrily. *Whoever did this knows where we live. They knew what they were doing. They had intended for the* John Galt *to sink—or to severely damage her, anyway.*

He left a quick note for Dave, explaining that he had been there and asking him to call him when the boat was repaired.

This time, he thought. *This time, they failed. But what would they do next time?*

Kari still wasn't home when he returned. He re-filled his coffee cup and decided against breakfast. Instead, he decided to take the Blazer and find Kari on her running route, pick her up, and go out for a bite to eat. She ran the same circuit nearly every day, rain or shine. More than once he had tracked her down in the vehicle. When he found her, she would either stop running and get into the Blazer or finish her jog by running downtown and then meet him for breakfast at *Kretchman's,* a small coffee shop.

The city was quiet and the streets deserted. There was no sign of Kari. He turned down the final street where he thought she would be and—

There she was, near the end of the street at Gordon Turner Park. Only she wasn't running, she was standing on the beach talking to someone. The wind blew her ponytail about and ruffled her nylon running pants and coat. The lake beyond was angry, and boiling whitecaps shattered on the sandy shore. Storm clouds hung like dark pinatas waiting to be ripped open, their contents unleashed in a torrential fury of rain.

He parked the Blazer, leaving it running as he hopped out and walked towards the beach. Kari and the other woman turned to look as he approached. Hair whipped in the gale. "Hi," Kari said brightly, giving Eric a warm hug and a kiss. "This is my husband, Eric" she said, turning and introducing him to the other woman. Eric smiled and extended his hand, and the woman did the same. *"Eric, this is Sharon."*

chapter 114

Don had slipped out of Eric and Kari's before dawn and returned to his cabin. Even at that early hour Duane had managed to corner him, and for once Don was grateful for his company and the offer of coffee. He was content to let Duane ramble on for almost two hours, throwing out "uh huhs," "nopes," and "didn't know thats" every few minutes to keep the comforting flow going.

Don finally excused himself, pleading the need for breakfast. After spending a few minutes needlessly straightening and arranging what little clothing he had, he decided to go into town, prompted by the sight of the broken dreamcatcher which still hung, crudely taped at a drunken angle in his window. "Need to go find me another one of those before tonight," he said aloud to himself.

The morning sky was ashen, and ghostly gray clouds haunted high above the treetops and buildings. Wind gusts shook the van as he slowed to a stop at a traffic light. A parking space opened up ahead of him and he slipped into it. *Even if the* John Galt *were operational,* he thought, stepping from the van, *I don't think we'd be out there today.*

He spotted a store window that was filled with dreamcatchers of all sizes, shapes, and colors. One was nearly two feet in diameter and was elaborately adorned with multi-colored beads and feathers. *Must be for those really terrible dreams,* Don thought. *Just what I need.* He stared at the curious shapes through the window for a moment and then went inside. Tiny brass cowbells jangled sweetly as the door opened, and the aroma of cinnamon incense filled the modest business. There were no other customers in the small, cluttered gift shop and, apparently, no clerk.

Don browsed for a few minutes before he heard soft leather whispering on the wood floor. He turned and was greeted by a small, gray-haired woman. Her skin was dark and embedded with deep lines of hardship. Long silver hair was pulled back in a ponytail and the snowy mane fell to the middle of her back. She wore a long, earth-tone dress, almost certainly made by her own hands. Intricate designs and patterns were woven into the fabric, and Don was intrigued by the amount of work that had gone into such a detailed work of art.

"Dreamcatchers are a gift of the Great Spirit," she said in a soft voice, hardly more than a whisper. Her speech was unique, conveying her heritage. Her eyes glowed, waltzing gently over Don's face. "Dreamcatchers are good for the mind and soul." As she spoke, she slowly brought both hands up and touched her forehead, then crossed her arms over her breasts.

"Who makes them?" Don asked.

"I make these," she answered, extending her hand and waving the length of the window. "I make these the old way. Many people make dreamcatchers fast to sell fast. My dreamcatchers take time," she explained. Don looked closer and noticed that her dreamcatchers were indeed different than the one that had hung in the window in the cabin. The one in the cabin had been made of string and plastic beads, but the dreamcatchers in her window were made with natural materials. The fragile webbing was made from long thin blades of grass woven inside a branch that had been carefully bent to form a circle. Instead of plastic beads, dried berries of many different colors and sizes were incorporated into the web. All the dreamcatchers were different; all individual and unique.

Don fingered one of the larger ones. The feather in the middle of the web trembled as he held the dreamcatcher in his hand, and it swung slowly back and forth in the window as he released it. His eyes stopped just below the larger one. It was about the same shape and size as the one he had broken in the cabin.

"How much is this one?" he began, as he turned to address the woman. She was nowhere in sight. He had not heard her walk away and he hadn't turned his back on her for more than a few seconds.

Well, this one will probably do the trick, he thought. He scanned other similar dreamcatchers, looking for a telltale string dangling a tiny white cardboard square. He found none. *Doesn't matter anyway. Can't cost that much and I've got to replace the one I broke.*

Christopher Knight

The dreamcatcher was attached to the window by a small piece of tape and a thread of monofilament fishing line. He held the dreamcatcher in his left hand and peeled at the tape with his right. It came away easily and he brought the small, carefully-crafted piece closer to his face for a more detailed inspection.

"That one not for you."

The voice startled him. The tiny woman had returned, holding a dreamcatcher in her hands. Once again he had heard nothing. No footsteps, no noise, nothing. "This is dreamcatcher for you."

She extended her hand and Don reached for the offering. This dreamcatcher was not as colorful as the ones in the window. It was brown and black, had no berries, and the web was sparse. Nor did this dreamcatcher have a feather. Instead, a dozen strands of fur were tied to a very fine strip of grass that hung from the epicenter of the web. Don lifted the hairs gently with his finger. They were coarse but not brittle, and were colored a mottled gray and black, darker near the narrow tips and light brown, almost creamy, near the thicker base of each hair. Don fingered the slender strands curiously.

"That is the hair of a timber wolf. The spirit of the wolf will protect you from evil," she said soberly.

Don gently touched the web of the dreamcatcher. "But, isn't the feather supposed to allow the good dreams through and the web supposed to catch the bad dreams?" he asked, confused.

"Dreamcatchers stop evil dreams from entering," she said, as she gently stroked the tiny bristles suspended within the web. "But the spirit of the wolf does not stop evil dreams from coming in." She raised her hand and placed it softly on Don's chest. Her eyes

were warm and caring. She smiled a caring, grandmotherly smile.
"The spirit of the wolf protects from evil dreams already inside."

chapter 115

"My husband is here fishing," Sharon said. "I just came up for a few days to visit." She scraped together the last of her eggs. Kari had invited her to join them for breakfast and Sharon had accepted. Her two new friends were good company, and helped to take her mind off her problems. The three had rode in the Blazer to the *Chateau Lodge*, and now they sat at a small table next to the huge glass windows overlooking East Twin Lake.

"What does he fish for?" Kari asked Sharon.

"You got me. I don't know much about fishing. Neither did Jimmy until a few years ago. Then he took a sudden interest and now he comes up here all the time with my uncle and another friend. I think they're more into the *party* aspect than the *fishing* aspect. Maybe that's what he's doing. Fishing for a party." Grins all around.

Eric vaguely took in that Sharon was from the Detroit area and this was her first time in northern Michigan. He nodded his head politely, as if paying attention to the conversation between Sharon and Kari, but his thoughts were miles away on the stripped bolts, the shipwreck, the bodies, the knife, then back to bolts.

"What does your husband do?" Kari asked Sharon.

He doesn't do jack shit, unless you count pumping himself full of Tetranobol and beating the hell out of me, Sharon thought. *Nope. Can't say that. What's something better? Oh, yeah.* "He works part-time at a Gold's Gym in Sterling Heights. He's into competitive bodybuilding. He's competed a few times and done fairly well. Oh! You know," she said, as she opened her purse. "I have a picture." Her hands stirred inside the leather bag. "Ha. Here it is. This is Jimmy." She pointed to an enormously muscular man, arms folded, leaning on a black Trans Am. "And him," she pointed to a man next to her husband, "is Phillip Keanan. Jimmy's fishing buddy. Two of the Three Stooges, if you know what I mean." She grinned. Eric and Kari leaned forward to look at the picture. Eric's eyes lit up.

"I've seen him," he said, pointing to Phillip and tapping the photo with his finger. "On the river. I've talked to him."

"You're kidding?!" Sharon exclaimed.

"Cheboygan isn't that big," Kari explained. "You're bound to run into just about everyone, sooner or later."

Sharon returned the photo to her purse and continued to talk about Jimmy's bodybuilding accomplishments and Kari listened and chatted along.

Eric sat lost in thought. He really wanted to dive again today and explore the interior of the ship. He also wanted to find out who else had been diving the wreck and who had sabotaged the *John Galt*. But the weather had deteriorated, and they'd have to wait till the front moved through. Slowly, he became aware that Kari was gently nudging him with her foot and Eric shook his head, returning his thoughts to the table.

"Sharon asked you a question," Kari said pointedly. Beneath the table, another leisurely jab tapped his shin.

"Sorry about that," Eric apologized. "Kind of lost for a moment." He smiled meekly.

"Sharon asked where you worked." It would have been easy enough for Kari to answer, but Sharon had directed the question to Eric.

Where I work. Hmmm. Gotta think about that. He grinned.

"I'm Kari's love slave. I'll do—"

Kari rolled her eyes and dipped her head. Sharon smiled. Eric smiled, then felt another tap on his leg.

"I'm a diver. Underwater welding, construction, recovery. Things like that."

If Sharon had noticed his inattentiveness, she didn't seem to mind. She asked the usual questions. *Ever seen a shark? How deep have you dived? Whaddya see down there?* And so forth. They were questions Eric could answer in his sleep and his mind began to drift away again. If the weather improved even a little, maybe they could try to make a dive that afternoon. That left the problem of no boat. Mike had kindly offered the use of his Chris-Craft, but it was in Cross Village and would probably need extensive preparations to make it seaworthy. By tomorrow the

John Galt would be repaired anyway. But Eric didn't want to wait until tomorrow. He wanted to dive *today*.

Eric sneaked a glance at his watch. It was nearing eleven. He excused himself to go to the restroom, stopping at a pay phone in the hallway. He called Dave. The phone rang a few times before the answering machine picked up and Eric left a message for Dave to call when he got the chance. He hung up the phone and returned to the table.

After breakfast they drove back in to town and dropped off Sharon at the *River Terrace Motel*. Sharon turned and waved, then disappeared behind the lobby doors.

"Well, what do you think?" Kari asked, as the Blazer pulled out into traffic.

"Sharon? Nice. Talkative. But very nice." He turned on the radio and scanned the stations for a weather report.

Kari nodded her head in agreement. "I think she's lonely. It sounds like her husband does an awful lot of fishing."

"Yeah. Sounds like an interesting guy, being a competitive bodybuilder and all that. I hope we get the chance to meet him sometime."

chapter 116

Eric dropped Kari off at home and drove over to Dave Shandler's for the second time that morning. Dave was working on the *John Galt* as Eric pulled in.

"Hey, got your note," Dave began, his deep voice booming from the deck as he waved a tool in the air. "You must've been here pretty early."

"No offense, but I wanted to see those bolts for myself," Eric said.

"What do you think?" Dave asked, not at all offended by Eric's need to confirm his diagnosis.

"Like you said, somebody loosened them. There's no doubt about that. The question is, who?"

"Well, I dunno 'bout that. But you should be back in the water by tomorrow. I'll give 'er a good check over to make sure nothing else has been screwed with."

"What are the chances of getting her back in the water today?" Eric asked, and then immediately wished he hadn't said anything. Dave had already gone out of his way to find the replacement shaft and had reshuffled his work schedule to fix the *John Galt* first, ahead of some of his other projects.

"Slim and none," Dave answered. "You took in a pretty good amount of water and your whole engine's gotta be looked at. I don't think there's any serious damage, but it's gotta be checked out." He saw the disappointment in Eric's face. "You *really* need it today?"

"Well, yeah. I've got a friend visiting. Gonna do some diving." He didn't offer anything further, and Dave didn't ask.

"Well, if it's just diving you need to do, I got an old fishing trawler down at the marina." He gestured with a quick sideways nod. "It's a little smaller than your boat and she ain't that pretty to look at, but she'll probably do fine. You're welcome to use 'er if you need to. She's gassed and ready to go. You gonna dive in this weather?" He finished the sentence by poking his thumb towards the river, where the leaves on the trees fluttered and spun in the early afternoon wind. The gusts rocked some of the trees violently, causing them to bend and sway towards the east.

"Well, not if it stays like this." He looked out and around, noting the swaying trees and the turbulent river. "But this is supposed to move out this afternoon. You really wouldn't mind if we used your boat?" Eric asked.

"Not at all," Dave replied. "I haven't used 'er much this year. It'll probably do 'er some good to get out on the lake for awhile."

chapter 117

When Eric told Kari about his idea, she was excited about diving, but she was a little apprehensive about the weather. "Are you sure you want to go out? I mean, with the way the wind is blowing and all?"

"It'll have to calm down a bit," he replied knowingly. "But look." Eric pointed to the trees on the riverbank. "The wind has already slacked off a bit. I'm sure the waves are still coming in, but it's still only one-thirty. By this evening, the lake will be a lot calmer if this front pushes through. Besides, I don't think we can wait 'til tomorrow. Someone else is diving that wreck and I'm sure they're the same ones that sabotaged the *John Galt*, in which case they know where we live. I want to know what's going on and why, and I think the answer is on that wreck."

"Well, from now on, we need to lock the windows and doors,"

Kari instructed. Until now, Cheboygan had seemed so innocent and previously they had never paid attention to locked doors or bolted windows. It was a sobering realization for both of them.

"What about going to the police?" Kari asked.

"Unfortunately, they wouldn't be able to help much. We have no proof, just a couple stripped bolts. Even Mike said that the police can't do anything except send a car over now and then during the night hours to keep an eye on things."

As they sat in silence, considering their options, the phone rang. Kari plucked it from its cradle on the wall. "Hello? Oh hi! . . . You found out *what?* Wow! Okay, yeah, he's right here." She handed the phone to Eric. "It's Mike." He took the phone from Kari.

"What's up, Dick Tracy?"

"Funny. Real funny. Lots, actually. I think we might finally be getting somewhere." Mike sounded calm, but Eric picked up an undercurrent of excitement in his voice. "I found an old story in the *Tribune* that may or may not have something to do with the wreck. But first, tell me: is there any evidence there was a fire aboard the *Brittany*?"

Eric thought only a moment. "No. Not that we've seen so far," he said. "But a portion of her starboard side is buried in the sand, and we haven't managed to get inside of her yet."

"Well, I found an article in the *Tribune* about a strange fire in Lake Huron. It was back in 1859, southeast of Bois Blanc Island. That's about the area of the wreck, isn't it?" Eric answered that it was, and Mike continued. "And 1859 is the year that Merman purchased the *Aurora* and the year her history seems to stop. It might not have anything to do with the wreck at all."

"You think it might have been a burning ship?" asked Eric curiously.

"The people who saw it described it as a bright fire on the water or in the water at night. They say it burned for about ten minutes before going out. At the time there were no reports of a ship foundering or going missing. One guy reported seeing two ships in that area at nightfall, shortly before the fire was sighted, but there wasn't anything more on that, either. I guess we're at a dead end with that one. I was hoping that maybe you'd tell me that you saw the indications of a fire aboard the shipwreck."

"Let's not close the book on that idea yet," Eric said. "It looks like we might have the opportunity to get a closer look at her again tonight. We're going to make another dive this evening if the weather eases up. Dave Shandler offered to let us use his boat. Want to come?"

"No, thanks," Mike said, declining with obvious reluctance. "I'd love to tag along, but Evelyn and I have plans for tonight. Thanks for asking. Sure would be fun." He was about to hang up when he remembered the phone call he'd made from the *Big Boy* restaurant. "Oh, I almost forgot. I called a friend of mine that still works for the department in Detroit. Vic Aronson. I asked him to trace Merman, or more specifically, Merman's descendants. Maybe they'll know something about the family history. But don't get too excited. It's only a long shot, and Vic's pretty busy."

"Right now, long shots are about all we've got. Let me know what he finds out." Eric thanked him for all his work and hung up.

From the kitchen he heard Kari turn on the shower, and the radio in the bathroom crackled to life. Eric stepped out the sliding glass door, walked across the grass to the river, and stood on the empty dock, staring down into the green-blue waters.

Who in the hell did it? Right in our own damn yard? The more he thought about it, the angrier he became. *Well, whoever you are, you aren't going to get away with it*, he vowed. Eric finished his drink, dumped the remaining ice into the river, and walked back up to the house.

chapter 118

When Jimmy awoke, the first thing he noticed was that Sharon was gone. He looked groggily at the clock. It was 12:20 . . . or 12:50. He couldn't tell. He rubbed his eyes and focused on the glowing red letters. *12:50.* He lay in bed staring at the ceiling. The pain in his leg seemed to have at least temporarily been banished by the Percodans.

He lay in bed a few more minutes before dragging himself to the bathroom. As soon as he stood up, his leg began to throb as the blood rushed to his lower extremities. He winced in pain.

Holy shit. This is a fucking doosey.

He opened the bottle of Percodans, poured three of the white tablets into his hand, thought for a moment, then returned the pills to the bottle. The Percodans made him drowsy and slow and he didn't like that feeling. He had a better idea.

He fumbled through his black leather shaving kit and found the tiny brown vial that he kept filled with cocaine. It was almost empty. *Shit*, he thought. *Not even enough for one good line,*

He tapped the small glass bottle on the sink, as if in doing so more powder would miraculously appear in the bottom of the little jar. None did. There was maybe enough to put on his gums, if he really stretched it. Disgusted, he tossed the tiny brown bottle back into his kit, then lifted his leg and placed it on the counter of the motel bathroom. Carefully, he peeled away the bandages that extended from his ankle to his knee, exposing his wound to the open air. The cuts and scrapes, now cleaned, were not as bad as he had thought. Only one laceration had been deep enough to require stitches. It was red and purple and swollen, and the wiry black stitches wrapped around his shin to his calf like a railroad track. Jimmy replaced the bandages, took a leak, and returned to the bed.

Where in the hell did she go? And why did she come up here anyway? The more he thought about Sharon, the more enraged he became. *Sometimes I just wish she would—*

The phone rang. He picked it up and lay back on the bed as he answered, closing his eyes. "Hello." His voice was tired. "Yeah. It's fine." Nods toward his leg. "Some stitches, no big deal." He paused a moment, listening. "All right. I'll meet you over at *Charlies*." Phillip had said that the weather looked like it was going to break and they were probably going to make another dive this evening.

Jimmy got dressed slowly, carefully sliding his jeans over the bandages. He grabbed the bottle of Percodans from the bathroom, just in case. If the pain got really bad, he would take a few. His leg still ached and he walked with a limp, but he had refused the crutches at the hospital. There was no way in hell he was walking around *anywhere* with those things needled under his arms.

He left the motel room, closed the door, and then stopped. *Sharon*, he thought. *She'll probably be back soon.* Normally, he would have just said *screw it* and left. But this time, pulled the plastic key card from his pocket, unlocked the door and went back inside. *I don't need her to come looking for me.* He scribbled a hasty note on the motel stationary and left it on the dresser table.

chapter 119

Don looked at the new dreamcatcher hanging in the cabin's kitchen window. He had purchased the one that had most resembled the one he had broken. He'd also wanted to buy the dreamcatcher that the Indian woman had showed him, the *special* dreamcatcher, but she told him that it was not for sale.

She *gave* it to him.

He held the dull-colored, unassuming-looking dream-catcher in his hand, contemplating where to hang it. *When did I start believing in this stuff?* he wondered with a grin of amusement.

Through the window he saw Duane in his trademark dirty blue coveralls and a white T-shirt. He was replacing the door hinges of an old shed that sat near the water's edge. Duane had just about every imaginable hand tool known to man stuffed into his pockets, and his faded blue denim bulged unnaturally from almost every portion of his body. He was so caught up in removing the door from its hinges that he hadn't seen the Caravan pull up in the gravel driveway, nor did he see Don as he walked across the grass and entered the cottage. Which was just as well. Don didn't feel like getting roped into a drawn out conversation at the moment. After looking about the tiny cabin for a suitable spot to hang his own personal dreamcatcher, Don decided that on the wall above his bed would be as good of a place as any. He searched the drawer next to the sink, looking for some tape or maybe a thumbtack. The drawer was stuffed full of handy items: candles, a book of matches, two pencils, a pen, a sewing kit that was missing needles, a small pad of paper, a transparent green Cricket lighter, a county map, an empty box of paper clips, a 1992 Cheboygan County phonebook, half-full metal container of Band-Aids—but no tape or thumbtacks. *Well, Duane will have some. Probably got the kitchen sink stuffed somewhere in those pockets of his.*

He looked out the window. Duane was nowhere in sight. The door of the shed was open, slowly swaying in the wind, partially removed and hanging only by one set of hinges at the top. The wind forced the door back and forth, and a gust whipped it against the side of the shed, almost ripping it from the single rusting hinge. Then, as Don watched in amazement, from behind the shed, a hammer took flight, arching up and then curving down, the stainless steel head plummeting into the grass. Don's eyes followed the hammer as it sailed through the air, hearing in his mind the dull *thud* as the heavy tool struck the ground. The handle stood straight up for a moment, then tumbled over, disappearing amidst the thick blades of grass.

Christopher Knight

What the hell? Don thought as Duane suddenly exploded from the far side of the shed, a blur of flailing legs and arms. Tools were falling out of his pockets as he swung his arms wildly, swatting his face and spinning around and around. He hopped up and down as if possessed by some unseen force, tormented by an evil puppeteer that was jerking and pulling at his strings. Tools flew from his pockets as he spun and slammed into the side of the shed. Another violent lurch forward, and he smacked into the old door, tearing the hinge clean off the molding. The door crashed to the ground and Duane stumbled over it, falling to the grass. He bounded back up immediately, still swinging his arms crazily about.

Don was already out the door and running across the lawn towards him. As he drew closer, Duane's strange actions suddenly made sense.

Wasps.

There were dozens of them, swooping and diving. They swarmed over Duane, viciously stinging his arms and neck. Then Don found himself under attack as well. *"Water!! Run into the water!!"* Don shouted, not sure whether Duane had heard him or not. *"Run into the lake!! The lake!!"* Finally, Duane understood and made a cumbersome dash across the sand. His arms sailed and thrashed about his head as he plunged into the water. He fell down and splashed the water about him, then ducked his head beneath the surface. The water was too shallow to cover him entirely, but it was enough to make the wasps give up their chase. As Don waded into the lake to help Duane, a wasp stung him as well, and he also leapt headlong into the water. He popped his head back up and looked for more of the demonic dive-bombers, but saw none.

Christopher Knight

Duane was kneeling in the water, cursing. "Damn those sonofabitches! Damn'em all to hell!!" Welts had already begun to form on his face, forehead, and arms. Don stood up in the water and waded to Duane, offering his hand to help him up. A smashed wasp was stuck in Duane's hair above his ear. Don reached out and flicked it off and the dead insect tumbled into the water, to be scooped up by a hungry bluegill or perch or bass. Both of the men bowed their heads warily and ducked low as a trailing wasp buzzed close by, then sped off.

"Are you allergic to bee stings?" Don asked. Years ago, he'd had a friend, Geoff Harding, who had died from just two bee stings. They had been playing and stumbled over a hornet's nest in the ground. Don had escaped getting stung, but the two that had gotten to Geoff were enough. Within minutes of being stung, Geoff's eight-year old body had billowed to the size of a beach ball, and he had collapsed and died on Don's front lawn, to the shock and horror of the half-dozen friends that had gathered around.

"Damn things," Duane replied, running his fingers through his wet hair. "No, I'm not 'lergic to 'em, the bastards. I'm gonna fix 'em though." He nodded toward the shed, then looked down at himself. "You betcha. Damn, those bastards *hurt!*" Duane squelched out of the water, looking at the welts on his arms, feeling his face and head. "Damn things really got aholda me. Jeez these things hurt." He looked up at Don and pointed, "Looks like you got a coupla hits yerself." Don nodded as he reached and felt the swelling lump on his neck.

"Just one. No big deal."

"Well, come on up to the house with me and we'll getchas some lotion, if it's still around. Haven't been stung by a bee in years."

"Actually, they were wasps," Don corrected.

"Bees, wasps, hornets . . . they're all the same. Bees is bees. Lil' bastards. Didn't even know they had a nest in that shed. Guess it was better that I found 'em though, instead of a guest. I'd have a lawsuit quicker than jack-shit if a customer got stung like this here."

"Maybe you could sue yourself," Don said, grinning. Duane let out a guffaw that bellowed out over the yard. "Hahaha!! Sue myself!! Now *there's* a good one!! And you know . . . there'd be some lawyer crooked enough to take my money and try it!! Sheesh! I bet I could sue myself for a couple million!!"

Duane's wife met the pair at the door. This was the first Don had seen of her since his arrival. She was a plump woman, and wore an apron that covered most of her light blue flower-patterned dress. Her graying hair was drawn into a bun. Her jaw dropped in amazement and then concern as the two men drew nearer.

"Oh for goodness sakes! What happened to you?"

"Just a few bug bites, that's all," Duane assured her, and then turned and winked at Don. "Nothing that an ice-cold beer couldn't take care of. Oh . . . this is Don Garrity. He's in cabin seven." Duane's wife smiled politely and stepped aside as the two men entered the house.

Duane returned from the bathroom with a bottle of calamine lotion, already in the process of liberally applying the cream to the welts on his arms, face and neck. He rubbed the white grease into his skin, then handed the bottle to Don, who dabbed a small amount on the raised bubble of skin on his own neck. The sting still hurt and Don thought that Duane must be in a lot of pain with nearly a dozen stings himself. But if they hurt, he didn't let it show. At the moment, Duane seemed more concerned with finding an ice-cold beer than he was with wasp stings.

"Come on. There's some beer in the 'fridge." Before Don had a chance to refuse, Duane had plopped a sweaty-cold Busch Light in his hand. Duane disappeared to change his clothes and when he reappeared he was wearing white boxers and a white tank top.

"I think I'm going to run over to the cabin and grab some dry clothes, too," Don said. He slipped out the front door, returning a few minutes later in a pair of dry shorts and a blue turtleneck. He followed Duane through the living room with its dozens of guns lining the walls, then onto a screened-in patio where Duane took a seat in an old aluminum lawn chair, motioning for Don to do the same.

Don stood for a moment too long and Duane sensed his hesitation. "Go ahead, it ain't gonna break," he said. "Got these on sale for two bucks apiece at K-Mart in 1978. You don't find bargains like that around anymore." Don sat down cautiously amid squeals and squeaks, waiting for the wobbly aluminum to give way and send him crashing to the cement floor.

Duane's wife entered, handed them each a plate of brownies with almonds and a fine coating of sugar on top.

"Thank you . . . " Don suddenly realized that he didn't know her name.

"Sally," she introduced, smiling pleasantly. Blue eyes glowed. "But Duane calls me Sal, among a few other things," she said, good-humoredly.

Christopher Knight

"She's my Honey-Bunch O' Love, that's what she is. Been married for thirty years." Duane sipped his beer and wiped his mouth with his hand, then grinned smartly. "Can you believe that? In love with the same woman for thirty years. Of course, If Sal here ever finds out, she'll kill me." He laughed at his own joke, and Sally shook her head in tired exasperation.

"He heard that joke on an old *Tonight* show years ago—long before that new fella, Johnny Carson, took over." Sal was unaware that the Johnny days were over and the Jay days were trumpeting along nicely.

Sally soon left the two men to their beers and brownies. Duane was still chuckling to himself as he raised his arms and surveyed the swollen welts, which already seemed to be getting smaller. Don listened to Duane talk for over an hour, about his service in the military and about his son who was killed in a car accident on his sixteenth birthday. Duane talked about growing up in the north country and then moving to Saginaw where he and Sally had lived for two years. He said that they had finally decided to semi-retire and buy these cottages on Mullett Lake. Only he said that he worked harder now than he ever had before in his life. "Always somethin' that's gotta git done," he said. "And besides that, if there ain't somethin' that needs to be fixed, fix it so there is."

Finally, after guiding the entire conversation single-handedly, Duane looked at Don and asked, "Not much of a talker are ya, young fella? You know, you look kinda tired. Been gettin' enough sleep? What's her name?" He grinned, winked at Don, and explained. "I noticed ya dinn't make it home last night. Figured you found yerself a gal."

Christopher Knight

"No, nothing like that," Don replied, grinning. "I was over at a friends' place. We were up a little late and I ended up sacking out on the couch."

"Sure, son, sure," Duane said, unconvinced. "Well, you jes better make sure you're not bringin' her home here." He lowered his voice and gave a wary glance over his shoulder. "Oh, myself, I couldn't give a horse's petoot. But the Missus . . ." He pointed his thumb and glanced in the direction of the living room. "The Missus'll raise holy hell," he explained, his voice lowering even more. "Oh, she won't tell *you* about it. But she'll stew all day over here at the house, quotin' from the Good Book, smackin' around dishes and raisin' a ruckus. I don't need it. And if *I'm* gonna hear about it, *you're* gonna hear about it. Sal's kinda old-fashioned when it comes to things like that. Me? Well, I'm a little more tolerant a' you younger folks. I remember when . . . " and Duane plunged headlong into yet another story of his life that segued into another, and then another. Don was unable to get in more than an occasional 'hmmph' or 'hmmm' and once he managed to get in an entire 'I'll be darned' before Duane started up again. No matter. Don liked him. Duane was honest and told it like it was. He was Fred Sanford, the Rifleman, and Archie Bunker all rolled into one.

"Oh. Almost forgot," Duane said. "The wife an' me'll be headin' outta town for a couple days, startin' tomorrow. I'm going to leave you a phone number of a friend of mine. You call him if anything needs fixin or somethin'. Course, I don't think you will, but just in case. Nephew is getting married, that son of a pup. Twenty-four years old." He took an enormous slug from his Busch Light and shook his head. "It's a damned shame. Too young. *Way* too young to be getting hitched like that. Only known the bride a couple months. Me an Sal, we got 'em a cheap toaster as a gift. Nine bucks. They got 'em up at Wal-Mart. No use in spendin' lotsa money when they'll prob'ly be splittin' up in a few weeks. Anyways, I'm gonna leave you this . . ."

Duane got up and returned a moment later with a small leather loop, the size of a bracelet. A dirty, bronze-colored key dangled from it. "Now, I wouldn't normally do this, but I plum fergot all about the weddin'. Gotta drive to Rockford, Illinois. Here. Key to the house." He handed the key to Don, who put it in his pocket. "Bob Wells . . . that's my backup maintenance feller . . . he's got one already. But you'll need one to get into the house to use the phone. And if yer needin' to make any personal calls yerself, you go right ahead, but write 'em down on a slip of paper and leave it near the phone, so we can add it to your bill. Damn phone company charges four cents every time we make a local call. Thieves, is what they are. Robbery plain and simple."

"Thanks," Don answered, touched by the gesture of trust. "But I'm sure that I won't need it."

"Prob'ly not, prob'ly not, but just in case you do. Bob's number is on the wall above the phone in the kitchen. Lives over in Topinabee onna other side of the lake. And don't lose that key. Besides Bob's key, it's the only spare we got."

Finally, after another Busch Light and more than a few of Sally's brownies, Don was able to slip away back to the cabin. Duane followed him out into the yard to retrieve his tools that had scattered from his person during his tumultuous dash to the lake. He picked them up cautiously, looking over his shoulder as if a wasp might attack him at any moment. He told Don he was going to wait until the evening when the insects were sleeping and then spray the wasp nest with Raid. Don returned to the small cottage and watched as Duane picked up the shed door that had been ripped from its frame and propped it against the shed.

Three o'clock. The sun poked through the clouds on and off in a desultory fashion, but the wind continued to blow and it still looked like it might rain. Don lay on the small bed and read until he fell asleep.

chapter 120

The rain is falling steadily and it is still dark when Daniel arrives on deck. Captain LaChance is at the helm. Daniel is certain that they must be getting close to the Straits and Mackinac Island by now. The cold drizzle runs down Daniel's face and creeps uncomfortably down his collar. He turns and sees the dark figure of Jack Malloy on the deck. Instantly, he remembers the odd encounter last night, the cold hand grasping his face, the glare in Jack's eyes in the candlelight. Jack turns, and begins walking toward him.

"Mornin' Daniel," Malloy says, as he passes the two men. He nods to LaChance who returns the gesture without a word. "Daniel, can you give me a hand over here?" Jack's voice is pleasant and Daniel follows him to begin his morning's work. Jack is his old self and as they work, he tells Daniel stories of his travels and explorations of lands far away.

Often throughout the day, Daniel wrestles with his conscience.

A thought surfaces, a pang of guilt, and he pushes it away, only to have it return moments later. He tells himself that it is too late, that he has already made his decision. Two thousand dollars, he reminds himself. But not even the thought of all that money can erase his betrayal of Captain LaChance, Jack, and the passengers. He dreads facing Jack and Captain LaChance as a traitor and a mutineer. Neither is Daniel so sure anymore that he is willing to become a fugitive so early in life. For the first time, Daniel admits to himself that he might have made a mistake.

The rain ends early in the evening and the wind diminishes to a mild breeze. Daniel is below deck when he hears Jack call out. "Captain! There's a ship southeast of Bois Blanc Island. Someone is signaling for help."

When Daniel arrives on deck, Jack is standing at the bow of the ship, gazing through a telescope. About a mile off the Brittany's bow, Daniel can make out a dark blotch on the horizon. The ship's sails were down and it appeared to be dead in the water.

His stomach twists and aches. His heart slams in his chest. This is it, he thinks. They are probably going to trick the Captain into helping them, and then rob the ship of its cargo.

LaChance joins Jack at the bow, and Malloy hands him the telescope. The Captain holds the scope to his eye for a moment, then puts it down and talks with Jack. From where Daniel is, he can't hear what is being said, but it appears that Captain LaChance has made the decision to offer assistance. He returns to the helm and altered course for the crippled ship.

Daniel feels sick. He wants to warn them, wants to tell them that it is a trick and that the ship isn't in trouble at all, that they are going to steal the . . . the . . .whatever it is below deck.

He walks to the bow and watches as they approach the ship in the distance. The tiny figures on deck grow as the Brittany draws closer. It will be dark soon, but the vessels would meet before night fell.

"Looks like she's got a problem," Jack says, suddenly appearing at Daniel's side. "Don't look like she's sinkin' though." Daniel remains silent. He notices for the first time that his hands are trembling and his ears are warm. Whenever he is nervous or scared his ears turn as red as summer strawberries. Daniel backs up a little so that Jack wouldn't see them.

But Jack doesn't even look at Daniel. Instead he lifts the telescope again and watches the ship in the distance. He holds the scope to his eye for a long time and then lowers it, not removing his gaze from the ship. "Well, it don't appear to be anything serious." He hands the telescope to Daniel. "Holler if anything changes. It'll take us another twenty minutes to get there." He walks away, leaving Daniel alone at the bow, staring blankly at the ship.

Daniel's thoughts race and his head spins. He thinks of Captain LaChance, how kind he has been to Daniel, and of fun-loving Jack, who is never at a loss for a good story. Daniel has betrayed them for two thousand dollars. He has sold out his new friends to some men that he hardly knows. But it is too late now. The deed is almost as good as done.

Although they are getting closer to the ship, it is getting harder to see it in the encroaching dusk. A lantern is lit in the distance, and then another. For lack of anything else to do, Daniel also finds a lantern and lit it, setting it next to him at the bow. Within moments, a moth swarms at the bright glass, begging to be closer to the tiny yellow flare glowing within. Tink. Tink-tink. The moth batters the glass again and again, mimicking Daniel's own drumming heart.

Christopher Knight

Tink.   Tink-tink. Tink.   Tink.   Like a moth to the flame, the Brittany edges closer to the unknown vessel.   Daniel wants to shout, to scream that the money no longer matters.   He wants to run and hide.   But it is too late.   Much, much too late.

Tink.   Tink.   Tink-tink.   Like a moth to the flame.

chapter 121

At six o'clock, Eric Randall decided that the wind had died down enough. He jumped in the Blazer and sped down to Gordon Turner Park. The waves were about two feet. *Hot shit,* he thought excitedly. *Looks like we're gonna dive tonight after all.*

At six o'clock, Ed Belmont stepped out of *Goodtime Charlie's* and looked around. The clouds had moved east and the trees no longer bent in the breeze. He went back into the bar and laid a twenty on the table in front of Phillip and Jimmy. "Let's dive," he said, and the three walked out of the bar, piled into Phillip's Dakota, and headed for the marina.

Ed, Jimmy, and Phillip were preparing the boat to head out to the dive site when Phillip saw the black Dodge Caravan pull into the lot and park. He didn't think much of it until the three passengers emerged.

Well, looky here, he thought. Phillip stopped what he was doing and watches the three figures on the other side of the marina. He tapped Ed on the shoulder and pointed, "Don't look now, but *you-know-who* just pulled up."

Ed turned slowly, glancing up nonchalantly. When he saw the three forms near the van, he dropped the line he was holding and reached for a cigarette. Jimmy emerged from the cabin and stood casually at the bow.

"Well, well . . . just what are you up to, Mr. Randall?" Ed sneered quietly. He watched the three as they began to unload equipment from the van. "Those bastards are goin' diving. That's what they're doing. They gotta be borrowin' somebody's boat."

"Shit," Phillip spat beneath his breath. He turned to Ed. "Now what?"

"We watch," Ed said coldly. "We just watch and see what their game plan is." The gray hair above Ed's ears swirled in the slight breeze.

"But what if they—" Phillip started to ask.

"Look at what they got," Ed interrupted sharply. "They ain't got anything for recovery. They're gonna go out, make one dive, and come back in. What are they going to get in one dive?" Ed's voice was calm, but it was obvious that he was much more pissed off than he was letting on. Phillip could almost see the anger boiling within Ed's bloated frame.

"They're going to get information, that's what they're going to get," Jimmy snapped. "They're going to see holes ripped in the hull and a portion of the wreck caved in. The wreck looks a lot different than the last time they saw it. Half of that fucking thing came down on top of me."

The three men busied themselves, staying out of sight in the Bayliner as Eric walked toward their boat. Randall seemed to be searching for something, as if he was unsure of where he was going. He passed within a few feet of the three men and stopped at the slip adjacent to the white Bayliner. An old trawler, painted a dark dirty blue, sat low in the water. Black and white seagull droppings stained the glass windshield and the top of the cabin. Dave was right, Eric thought, giving the weathered vessel a long look over. He hasn't used her much this year. Eric waved his arm toward the shore. "Over here," he shouted to Don and Kari. They looked in his direction and walked out on the dock towards him, each carrying an armload of wetsuits, masks, fins, and other dive equipment. Eric and Don returned to the van, each returning to Dave Shandler's boat with their arms filled with camera and video apparatus.

Ed Belmont, seeing the underwater video equipment, was getting more and more agitated by the moment. Those sons of bitches. They know. And it's only going to be a matter of time before they start hauling shit up. He watched as the last of the dive gear was loaded on the boat in the slip next to them.

"So what do we do?" Phillip asked quietly.

"I told you" Ed replied. "We wait. They'll be back soon enough. And we'll be right here when they come back. Then, we dive." Ed opened up a new pack of cigarettes and put one to his lips. Jimmy stewed quietly in the corner, his wounded leg stretched out.

In the slip right next to the Bayliner, Eric turned the key and the trawler's engine coughed and sputtered, belching a cloud of thick blue smoke out behind the boat. In another moment the engine roared strongly to life, and after one more burst of oily smoke, the engine idled and smoothed out. A breeze blew the wisping fog back towards the Bayliner and it drifted into the cabin. Eric could see the shapes and outlines of people in the boat and he waved over to them. "Sorry about that," he apologized. A figure in the Bayliner waved back. Eric, Kari and Don finished loading the gear and soon the trawler and its three occupants were gone, heading northeast towards Bois Blanc Island.

chapter 122

Shoot, Mike thought. The first thing he had done after walking in the door was to check the answering machine, but the little red light was not blinking. He knew it wasn't reasonable to expect Vic Aronson to call back so soon with any information, even though computers had sped the process up considerably. Years ago, Vic had had to physically search through filing cabinets to locate the information. Often, he had to go to the library or the courthouse and it sometimes took him days, even weeks, to locate the people he was looking for. Now, with computers and the internet, he could locate enormous amounts of information in a matter of seconds.

Mike trolled around the house at loose ends. He even tried, briefly, to do some writing. The result was the same as before—nothing. "To heck with this," he said aloud to himself, and went downstairs and dialed Vic's direct line at the department.

The phone rang nearly a dozen times and Mike was just about to hang up when it was answered by Vic's blunt voice. "Yello."

"Vic. Mike Felsing calling." He could hear people talking in the background, the tap of fingers on computer keyboards, and phones ringing. Suddenly, Mike was homesick for a moment. Other memories, more unpleasant ones, flashed quickly by, and his brief homesickness faded.

"Whaddya need." The voice would have sounded annoyed, even hostile, to anyone who didn't know Vic. But Mike had worked with him long enough to know that the gruff voice didn't reflect his personality.

"I was just wondering if you were able to find anything out about Merman's family. I know I just asked you this morning and all, but—"

Vic stopped him before he went further. "Haven't you checked your e-mail this afternoon?"

"My e-mail?" Mike asked absently. He'd never even thought about it. He had set up an e-mail box over two months ago when he had gotten onto the internet, but never got any mail from anyone, mostly due to the fact that he told very few people that he had an address.   Most of the mail he *did* receive was advertisements, solicitations for mortgages, work-at-home-and-get-rich-quick scams, offers for low-rate credit cards, and the like. "How did you know—"

"We have it on file. You included it when you filled out some of your updated insurance papers. We keep *all* that shit on file. You know that."

"E-mail. I hadn't thought of that. I don't get much e-mail," Mike admitted sheepishly.

"Well, you got a bunch now. Eight or ten pages of the family tree of Richard Merman. Call me if you don't find what you need." The two men chatted for just a few more minutes, then Mike thanked him and hung up the phone.

E-mail, he thought again, shaking his head as he went back upstairs.

chapter 123

The cool air gnawed at Don's face as he stood at the bow of Dave
Shandler's trawler. As they motored out to the dive site, Eric and
Don had cleaned some of the seagull droppings from the deck and
top of the cabin. Thirty minutes later, the problems of the last few
days vanished, as Eric and Kari once again swept their lights over
the wreck of the *Brittany*. The mini-sub had followed them down,
Don carefully guiding it from the surface in the wake of the diver's
bubbles.

Eric, unaware that he and Kari had become separated by the
current, was startled by a light that flashed two times. He and Kari
had long ago devised their own communication code under water.
One flash was to get attention. Two meant it was urgent. Three
was for an emergency—a signal that fortunately they had never had
to use. Now Kari was signaling him.

Urgent.

He swam toward the light to find Kari hovering in the water just off the port side bulwark. The mini-sub was just above them, and the bright light illuminated the deck and tossed eerie shadows over the ship. Kari pointed her light down along the port side of the hull. Eric could see the look of shock and disbelief through her mask. As he moved to her side, he discovered why.

The port side of the hull was literally in shambles. It looked like it had been ripped apart, chewed and gnashed by a bulldozer, chewed a little more, and been spit back out, slashed and torn. *What in the hell?* Eric thought, gliding closer to the ship. Pieces of the wreck lay on the bottom, scattered below what was left of the hull. Kari looked at him again, bewildered.

Eric tapped her shoulder, pointing to the mini-sub that hovered a few feet above them. Don had also discovered the damage and now he maneuvered the underwater camera to get a better look at the destruction. The brilliant, dome-shaped light on the front of the mini-sub lit up a large part of the port side of the ship. It looked as if someone had set off explosives and ripped holes in her hull.

This can't be, Kari thought. *This just can't be.* But she knew that it could. Treasure hunters, hell-bent on finding their riches, were capable of this and a lot more in just a very short time. The knife in the video indicated that someone else had also discovered the wreck, but to deface . . . no, to *demolish* . . . a major portion of the wreck was just too incredible to believe. On deck, Don had instructed them to *'give us your best National Geographic looks-of-wonder-and-amazement, with a lot of pointing and somber reflection. That's the shit that sells.'* Under the circumstances, it wasn't too difficult of a request.

Eric and Kari poked their heads inside a hole to get a better look, but so much of the ship had collapsed in on itself that it was impossible to make out anything but broken, rotted timbers. Thoughts raced through Eric's head. Someone else *had* discovered the wreck and they had mangled nearly a third of her.

Suddenly, he remembered the knife and realized that it might provide a clue as to who had done this to the vessel. Occasionally, divers would engrave their name or initials on their dive knives. If he could find the knife . . . .

He grabbed Kari's arm, pulled out his own knife and pointed toward the other side of the wreck. She understood. Eric sheathed his knife and both ascended once again, along the tattered hull and over the deck to the location where they had seen the knife on the video. The mini-sub followed at a distance, aiding in the search with a single, intense light. The knife had stuck out like a sore thumb before, but the currents must have moved some silt and sand around by now.

Eric and Kari swept the sand with their flashlights, hoping to catch a glimpse of the shiny stainless steel blade. Seconds ticked by.

Nothing.

Kari glided to the bottom and began to wave her gloved hands slowly and deliberately, back and forth, just over the bottom, creating swirls of silt and sand, being careful not to kick up too much at one time. Eric followed suit under the watchful eye of the mini-sub that hovered a few yards above them.

From the surface, Don Garrity watched through the monitor. He, too, was aghast and infuriated by the level of destruction. He watched in impotent rage as Kari and Eric searched for the knife, one hundred sixty feet below him. He knew that Eric was right on top of where the knife should have been. *But it's not there,* Don thought. *Whoever lost the knife came back. They came back and found it. After all, dive knives are expensive. Nobody would want to lose one—or, in this case, leave it laying around for someone else to find.*

Suddenly, fear surged through him and his hands began to shake. *What would happen if my brain decides to hitchhike to the land of Oz? What if I pass out cold again and fall overboard?* He looked around. A blue-and yellow life jacket lay in the corner. *Nah. That's not really necessary, is it?* After a moment of hesitation, he put the life vest on and snapped the buckles in front. *Well, at least if I fall overboard and drown, they'll be able to find Don the Blue-and-Yellow Bobber instead of Don the Khaki-and-Patagonia Anchor.*

He was lost in thought when Kari's frantic waving on the monitor brought him back into the galaxy, back to earth, the United States, in a state called Michigan, drifting in the water a few miles from shore. *The knife. She must have found the knife.*

He carefully guided the mini-sub lower, zooming in on Kari as she knelt on the chalky bottom, just a few feet from the *Brittany*. Silvery bubbles spun and whirled, disappearing as they began their ascent. Eric was beside her and both were intently studying the new discovery. *True-to-life National Geographic looks of wonder and amazement,* Don thought. He brought the mini-sub closer and zoomed in on what now lay in Eric's hands. Eric held it up for the camera and Don stared in amazement at the unbelievable image that filled the screen.

A solid gold crucifix.

chapter 124

The Brittany slowly edges closer to the dark ship that lay dead in the water. Daniel can see figures moving about on the other ship and he hears a voice shouting out instructions. Then he hears a splash. Bloop . . . swish. A pause. Bloop . . . swish. Another pause. A rowboat. The oars plop lazily into the lake, followed by the telltale sound of wood pushing water, and then silence as the oars exit the water and stroke back. Bloop . . . swish. Pause. Bloop . . . swish. Pause. Daniel's heart pounds, threatening to leap from his chest, and with every breath he feels like he is trying to drag a wet blanket into his lungs. His muscles feel weak and his bones ready to snap under his weight. He desperately wants to wake up from this nightmare. Suddenly, his stomach rises uncontrollably into his throat, and he leans over the rail and vomits, weeping silently. As he wipes his mouth with the back of his hand the metronomic rhythm of the oars of the approaching boat beat at *him like dark wings.*

Bloop . . . swish. He searches the dark waters for a shape or a movement. Bloop . . . swish. The rowboat isn't far off now, and the other ship is not more than one hundred feet away. Even in the darkness, the giant black shape of the vessel is visible, its sharp masts spearing up into the night sky.

Bloop . . . swish.

Daniel can see the dark silhouette of a small rowboat not more than thirty feet from the Brittany. He can't tell if there are two or three men aboard the small craft.

Jack has let out the sails and the Brittany is almost at a complete standstill.

Bloop . . . swish. The rowboat and its occupants inch closer. Daniel makes a giant effort to pull himself together. Deep breaths, relax, easy, slow . . . .

Bloop . . . swish. Bloop . . . .

The sound of a gentle bump indicates that the rowboat has reached the Brittany. Captain LaChance approaches the starboard gunwale and holds a lantern over the side, gazing into the shadowy darkness below. In another moment, Jack has secured the rope ladder and heaves it over the side of the ship, and it tumbles with a series of thuds to the passengers in the rowboat.

Suddenly, Daniel can't stand it anymore. His eyes well with tears and his face flushes with heat. His ears tingle. His knees wobble and every part of his body shakes, partly from fear and partly from shame. He will not be part of this. He isn't going to allow a band of ruthless men to take something that doesn't belong to them. He hopes that it is not too late.

"Stop! Stop!" he screams as he bolts toward Captain LaChance. "Pull the ladder back up! It's a trap! It's a TRAP!"

Captain LaChance and Jack look stunned. "It's a trick!! They don't need help! They just want to steal the chest!! It's a trap!!"

Daniel reaches the captain, grabs the ladder and begins to pull it up. He can see the grim faces of three men in the rowboat below, leering up at him in the glow of the lantern. As Daniel pulls at the rope one of the men below grabs the other end and holds it fast. Captain LaChance remains calm, apparently unmoved by this strange turn of events.

"Explain your problem or state your business, please," LaChance says sternly to the men in the rowboat. The reflection of his lantern dances on the inky waters and illuminates the faces of the three men.

The moth has found its way through a crack in the lantern glass, realizing its own mistake much too late. It flies erratically inside the confines of the invisible walls, smashing from one side to the other, then back again, finally and fatally coming too close to the blazing yellow core. The tiny insect erupts in a flash of flame that fades as quickly as it had appeared, a self-contained shooting star. The orange glowing ember falls to the bottom of the lantern, dims, and vanishes in an evanescent wisp of smoke. LaChance waits patiently for an answer, and the reply comes at six hundred fifty feet per second. Daniel sees the movement, the subtle draw, but he is powerless to do anything as Jack Malloy backs up a few steps and pulls a revolver from beneath his coat. In less than a second he levels the weapon . . . and shoots Captain Nathan LaChance right between the eyes.

Christopher Knight

chapter 125

"I've never ever heard of a Great Lakes ship carrying anything like this," Kari said in amazement. The three were seated in the cabin of Dave Shandler's trawler. Kari and Eric had ascended after finding the crucifix, which now lay on a table in front of them. They huddled over the gleaming object, transfixed. Eric had removed some of the sediment, revealing not only gold but precious stones, eight in all, set in the cross. The three were silent as they contemplated their find.

"It's possible that this had belonged to one of the passengers or crew," Eric said.

"Do you really believe that?" Don asked, glancing up and adjusting his glasses. "People don't carry around stuff like this. A necklace, maybe, or a bracelet. But not a solid gold tire iron."

"Come on, Don," Eric replied, shaking his head. "What are the chances of a treasure ship sinking in the Great Lakes? What are the chances of it even being here in the first place?" He picked up the artifact and looked at it in disbelief.

"It does seem hard to believe," Don mused. "But think about it. It would answer a lot of questions. Like why someone changed the name of the ship and made no record of it. It's probably why those people on board were killed. There's no other logical answer. Someone wanted the treasure on board the *Brittany* bad enough to torture and kill those people."

Eric reached into the cooler and pulled out three beers, handing one to Kari and Don. The sun had set and the boat was still anchored in the Channel over the dive site.

"It would also explain the knife," Don continued, after they had sat another few moments in silence. "It's obvious that someone else knows what's down there. Somebody lost that knife and returned and picked it up. They missed the crucifix because it was buried."

"By the looks of the wreck, if there had been any more treasure aboard, somebody's already found it. It's probably all gone by now," Kari said.

"I don't think so," Don said, stroking his beard. "The wreck was in perfect shape when you found it. I think that someone found it about the same time you did. There hasn't been enough time to salvage the entire wreck."

"If there's more of this down there," Kari said, picking up the crucifix, "it explains why someone sabotaged the *John Galt*. No wonder they don't want anybody diving on her. If someone is plundering the wreck, they'll be keeping silent about it. They've already vandalized one boat. What's next?"

They sat quietly for another few minutes before heading back to Cheboygan. As Eric stood at the helm, Kari's words echoed through his mind. *What's next?*

chapter 126

It was eleven p.m. when Phillip saw the lights of a boat approaching in the distance. A few late boaters—mostly fisherman—had returned during the last hour. But this time the low droning *chugugugugug* of the old engine announced that the divers were returning.

Jimmy was napping in the cabin below, and Phillip banged on the deck to wake him up without taking his eyes from the oncoming lights. Ed had passed the time sitting on the dock in a lawn chair, his huge belly hanging over the armrests. He'd chain-smoked nearly a dozen Camels, flicking the tiny butt into the water and instantly digging another cigarette from the pack.

The trawler slowed and turned into the marina. Ed struggled out of his chair and he and Phillip ducked into the cabin of the Bayliner, shutting off the lights. The three watched intently from the shadows of the cabin as the trawler chugged into the slip next to them. Its engine coughed wearily several times and finally stopped. A dim light burned inside the weathered cabin.

"Open the window a little more," Ed whispered, drooling smoke. "I can't hear them." Phillip leaned over and carefully slid the window open a few more inches. Inaudible voices mumbled from within the old trawler. Jimmy began to speak but Ed raised an impatient hand to quiet him. A woman came out of the cabin and leapt onto the dock. *It's the bitch*, Ed thought. *It's Old Lady Randall. Nice ass.*

Kari secured the boat, then hopped back aboard just as Eric and Don emerged from the cabin. Eric spoke in a hushed tone and three pairs of ears strained mightily to hear him from the adjacent slip. "This single piece has gotta be worth thousands," he said. "The historical value alone, combined with the weight of the gold and the set stones . . ." His voice faded as Eric and Don walked up the dock to move the van closer to the water. Kari stayed behind on the boat, sipping the last of her beer and staring up at the stars. She turned the object over and over in her hands, cautiously, as if it were fine china or delicate glass.

In the dark Bayliner, not ten feet from where Kari stood, Ed's blood boiled. His veins heaved with every strenuous beat of his heart. Beads of sweat formed on his neck and the collar of his shirt displayed a dark ring. *"Shit,"* he hissed under his breath. Every profanity in every combination rang through his head, pleading to come out, to escape, to rush rampant and uncontrolled, echoing out over the marina for everyone to hear. Rage, anger, resentment . . . the very core of Ed Belmont was rising to the surface and seeping through his skin. His hands were clenched so tightly his knuckles were white and he unclasped his hands, wiping the sweat from his palms on his shirt.

Son of a bitch. Son of a bitch. The words burned from his pores, raging over every inch of his body. *Son of a bitch!*

Two feet away, Phillip restrained his own indignation. He was pissed but confused. *They had been so close . . . so damn close*, he thought. Suddenly unbidden, he remembered what his older brother had always told him when he fell short or didn't quite measure up: "Close, but no cigar, Phil." When the two played basketball together, Phillip never won. His brother had been only two years older than Phillip, but was quite a bit taller. Every time Phillip went to shoot, his brother knocked the ball back into his face. His brother let him get a few points now and then and Phillip even came close to winning once in a while. "Close only counts in horseshoes, hand grenades, shit fights, and nuclear bombs, Phil," his brother had said. "Close . . . but no cigar." When his brother died of a massive hemorrhage from injuries suffered in a motorcycle accident, the doctor told them that they had been *close* to saving him but the internal bleeding was too bad and could not be stopped. *Sorry, Doc*, Phillip thought. *Close only counts in horseshoes, hand grenades, shit fights*, and nuclear bombs. *Close, Doc . . . but no cigar.*

Jimmy sat in the shadows of the cabin glaring at the woman as if his gaze alone could inflict great injury. He leaned slowly forward and reached into the black leather bag he had stuffed beneath the seat cushion and found the cold steel of his gun. Without taking it out, he gently ran his fingers along the barrel and back to the chamber in a listless, macabre foreplay. He felt the stiffness of the hammer, upright and erect. His fingers found the pleading tongue of the trigger and he wrapped one finger around it, gently and warmly, in a lover's impassioned embrace. He gripped it tighter, squeezing, squeezing. His finger licked the trigger as he stared at the shadow of the woman on the boat next to them. *Do you know how close you are to death right now, bitch? Do you have any idea?* He turned the gun over in the leather bag and held it in his palm, then grasped the handle again. He was ready to explode, ready to bring the gun to a climactic fury and unleash its seed in an erupting, fiery orgasm. His finger clenched the trigger. *You have no idea, chicky-poo. No idea at all.*

Footsteps alerted them that the two men were returning. "You hungry?" Eric asked Don. His voice was clear and audible in the cool night air.

"Yeah, I could eat," Don replied.

"We'll stop at *Pappas'* for a bite and a couple beers." Ed, Phillip, and Jimmy listened to the footsteps recede down the dock and waited until they heard the van start. Ed poked his head out of the cabin in time to see the taillights of the van flare as it pulled out of the marina and onto Huron Street. No one spoke, each privately seething in anger and frustration. Ed found his pack of cigarettes, rolled a cigarette between his fingers for a moment, then placed it to his lips. The obtrusive eruption of the match lit up the cabin for an instant until Ed shook the tiny torch with his hand, extinguishing the flame. The orange coal of the cigarette brightened as Ed inhaled and his whole body heaved as he exhaled.

Jimmy dipped into the refrigerator and opened a beer, not

extending an offer to the other two. Phillip sat unmoving. "What now?" he finally asked.

"What the fuck do you mean *'what now'?*" Ed spat. "We go get what belongs to us, that's what. Maybe we hadn't planned on a few of these things happening, but we should've known that it wasn't going to be a cakewalk at a Girl Scout fund-raiser. We tried to slow 'em down before and we underestimated them. Now they know what they've found. Fine. Let 'em keep it, whatever it is. It can't be much. They had no salvage equipment and the only thing they could have brought up is what they could have carried or put in a small bag. There's a shitload more from where that came from. Did you hear him bragging? Thousands, is what he said. Fine, let him have his 'thousands.' Hell, we oughta be thanking the assholes. They found a wreck that we've been trying to find for years." He took a drag of the cigarette, the smoke trickling from his lips and out his nostrils. "But now they've done their job. Thank you very much Mr. Randall and friends, we'll take over from here." His deep voice was quiet and controlled, the anger bubbling underneath now contained. He flipped the cigarette around in his fingers, watching the smoke slither away from the smoldering ember. He took another drag, inhaling deeply. "We just need a little time. So, if we can't slow them down," he breathed, "we just stop them. *Permanently.*"

chapter 127

Mike tried Eric and Kari's number for what seemed like the fiftieth time that night. *They must have gone diving after all,* he thought in frustration, tapping his fingers on the desk. After the fifth ring, the answering machine picked up, and Mike left his third message of the evening. He put the cordless phone down on the desk and then looked at his watch. Ten o'clock. *Just have to wait 'till tomorrow, I guess.*

Mike wasn't tired and after he had saved and printed the nine pages of e-mail he had received from Vic Aronson, he exited the program and opened up his word processing program. *Might as well try a little writing.* But once again the vast white desert lay before him and his hands rested on the keys, unmoving. The cursor seemed to shout at him from the white sea. He wrote a single sentence, stopped, deleted it, and began again. Start, stop, delete.

Start, stop, delete. No matter what he tried, his mind kept wandering; mainly to the newly-acquired information from Vic Aronson. His futile attempts at writing went on for nearly thirty minutes, until in utter frustration he exited out of the program and shut down the computer.

Nope. Not going to happen tonight I guess.

Mike stepped over to the window and opened it wider. He stood staring out over the calm waters of the lake for many minutes, lost in thought. His mind again drifted back to the e-mail Vic had sent him. He picked up the pile and read through them carefully again, stopping on the last page and reading the list of names over in his mind. "Well, that solves one question," he said aloud. He glanced at his watch. *Too late to call tonight, though. This is one call that will have to wait until morning.* He shut off the computer and joined Evelyn in bed. She was sleeping, and murmured something unintelligible as he slid next to her. The papers fluttered gently in the breeze from the window, their secrets patiently waiting for the dawn.

chapter 128

Phillip was sitting in the passenger seat of Ed's Ford Ranger, alternately watching the dark shape of the *John Galt* in the boatyard, Shandler's house next door, and the street, when he spotted the car approching. He ducked below the dash, banging his head painfully on the steering wheel as he did. He lay on the seat until he was sure the vehicle had passed, nursing his head and cursing. *Where in the hell is he?* he thought. Five minutes should have been plenty of time. *Come on, man . . . quit fartin' around.*

A police car approached on Main Street and he ducked down again, this time missing the steering wheel but hitting the armrest on the passenger door. The headlights of the police car swept the Ranger, filling the cab with blazing white light. As the light receded again to black, Phillip slowly raised his head. The police cruiser had passed. He again turned his attention toward the river, glancing at the glowing digital clock on the dash. There was no movement in the boatyard. *Come on, Ed.* Another glance at the clock. Ten minutes. It shouldn't take this long.

Hurry it up, Belmont. Hurry it up.

Ed, having completed his task, picked his way slowly through the boatyard. The grass was strewn with old, worn boat parts and, although the yard was flooded with moonlight, he still managed to stumble over several hidden obstacles. Once he slipped on the wet grass and went down heavily on one knee. Cursing under his breath, he waited immobile for several minutes for any indication from the adjacent house that he had been heard. There were none. He slipped quietly past the house, right beneath Shandler's bedroom.

That'll hold 'em for a while, he thought. *That just might solve our problem for good.*

Finally, Phillip saw his giant form walking down the driveway, hugging the bushes in a vain attempt to conceal himself.

"Piece of cake," he said arrogantly, climbing in to the driver's seat and starting the truck. "Piece of goddamn cake." He found his cigarettes on the dash and the book of matches on the seat, and lit one with a wide grin. "You gotta get what you can, while you can, as fast as you can, Phil ol' boy," he said, tossing the match out the window. "Let's get the fuck outta here."

The Ranger pulled out of the driveway into a deserted Main Street and headed away from downtown. Phillip sat quietly until Ed dropped him off at the marina where the Dakota was parked. Ed sped away into the night and Phillip leaned against the car a moment, looking out over the dozens of boats crowding the slips. *Six years*, he thought. *Six damned years and finally we're almost there.* He thought about the early days where their belief was all they had. The belief that a fortune was out there just waiting to be found, waiting for himself, Ed and Jimmy to discover her. Now the search was over. *Maybe Randall did do us a favor by finding the wreck*, he reflected. *We could have looked for another ten years and not found it. Thanks guys. Please accept tonight as a little token of our gratitude. Don't take it wrong, nothing personal.* He grinned and then shuddered in the brisk night air. As he started the car, Ed's words burned in his mind. *You gotta get what you can while you can, as fast as you can.*

chapter 129

When Sharon saw the Trans Am parked in the lot of the River Terrace she froze. *It looks like this is it*, she thought grimly. She had half-hoped he wouldn't be home yet and she could climb into bed and go to sleep. Jimmy could just drift in whenever and fell asleep next her. Then she could have dealt with this in the morning. *Maybe he's asleep*, she thought, but that possibility fled when she noted that the room light was on.

Sharon sat in the car for a moment trying to work up her courage. She was frightened, scared, and angry. She was angry at having to be so frightened. She wasn't at all unhappy that she was pregnant, in fact, she was more excited than she had ever been in her life. *Maybe Jimmy will be just as excited as I am and he'll finally settle down and not be gone for days at a time*, she dreamed. *Maybe*. She took a deep breath, opened the car door, and stepped out into the cool night air. *No time like the present, I guess. I'm gonna be starting to show soon anyway.*

The motel room door was unlocked and she gently pushed it open. Jimmy's clothes were piled in a heap at the foot of the bed and he had carelessly tossed his wallet and change onto the dresser. The shower was running in the bathroom. She felt relieved at buying even a few more moments to think. She looked around the room, trying to strategically plot where would be the best place to sit or stand. *Or hide,* she thought grimly. She opted for the lounge chair at the table near the window.

She could hear Jimmy whistling to himself, then the water was turned off and the clicks of the curtain rings and the gentle swish of the shower curtain opened and Jimmy stepped out. There followed the sound of the sliding and moving of objects on the bathroom counter and a short blast of water from the faucet. Jimmy clicked off the light and stepped out of the bathroom. He was wearing his sweats with no shirt, flexing his left arm as if it were sore. *Juice. Can't live without those damn steroids,* she thought.

He saw her immediately and he smiled his smug smile. Sharon felt her knees go weak and her courage fled. Then came back. Fled again. Off. On. Her bravery was being toyed with like a child playing with a faucet. On. Off. On. Off. On . . . .

Tell him, dammit. Tell him.

chapter 130

When Jimmy had walked in and found his room dark, he was hopeful. *Maybe the bitch went home*, he thought. But when he turned on the light and saw her suitcase still against the wall and her blue jeans on the bed, he knew he hadn't been that lucky. He figured that she had probably just gone to get something to eat. Hopefully, another day of being bored shitless and she'd figure that she's not welcome and go back home. *Just go back home, Sharon, and we'll all be happier. Me especially.*

Jimmy stripped and searched through his duffel bag for a vial of Tetranobol, a syringe, and a needle. He checked the vial of coke to make sure that it hadn't magically refilled itself while he was gone. It hadn't. He went into the bathroom, closed the door, and lifted his injured leg up and rested it over the sink. He removed the bandages carefully from his leg and stepped into the shower. The hot water felt good although the soap stung his cuts. He was feeling better. Things were finally beginning to go their way. *Wait 'til Randall finds out the surprise that's in store for him. I'd kill to be there to see his face,* he gloated.

He finished his shower, dried off, decided not to re-apply the bandages, and shot up the Tetranobol. He turned and twisted his torso to look at himself in the mirror. *Got to do some more work on my triceps. Gettin' kinda flimsy. And my shoulders, too.* He flexed. *Two hundred thirty pounds of twisted steel, that's what I am,* he thought with vain satisfaction.

He made a slight attempt at cleaning up the counter, but ended up shifting his toiletries to a more focused location. Picking up the empty vial of Tetranobol and the needle and syringe, he stuffed them in his leather bag. Sharon didn't say anything about the drugs, but he knew she didn't like it. He briefly wondered where she had gone, but found that he didn't really care. *What matters now is that we are on the verge of getting everything we've worked for during the past six years.*

He opened the bathroom door, killed the light, and stepped into the room.

Surprise.

chapter 131

Sharon. She was sitting quietly in the chair with a strange look on her face. He had hoped that he would be able to nod off to sleep without any conversation to interfere with his light-hearted mood. Now it was ruined. Worse, he could see that she wanted to talk. She did this about once a year. The old 'I'm-not-feeling-satisfied-with-this-relationship-and-we-need-to-talk' talk. He forced a smile and kissed her on the cheek.

"Hi," Sharon said. She tried to make it sound as casual as possible. Sharon held her breath and meditated upon a silent prayer. She looked at Jimmy, put on the brightest smile she could muster, and told him bluntly, as if relating that the furnace had broken or the TV wasn't working properly. "Jimmy . . . I'm pregnant."

There were no raised eyebrows, no ruffled forehead. No

flinches or gaping jaw. No wide eyes. Only a few seconds of hesitation while the entire scope of the matter came crashing down.

"Pregnant?" Jimmy muttered in disbelief. *Did she just say pregnant?* He had no desire to become a father, none whatsoever. Anger at her betrayal washed over him in a tidal wave of negative emotions. *A baby?* Images of a chubby infant toddling around in smelly diapers flooded his head. Echoes of nonstop crying and babbling reverberated in his ears. *A baby? A kid? No, that will never do. You're fucking kidding me, right?*

Jimmy looked at Sharon. She was studying his face, trying to get an idea, a hint, about what he was feeling. He felt her eyes searching his own, looking, intruding, trespassing in places where they shouldn't be. As if reading his thoughts, she took a deep breath and spoke again before he said anything. "I'm not getting an abortion. Not *again.*" Jimmy spoke, saying the exact same thing that every man since the beginning of time has said when he hears those words so unexpectedly. "Are you sure?"

"Yeah, I'm sure. Doctor Webber confirmed it last week."

Jimmy wasn't upset. He was much more than that. He was way beyond upset. He was pissed off in a way that he hadn't felt in a long time, if ever. *No, no, no. This fucks everything up. This was not supposed to happen. Not now. Not like this. Not when we're this close to salvaging the treasure.*

Then he did something that really frightened Sharon. She watched as he gathered all of his strength, every tiny bit he could muster in his Herculean frame—and he held it. He smiled and relaxed. Color returned to his cheeks. But underneath, Jimmy was boiling, his temper screaming to come out, to let fly and let all hell break loose. Sharon knew it. His anger was chained behind bars, screaming at the top of its lungs. *If you don't let me out, I'm gonna break the goddamn bars. Do you hear me? Let me out of here you no good shit-fer-brains idiot . . . ."* Charles Durand, long dead, tormented Jimmy from the depths of his mind, taunting and lashing, wailing and pawing at the cell that Jimmy usually kept closed and locked. With all of his force, all of his control, Jimmy held his father back. He pushed him aside. The hurricane force of fury raged on, but Jimmy found the eye, the eerie calm in the eye of the hurricane. Within it, the weather was tranquil and untroubled. In the eye, everything was okay.

He took Sharon in his arms and held her tenderly. He told her that he loved her, that this is what he'd always wanted, sweetheart. *Always.*

Now Sharon was genuinely terrified. For a moment she thought of leaving and running as far away from Jimmy as possible. This man was not Jimmy. In her arms was a man who cared, a man who shared her joy and excitement over this new life. He held her tightly and she held him back. She whispered that she loved him, and he told her that he loved her as well.

Was this really Jimmy?

Maybe everything will be all right after all, she thought wildly. Tears welled up in her eyes. Every emotional up and down that she had felt in the past few days sped by her again like a roller coaster, only now she was merely the innocent bystander, watching the speeding carts wheel by at break-neck speed, happy to let them go on their way without her. She would no longer be riding a roller coaster. She had two lifetime passes to the tunnel of love and she planned to use them every single day.

But as alternating currents of fear and hope surged through her, in the back of her mind, a persistent nagging voice intruded into this dream. She had learned not to trust Jimmy, no matter what he said. She tried to silence the voice by telling herself that he didn't mean to hurt her, that occasionally he just made mistakes. His temper just got the best of him sometimes, that's all. He really *was* a great guy. After all, she hadn't been beaten to a pulp for over four months now.

Jimmy caressed her back, not saying anything. Sharon was quiet as well, her tears running down her cheek and dripping down Jimmy's chest. *It's going to be all right. It will be. This time everything is going to be all right.*

chapter 132

Jimmy stared at the wall, holding Sharon in his arms. He had managed to restrain himself, to not let his anger seep through, to not let her see the burning in his eyes and the madness in his face. The monster remained in darkness, unseen and silent, waiting for its chance to come out. The hurricane swirled madly about him, but he remained untouched and unaffected in the tender eye of the storm. But too much was at stake now that they had found the shipwreck. He had to play it cool. He had to be calm. And it was hard. Jimmy was used to using his lightning reactions any way he wanted at anyone's expense, and discipline and self-control had never played much of a role in his life. *This is what I gotta do. We'll go to bed, screw like animals, and then I'll convince her that the best thing for her is to go home. Just go home and get some rest.*

Sharon backed away, her arms still around him. He could see the tear stains on her face, but she was smiling. She was telling him how happy she was, but Jimmy was no longer listening. He smiled and nodded his head when necessary, but he was a thousand miles away. Then he caught the end of a comment about how much she liked it up here, how the folks were so nice. "I met some really cool people this morning. Maybe we can all get together some evening, Jimmy. I think you'll like them. Their name is Randall. Eric and Kari Randall."

The roof was about to cave in on Sharon Durand.

Randall? Did she say Randall? Eric and Kari Randall? The smile slipped away from Jimmy's face, replaced by a scowling demon, a sinister beast that had risen from the bowels of the earth. Jimmy's self-control went out the window and his haughty discipline took a bus ride downtown. There was a dramatic shift in the winds as the eye of the hurricane passed and the full brunt of the storm threatened. Lightning flashed. Thunder exploded like nuclear warheads. Clouds drew back, preparing to unleash a blistering torrent of destruction. And in a split-instant, the storm ignited. Clouds erupted. A raging beast awoke and showed its vicious head, the teeth of a hundred demons snapping and snarling, wailing and bellowing over a sea of blood beneath a black sky.

chapter 133

Sharon wasn't sure how she came to be lying on the floor. The side of her head hurt and she shook it away. Jimmy was towering above her, a solid skyscraper of cement-hard flesh. *What did I say?* she thought in bewilderment. The thought was literally kicked from her mind as Jimmy brought his uninjured leg back and kicked with all of the inhuman strength he could gather, connecting just beneath her rib cage. Her tiny frame was lifted off the floor, landing nearly four feet away.

The pain was incredible. She clutched her stomach, gasping for air. Her tears came freely now and she was hyperventilating, desperately trying to fill her lungs with air after the killing blow to her mid-section. She tried to speak, tried to scream, but could not. No sound came from her mouth and she caught a quick glance of Jimmy as he came at her again. *Jimmy . . . no! Oh, please no!*

He grabbed her by the neck with one hand and lifted her to a standing position, holding her there. She was unable to stand on her own and he grasped her neck tightly, making it even more difficult for her to breathe. It had only been three or four seconds since the initial blow, but time was no longer measurable to Sharon. Or Jimmy, for that matter. For Jimmy, the clock had stopped, trapping him in a moment that was ageless and timeless. For Sharon, eternity sped through a twisting never ending vortex, each moment exactly as the same before, unchanged and identical to the previous nanosecond. Sharon was in the throngs of a hurricane.

With the iron grip of his right hand still wrapped around Sharon's neck, he grabbed her hair. Sharon felt her head was going to explode. He pulled her hair so hard that she was sure her entire scalp was going to be torn away. Just when she thought that the roots of her hair could no longer hold, Jimmy released his grip, only to bring his hand back like a freight train, his huge fist slamming into her ear. The thunderclap exploded through her entire body and she would have fallen to the floor again, except that he was still holding her up by her neck.

For an instant she passed out, coming to again as Jimmy finally let her collapse to the floor. She tried to speak again and only managed to exert a few tiny pitiful gasps and a bubbling sound from somewhere within her. The blow to the side of her head had caused a terrible ringing throughout her head and she grasped her ear, wincing in pain, feeling faint and dizzy again. *Jimmy, no more. Please God ... Jimmy ... no more ....*

Sharon tensed her stomach muscles in anticipation of the

coming foot, and the impact of the direct hit once again raised her body almost entirely off the floor. She landed on her back, limp and unconscious.

For Jimmy, was as if a tape were being rewound and fast forwarded in rapid succession. His thoughts raced and he was unable to grasp one before another came. He stared down at Sharon's unmoving body. Blood was running from the side of her mouth and ear. As he watched, a trickle of blood formed in her nose, bubbled, then ran down the side of her cheek. She stirred, but only for an instant, and Jimmy thought that she might be coming to, but her body faltered and she slipped back into unconsciousness.

Serves her right. Hangin' out with the fucking Randalls. She won't be doing that for a while.

His massive chest heaved with every breath. He stared down at the limp form of his wife on the floor.

Randall. Jesus Christ.

Jimmy picked up the phone and called Phillip at his motel. The phone rang a long time before it was answered. Phillips' sleepy voice croaked through the receiver.

"Phillip. It's me. Look, I need a place to stay tonight . . . No, she's here but we had a . . . a fight. Yeah, she's sleeping . . . Thanks. I'll be over in a few minutes." As he hung up the phone Sharon stirred again. He gathered up a few of his things, stuffed them into a bag, looped the *Do Not Disturb*' sign on the outer door handle and locked the door on his way out.

The bitch deserved it, he thought. *Got what was comin' to her, all right. Abso-fucking-lootely.*

Christopher Knight

chapter 134

The Cheboygan City Police dispatcher scratched his head. *Crazy*, he thought. *When it rains, it pours*. He had just taken the call and scribbled down the information when he heard a voice from the back office.

"What now?"

"Disturbance," the dispatcher called out. "At the River Terrace. Someone in one of the rooms said he heard a lot of loud banging. Sounded like a fight or something. Says it's all quiet now, but he said it was pretty loud."

The voice in the back room was silent for a moment, then responded. "Tell the night manager to handle it."

"That *was* the night manager. Says the room's all quiet now, but wants us to check it out. Says he knocked on the door but got no answer."

"Doesn't he have a key?"

"Yeah, but he wants to wait 'til one of us gets there," the dispatcher replied, sipping his coffee. "Says the guy that's been renting the room is kind of an oddball. One of them macho body-builder types."

There was a long, pregnant pause. Paper shuffled. A chair scooted.

"Yeah, all right," the unseen voice said without enthusiasm. "I'll go check it out." The voice sounded tired, or maybe just bored. "As if I don't have enough shit to do already. Call over to the State Police post and tell 'em they'll have to go bring in Randall by themselves. Have them come pick up the warrant here. It's signed and ready to go."

chapter 135

The bullet strikes LaChance just above the bridge of his nose, right between his eyes. His head jerks back violently and he falls to the deck, dead before his body crumbles to the wood planking. Daniel screams as a pool of blood forms around the Captain's head and runs between the thin cracks in the boards.

"You're next if you don't do what you're told," Jack says. "You got it?" The gleam from the lantern reflects in his eyes. They are ice cold and menacing like last night in the hold. He pulls the hammer back on the pistol.

Daniel doesn't say a word. He is too shocked by what has just transpired. The men in the rowboat are climbing up the rope ladder, and Daniel stands frozen, watching Jack, glancing at the pistol, then looking at Jack again. He sees in Jack's eyes something that he has never seen before: greed. Was this the man with the wonderful sense of humor, always smiling and laughing? Never in a million years had Daniel thought that Jack

Malloy would even be capable of such unspeakable treachery.

He looks down at Captain LaChance, the stain of blood on the deck now larger than the Captain himself. His eyes are open, staring blankly upward towards the dark heavens. Daniel looks back at Jack. He still hasn't answered his question.

"I'm gonna take that as a 'yes', Daniel, because you are a reasonably smart young man. All except for that stunt you just pulled a minute ago."

The three men are now on deck. In the frosty glow of the lantern, Daniel recognizes them. They are the men he had met on the docks, the men that had hired him to assist in the heist.

"Kill him," one of them says angrily. "All he's done is cause trouble. All he's gonna do is cause more trouble."

"Not yet. We need him," another says. Then, addressing Daniel, "Just what do you think you were trying to pull back there, huh boy? You thought you was gonna get away with that? Or maybe the Cap'n promised you some of the take?"

The five men are standing near the bow when one of the male passengers comes above deck, alerted by the single gunshot. When he sees Jack holding the gun he stops, then backs up a step. Then another.

"That's far enough," Jack commands. "Come back here." The man does what he is told, stepping into the glow of the lantern. The passenger looks at LaChance's body lying on the deck in a lake of blood.

"Go down below and bring everyone on deck," Jack orders. "Keep them calm," he warns menacingly, "because if there are any problems, I'll kill you and everyone on board. Understand?" The man looks at LaChance's body again and nods numbly. He stands there for a moment, watching the men. "Well? What are ya waitin' for?"

Christopher Knight

The passenger turns and is about to go below deck when Jack speaks again. "Hold it." The passenger stops, and slowly turns around to face him. "Someone go with him," Jack orders. "They may have a gun."

When they are gone, Jack confronts Daniel. "Sorry it has to be this way, Daniel, but it's your fault. I'm going to put this gun away 'cause I know that you're not going to be foolish enough to try anything."

"You're going to kill me anyway," Daniel says flatly. He feels unnaturally calm, as if he is watching the whole situation from outside himself.

"I probably should kill you after that stunt you pulled back there. But I'm gonna give you a chance to redeem yourself." He shoves the revolver back into his coat pocket. "You're gonna help us. And for your help, we'll let you live. No two thousand dollars, just your life. Got it?"

Daniel nods. "If you were part of it all along," he asks. "Why did you need me?"

"We hadn't planned on Merman's family," Jack explains. "We figured that it would just be myself and LaChance. When we found out that there would be more people on board, we thought we might need a hand restraining them. And we didn't have a lot of time. You've been around ships, you're quick, and up 'til today, you followed orders pretty well. And believe me, there are plenty of others who would have been willing to do it for two thousand dollars. You made an agreement and then you broke it, not five minutes ago. Matter of fact, we really didn't plan on hurtin' anybody. You might say that the blood of the Cap'n is on your hands."

Daniel gazes up. The North Star flickers high above him like a distant candle. A cloud passes over and it vanishes altogether.

Christopher Knight

chapter 136

The incessant pounding boomed hollowly through the house and awoke Eric with a start. He sat up in bed and looked at the clock. 3:30 a.m. *Who in the hell is that?* Kari slept serenely on; she had the ability to sleep through a war. He threw on a pair of sweats and a flannel shirt, buttoning it up as he walked down the hall. As he passed by the living room window, he caught a glimpse of a Michigan State Police car parked in his driveway.

Great. What now?

He turned the porch light on and opened the door. Two state troopers stood on the porch. He recognized one of the troopers as one of his high school classmates, Mark Stoddard. Not necessarily a friend, but the two men knew each other. Eric greeted him but Stoddard didn't acknowledge the greeting. The two troopers on the porch just stood there with a look of concern and regret on their faces, and Eric knew that something was terribly wrong.

"I don't imagine that this is a courtesy call, kind of a late night 'get-to-know-your-local-state-trooper' kind of thing, is it?" Eric asked, trying to lighten the blow he was sure was coming. What that blow was to be he could only guess.

"We're really sorry about this, Mr. Randall," one of the troopers said.

"Sorry about what?" Eric asked. "What's going on?" Kari had finally awoken and now she joined Eric at the door with a sleepy look on her face.

"Mr. Randall, you are under arrest for felony theft of state property, specifically artifacts and items from a shipwreck in the Straits Area Shipwreck Preserve."

Eric's jaw dropped open. *How did they know?* The crucifix was locked in a safe downstairs in the den. They had told no one. It was impossible.

"In addition, a felony charge of defacing state property will also be added, stemming from the same instance."

"Defacing state property?" Eric echoed, genuinely baffled. "You wanna tell me what the hell is going on here?"

"Mr. Randall, we got an anonymous tip that you stole some items from a shipwreck in the Straits Preserve. Earlier tonight, we searched your boat over at Shandler's boatyard, and we found . . . well, let's just say that you have some explaining to do. And a good attorney couldn't hurt."

"We haven't stolen anything from anywhere!" Kari said angrily. "What 'stuff' did you find on our boat?"

"It has to do with artifacts taken from the *North Hawk* wreck a couple years ago."

Kari and Eric were stunned.

"I have no idea what you're talking about!" Eric denied. "I've never stolen anything from any shipwreck and I've never even dived on the *North Hawk!*"

"Nevertheless, Mr. Randall you'll need to come with us."

Kari's grogginess had worn off and had been replaced by anger. "He isn't going anywhere! If this is some kind of—" Eric squeezed her shoulder gently, stopping her before she went any further. No sense in both of them getting arrested.

"Like I said, Mr. Randall—*Eric*—" Stoddard said with some sympathy, "it doesn't sound right to me either. My dad and yours were friends . . . but we still have to take you in. I'm sorry."

chapter 137

"Jesus, Lord in heaven . . . what happened to you?" Duane greeted Don as he sleepily opened the door. The sun was just coming up and the crispness in the air announced that it was going to be another picture-perfect northern Michigan day. Except that blocking his view of this particularly beautiful morning was a very sleepy-looking pissed-off Duane Everett. He stood at the door, clad in boxer shorts and a white cotton tank top.

Don ignored the comment and said nothing. He glanced at the clock on the wall. *6:00 a.m.* "You got a phone call, Duane continued harshly. "Says it's an emergency. Some 'Karen' or 'Carmen' or somebody."

"I don't know any 'Karen' or "Carmen'," Don replied, confused. He liked Duane and all, but not at 6:00 a.m. after a late night. He moved to close the door, but Duane reached out his hand and stopped it.

"Well, I don't give a yella' cornshit who they said they was. They asked for Don Garrity. Now, maybc I'm wrong, but I got a Don Garrity registered as one a my guests. And you bein' the only fella I have ever met by that name, I'm kinda thinkin' that they meant you. Course, I could jes tell 'em to go straight to hell, an' then botha us'll be gettin' more sleep. Which is it? And don't be taking your ol' sweet time with an answer either cause lemme tell you, you ain't got it. In two seconds I'm going back in, hangin' the phone up, and goin' back to bed."

Don waved his hand in the air. "Fine, fine. Hang on." But Duane was already walking away. Don quickly threw on his shorts and a sweatshirt and raced to catch up with him.

"Kari. That's her name," Duane remembered as they approached the front door. He opened it and walked into the house, not caring if Don was behind him or not. Don grabbed the door to keep it from closing on him.

"Kari? Kari Randall?" Don asked. Duane said nothing as he pointed to the receiver that lay on the kitchen table. The phone was a banana yellow, dirty from years of use, and the long yellow cord that dangled from the wall mount was tangled into a violent knot. Don picked up the receiver and put it to his ear. "Hello?"

"Don? It's Kari. They've arrested Eric."

Don wasn't sure he'd heard her right. "Eric arrested? For what?"

"It's bullshit, Don. It's all bullshit. I'm at the Sheriff's Department."

"All right. I'll be there in a few minutes." He placed the dirty banana back on the hook and looked around to thank Duane. He was nowhere in sight and Don figured that he must have gone back to bed. Don scribbled a quick note to both Duane and Sally, apologizing for the early intrusion, left it on the kitchen table, and closed the door quietly behind him.

He was fully awake now. *Arrested? Eric?* he thought again, as he put on a pair of jeans and a clean shirt. He hopped in the Dodge Caravan and sped off towards town.

chapter 138

Kari was sitting in the lobby at the Sheriff's Department, sipping a cup of coffee. Smudges remained where tears had streaked her face. She put her coffee down when she saw Don, hugged him briefly, and told him what happened. "They framed him, Don. Someone planted artifacts from a plundered shipwreck, the *North Hawk*, on the *John Galt*."

"Did Eric tell them that?"

"Yeah, he did. But they said that they had to bring him in anyway, and we should probably get a lawyer." She started to cry again.

"Well, it's obvious that whoever sabotaged your boat were the same ones that framed him. When are they going to arraign him?"

"At four o'clock this afternoon."

Don looked at his watch: nine hours from now. "Can he have

visitors?" he asked.

"No," Kari said. "Visiting hours are on Wednesdays and Sundays only. The only person who can talk to him is our attorney, Jennifer Brooks. She's busy today but she said she'd switch some things around to help us out. I'm supposed to meet her at her office at one o'clock."

"All right," Don said. "Then you've done all you can for Eric for the moment. Let's see if we can find out anything more about what the police found on the boat."

Kari rode in Don's van, and for the second time that morning, Dave Shandler was rudely awakened by a pounding at the door. The first time was when the two uniformed men stood on his porch. He had figured that *yes, indeed, someone had seen him growing those two marijuana plants in his backyard last summer and now he was in trouble.* But instead the cops had a search warrant for the Randall's boat. He had stumbled across the lawn, showed them where it was, and waited while they searched the *John Galt*. The cops had taken a few items from the boat, asked a few questions, and left.

Now, he was roused for the second time that morning by Kari Randall and another man. Dave invited them in.

Kari introduced Don, and the two men shook hands. "What exactly did the police find?" Kari asked.

"It looked like they found a ship's windlass, a couple old silver dollars, and something with the a ship's name on it, the *North Hawk*. It was as if they knew exactly where to look," Dave explained.

"But that's impossible!"

"I know," Dave continued, "but I watched 'em pull the stuff out."

"Didn't you tell them that none of that was aboard when you got the boat?"

"Quite honestly, Kari, I couldn't truthfully say one way or the other. My job was to work on the engine, not sift through the entire boat to see what you had. The cops asked me if I knew anything about it and I told them that the boat was in for repairs to its engine. I told them that I had been working on the boat and I hadn't come across any stuff like that before. I wish I could've told them something that would have helped you out a little more." He added apologetically, "I did tell 'em that this didn't seem like something you folks would do though."

"Do you have a security system?" Don interjected.

"No," Dave said. "I never thought I needed one. I just fix boats. I've never had any trouble before." He paused a moment, then added: "But I'm not really the one with the problems this morning, I guess. Except for the fact that I haven't had much sleep."

Dave Shandler didn't have much more to offer. He was disappointed that Eric had been arrested, and concerned that there seemed to be a good possibility that someone had entered his boatyard to plant evidence. But he was thankful that he hadn't been busted for growing the pot. That would have really messed up his day.

chapter 139

"The *North Hawk*!" Kari exclaimed, as the Caravan pulled back onto Main Street. She explained the significance of the *North Hawk* to Don including how the wreck had been found, what it was said to have contained, how it was tied up in court, and ultimately, how it had been plundered under everyone's noses, making headlines across the country. Not only *that*, Kari explained, but mocking writing had been carved into its hull.

"Well, it's pretty safe to say that Eric has been set up in a big way," Don said. "And I'm sure that it has everything to do with what we found yesterday evening. Whoever else has been diving on the *Brittany* is probably responsible for the plundering of the *North Hawk*."

"The question is . . . what's on the *Brittany* that they want so badly?" Kari wondered.

"I think the answer to that begins with the crucifix we found," Don replied.

Both were silent for a moment, trying to calm their thoughts and slow the dizzying possibilities and conclusions that were churning through their minds.

"You hungry?" Don finally asked.

"Yeah, I am," Kari belatedly realized. "I just don't know if I can eat."

"You should try," Don said. "You've got a long day ahead of you. Looks like we both do." He pulled into a small diner and while Kari nibbled on a bagel, he wolfed down a bacon and cheese omelet. Both had several cups of coffee. Kari was clearly tired, having been awake since three that morning, as was evident by the maroon pockets below her eyes.

"What did you tell your attorney?" Don asked, through a bite of omelet.

"Not much. I told her the police had found some stolen artifacts on our boat and that they had come to our house early this morning to arrest Eric."

"Why didn't they arrest you, too?"

"I don't know. I imagine they still could. They told me not to go anywhere."

They sat together in a long, tired silence. Kari sighed, "Well, it looks like we have some explaining to do about the *Brittany*. We're going to have to convince the police that those artifacts were planted in a deliberate effort to get Eric arrested."

"The only evidence we have are the stripped bolts," Don reminded her.

"What we *really* need to do is find out who 'they' are," Kari said.

Don paid the bill and they left the restaurant and climbed into the Caravan.

"Turn that way," Kari instructed, pointing as she clicked on her seat belt.

"Where are we headed?" Don asked.

"Let's go down to the marina," Kari replied. "Maybe our 'friends' have a boat there."

chapter 140

The marina was quiet. A few early risers were working on their boats, and numerous seagulls scattered the docks and grass. Kari and Don walked casually along, taking their time, trying not to appear overly interested as they inventoried the items on the decks of the vessels that bobbed in their slips. They were looking for dive gear or anything that would indicate that the occupants were doing more than pleasure cruising, although they both knew their adversaries would be more careful than to leave stray equipment lying around in plain sight. On the boat next to Dave Shandler's dark-blue, seagull shit-splattered trawler, a fat whale of a man lay sprawled asleep in a chair on the deck. Don pointed to the tattoo on his arm and whispered, "I'll bet the Disney people really like that one." Kari giggled, and they kept walking, checking out the other boats in the marina. They stopped at the end of the dock.

The Laurentian Channel

To the south, the huge Coast Guard cutter *Mackinaw* was anchored in the river. Beyond that, the river wound beneath a drawbridge and through town where it would finally meet Mullett Lake, the first in the chain of lakes that stretched all the way to Petoskey. To the north, a red and white lighthouse sat at the base of the breakwall. The cement slabs reached out into the lake, capped off by yet another, smaller lighthouse at the end. This morning, a few fisherman sat idly on the wall, lines in the water, waiting. Bois Blanc Island was visible as a thin band of trees several miles into Huron.

Kari surveyed the marina. Most of the slips were filled, and she wondered which boat could be the one. She felt they had to be here, somewhere. Yet, so far, they didn't see any evidence of dive gear on anyone's boat.

"Come on," she said to Don. The two walked on the dock and headed for the parking lot.

Ed saw the two approaching again, closed his eyes and snored convincingly. After they had walked past, he opened one eye and watched them until they had reached the parking lot. *Awww*, he thought, *leaving so soon?*

chapter 141

Four rings. Mike glanced at the clock, wondering if it was too early.

Five rings.

I'll give 'er a couple more. If she doesn't answer by the tenth one—

A fragile voice on the other end of the line interrupted his thought. "Hello?"

"Hello . . . Mrs. Jewell?"

"Yes?" the voice on the other end of the line peeped.

"My name is Mike Felsing. I'm sorry to bother you at this hour. I hope I didn't wake you up."

"No, that's quite all right. Can I help you?" she replied politely.

"I'm doing some research on a ship that belonged to a relative of yours, a Richard Merman," Mike said, holding his breath. There was a pause. Then:

"Oh, yes. Richard Merman was my great-grandfather, and he did own a ship for a short time," she said pleasantly. "You know, you're the second person that has been interested in that ship."

Second person? Mike thought. He paused. "A second person, Mrs. Jewell?" he asked carefully.

"Oh, yes. It was five . . . maybe six years ago. A young man came to my house. He was looking for information about that ship too. He told me he was doing some research for a college paper."

"Do you remember his name?"

"Hmmmm. Phillip Kingsley, I think. No, that's not right. Maybe . . . Killington. No, that's not it either. Just give me a moment. I may be old but my memory is very good."

I'll give you as many moments as you need, Mike thought, clutching the phone tightly.

"Keanan. Yes, that's it. Phillip Keanan. Nice young man," Mrs. Jewell said finally.

Mike realized he had been holding his breath, and as he let it out he was barely able to restrain himself from whooping in delight. He scribbled the name down on a sticky-note.

"Do you recall anything about the ship? Anything about your great-grandfather?"

"No, I'm afraid I couldn't tell you much."

Mike was disappointed. He'd hoped that perhaps the old woman would be able to give him some more information. Specifically, what was aboard the *Brittany* when it went down. But Abigail Jewell didn't seem to know much about Merman or the ill-fated ship. But—

"I do know that my great grandfather kept journals, though," the old woman mused. "They're probably all still in the attic where my father had placed them years ago."

Journals? Richard Merman kept journals?

The two talked for another ten minutes. Mike thanked Mrs. Jewell for her time, hung up, and immediately called Eric and Kari but the line was busy.

chapter 142

Be-EEP. Be-EEP. Be-EEP. Be-EEP. The phone buzzed in Kari's ear. "Mike's line is still busy," she said, hanging up the phone, obviously unaware that she was trying to call Felsing at the same time that he was trying to call her. She made another pot of coffee and sat down at the kitchen table. Don was staring out the window, watching a boat plow slowly downriver. Kari watched him watching the water.

"What happened Don?" she prompted gently. "What happened that day under the ice? Did you get narced?" He shot a nervous glance in her direction, then returned his gaze to the river. It was an odd question, since Kari had been there on the expedition. Not under the ice, of course, but she had been there. She knew what had happened. The question Kari posed wasn't 'what happened?' as much as it was 'what happened to *you?*'

Don didn't answer for a long time. The coffee machine gurgled and sputtered. Don stood and walked to the sliding glass doors, staring at nothing in particular. A glance here, a look over there. Finally, with a sense of overwhelming relief, he sat down at the kitchen table and began to tell her about the nightmares and the flashbacks. Everything spilled out in a flood that he couldn't have stopped even if he had wanted to.

Kari let him finish without interruption. "So, it wasn't low blood sugar?" she asked.

"No, but the blood sugar explanation was easier than telling you what was really going on. It doesn't help that I myself don't even know what's going on. All I know is that there is a black hole in my brain where something has been erased or suppressed," Don said in frustration. "Maybe you can tell me what happened, Kari. Then I won't have to pay anybody else a hundred bucks an hour to find out," he said, smiling weakly.

"You really want to know?" she asked.

Don looked out the window. A small fishing boat was making its way upriver, its two occupants clad in orange life vests. A boy of about twelve sat on the opposite bank, holding a fishing pole in one hand a sandwich in the other. Don looked back at Kari. "Yeah," he replied, nodding his head. "Yeah I do."

Kari refilled their coffees. "Okay," she began.

chapter 143

"Hot shit!" Phillip's voice woke Jimmy, and he stirred in the chair he had been crashed out in for the better part of the night. Sunlight streamed through the cracks in the curtains. He opened his eyes. Phillip was standing up. "Check it out," Phillip said excitedly. He pointed to the radio and they both listened. *"Local diver, Eric Randall, was arrested this morning after an anonymous tip led authorities to a boat owned by Randall. Michigan State Police confiscated numerous artifacts from the Night Hawk which was plundered of her cargo and vandalized a few years ago. Arraignment will be later this morning in 87th District Court. If convicted, Randall faces a minimum ten thousand dollar fine and ten years in prison. Also overnight, police—"*

"How about that!" Phillip crowed. He flashed an arrogant smile. "That son of a bitch isn't going to do much diving now!"

"You sure nobody saw you and Ed?" Jimmy asked warily.

"Nobody's around that time of night," Phillip gloated. "Not in this town. It was a piece of cake. We were in and out in ten minutes. Besides, it sounds like *you* ran into more trouble than *we* did."

"Oh, that," Jimmy said, waving it off. "Just a little disagreement. I think Sharon will be heading back downstate today. Thanks for letting me crash here."

Phillip was sickened but said nothing; he knew what Jimmy's 'little disagreements' usually entailed. "Ed is down at the boat. He spent the night there keeping an eye on that boat Randall borrowed in case they decided to go diving again. They didn't, but we're diving tonight as soon as it gets dark."

chapter 144

It's over, Sharon thought miserably. *This time I swear to God it's over.* She lay in bed, peering through the window as the sun rose. When the police and the night manager had shown up last night, she had crawled painfully into bed, pulled the covers over her head, and ignored the heavy knocking at the door. The night manager finally used his key and peered hesitantly around the cracked door and into the room. "Pardon us, ma'am," a voice said apologetically. "But we had a report of a disturbance coming from this room. Is there a problem?" His eyes scanned the room, but he saw nothing out of order.

Sharon did her best *'you-just-woke-me-up-and-I'm-groggy'* voice. "I . . . I got up to go . . . to the bathroom . . . and knocked over a . . . chair."

"Are you sure you are all right, ma'am?" the voice asked again.

"Mmm. Me? Fine . . . I'm fine." She was having a hard time breathing.

"Well, okay. Sorry to bother you."

"Mmmm. Good-night."

The cop and the night manager closed the door. Sharon heard mild laughter as the two departed. She lay in the dark motel room, the glare of a streetlight outlining the gaps in the closed curtain. *Why did I do that? Why didn't I tell them what happened? Why didn't I tell them I just got the living shit beat out of me and I'm pregnant and probably need to go to the hospital?* But she knew why. She was terrified of Jimmy; he always had an angle on everything and if the cops hauled him away, as soon as he got out he would come looking for her—and he would find her.

She started to cry and she held her pillow tightly, sobbing in the darkness, feeling alone and afraid, until she fell into a troubled and painful twilight sleep.

She awoke hours later, still curled up in the fetal position in which she had fallen asleep. She was afraid to move. Her head throbbed from the blows to the side of her head. Her chest hurt and she was still having difficulty breathing. Dried blood was caked under her nose and around her mouth. Worse, her abdomen throbbed dully and she felt a slow wetness growing between her legs. *No*, she thought desperately, *not the baby! Not again.* All these years she had let Jimmy get away with beating her, but now her baby might be reaping the awful fruits of her indecision. Tears welled up in her eyes and she sobbed raggedly, curling deeper into a fetal position in an attempt to disperse the pain that racked her.

Christopher Knight

It's just a bunch of cells, that's all, she thought, trying to console herself. *A bunch of cells that were multiplying and growing, that's all. Just like last time. Just like the abortion.*

She sobbed, burying her face in the covers.

chapter 145

Don Garrity was ass-deep in hell. He hadn't really planned on being there and had he known of the travel arrangement ahead of time, he would have called his agent and swapped his tickets for a more amiable destination—like the surface of the sun or something. Anywhere would have been better.

Kari began gently, telling him what Eric had told her about the dive. Eric had slipped into the frigid water first. The temperature beneath the surface was thirty-six degrees. After filming Eric dropping down through the jagged, glass stalactites that stretched into the depths, Don had followed him as he descended into the amazingly clear water in search of the wreck. They were wearing drysuits on this dive, beneath which they wore thick cotton underwear. Nevertheless, it would still be a cold dive.

At two hundred feet Eric looked up. Don was hovering a few

feet above him, shaking the camera, turning it around in his hands puzzled. Don brushed at the camera housing with his thick gloves, apparently trying to dislodge a piece of ice from the zoom lens. Failing, he pulled his dive knife from its sheath. The shiny blade glowed in the dim light. Eric watched as he dislodged a fragment of ice from the camera housing and attempted to return the knife to its sheath on his leg. He watched in horror as Don fumbled while attempting to re-sheathe it.

"Don! Be careful! Don't cut—" Eric had shouted through his regulator. But it was too late. Air bubbles swarmed around Don as the piercing cold water rushed into his suit. The air in his suit boiled out of the four-inch slice in the suit's leg and immediately Don began to sink. He panicked and let go of the camera and it sank as well, falling straight to the bottom like an orange torpedo.

"Oh, God," Don moaned from his seat at the kitchen table. "I remember some of it now." His stomach reeled drunkenly and he staggered over to the kitchen sink, not sure if he could make it to the bathroom. After the spasm passed, he put his head down on the cool surface of the counter and was surprised to find tears in his eyes. Regaining composure, he returned to the table.

The frigid water had raced through the hole in his dry suit, numbing his body. He reached for the lifeline clipped to his waist. He grabbed the rope with both hands and gave three quick tugs. Emergency. It was a last resort. The line was meant more for the divers to find their way back to the hole in the ice than it was a rescue line. But it was immediately apparent that something was wrong; the line was limp in his hands. He had pulled again, three quick tugs, but the rope just coiled about him as he twisted and turned. Only a few seconds had elapsed since he had sliced open his suit, but in those few moments he had become entirely disoriented. He had swung the knife wildly about him, hoping to cut the line, to release himself. He had felt something resisting the knife and thrust again in a hard, sweeping motion only to find water rushing into his mouth. He had choked violently and, grabbing his regulator hose he found with horror that he had cut it. Water filled his mouth, his throat.

Don lifted his head from the counter to find Kari hugging him, trying to soothe him like a child who had fallen and suffered a bad cut. "Eric saw you struggling and realized what was happening. When he saw you cut your air hose, he was already on his way to you. He didn't dare get too close because you were flailing around so wildly with your knife. So he pulled on the line and—"

"Kari, I stabbed him, too," Don said miserably. "I panicked and almost killed both of us."

"I know, Don," Kari confirmed. She squeezed his shoulders and stared into his eyes. "But he knows that you didn't mean it. You panicked, Don. Eric said that you didn't know what you were doing."

"What happened next?" Don asked, not sure if he wanted to know. "I don't remember."

"Eric hit you hard and knocked you out. It helped that you were already almost unconscious from lack of oxygen. He brought you straight up. The mix you were breathing probably prevented you both from getting bent. That, and the fact that you had only been beneath the surface for a few minutes. Luckily, there was a doctor on the research team. You were both evacuated to the mainland by helicopter."

"I remember being in the hospital in Reykjavik," Don said, slumping into a chair at the kitchen table. He reached for his cup of coffee, but his hand shook so much that when he raised it to his lips, the liquid spilled into his lap. He put the cup back onto the table.

"Are you okay?" Kari asked gently.

"Yeah, I think so," Don said hesitantly. Kari sat quietly across from him, not knowing what to say to comfort him.

"What happened to Eric?" Don asked.

"Stitches," Kari replied. "That's all, Don. He was okay. He needed thirty four stitches."

Thirty four stitches, Don thought in horror. In his mind he relived the panic, the extreme horror. He had lost it. He had been a good diver, a safe diver, and he thought that he would be able to handle any situation in the water. But each critical mistake compounded the next, then the next. It was a series of mishaps that led to a loss of control as he realized that he was going to die. It would be his last dive, his last breath. He had heard of divers that had panicked, lost in a confused whirlwind of terror and dread. Don never thought that he would find himself in the same situation.

"Would you like a glass of water?" Kari asked, bringing him back to the present.

"Right now, I don't want anything to do with any water," Don said, smiling weakly.

That's good, Kari thought. *It's a step in the right direction if he can joke about it.* "More coffee then?"

"Sure," he said, nodding. Kari stood up just as the phone rang.

chapter 146

Eric lay on his bunk worrying more about Kari than himself. The arrest and the charges were ridiculous, but the fact that they had been so blatantly set up was disturbing. Whoever was trying to curtail their diving was resorting to drastic measures. Eric didn't hear anyone approaching until a voice boomed through his cell.

"Well, well. Eric Randall. Next thing you know, we'll be picking up Norman Rockwell on child abuse charges. What brings you to our fine establishment?"

"Just visiting, Bill," he said, stretching and placing his hands behind his head. He knew Sheriff Bill Tyrell. Not real well, but enough to buoy a cordial conversation. The sheriff remained on the other side of the bars.

"What in the hell is going on here?" Tyrell said, lowering his voice. "The troopers say they found some artifacts from the wreck of the *North Hawk* on your boat."

"Yeah, well, they may have found it there, but that doesn't mean I put it there. I've never even dived on the *North Hawk*. Maybe you can put a good word in for me so I can get the hell out of here."

"I'm afraid my good word isn't going to do much, Eric. These are felony charges. I'll help you if I can, but my advice to you is to get a good lawyer. They aren't going to be throwing *these* charges out. Hell, I've got both of the Detroit papers and *USA Today* wanting to talk to me. And some big shot at NBC in New York has called, not to mention the local boy scouts from the network affiliates that have been camped outside most of the morning. You're big news, pal."

Beautiful, Eric thought. *Just beautiful*. He looked at his watch, mentally counting down the hours until he would be arraigned. The seconds ticked by like decades, and it drove Eric mad. Every moment in the tiny cell was like a year. But, if all went well, he'd be out of jail later in the afternoon.

Might as well try and relax a little bit. He had been awake since the knock on the door early in the morning, and he had been wired and tense. There was nothing he could do now, and he finally allowed himself to loosen up. After a while, he fell into an uncomfortable sleep.

chapter 147

Mike dialed Eric and Kari's number and tucked the receiver to his ear while he popped a bagel in the toaster. Evelyn was up now, and he poured her a cup of coffee. Mike was relieved to hear the phone ring on the other end of the line instead of the busy signal he'd received all morning.

"Hello?" Kari answered.

"Kari. It's Mike. Boy, have I got news for you."

"Me first," she told him, and explained what had happened to Eric.

Mike was shocked. "I'll be over as soon as I get dressed," he said, after Kari finished speaking. "But I just got off the phone with Merman's last living relative. Guess what the woman's name is?" Mike asked, relishing his moment of triumph. "Abigail Jewell." He paused. "But get this. Richard Merman re-named the boat after his granddaughter. The name was passed down to his great-granddaughter . . . Abigail Jewell."

"I don't—"

"Abigail *Brittany* Jewell," Mike finished proudly. He heard Kari gasp.

"What does she know about the ship?" Kari asked.

"Apparently, not much. But here's another thing: she said that several years ago, a man visited her. He was interested in the ship. Said he was doing some research for a college term paper or something. His name was—" Felsing paused as he flipped through his notes. "—here it is. Phillip Keanan."

At first, the name skipped by her, not registering. It was oddly familiar, somehow, somewhere. *Phillip Keanan. Where have I—* Suddenly, it hit her, and the name seemed to clang in her head. She knew. She knew that name, she knew what he looked like. Phillip Keanan was the name of the man in the picture that Sharon Durand had showed her and Eric. Phillip Keanan was a friend of Sharon's husband, Jimmy.

"Does the name ring a bell?" Mike asked, feeling Kari's stunned silence on the other end.

Was it possible? she thought. *No. It can't be the same. Yet, Phillip Keanan wasn't a very common name. They have to be one in the same. They have to be.*

"Kari?" Mike asked, after her tense silence.

"What?" she breathed. "Oh. Sorry. Yes. I mean—I think I know who he is."

chapter 148

"Let's go."

Kari spoke to Don without looking at him, hurrying to the counter to snatch up the car keys.

"What?" Don asked. "What is it?"

"I think I know who might be diving on the wreck. And who planted the *North Hawk* artifacts on the *John Galt*. Come on."

"What? Who?" Don said, snapping to his feet.

"I'll tell you on the way."

Minutes later, they were on their way to the *River Terrace*.

"Eric and I met a woman the other day at Gordon Turner Park. She seemed nice, a bit lonely, though. I talked with her for a while and invited her to breakfast. She showed me a picture of her husband and another guy named Phillip Keanan. Mike Felsing told me that a man with that same name visited Abigail Jewell several years ago, asking about a ship her great-grandfather owned."

"What do you know about this Keanan guy?"

Kari shook her head. "Not much. I mean . . . I know what he looks like, and I'd probably recognize him if I saw him. He's got dark hair. Medium build. Actually, quite good looking. But Sharon Durand didn't say much. Just that her husband and Phillip Keanan were fishing buddies."

"Yeah," Don snorted. "They're fishing buddies, alright."

"And get this. Eric *talked* to him."

"Who? Keanan?"

Kari nodded her head as she stopped for a traffic light. "On the river. Says he was going upstream and asked him what he was diving for. Apparently, Phillip Keanan saw us diving the wreck. He asked Eric what we were diving for."

"What did Eric tell him?"

"He just said that we were practicing some deep dives. Nothing in particular. He sure wasn't going to say anything about the shipwreck." The light turned green and the Blazer roared through the intersection. "I want to find Sharon Durand. I wonder what she knows. Maybe she's behind all of this."

"Maybe we should wait until Eric gets out of jail," Don advised.

"Right," Kari smirked, glancing over at him.

"Yeah, I know. It was just a suggestion. Where are we headed?"

"The *River Terrace* motel. That is where Sharon Durand is staying."

chapter 149

It was a supreme struggle just to move, let alone get up from the bed. Sharon was certain that several of her ribs must be broken, as she was only able to manage slow, shallow breaths without wincing in extreme pain. *And my stomach. So help me Jimmy, if I lose the baby because of this, I will kill you.* She crawled to the edge of the bed and swung first one and then her other leg to the floor. *So far, so good.* As she slowly sat up, pain struck her like a lightning bolt. A sharp, unexpected twinge jolted her lower abdomen and she fell back into the bed, tears of frustration overflowing once again, streaking her cheeks and staining the pillow.

She felt a hot surge of anger, and she fed off it, using it to help lift herself to an upright position. She ignored the biting, burning pain and concentrated on dealing with waves of dizzying nausea that enveloped her. As she blotted her tears away with a corner of the bed sheet, she felt the hardened flecks of blood on her face. Locks of her black hair were glued together by dried blood. She looked at the pillow, which was also stained with dark brown spots. *Hah! Explain that to the cleaning lady, Jimmy*, Sharon thought. *It looks like someone sacrificed a goat in here.*

The walk to the bathroom was strenuous and slow. Her body ached with every tentative step and she wondered if she was going to be able to make it out of the room and to her car without falling. The warm washcloth felt good on her face and when her face was clean she assessed herself in the bathroom mirror. Besides a swollen, split lower lip and a red swelling on her cheekbone her face didn't look too bad—at least not as bad as it felt. She covered the red swelling along her cheekbone with make-up. Another sharp, unanticipated twinge of pain jabbed at her lower abdomen, causing her to nearly crumble and fall to the bathroom floor.

Slowly and cautiously, she gathered her few belongings, packed them into her suitcase, loaded it into the Grand Prix, and left the *River Terrace*. She drove through town and checked into the *Continental Inn*, just three blocks from the Cheboygan marina.

chapter 150

After not finding Sharon Durand at the motel, Kari and Don returned to the house. The motel clerk hadn't been able to give them much information, except the fact that he didn't have anyone by the name Jimmy Durand registered. Or Sharon Durand, for that fact. But Kari had given the clerk a physical description, and he said that it *did* fit two of their guests. Especially the bodybuilder, who he seemed to see frequently in the past few days. Room 213, he had said. Their repeated knocks were unheeded. Of course, Kari and Don had no way of knowing that they had missed Sharon Durand by mere minutes.

Felsing arrived at the Randalls just as Kari had hung up the phone with their attorney, Jennifer Brooks.

"They've moved the arraignment to tomorrow," she said, visibly upset. "There's some kind of scheduling conflict with the judge."

"Can they do that?" Don asked. "Schedule something like that, and then move it all of a sudden?"

Mike nodded. "Happens all the time. But they have to arraign him within seventy-two hours. If he's not charged by then, he'll have to be released."

"Well, there's no chance of that," Don concluded. "So I guess we wait."

Don filled Mike in on the discovery of the crucifix while Kari retrieved it from the safe. It lay on the table before them, gleaming. To Kari, it had come to represent both an accusing finger and the key to the mystery of the *Brittany*.

"Tell us more about Abigail Jewell," Kari said.

Mike's eyes flared, a spark of fire coming to life from deep within. *Once a cop always a cop*, he thought proudly. "Abigail *Brittany* Jewell," he said with relish, adding emphasis to her middle name. Mike filled them in on Abigail's account of Phillip Keanan's visit and his interest in the ship as well. "She's apparently got quite a bit of family history tucked away in boxes," he said. "It may or may not have anything to do with what's going on. But too many coincidences are beginning to fit together."

"I think we might be getting closer to our adversaries," Don said quietly. He stood up. "I'm going to go down to the marina. It's probably hopeless, but I'll have a look at every single boat that heads out or comes back today. If I see something, I'll let you know."

"I'm going to St. Clair Shores," Mike announced. "There might be something in one of Abigail Jewell's boxes that may tell us something."

"And I'm going to try and get some sleep," Kari said wearily. "I'm no good to anyone falling off my feet."

chapter 151

Mike rang the doorbell again. He had waited a long time after the first ring and no one had come to the door. The red brick house looked strangely quiet with the garage door closed and the curtains drawn. No sounds emanated from within. He turned and watched a dozen sparrows dart among the branches of a single, large white birch tree in the center of the yard. Across the street, a man was tinkering with his sprinkler system, and in the driveway of the house next to that one, an old blue GTO in beautiful condition was jacked up by the front. Mike could see the bottom half of a body protruding out from beneath the car and an occasional hand swinging out from underneath to blindly reach for a tool laying near the body's side.

He had made the trip from Cheboygan to St. Clair Shores in a record three hours. Thankfully, he had missed all of the highway construction and, being it was mid-week, he'd also missed the heavy weekend traffic. Now he stood on the porch of Abigail Jewell's home, in a cookie-cutter rural American neighborhood.

He reached for the doorbell, then decided to wait just a few more moments before ringing it again. She had said she would be here. After another moment he pressed the doorbell again, just as the door opened. Abigail Jewell stood in the doorway, her eyes looking past him, unfocused and unseeing.

She's blind, Mike thought immediately. *She can't see a thing.* She invited him in and he was surprised at her agility as she moved around the house. She was a tiny woman and Mike guessed her to be about eighty, but she carried herself gracefully with an air of physical confidence. Her visual impairment didn't seem to be much of a hindrance at all.

Nearly two hours, two croissants and three cups of imported gourmet coffee later, Mike stood bidding her good-bye in the small, bright living room. "You're sure you don't mind me borrowing these pictures and the book?" he asked the old woman. He held an old, leather-bound book that he'd found in the attic, some loose papers, and a few old photographs.

"Not at all," she replied, her voice cracking. "It's been some time since I've read a book," she smiled.

Yeah, that's probably right, Mike thought. "I will return them as soon as I'm done with them," he promised.

"That'll be fine, fine. Just fine." Mike thanked her again, and turned to walk back to the car. He heard the door close behind him, and he shot a quick glance back.

Holy cow, he thought, almost running to his car. *Holy cow. It all makes sense.* His heart was pounding and his hands were shaking as he pulled the wad of keys from his pocket and unlocked the car door.

chapter 152

Don just needed to be alone, to relax and think. He sat on the soft grass near the river, the blades tickling his bare legs in the late-morning sun. He took his shoes off and lay on his side, watching the boats as they left their slips. Before staking out a spot on the lawn, he had checked with the harbormaster to see if there was a boat in the marina that was registered to a Phillip Keanan. There wasn't.

Don closed his eyes, taking in the sounds of the marina. Given the events of the morning he had had little time to think about what had happened to him, but now he forced himself to. He was determined to deal with it this time, and not push it away. Not again. He re-lived the entire experience again, the terror, the fear, the incredible horror. He felt the pain, the anguish, and the desperation that he had buried so deeply for so long. The hidden fears and secrets that he had suppressed after the accident were now as clear as if the dive had just happened yesterday. He felt himself beginning to sweat again, and felt the flood of anxious, frantic thoughts. The warm breeze licked at his hair, but he only felt the piercing chill of the ice water lunging at him.

He had snapped like a dried twig under the ice. He had lost it in an emergency situation and it had nearly cost him his own life and the life of a good friend. Don tried to remember the exact moment that he decided to forget what had happened, but couldn't. It was as if the memory had a mind of its own, making the decision to hide itself away. *But it's all right now*, he thought. *It's over, it's done. I know what happened. I may not know why but at least it's no longer a mystery.*

Don opened his eyes and squinted in the bright sunlight. The world suddenly seemed new, more colorful and defined. The trees were greener and more alive, the white hulls of the boats in their slips were being caressed by the deep blue-green waters of the marina. He felt he could reach up and touch the pristine blue sky suspended above him like the canopy of a massive tent.

The clang of a ship's bell rang lazily in the distance, signaling the departure of the Bois Blanc Island ferry. He watched as the big boat plowed past like a giant sloth inching through the waters. Its wake rolled through the marina and gently rocked the boats moored in their slips so that the tall masts of sailboats waved to and fro. *It's over*, he told himself. *It's done.*

But somewhere deep inside he knew that it wasn't.

chapter 153

"I've changed my mind. We're diving now." Ed was standing at the stern of the Bayliner, looking out over the marina. "It's still early and I'll bet they're running around like goddamn chickens with their heads cut off." He was wearing mirrored sunglasses and smoking, and now he tossed the half-smoked cigarette into the water as he turned to prepare the boat. "They'll be tied up at least 'til tomorrow."

Sharon lay on the double bed in her new room at the *Continental Inn*. She was exhausted. The short drive from the *River Terrace* had seemed to take hours and she had flinched in pain when the car went over even the slightest bump. The desk clerk at the *Continental Inn* had given her a strange look as he surveyed her swollen face and reddened eyes. She had discovered that a tooth was loose as well. She had swallowed four ibuprofen caplets to help ease the pain and stop the swelling.

Car accident, she had explained to the man at the reservation desk. The explanation seemed to satisfy him.

She ran her fingers through her hair as she lay back on the pillow in the motel room. *The bastard*. In her mind, she became a giant, twenty feet tall, with fists the size of basketballs and legs like telephone poles. One swift kick sent Jimmy flying through the air, over a couple houses, against a tree, and tumbling back on to the ground. He tried to run, but she jumped over a house and picked him up by the back of his shirt collar, the way a mother wolf picks up one of her pups. Gently, cautiously . . . at first. Then she lifted him high up into the air and dangled him there for a moment, listening to his incessant whining and begging for her to stop. She laughed, a deep throaty roar, then dropped him, knocking the wind from him in a dull, heavy thud. He slowly got to his feet and tried to run again. This time she kicked him, cornering him against a building, listening with great pleasure as he screamed in pain, pleading for her to quit. She heard his bones crack with every kick, like she had stepped on a pile of dead branches. *How do you like it, Jimmy? How does it FEEL? Does it feel GOOD? Oh . . . can't decide? Well, how about another free SAMPLE?* And again she swept her giant arm across him, knocking him twenty feet and sending him tumbling even further. A trail of blood followed him through the grass and across the street, where he lay in agony, still and unmoving. *Ya like that, Jimmy? Do you like it?* She towered above his lifeless figure, laughing and taunting him, daring him to move, to try and run away. *How 'bout it, Jim? How about another round? You know . . . one for old times' sake?* When he didn't move, she raised her leg high above him and brought it down in one final, crushing blow. She could hear his bones and flesh giving way beneath her car-sized feet, could hear his last pathetic, pleading cries and whimpers of pain, and it gave her enormous pleasure. Small white twigs protruded from under her gargantuan *Reebok* cross trainers and a pool of blood began to form, staining the bright white sole of her shoe. His final shouts and cries diminished to pained gasps and gurgles, and then vanished completely. She lifted her foot and smiled at the crimson and cream mesh of unrecognizable tissue at her feet. *How do you like that, buddy-boy? The shoe's on the other foot now, isn't it?* Then she laughed at her own pun, and brought her foot down again on the pile of pink, mushy tissue, splattered and nearly flattened on the pavement below her.

She opened her eyes and the tattered, bloodied image of what was left of Jimmy faded and she began to cry in deep choking sobs. She pulled the limp cotton pillow to her face and wiped the tears from her face for the umpteenth time that morning. Only a trace of makeup remained, smudging the pillow lightly with faded dirty stains.

Christopher Knight

chapter 154

Don lay in the grass, propped up on his elbows, idly watching boats coming to and leaving from the marina. A wave of distant applause filled the air. Across from the marina a children's soccer game was in progress. Ducks muttered to themselves as they bobbed in the flat waters. A few large mayflies glittered in the sun, fluttering about like delicate, crystal fairies. A big white Bayliner was backing out of the slip adjacent to Dave Shandler's trawler. Don recognized the huge man at the helm as the man he and Kari had seen sleeping on the deck that morning. He smiled as he remembered the obscene Mickey Mouse tattoo on his shoulder. Two other men were working on the boat. One lifted something on his shoulder and went below to store it.

Wait a minute.

A bead of perspiration ran down his forehead and on to the

metal frame of his glasses, dribbling down the inner side of the glass lens. He hastily pulled them off and wiped the smear away, quickly putting them back on and kept watching the boat as it left the marina. The man had picked up an air tank and taken it in to the cabin of the boat.

Then, like a gear slipping into place, a sudden memory struck Don, and he froze.

The two men near Eric and Kari's! At night! The ones that ducked off the road when I turned the corner!

It could have easily been one of the men. Very large, gargantuan. Not many people were likely to fit that description. Not as well as this guy did.

Don's gaze followed the Bayliner as it chugged out of the marina and into the river. He looked for a name of the boat, but there was none. *That's them,* he thought anxiously. *Has to be. Has to be them.* He stood up and walked rapidly, almost running, to the van.

chapter 155

The shrill double chirp of the phone awoke her on the first ring. Kari's thoughts were clouded as she reached across the bed for the phone. A strong afternoon sun seared the edges of the window pane and sent sharp streaks of white-hot rays burning around the outline of the curtain. "Hello?" she said groggily. She rubbed the sleep from her eyes.

"Kari?"

"Hi, Mike." She looked at the clock and yawned. *5:07 p.m.* "Wow. I didn't think I'd sleep that long."

"Remember when I said that Abigail Jewell was the great-grand-daughter of Richard Merman?" Mike interrupted.

"Yes."

"Well, guess what. Richard Merman kept a journal." His voice was smug with satisfaction and trilled with elation.

"Yeah?"

Twenty minutes later Kari hung up the phone, placing it on the table next to the bed. She was wide awake now. *Oh my God,* she thought. Her mind whirled. She couldn't believe it. *Oh my God,* she thought again. Suddenly everything clicked. She wished she could tell Eric what she had just learned but realized with a pang that it would have to wait until tomorrow.

She heard a car pull into the driveway, its tires screeching as it came to an abrupt halt on the pavement. She got up out of bed and was putting on her sweats when the doorbell rang.

"Just a second," she shouted as she jogged barefoot down the hall to the front door.

A thick, humid glaze hung in the air as the afternoon sun beat down. Don stood on the front porch, clad in a pair of shorts and a faded yellow tank top.

"Sorry to wake you up," he said quickly, as Kari opened the door.

"You didn't," she said. "Mike just called a few minutes ago. I was already up when you got here."

"I know who's been diving," he exclaimed, almost out of breath, unable to hide his excitement.

"And I know *why,*" Kari said, closing the door behind him. "Wait till you hear this."

After calling Kari, Mike hung up the receiver at the pay phone outside of the Marathon convenience store in Gaylord, an hour south of Cheboygan. Within a few minutes he was back on I-75 again, streaking north, his thoughts whipping by faster than the trees along the interstate. He looked at the old worn book lying on the seat beside him. Deep scratches gouged the soft leather binding and the top right corner looked as if a mouse or a rat had taken a few nibbles before deciding that he would be better off sticking to cheese or stale bread. There was no lettering on the cover of the book, just the blank dirty brown of aged cowhide. The pages inside were yellow and brittle and the book gave off a strong, musky smell that seemed to leap from the pages the instant he had flipped open the cover. The stiff pages were filled, front and back, with thick writing carefully written in black ink.

Mike could see the writer in his mind, sitting at his desk late at night. An oil lamp would have glowed atop a cluttered desk as the man wrote carefully with an old pen, dipping the end every so often into a small bottle of ink that sat off to the side of the open journal. It must have been a painstakingly slow process as Mike didn't see many places where a word or letter had been scratched out. Merman must have been clear with his thoughts, thinking his words out carefully before putting them down permanently on the pages beneath his fingertips. *And what words they are*, Mike thought, shaking his head. He let out a whistle. It was all coming together.

chapter 156

Ed, Phillip and Jimmy hadn't noticed the figure on the grassy bank watching them as they left the marina. Jimmy picked up one of the air tanks that Ed had filled and stowed it out of sight. Phillip stood at the bow in cut off denim shorts and a white T-shirt, one hand in his pocket, the other holding a can of Pepsi. Ed's cigarette dangled from the corner of his mouth, the thin trail of smoke curling around his cheek and fading away, dispersing into the air behind him. Soon, the boat was moored at the wreck site. Ed and Phillip suited up and plunged into the water.

All right, all right . . . where in the hell is it? Ed thought, as he waved his flashlight beam over the wreck. He inspected the damage the wreck had suffered during Jimmy's last dive. *The son of a bitch really tore things up.* Phillip glided up next to him and also looked inside the ship. He shined his light down along the hull and noticed that the soft debris of the bottom had been recently disturbed; clumps of sand and silt were scattered unnaturally over a small area. Dirty brown globs of mud lay piled in disarray, as if a child had been digging in a sandbox. The two divers descended along the hull, their flashlight beams trained on the murky bottom. Ed slowly lowered his knees into the sludge and carefully swept his hand through the already disturbed area. Chunks of clay-like debris fell between his fingers and tumbled back to the bottom as he slowly moved his arm back and forth. Phillip did the same. They found nothing.

Phillip looked at Ed's face behind the thick glass of the facemask and shrugged. Ed turned on his knees and faced the huge hull of the ship, which towered like a submerged skyscraper above him. He exhaled, and the silver bubbles glowed in the dim light and began their churning ascent to the surface. Then he shined his light along the bottom, where the hull of the ship and the sand met. Phillip dug in the fine silt that lay caked near the hull. He grasped a handful of the soft sludge and let it dribble through his hands. A cloud of sediment quickly enshrouded him, swirling and whirling like an underwater dust storm.

His hand brushed something in the silt. He pointed his light at the spot and turned it on and off once to attract Ed's attention. Both lights were now trained on Phillip's hand as he sifted the silt carefully. *There.* He felt his gloved hand bump something again. Something small like a stone or . . . *Got it!* He grasped the object with his hand and pulled it out of the mud. It was heavy, about ten inches long and the diameter of a hammer handle.

Ed grabbed it from Phillip's hand and began to scratch at the object with his knife. Clusters of blackened debris fell across the blade as he scraped harder. Ed wiped at the object with his glove, then began scraping again. Suddenly he stopped, holding the object further from his face. Phillip drew closer and looked. A strip of the sludge had been wiped away and a dull gray sheen shone through.

A silver bar.

chapter 157

On the boat, Phillip held the silver bar in his hand and stared at it in disbelief. "Son of a bitch," he said in awe. The bar was still dirty from years of being buried in the sand and water, but the sun caught a sliver of shiny metallic gray where Ed had scraped it with his knife. It glistened in the bright sun, the sweat and work of six years glowing in his hands as he held it before him.

Ed cut his elation short. "We haven't found jack shit." A fresh cigarette protruded from his mouth, and he lit it, exhaling the smoke through his nose. "We found a silver bar. That's a start. But we found the damned thing in the *sand*. It was supposed to be in a chest or a crate. Now it looks like the shit could be scattered all over the bottom of the lake. What's your fucking book say about that?" He looked at Phillip with a challenging glare.

"You read it yourself," Phillip replied defensively. "You know what it says. Maybe the chest broke open as the ship sank. How the hell should I know?"

"Let me have a look at that thing," Jimmy demanded. Phillip handed the bar to him and Jimmy whistled as he stroked the object in his hands in a passionate, almost sexual gesture.

"You know as much as I do. Why don't you take a stab at what happened, Mr. 'I-know-everything-treasure-finder'," Phillip said sarcastically.

Ed smiled unpleasantly. The fine gray hair over his ears tossed in the hot breeze and he brought the cigarette to his lips again and took a long drag on it. "You know what I think," he said. "I think you need to find the rest of that diary. I think that you need to find out exactly what happened to the ship and the chest."

"I told you," Phillip snapped. "There wasn't anymore."

"Well if that was it, then the wreck would be intact, with a chest full of gold and silver and diamonds. Now, correct me if I'm wrong, but we just found a silver bar *outside* of the ship. That tells me a few things. One, all the crap ain't in the chest like it is supposed to be, and two, if it ain't, then something happened aboard that ship that we don't know about. Something that wasn't written about in that book." His eyes narrowed as he took another hit from the cigarette. "And three, if that's the case, we got one hell of a salvage operation ahead of us. If we gotta dig through all kinds of shit to find the cargo, there's no tellin' how long it may take. Like I said—I think you gotta find the rest of that journal."

Phillip ignored him and looked at the dirty silver bar in Jimmy's hands. Jimmy had been rubbing some of the blotchy tarnish away and the bar had become much more defined. Faint, but unreadable, letters had begun to appear.

Ed stripped out of his wetsuit and allowed it to crumple in a heap at his feet. "Your turn," he said to Jimmy, who had already handed the silver bar back to Phillip and begun to put on his own wetsuit.

chapter 158

Phillip dialed the number from his motel room and held the phone to his ear with his shoulder, using both hands to clean off the papers and empty *Arby*'s bags that had begun to build up on the table by the bed. They had returned to the marina after Jimmy had finished his dive. Jimmy had found two more silver bars, both buried in the sand near the ship. *No, no, no*, Phillip thought. *This is not the way it should be at all. It shouldn't be scattered about on the bottom of the lake.*

The phone buzzed in his ear, ringing for the seventh or eighth time. *Hell, she's probably dead by now*, he thought. He gathered the wrappers and papers in his hand and tossed them in the small metal waste bin next to the dresser. Then he heard the receiver being picked up, but no voice came. He was about to speak himself when the tiny voice finally squeaked in his ear.

"Hello?"

"Hello, Mrs. Jewell," he said in a pleasant, easy tone. "This is Phillip Keanan. Maybe you remember me. A few years ago, I was doing some research on a ship and . . ."

"Of course," the fragile voice interrupted. Phillip paused, thinking she would continue. When she said nothing more, he began again. "Well, I'm continuing with my research. I was wondering . . . do you still have those boxes? The ones with the old pictures and letters?"

"Why yes, of course," Abigail said brightly.

Phillip breathed a sigh of relief. "I was wondering," he continued, "If I came down tomorrow, could I take another look through some of those papers?" He paused as his mind raced for an explanation. "I'm still trying to make a positive identification. I think that I might have found your great-grandfather's ship."

"I'm afraid that won't be possible for a few days. There was a man here just this morning looking for information about it, and he borrowed a box things."

Silence seeped through the lines, winding through the wires, underground, through trees, and over telephone poles. "A man?" Phillip asked cautiously. *"Today?"* He was dumbfounded.

"Yes," she continued. "This afternoon. A very nice man. He even found a few things that he said would be helpful. Some pictures . . . and a volume of my great grandfather's diary. I thought that all had been lost years ago."

Phillip's heart plummeted. *So there had been more*, he thought, cursing himself for not taking the time to look further after he had found the first volume. *And what 'man' could she be talking about? Randall was in jail.*

"A young man, Mrs. Jewell? Thirty-five? Forty?"

"Oh no," she replied. "He sounded older than that. Maybe in his sixties."

The description didn't at all ring a bell. "Well, maybe he could help me out," he said carefully. "Do you have his name? Maybe I could get in touch with him and we could share information."

"Oh yes," she said without hesitation. "It was Mike Felsing. He lives in Cross Village up north. He drove down this morning and left a short while ago. He borrowed my great-grandfather's journal for a few days."

"Do you know how many volumes there might have been?"

"Mr. Felsing asked the same thing. I can't say for sure. He said he had found just the one. I'm sure that I don't have any more around the house. If they're not in the attic, I'm afraid that any others must have been lost."

"Thank you, Mrs. Jewell," Phillip said, and he hung up the phone, immediately reaching for one of the yellow phone books in the table drawer. The thin sheets rolled easily beneath his fingers. Easton. Ellington. Elzinga . . . He turned the fine pages more slowly. Fairbanks. Fawcett. Faylor . . . The names rolled beneath his searching finger. Feeney. Feldman. Felrand . . . Felsing, Michael. A phone number as well as an address were listed. Phillip circled the name with a pen, dropped the open book on the bed, and picked up the phone.

chapter 159

The four passengers huddle on the deck, bathed in the dim glow of a lantern. After making sure they were all there, Jack stares at them coldly for a moment, then orders them taken back below deck to be tied up together in one cabin. Daniel and Jack are once again alone on the deck.

"Well, Daniel, want to take a look at what you can't have?" Jack laughs cynically. Daniel doesn't move or speak. He still can't believe that Jack could be capable of such unspeakable, cold treachery. "Go," Malloy orders, pointing to the main hatch. Daniel warily takes a step, wondering how he ever got wrapped up in this mess. And more importantly, how he's going to get out of it. One thing he is certain of: he is sure that the men have no intention on letting him live.

Jack follows Daniel in the glow of the lantern. In one of the cabins, a lantern cast a dim light in the dark corridor. Daniel can hear laughter and loud talking. He steps through the doorway into the cabin. The men stop talking and one reaches for his gun. After seeing Jack step through the doorway right after Daniel, the man puts the gun away.

They are gathered around the large wooden crate. The other smaller boxes have been hastily tossed aside and the chest is now open, its locks cast away and the chains scattered carelessly on the floor like iron snakes. The faces of the men are glowing with triumph. They have a look of awe and excitement, and their eyes are alive in the flickering light of the lantern. A bottle of whiskey is being passed around in celebration.

"Go ahead," Jack says, nudging Daniel. "Take a look."

Daniel hesitates for an instant, glances around at the circle of men. Then he steps forward into the glow of the lantern, peering into the chest.

Christopher Knight

chapter 160

"They're out there right now!" Don said excitedly as he stepped through the front door. After he watched the Bayliner leave the marina, he had raced back to find Kari. "I saw a boat with no name leaving the marina. Someone on board lifted an air tank and stowed it away in the cabin. They were divers."

"How many of them were there on the boat?" she asked.

"Three, as far as I could tell. You know that big guy we saw this morning? The guy with the tattoo?" He paused, and Kari's eyes narrowed for a moment as she tried to recall who he was talking about. So much had happened that morning that she wasn't sure who Don meant. "Down at the marina," he prompted. "Sleeping in the chair. Remember Mickey Mouse? You know . . . the finger?" Don pointed to his own shoulder. Kari suddenly nodded her head in acknowledgment. "They were in the slip next to

Dave's boat!" Don exclaimed. "And what's more . . . I think it could be one of the guys that I spotted when I left your house the other night."

Kari looked perplexed. Don shook his head.

"Sorry. I didn't tell you. I guess I didn't even remember it until I saw the guy at the marina with the air tank." He explained how he'd spotted the two figures in darkness, and how they had slipped out of sight when the van had surprised them.

Kari's eyes lit up. "That makes sense," she said. "They were probably the ones who vandalized John Galt."

"Not probably. I would say certainly."

"Let's go," Kari said, running into the living room to grab the pair of binoculars on the mantle. "We'll be able to see them from the north end of the Cheboygan State Park. I'll tell you what Mike found out on the way. You're not going to believe it!" Within seconds they had scrambled into the Blazer. "Mike called from a pay phone," Kari explained as the vehicle spun out of the driveway. "In Abigail Jewell's attic he found part of a journal stuffed away in some papers. They had fallen behind a book case, and the journal has probably been there for years. Merman wrote at length about some 'cargo' that he was shipping to New York and how someone had been following him. Merman himself must not have been aboard the Brittany because he wrote quite a bit about how the ship was late in reaching New York and how he was worried that the men who had followed him had somehow found out about the ship and stolen the cargo."

"What was the cargo?" Don asked, as he made the turn onto Main Street.

"Are you ready for this?" Kari said, her eyes glowing. "Treasure! Honest to God. You were right, Don! According to what Merman wrote, that crucifix we found was only part of it. Mike thinks that there must be at least one more volume before this one because this journal picks up in mid-story."

Don looked incredulous. "And what's the story?"

"Merman and some other men had been in Florida and there was a bad hurricane. The storm washed ashore a portion of a Spanish galleon that had been wrecked a few miles off the coast. They found gold, silver, and precious stones—a lot of it—among the wreckage. They divided the treasure between them and Merman was on his way back to his home in Chicago, when someone found out that he was carrying this fortune and began to follow him. After that Mike was only able to skim but he did find a torn partial list of the cargo. It mentions gold."

Don raised his eyebrows. "How much?"

"It doesn't say," Kari replied. "But it does say that there were also Columbian emeralds aboard." Kari stopped, waiting for Don's response.

"I'm not really familiar with—"

"Columbian emeralds are very precious stones," she continued. "They're a beautiful, deep green. There were nearly two hundred of them on board the Brittany."

"What are they worth?" Don asked, holding his breath.

"Two hundred Columbian emeralds would probably go for about fifty million dollars today," Kari said with mock casualness.

chapter 161

"They're there, all right," Kari said bitingly as she held the
binoculars to her eyes with one hand and shielded her eyes from the
sun with the other. The beach was packed with afternoon
sunbathers and swimmers and a dozen radios blared music, each
one playing a different station. Don caught bits and pieces of songs
by Garth Brooks, Soul Asylum, Stone Temple Pilots, and that
annoying All Right Now by Free that had, at one time, been a great
anthem until it had been overplayed by every rock station in the
country.

Every so often the sweet aroma of coconut suntan oil tickled his
nostrils. A man and a woman were having a not-so-successful
game of frisbee. The wind kept taking the disc, carrying it over the
beach and up to the parking lot. A brown Rottweiler, soaking wet,
made its rounds among the people spread out among their towels,

hungrily devouring scraps and hand-outs.

"They look like they're anchored," Kari continued, speaking slowly. "Unfortunately, I can't make out much more." She handed the binoculars to Don. He took his glasses off and raised the binoculars to his eyes.

"You want to wait for them to return?" he asked, lowering the binoculars and handing them back to her.

Kari shook her head. "Too risky. I don't know what would happen if they saw us. I've got another idea."

They hopped back into the Blazer and sped back into town to the marina. Kari got out and went into the harbormaster's office, returning a few minutes later. "The slip next to Dave's is leased by a man named Ed Beech. He's had it for a few years. A 'fisherman.' Or so the harbormaster says."

She hopped back in the Blazer, wheeled out of the marina and headed back to the house.

chapter 162

Eric had not taken the notice of his delayed arraignment well. When Sheriff Tyrell brought him the news, he jumped up and said angrily, "What in the hell do you mean, a scheduling conflict?"

"Look, Eric," the Sheriff said, raising his hands. "This happens quite a bit. There is nothing I can do. Getting upset is counterproductive."

Eric had tried to remain calm through the entire ordeal, figuring that, even if he was charged, he would be out of jail by late afternoon. The news of the delay was the final straw and sent him into a rage. "I am not upset!" he yelled. "I'm totally pissed off! First off, I get yanked out of bed at three o'clock in the morning and arrested for something I didn't do and now you're telling me that my arraignment has been postponed because the judge has a damn scheduling conflict?" His face was damp with perspiration, his temples throbbed, and his cheeks were flushed with anger.

Tyrell crossed his arms and stood quietly until Eric finished. "Eric, do you think we like this?" he asked quietly, staring directly into Eric's eyes as he addressed him. Eric fell silent. "This doesn't sound like your style. Not that I would even recognize your style if you had one, but I don't think you're stupid enough to leave stolen property on your boat or to deface a wreck in the Preserve. I don't know you real well, but I know you well enough to know that something isn't right here.

"But the fact is we gotta play by the rules. Hell, if it were up to me, I'd send you home and say come back tomorrow for the hearing. But it's not up to me, and I have to enforce the rules whether I like'em or not. I hope you understand that." He turned and walked away before Eric had a chance to say anything more.

Yeah, well try being on the other side of the bars once in a while, Eric thought disconsolately, sitting down on his bunk. The Sheriff was right, and he would just have to deal with it. One night in the county jail couldn't be that bad. At least that was what he hoped.

chapter 163

Phillip dialed the number of Jimmy's hotel room, let it ring a dozen times, then hung up. He stared at the open phone book on the bed, then tore out the page with the Felsing listing on it, folded it, and stuffed it into his pocket. To hell with it, he thought. Jimmy will find out soon enough. He grabbed a sweatshirt from a laundry bag and left.

Ed had returned to the boat first. After their first dive, they had headed back to the marina so that Ed could refill the air tanks with the compressor at his cabin. They unloaded the tanks in large duffel bags and threw them into the back of the late Paul Sprague's Ranger. The Ford was once again parked in the lot when Phillip returned, but Jimmy's Trans Am was absent. Ed was in the cabin, sorting and separating the lift bags that would be used to retrieve the treasure at the bottom of Lake Huron.

Phillip reached into his pocket and unfolded the thin white page, laying it on the table in front of Ed. When Phillip didn't offer an explanation, Ed asked, "I give up. What is it?"

"I called the old lady down in St. Clair Shores. She says that a man was there asking about the shipwreck. Today."

Ed stopped what he was doing and picked up the page.

"He found another part of the journal," Phillip said quietly. He wasn't sure how Ed was going to take the news. They had bickered occasionally about whether or not there were more volumes of Merman's diary, but Phillip had assured him that he had searched through everything and if there had been, he would have found it. Now, with obvious proof that he had been wrong, he was waiting for Ed the Madman to appear, to rant and rave and scream. The air in the cabin was thick with tension.

"Well, this changes things," Ed said calmly, placing the torn page back on the table and resuming his work on the lift bag. Phillip could almost hear the rushing sssssssss of escaping anxiety from the cabin. When Ed had no more to say, a wave of relief surged over him. He was sure Belmont would have exploded in fury.

Ed pushed a lift bag aside and picked up the torn page again and read the circled name aloud. "Felsing." He sat down in a chair, the thick plastic legs bowing and creaking under his enormous weight. Two flabby tires rolled over the chair's armrests. He reached for his pack of cigarettes, still holding the torn page in his hand. "Michael Felsing," he continued pensively. "That exchange is Good Hart or Cross Village. Southwest of here about forty miles."

"The old biddy said this guy was older," Phillip offered. "He came by himself. She said he called her this morning and drove down this afternoon. He borrowed a few things and said he'd return them soon."

"No matter," Ed snorted, taking a drag from the Camel. "It's a little late for anybody else to be doing their homework. By the time they figure out exactly what's down there, we will have already saved them the burden of bringing it up. If we get our asses in gear." He turned and looked out the cabin window, breathing a cloud of smoke into the glass. "Where the hell is Jimmy?"

chapter 164

When Jimmy got back to his room, Sharon was gone. Good, the bitch went home, he thought with satisfaction as he inspected the empty room. He looked at the blood-stained sheets and pillows. Shit, she didn't even have the decency to clean up. He bundled the sheets into a large ball. Can't let room service see these, he thought, carrying them around the room as he wondered what to do with them. Screw it, he decided. I'll throw 'em out and buy some more. He tossed the bundle of sheets and pillowcases down near the door and stepped into the bathroom.

His leg was throbbing again and he pulled up the leg of his sweat pants and pulled off the bandages, laying his injured leg over the side of the bathtub. The warm water felt good and he let it run for a moment as he inspected the stitches. The gash looked like it was healing and the other cuts and scrapes had scabbed over. He shut the water off and dabbed his leg dry with a towel. There had been a few moments of anguish when he put his wetsuit over the wounds, but the discomfort went away when he dived. The deeper he went, the increasing pressure would keep the throbbing down. By the time he had made it to the wreck, the pain had virtually gone away.

He turned to flex in the mirror, to make sure that he hadn't lost any muscle mass over the past day or so. He stared. He hadn't noticed the writing until now.

"Well, you little bitch," he said quietly in a mocking, inimical tone. "You've got some balls, all right."

Sharon had defaced the mirror with deep red lipstick and the words spanned the entire mirror, distorting his reflection. In big, twelve-inch size letters, Sharon had left him a two-word message: YOU'RE DEAD.

The mirror gave the letters the appearance of being doubled, as if they had been written over top themselves. Jimmy stared, shaking his head. He tried wiping off the lipstick but it just smeared and he threw the washcloth down in disgust. He looked at the message for a long moment and then stepped out of the bathroom and closed the door.

chapter 165

The men watch as Daniel steps closer to the open crate. Their eyes burn like fire in the light and he likens them to the demons he had heard so much of in Sunday school. Their shadows grow long on the floor and against the wall; dark, ominous and swallowing everything in their path. These are the men who had given him one hundred dollars and had promised him a lot more. The ones he had so foolishly believed. They sneer at him as he approaches the box and he averts their gaze and looks into the open chest.

The brilliance that radiates from the inside of the chest is dazzling and he has to squint to see clearly. He has suspected something of the sort, but certainly not to this extent. Daniel had expected gold, but he is totally unprepared for what he was looking at now. Gold there is—in the form of bars and jewelry inlaid with glittering gems. But there are also silver bars and medallions, gold coins, and large, loose stones of a luminous green. Daniel has never seen such a sight in his life. The gold and silver reflect the gleam of the lantern, bathing the tiny cabin in a phosphorescent glow. The men catch his incredulous gaze and one of them laughs.

"Too bad you didn't just do what you were told, eh boy?" one of them asks. The men laugh and the harsh sounds push into every corner of Daniel's brain. Dirty yellow grins flash in the lamplight and the faint pungent smell of whiskey drifts to his nose. The laughter continues for only a few seconds, but to Daniel it seems like it is much longer than that. The jerking motions of their necks, the slow bobbing of their heads, their eyes and mouths opening and closing in uncontrollable laughter seem to happen in slow motion.

He turns and looks at Jack, who is smiling as well. Not the easy, sincere smile that Daniel has known, but an evil malevolent grin, above which his wicked eyes burn with greed. Suddenly, Daniel knows that even if he had done as he was told, he would have been killed. And he knows that even if he did what he was told now, he will still be killed. The sinking feeling in his heart makes him dizzy. There is no way out.

Jack and the men open up some of the smaller wooden crates, emptying their contents on the floor. Dishes, plates, cups, and other household items tumble out haphazardly and some break as they strike the hardwood planks. The men kick the debris away and stack the smaller, now empty, boxes to the side. Carrying the entire chest would be out of the question. Even if they forced the two male passengers to help, they probably would not have been able to lift it. It will be easier to load the treasure into smaller boxes and carry them away one at a time. After nearly two dozen small crates have been open, emptied, and stacked, the men figure that they had enough to carry away the contents of the large crate.

Daniel stands and watches, his face blank and glowing in the cool lantern light. He thinks about running, fleeing into the

Christopher Knight

darkness of the corridor. But where will he go? He wouldn't make it to the dinghy in time and besides, even if he did make it, they could easily shoot him as he tried to row away. The possibilities fly through his mind, but he knows it is hopeless.

"Over here." One of the men points to Daniel and motions for him to come closer. Daniel wordlessly does as he is told. "Pick that up and carry it out on to the deck," he orders Daniel. "Put them all together where the dinghy is tied up."

Daniel picks up the crate. It is incredibly heavy. The other men, including Jack, also pick up a crate and follow Daniel out of the cabin and down the hallway. As Daniel walks, his mind whirls, trying to think of any means of escape. But none come. There would be nowhere to hide on the ship. And if he leapt overboard and was able to get away, he knew he wouldn't be able to swim the several miles to shore.

The contents of the chest fill nineteen wood boxes that are soon stacked next to one another on the deck of the ship. Jack comes up through the main hatchway. "Let's get moving," he snarls. "We've spent too much time here already." One by one, they lower the crates to the dinghy. After four of the heavy wooden boxes are loaded, two of the men board the small boat and row it over to the waiting ship. The entire process is painstakingly slow, but after two hours only a single crate remains on the deck. The dinghy is now moored at the other ship, and the men are unloading the two crates. In a moment they will be coming back for the last of the treasure.

The remaining man addresses Jack. "What about them?" he nods to the main hatch, alluding to the four passengers below. Jack says nothing.

chapter 166

The tattered, worn book lay spread open on Mike's desk next to the dark monitor of his computer. He had returned only a few minutes ago and was now poring over the journal in detail. The pages were brittle and he turned them slowly, skimming the stiff writing but trying not to miss any important information. He slowed when he came to a sentence or word that was distorted.

In some places the black ink was dry and clear, but in others it had smeared, as if stained by dampness. His heart beat faster as he read. This was what he'd been longing for, what he'd needed for a long time: some kind of mystery or adventure to add a spark to his life. He hadn't realized how much he'd really missed his days of detective work until now. The drama rushed back to him like a sudden sweeping cloudburst, each warm droplet of rain a possible solution, a possible answer, to be pondered over and carefully examined.

Finally, Mike closed the book and carried it gently with both hands, like it was precious china ready to crumble with only the slightest mishap. Evelyn had left him a note saying she had gone to Harbor Springs for a few hours. He left his own message on a yellow sticky-note, posted it on the telephone, and headed for Cheboygan.

chapter 167

Sharon sat on her bed looking out the window at, but not seeing, the beautiful day. The late afternoon was hot and the air conditioner hummed quietly on the other side of the room. She turned and looked into the wall mirror. Her swollen red eye had turned a dark purple-black but her swollen, split lip was receding.

The heat hit her the moment she walked out the lobby doors. The acrid smell of burning pavement made her woozy. She paused, took a deep breath, and the feeling passed. Then she crossed the road and entered the corner convenience store, turning immediately to the tall spindle carrying hundreds of sunglasses. She chose the darkest ones she could find and put them on. Then she chose a red baseball hat from another rack without even looking at it and put that on as well, tucking her long black hair under it. The clerk gave her a smile and then a questioning frown as he looked her over. He stared at her face a moment, then looked away and began tapping the keys of the cash register. Sharon paid for the sunglasses and hat without taking them off.

"Sure is bright out there today, huh?" the clerk said. Sharon managed a slight smile but said nothing, turning her head slightly and looking out the large, plate-glass windows. A car caught her attention and her heart fell into her stomach. A black Trans Am was cruising slowly by in front of her motel. Sharon's pulse began to race furiously as she identified Jimmy's shape through the tinted windows. *Oh, God, he's gonna turn in. He knows I'm at the Continental Inn.* But the Trans Am continued on down Huron Street, toward the marina. He hadn't spotted her car, but she told herself that she would have to be more careful. She needed Jimmy to think that she had left for Detroit. *Don't want to spoil our fun so soon, do we?* she thought.

She glanced at the clerk. He was standing behind the counter holding her change out, smiling patiently. "That's a nasty swollen lip you got there," he said. "Howdja do that?" She ignored the question, took her change from him and left. The Trans Am was still visible on Huron Street and she stood in the open door of the convenience store until it turned into the marina.

Be careful, Sharon, she told herself. *Be careful.* It only took five minutes to walk to the marina, even moving as slowly as she was. She walked on the shoulder of the road and kept her head down, wary of any cars that approached her. Ed and Phillip were probably around somewhere, too, and she didn't want to be seen by them either.

The sun scorched her back and shoulders through her white

blouse. She'd always had a preconceived notion that northern Michigan was cold all the time. "Not today," she said aloud to herself, and wiped the sweat from her forehead. A car approached her from behind and she looked away as it sped by, in case any of its occupants had been looking at her as they passed. When it had gone a short distance, she turned back to get a look at it, half expecting to see Ed's beat up red Ford Ranger or Phillip's truck, but it was neither.

She reached the marina, walked to the water fountain, and bent down to get a sip, trying to be as inconspicuous as possible. She straightened up and scouted the parking lot surreptitiously. All three cars were there. The Trans Am was parked in the corner of the lot in typical Jimmy Durand fashion, taking up two spaces. Ed's Ranger and Phillip's Dodge Dakota were parked side-by-side. Sharon took a deep breath and looked over the boats moored in their slips.

No Jimmy, no Ed, no Phillip, she noted in relief. She looked carefully for the boat that she had seen Jimmy on two days ago, but she wasn't sure if she would recognize it. When she was sure that they must have already left the marina, she began to walk towards the Trans Am.

Damn, she thought, stopping half-way through the parking lot. *I forgot to bring my duffel bag. How could I be so stupid!* She turned and looked around, towards the marina entrance, wondering if she should go back to the motel. *No, not enough time. Might not ever get another opportunity like this one. I'll just have to make do with what I can.*

She reached the Pontiac and peered inside through the dark

tinted glass, hoping that Jimmy might have left one of his gym bags in the back seat. Styrofoam coffee cups and wrappers flooded the floor, along with a pair of jeans and an old flannel shirt that had been used as a rag. But there was no bag of any kind.

"Shit," she said quietly. She looked around. On the far side of a small portico were two dark green heavy-duty vinyl trash cans with lids. *Maybe there's something in there that will work*, she thought, and walked over to the can and lifted one of the lids.

The smell was horrific. Hundreds of flies poured into the air, buzzing about her face and whirring in the air about her. She swept the flies away with a stroke of her arm and looked into the barrel. It was filled with scraps of food and plastic wrappers. A hamburger coated with a layer of gray-green fuzz lay on the top, covered by dozens of stubborn flies that were either to lazy to fly away or just didn't want to give up a good spot at the buffet. Next to that, a black rotting banana peel sat like a spider, its legs curled and twisted underneath itself. Her eyes caught a piece of brown under the piles of debris.

If that's what I think it is, it just might work, she thought. She reached into the can and the remaining flies on the piece of meat took to the air. One of them lit on her nose, and she quickly brushed it away, shuddering in disgust.

A shrill, piercing voice suddenly came out of nowhere, and she jumped, almost dropping the garbage can lid. *"Mommy!!"* he screeched. *"Mommy!! That man is eating stuff from the garbage can!! Mommy, look!"* Sharon turned to see a small child about five feet away, pointing at her. She froze.

"Kyle! Get over here this instant!" The voice, faint but firm,

came from an unseen face in one of the many boats. The boy dropped his arm, took one last look at Sharon, and ran off towards one of the boats in the marina. *That's right kid,* she thought. *You saw a man eating garbage today. Remember that.*

She grabbed the small piece of brown paper that was buried under a mountain of rubbish. The bag was spotted with grease, and she held it up distastefully between her index finger and her thumb. *A little dirty, but it'll do,* she decided. She placed the lid back onto the garbage can, walked back over to the Trans Am and tried the door. It was locked.

Walking to the front of the car, she put her hand under the bumper, feeling across the fiberglass spoiler for the familiar piece of duct tape. It was caked with dirt and didn't peel away easily, but it finally gave way with a loud *sssshhhhhhttt* like the sound of tearing cloth. She held the tattered piece of tape in her hand and pulled the spare key off the sticky side. The key slid into the lock and turned easily. She opened the door, jumped quickly inside, and closed the door.

The inside of his car, as usual, was a mess. Coffee cups, wrappers, newspapers, and even one of his spent syringes from shooting up the Tetranobol were flung carelessly on the floor on the passenger side. An assortment of cassette tapes, from Judas Priest to Blue Oyster Cult lay slathered across the passenger seat, baking in the sun. She recognized *Agents of Fortune* by Blue Oyster Cult as one that she had bought years ago. She thought she had lost it, but here it was, worn and dirty without its case. She picked it up, turned it over in her hands and contemplated taking it back. *No,* she thought, putting it back on the seat. *Go ahead and listen to it a little more, Jimmy. It might be the last music you ever hear.* *Remember* Don't Fear the Reaper? *If I were you, I'd be a little afraid. I'd be a lot afraid, Jimmy, if I were you.* The tune drifted through her mind as she reached beneath the front seat, pulled out the Smith & Wesson .38 caliber handgun and put it in the dirty brown paper bag.

chapter 168

Sharon returned to the motel without incident. There had been a nervous moment when a city police cruiser had passed, eyeing her suspiciously, glancing at the bag. She turned after he passed and the cop touched his brakes and she saw him glance into the rear-view mirror. Apparently satisfied, he continued on down Huron Street, probably just making his afternoon rounds of the park and the marina.

The clerk at the motel didn't recognize her as she walked through the lobby and she pulled out her room key for him to see. He nodded in bored confirmation and she stepped into the elevator and pressed the faded red '2' button on the panel. She was uncomfortable carrying the gun around and the sooner she was back in her room the better she would feel. The steel doors slid open and to her relief, no one was waiting to enter the elevator.

The second floor was also empty.

She entered her room and closed the door, then pulled the gun out and lay it on the bed. Sharon had never liked guns and had protested vehemently when Jimmy had purchased the two Smith & Wessons. "Why do you need two?" she had asked. "One is bad enough." He had never given her an answer. She knew that he kept one under the car seat and carried the other with him, usually in his gym bag. Both firearms were registered, but Jimmy had no permit to carry one either in his car or concealed on his person. It remained a mystery to her why he felt he needed such protection. One look at Jimmy and nobody was going to mess with him anyway.

It's the other way around, she thought. *People need protection from Jimmy. I need protection from Jimmy.*

She picked up the gun and felt the cool steel in her hands, running her fingers down the barrel. She hefted it and pointed it at the wall like she had seen cops do on TV. She brought her other hand up and held the gun with two hands, sighting at her own image in the mirror. She lined up the sights and gazed down the barrel of the .38, staring down the battered face in the mirror.

"People need protection from *you*, Jimmy," she said aloud. "But not for long. We'll be taking care of that real soon, Jimmy Durand. Real soon." She wrapped the gun in a white hand towel and carefully put it between two of her shirts in her suitcase.

chapter 169

The cell was hot. Eric sweated and tried to keep his thoughts in order. He was still upset at himself for his silly outburst at the Sheriff earlier that afternoon. But then again, he had a right to be pissed off. He had been framed, just like in some TV drama. He still couldn't believe that it was happening. He thought about telling Tyrell the whole thing up to when they had found the crucifix, but he decided against it, at least for the time being.

A door slammed shut at the other end of the hall and he heard footsteps approaching. The deputy put his key in the lock and opened the cell door. "Your lawyer's here. Come on." The deputy led Eric out of his cell and down the hall to a small room. Jennifer Brooks waited for him at a single table with two chairs. She was a thin woman, with the strong chiseled features of a triathlete. Short, dark brown hair. She wore very little make-up, and the only jewelry she wore was her wedding ring and a gold watch; an anniversary gift from her husband. While working she was all business, and today was no exception.

Eric took a seat across from her as the deputy closed the door and the two were alone. Jennifer extended her hand and Eric took it, smiling.

"Well, Eric, when you decide to make the news, you do it in a big way," she began. "I'm sorry that I couldn't make it earlier."

"No problem," Eric said, managing a smile. "It's not like I'm going anywhere."

"I just came from your house after talking with Kari. She gave me this to give to you." She reached into her briefcase and pulled out a sealed envelope. Eric read the contents, wide-eyed, and gave it back to Jennifer. He sat back in his seat and looked up at the ceiling, as if pondering the possibilities. Then he frowned and tilted back towards the table. Jennifer sat quietly, watching him, waiting for him to begin.

"A couple of weeks ago," Eric began, "we came across a shipwreck out in Lake Huron." He told her everything including the recovering of the gold crucifix. She listened intently while he spoke.

"How many people know about the wreck?" she asked in dazed amazement.

"Apparently more than we thought. But from our end, it's just myself, Kari, Don Garrity, Mike Felsing and his wife."

The two talked for another thirty minutes before Jennifer left, saying she'd be back tomorrow morning for his arraignment. The deputy led Eric back to his cell, locked the door, and left without a word.

Eric lay back on his bunk with his hands behind his head, re-reading Kari's note in his mind. She had written that Mike had found Richard Merman's journal and the cargo it described. He was having a difficult time believing it. He laughed out loud, wondering what Jennifer Brooks had thought when he told her the story. Probably thinks I need a shrink, he thought. I wouldn't blame her if she did, either. A treasure ship? In Lake Huron? Sabotage? Pirates?

But everything was beginning to make sense to Eric. Columbian emeralds worth fifty million dollars? No wonder somebody didn't want them diving on the wreck. The saboteurs could be diving themselves, right now, plundering the wreck of all its valuables. They had already destroyed a major portion of the wreck. He was certain that they would stop at nothing to retrieve the cargo from the *Brittany*.

Suddenly he sat straight up on his bunk, eyes wide open, as a terrible thought struck him.

No! She wouldn't do it, would she? She wouldn't dive on the wreck alone, would she? He told himself that she wouldn't try it. He told himself that she knew that it would be too dangerous. *Don't do it Kari. Please, don't do it. Wait 'til I'm outta here.*

chapter 170

Mike, Don, and Kari sat around the kitchen table as the sun sank in the evening sky. The sliding glass door was open, and a warm breeze drifted through the screen. Merman's journal lay open on the table and Mike flipped through the pages, leaving slips of paper between a few of them, marking spots that he wanted to come back to. "Well, we know a few things for sure," he said. "Merman doesn't know what ultimately happened to the ship. In the first few pages, he says that the ship is four days late and he has begun to fear the worst. There are pages and pages of emotional turmoil. He writes constantly of not knowing what to do. He has children aboard the Brittany. I think that if we had the previous volumes, we would have a lot more answers than questions."

Don stroked his beard. "What about that cargo list? Does it say anything more about what exactly the cargo was?"

Mike pulled a loose piece of paper from the back of the old book and handed it to Don. "The only thing I can make out is this." Mike pointed to the clear writing at the top of the page. "The rest must have gotten damp because it's too obscured to make out." He pointed to one word near the middle of the page, "That looks like the word 'gold.' What do you think?"

"It sure looks like it," Don agreed, handing the brittle, yellowed paper to Kari, who scanned the page but said nothing. She handed the paper back to Mike.

"What about the value of the emeralds?" Kari asked.

Mike nodded confidently. "Yes. If anything, my estimate is low. Merman must have really hit the jackpot in Florida. Especially if this is only a partial list of what they found. It looks like the rest of the list is included with the previous volume."

Mike left, promising to return tomorrow for Eric's arraignment. Kari and Don sat alone at the table. Kari got up and brought back two beers from the kitchen and handed one to Don. He held the cold bottle in his hand, peeling at the label. They sat in silence, listening to the evening sounds drift through the open sliding glass door. A sprinkler system droned from a nearby yard, and a few houses down the neighborhood kids had gathered for a boisterous game of Kick the Can. Don set his beer on the table.

"Fifty million dollars worth of emeralds alone," he said. "All sitting on the bottom of the lake."

"We can find it before they do," Kari said confidently, finishing her beer. She gazed at him knowingly..

"No. Huh-uh," he said emphatically, shaking his head. "Don't even go there. No way in hell."

Christopher Knight

chapter 171

Phillip and Jimmy dived together first and found three more silver bars. The three bars weren't heavy enough for them to use the lift bags and Jimmy carried them up in his mesh bag.

Back on the surface, Ed's passive demeanor was slowly beginning to change—for the worse. "What are you talking about? *Three bars?* That's all you found?" He held an unlit cigarette and sucked on it without seeming to realize it wasn't lit. "We're running out of time. If we don't get that shit tonight, we may not get it at all."

Jimmy had been carefully peeling his wetsuit away from around his injured leg. He glared at Ed. "For somebody who's in such a big damn hurry, I don't see you with a wetsuit on," he snapped, then froze in stance, challenging the huge man. *Come on, you fat old bastard,* he thought. *Do something. Do something and I'll rip your fucking lungs out and shove 'em up your ass.*

Ed looked at him for a moment in disgust and then tossed the unlit cigarette into the lake. Without a word he began to don his wetsuit.

Ed found nothing. After returning to the surface the three stood on the deck in the fading evening sun. Ed took the last sip of his beer and tossed the can carelessly into the cabin. The can clanked lightly as is bounced off a chair and rolled to a stop in a corner.

"That shit's down there somewhere," he said angrily. "But it's not on the ship. I'll bet it's scattered all over the bottom of the damn lake."

"Well, if we can't find it, I doubt that Randall is gonna have any better luck," Phillip said.

"The problem with Randall," Jimmy said carefully, "is that now he *knows* what's out here. And he knows that someone deliberately set him up. God knows who else he's told." He looked directly at Ed. "Maybe we acted a little too hastily in trying to stall him."

Ed took the comment as a direct assault to his intelligence. His nostrils flared and his eyes widened. He turned and faced Jimmy. "Let me tell you something—"

"Yeah, go ahead!" Jimmy snarled, stiffening. "Tell me something, Ed!" He had been leaning against the railing and now he snapped straight up and took a step towards Ed. The situation was beyond explosive. Jimmy and Ed squared off just inches apart, neither one flinching. The tense confrontation was about to break wide open when Phillip, never before the peacemaker, spoke up nervously.

"Hey, this isn't helping us one bit," he said, putting his hands up. "We just need to keep out of sight and pay attention to when they dive. Maybe if we lay low they'll think we're gone. Then we could dive at night without them knowing."

Ed and Jimmy didn't flinch, silently challenging each other to make the first stupid move. Eyes glared and burned. Phillip wasn't even sure if they had heard what he said. The stress of finding the wreck and then only finding a tiny portion of the treasure had been quickly taking its toll on the emotions of all three men. Even Phillip was tense, but not as much as Jimmy and Ed, who were just about to rip one another limb from limb. Phillip thought that Jimmy would probably tear the fat old man to shreds, but then again, Ed had surprised him often enough before. Phillip thought that if there was anyone that would be able to hold their own against Jimmy, it would be Ed.

"I gotta better idea," Ed said, not taking his eyes off of Jimmy. The air seemed to hum between them like a high tension wire. "We just let that bastard find it and bring it up for us." He turned away from Jimmy and both men relaxed a little.

"What if he told the cops?" Phillip mused.

"Randall hasn't told the cops," Ed sniggered, finding his pack of cigarettes and shaking a cigarette from the pack. He lit it, tossed the match into the lake and exhaled the smoke. "He hasn't and he won't. Because if he tells the cops he'll get nothing. Zippo. The wreck will become property of the state and all those millions of dollars in gold and silver and rocks will be on display in a museum." A gray ash fell from the tip of his cigarette and tumbled down the front of his white tank top. He brushed it away absently and continued. "He'll be out of jail as soon as he's arraigned. As soon as he gets out, you can bet he's gonna dive again." Ed took another drag from his cigarette and pronounced, "Yep. That's what we'll do. I think we've done about enough work. I think it's time to let someone else put in their share of the effort."

"And what about that other guy? Felsing?" Phillip asked. "He still has the other part of the journal."

"Even better. Hopefully, it'll tell them exactly where they need to look. Like I said, let *them* do the work. From now on, we'll stay clear of the marina and out of sight. We'll keep the boat at the northeastern tip of Bois Blanc Island so we can watch the dive site but not be seen." He paused, and the tip of his cigarette glowed in the encroaching dark, "Then, we'll relieve them of the burden of ownership."

chapter 172

Don had tried to reason with Kari but she was adamant. "If we wait until tomorrow to make another dive, it might be too late," she argued. "We have to dive *now,*" Don. Then she caught herself. "*I* have to dive, Don. Before it's too late."

Don gave in largely because she had made it clear that she was going to dive with or without him. Reluctantly, he finally said he would go along and follow her down—with the underwater camera.

"But I have to run back to the cabin to get some warmer clothes," he said. "I'll meet you back here in thirty minutes." As the Caravan pulled out of the driveway, he saw Kari sitting impatiently on the porch already counting the minutes until his return.

The final rays of sun were bleeding through the trees as Don turned into the driveway to his cabin. He walked across the grass and opened the door to the small efficiency cottage and turned on the light over the sink, packed a few articles of clothing into his duffel bag, and set it by the door.

Don looked out the window at Duane's house. It was dark and the curtains were closed. Picking up the key Duane had given him, he left the cabin and strode quickly over to the empty house.

Don felt guilty entering Duane's home without him present. He felt blindly on the wall for a light switch. He found it and the room brightened, silent and empty. *Cripes*, he thought, as his eyes scanned over the dozens of guns hung on the wall. *Which one was the one he kept loaded?* Experimentally, he took a pump shotgun from the wall, racked the chamber, and put it back down.

Nope. Not that one.

He picked up another, a heavy twelve-gauge and racked it. A shell ejected, tumbling through the air and landing on the floor with a thud. The three-inch cylinder, brass and red, bounced at Don's feet before rolling and coming to a stop at the leg of a small table.

Bingo.

He racked the chamber again, but no more shells ejected. Don glanced around the room, hoping to see a box of shells on the mantle or somewhere in plain sight. There were none.

He picked up the single shell, re-loaded it into the shotgun and quickly left the living room, turning off the light and locking the door behind him. He wasn't crazy about the idea of Kari diving, especially at night. And he certainly wasn't crazy about the possibility of encountering the three men he had seen earlier today. The thought of having a shotgun provided some added comfort, but not much.

Please don't come home early, Duane, he thought, walking quickly across the lush green lawn. The sun had slid beneath the trees on the other side of the lake. Damp grass whispered beneath his feet as he trudged on, the shotgun under his arm. *Stay in Rockford another day . . . or anywhere, for that matter. But please don't come back early, Duane.* He laid the shotgun carefully on the floor of the Caravan, checked to make sure the safety was on, and covered the gun with an old blanket.

The kitchen light was on and the cabin door was still open. Don walked back inside to make sure that he didn't need anything else. After a quick scan of the room, he picked up his bag and turned off the light. The crunch under his foot stopped him before he got out the door. Even before he turned the light back on, he knew what he'd stepped on.

Shit. Not again.

Crushed by his weight, the dreamcatcher—*his* dreamcatcher—lay at his feet, broken and twisted, the fragile twig snapped in four places.

"Where the hell did you get this?" Kari said, staring at the shotgun that lay in the van, which was parked and running in the driveway. It was now completely dark and after the equipment had been loaded into the Dodge, Don had pulled back a portion of the blanket exposing the barrel.

"The guy who owns the resort is out of town," Don replied soberly. His eyes met hers. "I kind of borrowed it. Just to be on the safe side."

chapter 173

The night was clear and the air was warm and still. The stars twinkled by the millions as Dave Shandler's boat chugged lazily towards the Channel. They were going slowly, watching the darkness in front of them. When Kari and Don had arrived at the marina, the slip next to Dave's boat was empty. The other divers could still be at the dive site, but as Don and Kari looked out over the dark lake it was impossible to tell. Kari steered the trawler and Don stood on the bow, keeping a nervous, careful watch. The shotgun wasn't much more than a token comfort, but getting it on the boat without anyone seeing it had been easy. Kari had a dive gear bag that was a full six inches longer than the shotgun and it had fit nicely inside, along with her wetsuit, vest, and regulator.

Kari called quietly out from the helm, "See anything?"

"It's too dark to be sure," Don said. "But I think they're gone.

I don't see any sign of their boat."

"We're here," Kari said as she cut the motor and the aging engine groaned and died instantly. The night became very quiet, with only the sound of water gently lapping against the hull. The darkness overtook them. In the distance a few scattered buoy markers and lighthouses blinked, warning of dangerous shoals or reefs. The salty trail of the Milky Way twisted overhead, and from somewhere high in the sky, the faint buzzing of a small plane could be heard. Twenty miles to the northwest, the Mackinac Bridge spanned the Straits, ordained with hundreds of glimmering lights. Don could hear Kari fumbling with something in the dark cabin. Moments later, she appeared on deck. "Anchor's out," she said.

"Are you sure you want to do this?" Don asked, even though he knew that she wouldn't change her mind.

Kari ignored him. "Come on. Help me suit up."

"Okay, turn it around and cut the engine," Ed ordered. Jimmy shut down the engine and joined Ed and Phillip at the bow. All three peered into the black night that enveloped them. It was completely dark except for the lights of Cheboygan that glittered a few miles off, and the lights of the Mackinac Bridge to the west. Minutes earlier, the three had been preparing to leave the dive site when they heard the faint sound of a boat's motor approaching. The fact that the vessel was running without its lights told them all they needed to know. Jimmy had fired up the Bayliner and headed slowly northwest towards Bois Blanc Island until Ed ordered him to stop the boat.

They listened, straining their ears in the dark night. The muffled growling of the approaching boat drifted over the lapping water for about a minute, drawing nearer. Then it stopped. Ed lit a cigarette, cupping the match in his hands before blowing the tiny flame out and tossing it overboard. It hit the water with a *pfffftt* just as he pulled the cigarette from his lips. He cleared his throat softly. "We'll stay out of sight and wait here for a while. Drop anchor so we don't drift into them."

chapter 174

The shouts and screams make Daniel cringe. "No, God! Please, no!! Please!" A man shouts in protest and then let out a sickly, inhuman wail. It reminds Daniel of the sound of a dying rabbit, mortally wounded, yet still kicking and writhing frantically. Years ago, while hunting with his father, he had shot a rabbit in the hindquarters. The rabbit, unable to run, had used one leg to propel itself straight up nearly four feet in the air—all the while shrieking a shrill, gut-wrenching cry. Young Daniel had been horrified and he had stood paralyzed as he watched the maimed animal kick and screech. His father ordered him to put the animal out of its misery by grabbing it and swinging its head against a tree, but Daniel couldn't budge. The piercing, sobbing shrieks were more than the eight-year old Daniel Hawthorne could stand and he began to cry. Disgusted, his father had grabbed the rabbit and swung it by its hind legs, smashing the animal's skull on the closest tree. It was more than two years before Daniel got up the nerve to go hunting again.

The two male passengers below deck had apparently tried to overtake the other men. They succeed only in infuriating them, drawing even more severe punishment than planned. The continuous screams from below deck are horrifying. Loud thumps emanate up through the main hatch as the screaming becomes more and more intense. Daniel covers his ears, trying to block out the terrible sounds. The men are playing with the passengers, like children playing roughly with their toys, having their few moments of destructive fun before going on to the next toy. Then the screams begin to die down. A woman is sobbing uncontrollably, begging and praying for mercy. The men are silent now and the only sound was the woman's painful whimpers. Then she abruptly falls silent as well.

Then another sound fills the night—the sound of splintering wood. Daniel can feel the vibration of each strike as it reverberated though the ship. The thundering of axes continue for nearly five minutes before he hears one of the men shout from below. All the screams from below deck have ceased and all Daniel can hear is the rushing water as it enters through the huge holes the men have punched in the Brittany's hull. They are going to scuttle the ship. The three men appear out of the darkness, their faces glowing in the dim lantern light.

"Let's go," Jack says quietly. He looks at Daniel. "Well, Daniel, the only thing I can promise is that this is going to be a lot easier for you than it was for the others." His voice is cold as he reached into his overcoat pocket.

Daniel has known that this moment would come and as soon as Jack's hand disappeared inside his overcoat, Daniel springs. He doesn't believe he will actually get away or that he will live more than a few precious seconds, but he is going to make those seconds count. If he is going to die, then he is going to die giving Jack and the other men something to worry about. He is going to spoil their party, wreck their joyous celebration, and if he lives to see the expression on their faces for one split instant, well . . . then it will be worth dying for.

In three giant steps he is upon the lantern at the mainmast, the metal rung clenched tightly in his fist. The other men, surprised at his quick move, are slow to react. Jack has his gun in his hand and is bringing it up, but it is too late. Daniel's arm is already in motion and with all his strength, with what he knows will be his final burst of power before he leaves this earthly world, he lets the lantern fly. The single dot of light arcs high in the air, spinning and turning in the night sky. It reached its peak and begins plummeting downward, spiraling and picking up speed. The men turn and watch helplessly as the lantern shatters, exploding on the other ship fifty feet away. There is a loud pop of splintering glass, a low woooooohhh, and then a bright flash lights up the ship. In seconds, flames are reaching above the deck and scaling the mizzenmast.

"You little son of a bitch!!" one of the men shouts, charging Daniel and knocking him to the deck. Daniel rolls away and pushes himself to his knees. A gun barks, and a bullet hits him square in the stomach. He falls forward onto the deck, crawling into a fetal position, drawing his body close. Jack takes a few steps forward and from point-blank range, fires again, the second bullet striking Daniel in the back of his head. Daniel's head disintegrates in an explosion of hair, tissue, and bone fragments.

"Let's go!" Jack shouts frantically. "Move! Move! Let's go!" Two men quickly scale the rope ladder and drop into the dinghy. Another tries to hand them the last wooden crate, but loses his footing. The wooden box smashes into the hull of the Brittany, *jarring its lid loose and spilling its contents into the water below. "Leave it!" Jack screams. "Get over there! Get that fire out!!" The flames are spreading rapidly and the two men begin rowing frantically toward the burning ship. The dinghy is not built to handle more than two people at once and Jack Malloy and the other two men toss their coats aside and plunge feet-first into the water, swimming behind the dinghy in the darkness.*

The man rowing the dinghy is pulling in long, savage strokes. The tiny rowboat reaches the flaming ship and the two men clamber aboard, running towards the rising flames. They begin lowering buckets into the dark lake as the other three men finally reach the ship. They swarm up the rope ladder and climb aboard. The four men concentrate on the fire, while Jack works furiously to get the ship under sail. There isn't much wind, but Bois Blanc Island is only a short distance to the north. If they can't get the fire under control, perhaps they can make it to shore and strand the ship in the shallows, where it would be easier to salvage the cargo.

Two men set up a production line of water, one lowering buckets with a rope, one carrying a bucket to the blaze. The other two try to extinguish the burning wood by beating the flames with tarps and blankets. But the fire continues to spread and Jack shouts out orders from the helm as the situation worsens. The flames have spread below deck and it is all too apparent that the men are fighting a losing battle.

"The boxes! Get them in the dinghy! Load up the dinghy and we'll head for the Island," Jack shouts. One of the men abandons his bucket and goes to the bulwark. His shout of despair rises into the heavy night sky. The dinghy is gone. In their haste, the men had forgotten to tie up the small rowboat and it, as well as the ill-fated Brittany, are now nowhere in sight.

chapter 175

Mike rubbed his eyes and glanced at the clock on the wall. 10:00 p.m. That's enough for tonight, he thought. He began to close the journal when his eye caught something. Wait a minute, he thought. The entry was near the end of the journal and he must have missed it on his first run through it. He began to read quickly, becoming more excited as he went along. Finally, he picked up the phone to call Kari.

"Kari?" Don said into the darkness. He had heard Kari surface twenty feet from the boat, but couldn't see her. He heard the sound of splashing as Kari swam towards the trawler. "Kari?" he called again. She was next to the boat now, grasping the aluminum ladder with one hand and Don bent over the side to help her with her gear. "Did you find anything?"

"Nothing," she said, in a strained voice. Then she added,

smartly: "Nothing . . . except a silver and a gold bar. Help me get them into the boat." Kari hefted a small lift bag toward him and he hauled it with difficulty over the railing. It held two dirty objects, each about eight inches long.

"Holy Jesus," Don whispered excitedly, lowering the bag gently to the deck. Then he leaned back over the side of the boat and pulled up Kari's tanks, vest, and weight belt. She climbed up the ladder as Don knelt on the deck, examining the bars. "Where did you find these?"

"North of the ship about fifty feet or so. They were buried in the muck and I only found them by pure luck. Since the gold crucifix wasn't actually on board the ship, I figured that maybe the cargo had spilled overboard while the Brittany was sinking. So I just went exploring out a ways from the ship and there it was. I got narced a little bit and had to come up."

Narced, Don thought, recalling his own experiences with the toxic effects of nitrogen narcosis. Not a pleasant feeling to have, especially diving alone.

Kari piled her wetsuit in the corner and stepped into the cabin to dry off. Putting on a pair of sweats and a baseball cap in the darkness, she fumbled with the drawstring as she walked back on to the deck and kneeled next to Don. The penlight wasn't very bright, but he didn't want to use anything brighter for fear of being seen. One of the dive flashlights would easily be spotted from shore if someone was looking and knew what to look for. And they just might be looking right now, Don thought.

Kari picked up the silver bar and wiped away some of the sludge. "Unbelievable," she whispered in fascination.

"Yeah," Don replied, picking up the gold bar, which upon inspection, wasn't a bar at all. Like the crucifix it was embedded with stones. "I wonder how much of this stuff is down there," he said wonderingly.

"There's no sign of the Columbian emeralds so far. But if this stuff is scattered all over the bottom like I think, we're going to have our work cut out for us."

chapter 176

Ed, Jimmy, and Phillip had watched the activity on the distant trawler and were close enough to see the small flare of the penlight, tiny and blurry in the distance. "They found something," Ed snarled quietly. Jimmy was about to speak when they heard the engine start up. They listened without speaking as the coughing motor of the trawler diminished in the night.

"Why didn't they stay to get more?" Phillip asked, bewildered.

"I'll tell you why," Ed hissed. "Because that shit's just lying around on the bottom. I'll bet when the ship went down, the cargo busted loose and scattered it all over the bottom. They just happened to get lucky and find a little bit of it. Jimmy, we got any full tanks left?"

"Just two," came Jimmy's reply from the darkness.

"Two's enough. Get the boat back over the dive site. I'm going back down."

A mosquito bit Sharon on the cheek and she slapped it, rolling the tiny bug away with her palm. Damn things. Can't get away from them. She had arrived at the marina shortly after sunset. All three of their cars—the Ranger, the Dakota, and Jimmy's Trans Am—were in the parking lot.

Good. Still fishing. After a quick look around to make sure no one was watching, she had slipped into the thick bushes that lined the grassy area around the marina. It was hard to get comfortable, but after a minute she managed to settle back against a branch. *This will work just fine,* she thought smugly. *Come on Jimmy.*

Her hand gripped the gun she had stuffed under her sweatshirt. She had tucked it into the waist of her jeans and pulled her sweatshirt over it. A few cars had driven by as she walked along Huron Street, but no one paid any attention to her. It was a nice night and many people were out for a walk. She had even smiled and waved at a couple of the cars and other walkers that passed by.

Jimmy's Trans Am was parked directly in front of her, just a few yards away. She sat quietly for a long time, shifting a tiny bit every now and then into a more comfortable position. Another mosquito bit her on her forehead and she smacked at it. Normally, the mosquitoes would have driven her crazy, but tonight she had considered them no more than an annoyance, only smacking at them absently as they landed. There were more important things on her mind. She could deal with the little vampires.

A boat slid quietly into its slip and after a few minutes, Sharon heard the creak of footsteps on the wooden docks. She peered through the dense branches. A person came into view and from the silhouette, she could tell that it wasn't Jimmy or Ed or Phillip. The person passed a few feet from her hiding place and Sharon tensed, her finger on the trigger of the gun. After the person passed, she relaxed a bit. *It won't be long now,* she thought. *He's got to come back sometime. I'll wait all night if I have to. And it'll all be worth it.*

chapter 177

"Nothing." Ed had returned to the surface and lifted his mask over his face, spitting his regulator out of his mouth. "I looked all over the place. I didn't find shit. They either got lucky or they know exactly where to look. Or both." His tongue was an angry lion, seething with anger.

"We need to fill the tanks," Jimmy said. "They're all empty."

Ed climbed onto the boat and shed his gear. He lit up his ceremonial post-dive cigarette. "Well, let's get back to the marina. They're not going to be back until tomorrow. I'll fill the tanks at the cabin. We can grab the air compressor and bring it out on the boat with us, so from now on we can fill the tanks without heading in. Then we'll take off and head for the other side of Bois Blanc."

Shortly past midnight, the big Bayliner, a slow moving white ghost in the blue moonlight, crept out of the darkness of the lake and into the marina, gently nudging into its slip. In the next slip, to their relief, the Randalls' borrowed beat-up trawler rested, silent and dark. Jimmy jumped onto the dock and tied up the Bayliner, and Phillip unloaded the tanks onto the docks. The bright orange-and-yellow tanks were concealed in heavy-duty nylon bags.

"I'm going to run to my car and get something," Jimmy said, turning.

"Don't go away empty-handed," Ed hissed. "Help us get these tanks to the truck." Jimmy stopped abruptly and returned to the boat.

chapter 178

The red message indicator light was blinking as Kari walked into the kitchen. She set the bars down on the counter, lining them carefully up alongside each other. She pressed the button and the machine whirred to life. Beeeeeep . . . click. "Kari, it's Mike. Give me a call as soon as you get in. It doesn't matter what time it is. Got some more news." Click. The machine reset itself and stopped. Kari plucked the cordless phone from the wall.

Mike Felsing was in bed when the phone rang. He had kept the portable receiver with him and he picked it up off the night table after the first trill and put it to his ear. "Hi," he whispered, knowing it would be Kari. "I wondered when you'd get back."

"Don and I went diving. We found a silver bar and a gold bar inlaid with gems. It's incredible. And we found it north of the wreck, a little ways away from the ship itself."

"Yeah, well, this is just a guess," Mike said. "But I don't think you're going to find too much more."

"Why is that?" she asked.

"I came across something in Merman's journal that leads me to believe it's not there. Or, most of it anyway. Do you remember the article I had found about the strange fire seen over Lake Huron in 1859?"

"Yeah. At night."

"That's the one. Well, Merman mentioned that fire near the end of the volume. He wrote that he had read about the fire in the paper and he was certain that the fire was a burning ship."

"But there's no evidence of any fire on the wreck at all," Kari reminded him.

"The Brittany didn't burn," Mike replied. "The ship that was stealing her cargo did. I think that the ship that was being used to haul away the cargo caught fire and burned. I'll bet the gold and silver you've already found is just some of the cargo that had been carelessly knocked overboard in the transfer between the two ships."

"So, you think there might not be any more?"

"Hard to say. But remember the article from the Tribune? A man reported seeing two ships shortly before dark just before the fire began. I think it was the second ship that caught fire, burned, and sank. I think that there's another ship out there. And I think that's the one with the treasure on board. I'm going to go back to the library tomorrow to see if I can find out any more on that fire."

Kari told him about the boat they had seen in the Channel earlier that day that had been moored in the slip next to Dave Shandler's boat.

"Did you see the boat tonight when you went diving?"

"No. It wasn't in the slip and we didn't see it out on the lake. Don is spending the night on Dave's boat in case they come back."

"He's on the boat?" Mike asked, alarmed. "Tonight? What is he going to do?"

"Nothing," Kari replied. "He's hoping to get a better look at them if they come back. Don't worry. You can't see inside the cabin of Dave's boat. Don will be careful."

chapter 179

Sharon had been dozing. In her dream, she had killed Jimmy, but he had returned. She saw his eyes in the people she met on the street. She saw him lurking in the shadows in the alleys and had heard him call her name from a busy street corner. She had gotten rid of him, but she hadn't really gotten rid of him. He was still around, waiting for her, following her, watching her.

She snapped awake as she heard the low droning rumble of a large cruiser. Not long ago she had been surprised to see Kari Randall emerge from a boat and walk right past her. She almost popped out of the bushes to say 'hello' but thought it best to remain where she was.

She shifted around on the damp ground to get a better look at the boat that was arriving. Her body ached from being cramped in the same position for so long and her legs were tingling. She tried to stretch without making too much noise, keeping her eyes focused straight ahead through the bushes, watching the boat dock. And the first thing she saw was—

Jimmy. His size and form was unmistakable. He jumped off the boat and onto the dock and secured the line. *There you are, you son of a bitch. Come on, Jimmy. Come closer.* She watched Jimmy's huge form as he carried a large bag up the dock and over to Ed's truck. He was only ten car lengths away. *Over here, come over here. Come over here and get your surprise, Jimmy Durand.*

Jimmy tossed the heavy bag into the back of the pickup, turned, and began walking towards his car. That's it, just a little further—

Sharon was surprised to find herself shaking. Her heart was pounding, her muscles were tense, and her breath rapid and quick. She pulled back the hammer of the revolver and brought the barrel up from where it rested on her leg. *Say good-bye, asshole.*

Suddenly Jimmy stopped in his tracks. Sharon froze, afraid that he may have heard the tiny click of the hammer. He turned around and started to walk back towards the boat. Sharon held the gun up and leveled the barrel. No, too far. She was more afraid of missing him than she was of getting caught. For her, getting arrested went with the territory. If she did manage to get away, well, that would be a bonus. Her main concern was to make Jimmy Durand deader than a doornail. Not that she didn't want to give herself a fighting chance at fleeing; but jumping out of the bushes just to get a better shot wasn't going to help her in the escape department.

He'll be back, she thought. *Just hang tight, girl. He'll be back.* She lowered the gun.

"Let's get these last four loaded and get them back to my cabin." Ed picked up a bag containing two tanks, as did Jimmy.

Phillip lay down on a couch in the cabin. "I'm going to hang here and snooze for a while," he said, putting his hands behind his head.

"Yeah, you do that," Ed said sarcastically, his weight causing the boat to rock to and fro as he stepped onto the dock. Jimmy and Ed walked through the marina and across the parking lot, put the remaining two bags into the back of the truck and hopped into the cab. The engine sprang to life, and the late Paul Sprague's Ford Ranger left the marina.

chapter 180

The noise jolted Phillip awake from his sleep. He sat up on the couch in the darkness and looked out the window, shaking the grogginess from his head. He stood up and stepped closer to the window, cautiously peering out at the quiet marina around him. Nothing moved, except for the slight rocking of the boats as they shifted easily in the water.

There it was again. *A bump.* This time, Phillip knew instantly where it came from—the boat in the slip next to him—the boat the Randalls had been using to dive from while the *John Galt* was in for repairs. Someone was aboard that boat and they might have heard them talk about refilling the tanks.

Phillip backed away from the window and looked around the cabin, searching for Jimmy's bag. He found it in the corner next to a blue-and-yellow dive gear bag. It was unzipped, and he fished around in it until he found the gun.

Come on back, Jimmy. Come on back. Sharon crouched in the thick bushes, out of sight, waiting for the Ranger to return. She'd heard Ed and Jimmy speaking, talking about getting something from Ed's cabin and bringing it back. Fine. She could wait.

She rested her hand on her belly, thinking of the tiny life that she hoped was still growing inside of her. A tear rolled down her cheek, and she wiped it away with the sleeve of her sweatshirt.

A sudden noise surprised her. Glass had broken somewhere, she was sure of it. In one of the boats moored in the marina. She moved a branch to give her a clearer view.

The warm, midnight air was very still. The white lights that dotted the small harbor cast short shadows over the docks and boats in their slips. Hundreds of moths and other insects swarmed around the bright lights, battering themselves on the plastic lens covers. A bat zipped beneath one of the lights, appeared quickly again as it flitted beneath another light, and then disappeared into the darkness. Nothing else moved. After a moment, she let go of the branch and leaned back against the thin trunk of one of the bushes.

She would have missed the movement altogether had she not glanced up at just the exact moment. Someone was moving slowly in the shadows near one of the boats. Phillip? *What in the hell is he doing, sneaking around like that?*

Don lay in the dim light of the cabin, momentarily disoriented by his surroundings. He cursed himself silently for falling asleep.

Christopher Knight

He had wanted to stay awake to see if the boat in the next slip returned and he had thought that if he lay down on the hard floor, he would be so uncomfortable that it would prevent him from accidentally dozing off. But he had fallen asleep anyway.

The boat shifted and sank down a tiny bit and Don heard a footstep on the deck. He sat upright on his elbows quickly as the cabin door sprang open and a beam of light hit him in the face. He saw nothing but a shadow behind the bright beam and the outline of a dark gun pointed menacingly at him, cold and steady, as the man whispered loudly, his voice intense. "Don't move. Don't even fucking move or I'll kill you."

chapter 181

The flames leap into the night sky, licking higher and higher, illuminating the hellish cloud of smoke that billow up from the doomed ship. One of the sails catches fire and it quickly burns in a brilliant flash as the inferno spreads around the ship. The vessel starts to list and the men, realizing that saving the ship is hopeless, decide to save the cargo by engineering some type of crude raft.

"Hurry up!" one of them screams. "Tie together some boards and make a raft!" Orange sparks twist and rise up through pillars of black clouds, riding high into the thick debris-filled air as the men begin tearing the ship apart with whatever tools they can find. If they can strap together enough lumber, they will be able to float at least a portion of the cargo and hopefully make it to the nearby south shore of Bois Blanc Island.

The ship is now almost totally engulfed in flames as the men race furiously about the ship trying to collect the crates in one place. The ship, already listing badly, suddenly groans and capsizes without warning, slipping sideways into the water. The flames are extinguished with loud hisses as burning wood meets water. Within moments, the entire ship vanishes in a maelstrom of debris and hissing sparks.

One man is knocked unconscious by a piece of falling wood and he falls into the water, his lifeless form bobbing in the dancing shadows of the doomed schooner. Two other men are trapped under a falling mast, the last swept into the dark lake in a tangle of rigging. All scream in horror as the ship goes under, sinking into an inky sea. Jack takes a deep breath and prepares to leap from the burning deck but as he does a portion of the deck twists and gives way. Jack, his leg trapped in the debris of the deck, rolls with the ship, thrashing wildly as he plunges beneath the dark waves, trapped in a cold, black water coffin. His struggle is in vain. Within minutes, the schooner lay at the bottom of Lake Huron, carrying five new souls to their eternal rest—and one incredible payload.

chapter 182

Sharon watched Phillip disappear into the cabin of the big boat next to the dirty blue trawler. A few moments later another man appeared on deck followed by Phillip. *That's strange*, she thought. *It's a little late for visitors.* She watched the two men climb aboard the Bayliner and vanish into the cabin. She kept a close eye on the darkened Bayliner but nothing more happened.

Twenty minutes later she heard the sound of an automobile approaching. Headlights broke through the hedges near the entrance, scattering shadows across the lawn, the portico, and along the wall of the harbormaster's office. The vehicle turned from Huron Street into the marina, then passed directly in front of her and stopped in front of the docks.

Her hand squeezed the gun tightly, as she anxiously watched the two occupants exit the truck. The bed of the Ranger was heavily laden with a large machine that Jimmy and Ed struggled to unload onto the docks. It took the two of them to carry the lawnmower-sized machine down to the slip and onto the boat. Then both men went below deck and did not return.

The Ranger wasn't parked too far from where she knelt, concealed in the dark shrubbery. Although it was out in the open, the light wasn't as bright in that spot as it was elsewhere in the marina. She tucked the revolver beneath her sweatshirt, stumbled to her feet in the thick brush and pushed away the stiff branches. Keeping her eye on the big white boat at the far end of the dock, she slipped out of the cover of the bushes. If she could get to the Ranger and use it as cover, then she would have a good shot at Jimmy if he came back to retrieve something from either the truck or his car.

She crept along the grass, hunched over, trying to keep low and out of sight. She crouched behind the rear tire of the Ranger and slowly raised her head, peeked over the truck bed and looked down the docks towards the Bayliner. Nothing moved. She turned her head slowly, surveying the other boats in the marina. All was silent, calm and quiet in the dark early morning hours. Then a dull glint in one of the bags in the back of the truck caught her eye. Reaching in slowly, she turned back a portion of the unzipped bag.

Two stainless steel yellow tanks lay side-by-side in the bag. *Air tanks?* she thought. *What do they need air tanks for?* As she flipped the bag closed another object caught her eye. A large tarp lay beneath the bag and a grip-like handle protruded from under the canvas. She peeled back a portion of the tarp. *Spearguns? Now what would they need those for in Lake Huron?*

chapter 183

"He was in the boat all along, watching and listening to us," Phillip said quietly. "I didn't have any choice."

Don sat in a chair in the dark cabin of the Bayliner, while Ed, Jimmy, and Phillip stood over him. They glared at him for a moment without saying anything.

"What's your name?" Ed finally asked.

"Don. Don Garrity." Don's voice was nervous and tense.

"Well, Don Garrity," Ed continued boastfully, "I don't suppose you know exactly where that cargo is, do you?"

Don shook his head as the fat man lit a cigarette. He couldn't believe the enormous size of the him. The man standing next to him was huge too, but differently. Even in the dark, Don could see blood pumping through the bulging veins on his neck. The man had his arms crossed and they looked like bent fireplace logs. The other man, the one who had discovered him on Dave Shandler's boat, seemed edgy and nervous. The gun in his hands clearly made him uncomfortable. He was thin with dark brown hair and about Don's own height.

Phillip Keanan, Garrity thought. *That must be who it is.*

The fat man turned and tapped his cigarette on the edge of an ashtray, his face expressionless. "I guess it don't matter. Looks like you'll be going on a little road trip with us, Mr. Garrity." Don wasn't sure what the man meant, but he was pretty confident that he wouldn't like it.

Jimmy found some rope and tied Don's hands behind his back, placing a piece of duct tape tightly over his mouth. Then, after thinking about it a moment, he bound his ankles together with the tape as well.

Ed stepped off the boat and walked along the dock back to the truck, picked up the bag containing the last two air tanks from the truck bed, and then reached under the tarp. *What the hell?* He looked suspiciously around the well-lit marina. *Son of a bitch. Shoulda loaded 'em into the boat instead of leavin 'em in the bed. Damn kids.* He looked around the marina again and seeing no one, picked up the items and started to carry them back to the Bayliner.

As he walked to the boat he sensed that someone was watching. The coarse gray hair above his ears tingled and he turned his head from side to side. He looked slowly around the parking lot, at the parked cars, at the darkened windows of the harbormaster's office, and the boats tied up in their slips. *Where are you, whoever you are? I know you're there. It's just a matter of finding you. Come out, come out wherever you are . . . .*

Sharon hunched lower beneath the thick branches. Ed was standing only ten feet from her. *Had she made a noise? Why was he looking around like that? Did he know that she was there?* She didn't want to have to kill Ed, but if she had to, she would. Ed seemed to be looking right at her . . . or at least the dense brush around her. She could see his bulging eyes darting over the branches. Her heart pounded as she drew a slow breath and coiled her finger around the trigger of the revolver. *Stay away, Ed. This isn't for you. I don't want to do this. Just please . . . stay away.* Sure, he was an asshole, and a pig, and just about every other name she could conceivably think of, but none of that justified shooting him. She watched his icy gaze as he scanned the thicket. He must have noticed the spear gun was missing. Her pulse was racing and she tried to slow her rapid breathing, certain that he would hear the inhaling and exhaling of the air from her lungs. Her heart crashed like thunder and her breath sounded like the deafening roar of gale force winds. She could only hope that the harmonious chirping of frogs and crickets would drown out her own sounds.

Ed took a step forward and stopped. Sharon's finger tightened around the trigger. *Don't, please, no closer . . . .* Suddenly, satisfied that there was no one hiding in the bushes, Ed turned and lumbered back to the truck, locked the doors and walked back to the boat. Within minutes, Sharon heard the engine of the white Bayliner grumble to life as it left its mooring and slipped into the darkness.

Christopher Knight

chapter 184

Kari poured a cup of coffee and dropped the newspaper on the table. The sun was just beginning to peek through the trees. A bagel popped out of the toaster and she placed it on a napkin, picked up her coffee and sat at the table, spreading out the morning paper. *No, if there's anything in there about Eric, it'll just piss me off more. Best leave well enough alone.* She folded up the newspaper and dropped it into the rack next to the wall.

5:50 a.m. Still a lot of time before the arraignment. She almost dropped her bagel as a thought hit her. *Don was still at the boat in the marina!* She had forgotten that he had spent the night on the boat and she was to pick him up this morning. Dressing quickly, she took another sip of coffee, left the cup on the counter, snapped up the Blazer keys from the table and headed for the waterfront.

A few people were already up and about and a fishing boat was leaving its slip as Kari whirled into the marina. Dozens of sleepy gulls sauntered groggily near the shore, the more alert ones already wheeling in the sky.

Kari left the engine running as she walked along the dock towards the trawler. The boat that had been in the slip next to Dave's was still gone. Relieved, she stepped onto the deck. "Wake up, sleepyhead," she said, opening the cabin door and poking her head into the cabin. "Time to—"

The cabin was empty. Don was gone.

Mike was already awake when the phone rang. Kari told him that Don wasn't on the boat when she had gone to pick him up. "Have you looked around the marina? Maybe he went for a walk. Check down by the park. I'm sure he's around there somewhere," he reassured her. Kari hung up the phone, trying to remain optimistic, but she was already certain that she wouldn't find Don at the park or walking around somewhere. He would have called or left a note in the trawler.

Mike could tell by the worried look on her face that she hadn't found Don. It was almost eight o'clock, and she and Mike were standing in the parking lot outside the courthouse. "I looked everywhere," she said, her voice strained. "I waited around the marina and looked in the park. He never showed up. But the boat that was next to us in the marina is back at the dive site."

Christopher Knight

chapter 185

The arraignment took an hour. Eric pleaded not guilty to all charges and was released on his own recognizance. Kari told him about Don's disappearance. Mike headed out to Everett's cottages to see if Don was there, while Eric and Kari went back to the house, hoping to maybe find him there. The three of them, Mike, Eric, and Kari, met at the marina some thirty minutes later.

"We didn't find him," Eric said. "And that boat is still out in the Channel."

"What are you thinking?" Mike asked, knowing full well what Eric had in mind.

"I'm thinking we go out there and find out what the hell they're doing." He turned to Kari. "Mike and I are going to take Dave's boat. You stay here."

"The hell I am!" Kari insisted adamantly. Her eyes flared. "I'm going with *you.*" Eric knew that it would be pointless to argue.

"Eric, maybe it would be better to let the police handle this," Mike said apprehensively.

"I think the police have handled enough already," Eric replied in a salty tone.

Felsing gave in. "Yeah, well it didn't do me much good to argue with your father, either," he answered, shaking his head and sighing.

"Let's go," Eric said, and the three hurried to the old blue trawler moored in the slip. Kari untied the lines while Eric started up the engine. The motor sputtered and spit, then revved to life, its trademark cough of blue exhaust wafting up from the stern. Mike had gone down into the cabin and he popped his head back out.

"I don't know if this means anything," he said. He held up a broken glass, stained with dried blood. "Maybe Don cut his hand and went to the hospital."

Eric looked at the broken tumbler and shook his head. "He would have called."

Kari was just about to untie the last line when Eric shouted to Kari above the loud groaning of the old motor. "Kari! There's a toolbox in the back of the Blazer. Bring me a screwdriver and the vice grips from the first drawer." She wound the line and dropped it on the bow, and Eric watched her as she walked down the dock. When she was almost to the Blazer, he threw the boat into reverse and backed out of the slip. Turning the boat quickly, he dropped the engine into gear and chugged out of the marina, shooting a glance back over his shoulder. Kari had seen the boat leave the slip and now she was running up the dock toward the departing trawler.

Christopher Knight

But she was too late—the boat was already fifty feet from the slip.

"You are going to have one upset wife to deal with," Mike exclaimed over the grumbling engine.

"Yeah, well, I don't want her out here. Not when we don't know who the hell we're dealing with." He turned the boat into the mouth of the river and out into Lake Huron.

"There she is," Eric said, pointing to the white dot far out into the lake. "Still there."

chapter 186

Kari was livid. She had just gotten to the Blazer when she heard the strained moaning of Dave Shandler's trawler as it backed out of the slip. *That son of a bitch! He's leaving without me!* She stood staring after the departing trawler in helpless fury. *Damn him*, she thought. *I should have known better.* She turned and sprinted back to the Blazer, hopped inside and turned the key. The engine roared to life and she wheeled around.

"Well, Eric, you're in for a little surprise," she said aloud as she sped up Huron Street towards town.

Traffic was snarled from several detours that had seemingly popped up overnight. The downtown streets were being tore up and repaired, and orange signs led cars through a maze of back streets. Vehicles were backed up for several blocks in some places.

"Come on, come on," she said aloud as the Blazer waited its

turn at an intersection.

Dave Shandler was outside working in the yard when Kari pulled into the driveway. Black, inky grease stains ran up his bare arms and hands and dark smudges criss-crossed his face. About the only place on him that wasn't dirtied by oil was his long, thick beard. When he saw Kari coming down the driveway in the Chevy he put down his tools and straightened up. The Blazer scrunched to an abrupt halt on the loose gravel.

"Hi Dave," she said, rolling down the window and staying in the Blazer.

"Mornin'," he replied. "Read all about Eric in the paper today. How's he doin'?"

Kari ignored the question and looked around the yard and across the river, then back to Dave. "By any chance is the *John Galt* fixed yet?" she asked hopefully.

chapter 187

Their morning dive had been fruitless. First, Phillip and Ed had descended upon the wreck and scoured the area around the foundered ship. After finding nothing, they returned, increasingly frustrated. The eastern sky was beginning to lighten, and the sun would be up soon. They wouldn't be able to stay in the Channel much longer if they didn't want to be seen.

Ed was making the second dive alone when, nearly one hundred yards from the wreck of the *Brittany*, he spotted something in the beam of his flashlight. *Well, what have we here?* The dark form looming in front of him was nearly his own height and twice his width. He swept his light over the charred wood. He waved his hand over it and a cloud of greenish-brown silt burst up, swirling and billowing in the water around him. *Burnt*, Ed thought. *Burnt to a goddamn crisp.*

He pushed at the wood and a large chunk fell way, enveloping him in an even larger explosion of silt. *Just a piece of shit from a burned ship. Could have drifted here from anywhere, knowing the currents in the Channel.* The light didn't penetrate more than a foot in the whirling debris, and Ed drew closer to a part of the wreck that wasn't burned. The small structure was undefinable and could have come from any portion of a ship, but something about its shape made him take a closer look. It was a half-burnt box. The box was warped and bent, but the lid was still on it sealing its contents from view. Ed pulled his knife and forced the blade through a slight crack in the crate, twisting it back and forth. The wood around the blade easily split apart and fell away, exposing its contents.

Well I'll be a sonofabitch, Ed thought smartly. *How 'bout that?*

Jimmy watched the water boil on the surface twenty feet off the starboard bow and he waited for Ed's huge head to pop up in the center of the disturbance. *Wait a minute, that's not right*, Jimmy thought. *There's too much air coming to the surface. Way too much air. Something's wrong.* He yelled for Phillip and the two stood on the deck, watching the bubbles anxiously.

Then from beneath the churning water, a bright red shape loomed, as if ready to explode out of the water and take flight. Then the red nylon of a lift bag broke the water's surface. It looked like a giant red rubber ball, mostly submerged, dangling just beneath the water line.

"Holy shit! He found something!" Jimmy didn't wait to put his wetsuit on and plunged headlong into the water. He reached the balloon almost instantly, encircling the big red sphere protectively in his arms. "Throw me a line!" he shouted, waving an arm at Phillip. "I'll tie it up and we can pull it over." Phillip tossed out a line and Jimmy dived beneath the surface and tied it to the ropes of the bag. He surfaced, and Phillip began to pull the heavy weight through the water as Jimmy swam quickly back towards the Bayliner.

"Look at that shit!" Phillip exclaimed, standing over the open canvas bag, its contents now strewn across the deck. Jimmy was on his knees going over the items one by one, picking them up, looking at each one, and setting them back down. The array of artifacts was spectacular. Dozens of gold coins, bars, and pieces of jewelry shined like new in the early morning sun. A few silver bars and some dirty green stones also lay piled in the heap. The bag had weighed nearly sixty pounds.

"Son of a bitch," Jimmy whispered, holding up a gold necklace laden with precious stones. Phillip dropped to his knees and picked up a handful of coins, shaking them lightly in his palm. "We found it! Shit! We found it!!" he said, slapping Jimmy on the back. "We're rich! We're so damn rich it's sick!" He lay the coins back on the deck and picked up a necklace. He leaned over to look in the cabin. Don was bound to the seat, leaning over to the side, trying to get a look at the items strewn about the deck.

"Hey!" Phillip yelled to him. "Wanna see what you guys missed out on?" Phillip stood up and walked in to the cabin and dangled the necklace in Don's face. Don stared, and looked up at Phillip. "And it's all ours," Phillip taunted. "Finders keepers, losers weepers." He laughed and snatched the necklace away from Don's face, returning to the deck where Jimmy still knelt, still overwhelmed at the find.

Ten minutes later, after he'd completed his decompression stops, Ed's head popped to the surface some ways out and Phillip started up the Bayliner and motored over to him. "You found it!" he yelled, as he approached Ed in the water. He cut the engine, and Ed climbed up the ladder at the stern.

"Yeah, well, don't get too excited," Ed said crossly. Phillip's smile disappeared. "What do you mean? We found it! *You* found it!" he exclaimed, pointing to the items on the deck.

"I mean that's it. That's all there was. I found it near some burned wood. Just like I thought. Someone loaded it all onto another ship and it burned. That wreck could be anywhere."

"So, we'll look for it," Phillip said, the smile returning. "It can't be too far. We've got time!"

"Not anymore we don't." It was Jimmy. He was still crouched down on the deck, but his eyes were staring off into the distance, towards the southwest. He lifted his arm and pointed. A tiny blue speck was visible, moving towards them.

chapter 188

"It's the Bayliner," Mike said, as he gazed through the binoculars at the white dot in the distance. Eric was pushing Dave Shandler's trawler as fast as it could go—which was infuriatingly slow. Mike put the binoculars down and let them rest around his neck by the strap. "Are you sure they're over the wreck?"

"Positive," Eric replied, nodding. "They're right in the Channel. Damn, this thing is slow. Are they moving?"

Mike raised the binoculars up again. "Doesn't look like it. They appear to be . . . no, wait a minute. Someone just climbed on the boat. There's someone lifting a tank and a vest on board. They're diving, all right."

They haven't seen us yet, Eric thought. *As soon as they do, they'll be gone in a shot. And there's no way we'll catch them with this thing.*

A half-mile from the Bayliner, Mike raised the binoculars again. "Now what's this?" he exclaimed. Eric squinted in the sunlight, trying to see what Mike was talking about. "They're *fishing*. They've got downriggers out."

"They're not fishing," Eric sneered. "Maybe they want us to *think* they're fishing but they're not."

Felsing lowered the binoculars. They were getting close enough to see people moving aboard the Bayliner. A huge fat man was at the stern, fiddling around with a large net. Another man came into view, then disappeared into the cabin.

"It doesn't look like they're too anxious to move," Mike said.

The trawler slowly approached the Bayliner which was still sitting idle in the calm water. The fat man waved, but neither Mike nor Eric returned the gesture.

Eric swung the trawler behind the Bayliner and began to approach her on the port side. The heavy-set man pointed and waved at the downriggers. Eric ignored the gesture and kept approaching the vessel. The fat man began reeling in the downriggers.

Yeah, sure, Eric thought. Fishing with downriggers while you're dead in the water. Real convincing.

The fat man shouted to them. "Slow down! Slow down!" he boomed, gesturing with the palm of his hand. Eric cut the motor and the trawler slowed, gliding up right next to the Bayliner. Mike threw a line across and the dark-haired man caught it and secured the boat.

"How's the fishing," Eric sneered, making his sarcasm known. He stepped away from the helm and stood at the side rail of the trawler, not three feet from the huge man in khaki shorts and a white tank top.

"Not bad, not bad," the fat man answered. "Nothing yet this morning, though." Leaning over the railing of the Bayliner, he extended his hand in greeting. "Ed Beech."

Eric didn't move, keeping his hands at his sides defiantly. "I don't care who the fuck you are. All I wanna know is what kind of game you think you're playing."

The fat man seemed genuinely taken aback and he recoiled his hand slowly. The smile left his face and ripples formed on his forehead. Feigned surprise swirled in his bulging eyes. "I don't know what you're talking about."

Eric thrust his finger at him menacingly. "You know damn well what I'm talking about!" he roared. "I'm talking about messing with my boat and putting that shit in it and setting me up! That's what I'm talking about!" Eric was furious; he was one step away from jumping onto the other boat's deck.

"Hold on a minute," Ed said. "I think you've got us confused with somebody else."

"The hell I do," Eric retorted, regaining some of his composure and lowering his voice. Mike had finished tying up a line and now he joined Eric, standing next to him.

That was what Ed was waiting for. There didn't appear to be anyone else on the trawler besides the two men, and Ed needed them both to be together in plain sight. He didn't want one of them running into the cabin and radioing for help.

"I think I can clear this up," Ed said calmly. A clown-like smile emerged between his round cheeks. "This is just a simple misunderstanding, that's all." He turned and called into the cabin. "Jimmy? Can you come here a minute?"

Jimmy appeared clad only in his shorts, his hair still damp. Eric and Mike found themselves staring at a human wall of bricks.

And the barrel of a gun.

chapter 189

"I hope this straightens things out a bit." Ed was no longer grinning. "Both of you get aboard our boat—and no fast moves. You first," he said motioning to Eric. Eric and Mike did what they were told. "By the way," Ed leered, his yellow teeth flaring between two monstrous cheeks. "A friend of yours dropped by to say 'hi' last night."

"Where is he?" Eric asked defiantly. "He'd better be all right."

"Oh, he's fine. You might say that he 'duct' out for a while." Ed nodded his head in the direction of the cabin, and Eric took a step forward. Jimmy waved a warning with the gun and Eric stopped. He looked down into the cabin and saw Don, sitting in a chair, hands tied behind his back, his feet bound by duct tape, and a strip of the same pressed tightly over his lips. Other than that, he looked to be all right.

"Get away from there," Ed said angrily. "Get back over by the railing." Eric moved away from the cabin under the close surveillance of Jimmy.

"Now. Let's can the bullshit. You been lookin' for something. We been lookin' for something. This look familiar?" Ed reached into a canvas bag and pulled out a handful of gold coins and a gold bar. "This look like somethin' ya been tryin' to find? Then maybe you wouldn't mind savin' yourself an awful lot of trouble and tellin' me where the rest of it might be."

"I have no idea," Eric replied sharply.

"Wrong answer. Jimmy?"

Jimmy raised the gun. Every muscle in his body rippled with the movement and the mountainous veins in his shoulders stretched and splintered down his arms.

"I'm telling you, we don't know where it is," Eric reiterated. "We only found a gold crucifix near the wreck."

"And, of course, whatever was found last night," Ed replied. "Of course, you wasn't in on that little excursion being that you were a little 'indisposed'. But I know that somebody found some more last night. 'Cause we were here, too."

Mike Felsing spoke up. "I don't think that there is much, if anything, aboard the *Brittany.*"

"No shit, Sherlock," Phillip hissed. Felsing ignored the remark.

"There appears to have been another ship that was involved. Apparently, both ships sank. One burned. Going by what we know, my best guess is that any cargo was aboard that ship."

A long silence passed. Ed pulled out a cigarette, the last one in the pack, and placed it to his lips. Felsing's explanation made sense, considering that the artifacts he'd found earlier were in a box that had shown fire damage.

He crumpled the empty paper and cellophane container and tossed it into the water, not taking his eyes off Eric. The two stared at each other—Eric ashen with both fear and anger, Ed arrogantly confident. Ed smiled as he lit the cigarette, tossed the match into the water between the small crack of space that separated the two boats.

Phillip approached Ed and whispered quietly to him. Ed nodded his head and Phillip clambered aboard the blue trawler and disappeared into the cabin. Eric heard a loud smash and a splintering of wood. He turned to see Phillip emerge from the cabin with what had once been the trawler's radio. The microphone dangled from a coiled black cord and a large portion of the radio itself was dangling loosely from the side.

"I think what we have here is a failure to communicate," Ed said cynically, pointing to the radio and laughing at his own pun. "We wouldn't want you to try something foolish like order a pizza or something," he continued, his belching laughter echoing over the water. Even Jimmy chuckled a bit as Phillip dropped the broken radio over the side of the boat. It hit the water with a heavy *sploosh* and disappeared into the depths.

"Now, we're gonna search this Channel 'til we find that other ship—the one that burned. And we're gonna find it. Then you're gonna help us retrieve the rest of the treasure. Phillip, take Randall back to the trawler and tape him up," he ordered.

Phillip obediently duct-taped Eric's hands tightly behind his back, then pushed him over the gap between the two boats and sat him down in a chair in the trawler's cabin before binding his feet. When Phillip finished with Eric, he clambered back aboard the Bayliner and duct-taped Mike Felsing. "If there's anything we can do to make you more comfortable, don't hesitate to ask," Phillip said sarcastically, in his best flight attendant voice. Don and Mike glared at him.

"Let's go, let's go!" Ed said, raising his voice from the stern. "Jimmy, start filling those tanks." Jimmy shoved the barrel of the .38 into his denim cutoffs and went about the task of re-supplying the tanks.

Phillip climbed back aboard the trawler and went into the cabin. He reappeared shortly carrying a bright yellow tank. "Hey! They've got six more tanks over here! All full!" He carried a single tank to the side of the trawler and handed it to Jimmy, returning to retrieve the other five.

Eric watched Phillip as he lifted the tanks one-by-one and carried them out onto the deck. Each time Phillip was out of sight, he tried to wiggle his hands loose, but the duct tape was too strong and wrapped too tight. It was impossible to break his hands or legs free from the sticky binding material. Their situation was looking grimmer by the moment. *Well, at least Kari isn't here*, he thought. *At least she's safe.*

The grinding lawnmower-like sound of the gas air compressor droned steadily. The two boats were still tied together. Ed had decided they would move back and forth across the Channel, one hundred feet apart, until something came up on the depthfinder.

"Ed!" Jimmy yelled over the noise of the droning compressors.

Ed leaned around the cabin from the bow and looked back to where Jimmy was gazing towards the south through a pair of binoculars.

"What?" Ed replied, annoyed.

"We got company."

A small white dot, barely visible on the blue-green water line, was coming towards them. Ed joined Jimmy at the stern and took the binoculars from him.

"Yeah, I guess you'd call that company," he said finally, after taking a long look. "Jimmy . . . shut off those compressors. Phillip, help me get a couple of those chairs onto the deck. We're gonna have ourselves a little welcoming party."

Christopher Knight

chapter 190

The *John Galt* moved swiftly through the water. Dave had finished the repairs and had refloated it shortly before her unannounced arrival. It was now speeding northeast towards the two boats tied together in the Channel. Water sprayed off the bow as the vessel slid through the water, leaving a churning trail of turbulent white foam in its wake.

Kari focused her binoculars. To the naked eye, the two boats were a single speck, but with the binoculars she could see that the boats were tied together. She was still too far away to make out anything else. *Eric will be pissed*, she thought. *But that's too damn bad. He shouldn't have left me there like that.* She mentally estimated how long before she would reach the two boats in the Channel. *Twenty, maybe twenty five minutes max at this speed.*

Almost here, thought Ed. He called out to Phillip and Jimmy. "All right, you two get into the cabin. Turn the radio on and play some music. And for Christ's sake, hand me a beer and a bag of chips or something." He sat down on one of the chairs, which creaked alarmingly. Phillip handed him a beer and then returned to the cabin. Jimmy turned on the radio and Van Morrison's *Tupelo Honey* drifted through the midday heat.

Ed relaxed, leaned back, and sipped on his beer. "Phillip. Tell me a joke."

"A joke?" Phillip repeated.

"A joke," Ed said confidently. "A real belly-rubber."

Kari had tried to reach Eric on the radio, but she received no response. That was strange. Both he and Mike had to have spotted her coming toward them. And Eric always had the radio on.

She slowed the John Galt as she approached the two boats. The pitch of the engine dropped and the boat slowed rapidly. She was a hundred yards away. Dave Shandler's trawler was closest to her, the Bayliner was on the other side. She approached slowly from the south.

Where is Eric? she wondered, her alarm growing. And Mike? And why didn't they answer the radio.

A giant of a man came into view, with wild wind-blown tufts of gray hair just above his ears. He was the one she and Don had seen at the marina. He was sitting in a chair, just behind the cabin, a beer in hand. He appeared to be . . . laughing? They're partying?!?! What in the hell is going on? The fat man turned in his chair and looked her way. She caught broken fragments of music over the hum of the engine.

Beer in the morning, she thought cynically. Well, I'm sure it's five o'clock somewhere.

The man waved her to come closer, then turned back to the cabin, laughing, and took a swig of his beer. Kari cautiously slowed the John Galt even more. A man came out of the cabin, smiling and waving a beer, tipping it in her direction as if he were toasting her. Phillip Keanan, Kari thought, recognizing him from the picture Sharon had showed her. What in the hell is going on here? she thought again.

The John Galt was now just twenty yards from the two boats. There was still no sign of Eric or Mike, and Kari's uneasiness swelled.

Something's not right. Something is not right at all.

She throttled down the boat and began to turn it around. She picked up the microphone. Enough was enough. It was time to radio for help. She keyed the mic and was about to speak.

A sudden explosion ripped through the air and Kari jumped and turned. She dropped the microphone, and it dangled loosely from its cord.

Another man had appeared on deck. He'd fired a pistol into the air, and now the barrel of the gun was thrust against Eric's head. The fat man was waving her to come.

There was nothing she could do but turn the boat around.

"Slow!" Jimmy Durand shouted as the John Galt neared the two boats. "Go slow or I'll blow his fucking brains all over the lake."

Kari slowed the boat and it glided up next to the Bayliner.

"Throw that line over here now," Jimmy ordered. Kari did so

and Phillip tied the John Galt to the boat. "Get over here! Now!" the fat man demanded. When Kari didn't move, Jimmy Durand pulled the hammer of the revolver back. The barrel of the gun buried in Eric's temple. Kari nervously stepped over to the deck of the Bayliner.

"Mrs. Randall, I presume," the fat man said happily. "Welcome. The more, the merrier, that's what I always say."

chapter 191

Sharon had lain in wait in the shrubs until almost dawn and when the trio had not returned, she decided to head back to the motel. It would be too dangerous to try and hide out for the entire day.

As the sun crept up over the eastern horizon, she stuffed the gun back under the front of her sweatshirt. She peeked through the bushes to make sure no one was around. *And what am I going to do with this?* she wondered, staring down at the speargun between her feet. She wasn't sure why she had taken it from Ed's truck in the first place. She decided to leave it where it was in the bushes, doubting that anyone would see it in the thick foliage. She could retrieve it later tonight.

She slipped unseen out of the thick shrubbery and walked casually out of the parking lot and onto the shoulder of Huron Street. She was about half way to the motel when a massive cramp struck her like a baseball bat in the stomach, doubling her over and forcing her to her knees, bringing tears to her eyes. It happened so suddenly the gun fell out from under her sweatshirt to the gravel in front of her. On her knees at the side of the road, she doubled over in agony and vomited.

God, no. Please . . . no . . . .

The next spasm knocked her to the ground. She lay in a fetal position with her head on the pavement and her body curled on the shoulder of the road, sobbing in pain. When the cramping eased a bit, she tried to get up, but the motion caused another cramp to reel through her abdomen. She lay on the side of the road for another minute before she tried to move again. She made it to her knees and looked up Huron Street towards town.

She stuffed the gun back under her sweat shirt and tried to stand up. It was painful and difficult, but she managed. She walked cautiously, the loose stones and dirt crunching beneath her sneakers. She kept her hands tightly on the gun pressed against her skin below her breasts, trying to make it look like she was keeping her hands warm in the early morning chill. The cramps were coming in waves, the more severe ones causing her to jerk forward. She felt a warm wetness in the crotch of her jeans.

So help me God, Jimmy Durand, you will burn in hell forever. She kept walking, her anger and infuriation fueling her. Each step caused pain, each dizzying jolt caused even more blind determination.

After what seemed like a year later, she crept into her room at the motel. Her head was spinning and the cramps were almost continuous. The door closed behind her with a loud thud and she stumbled forward, holding onto a table for support. She focused her vision on the bed, let go of the table, and took a small step. She didn't make it. Her knees buckled and she crumpled to the floor.

She swam slowly into consciousness. The sun struggled to pierce the drawn curtains and Sharon lay on her side for a moment, momentarily confused.

Motel. Yeah. I'm at the motel. The events of the previous night started to come back to her: laying in wait at the marina, the mosquitoes, the gun, Jimmy, the speargun, walking back along the road in the early morning, the cramps. *The cramps!*

She rolled onto her back and sat up, feeling the sticky dampness in her panties. She looked at her jeans and was shocked to see that blood had soaked through the denim and a large stain swelled around her crotch area. The dizzy feeling returned, but she fought it, breathing deeply and slowly. Using the table for support she stood up. The walk to the bathroom was slow and difficult; every muscle seemed to be connected to her stomach and the pain was excruciating. She closed the door of the bathroom, leaned weakly against the sink, and cried.

chapter 192

"Jimmy, you take the old guy with you in the *Galt*," Ed ordered. "Phillip, you take the blue trawler with Randall. I'll keep these two here. You might say that they're our insurance policy." He glanced back into the cabin. Kari now sat next to Don, also bound by duct tape. Phillip had to cut the tape binding Mike's feet together so he could step aboard the *John Galt*. Then he ripped the radio out of the *John Galt* and tossed it overboard.

"If you find something on the depthfinder, mark the coordinates first, then stop and flag me," Ed called. Jimmy untied the *John Galt*, Phillip untied the old trawler, and the two boats drifted away from the Bayliner before both fired up their engines. Ed pulled in the Bayliner's anchor and then he too started the engine. Jimmy gave a thumbs up and Phillip waved.

The search was on.

Phillip was the first to signal. He marked the coordinates, stopped the boat, and flagged Jimmy and Ed, who immediately brought their boats alongside the trawler. "Found something. Right below us. Pretty good size by the looks of it." Ed circled the area with the Bayliner and found the same formation on the bottom scanner, in about one hundred feet of water.

"Piece of cake," Ed said. "I'll go check it out." He suited up and within minutes was underwater. Ten minutes later he returned to the surface. "Nothing but rocks," Ed shouted as he broke the surface. He got back in the Bayliner, took off his diving gear, and the three proceeded with the search.

chapter 193

By seven that evening they still hadn't found the burned ship and the three searchers were becoming edgy. All were tired from lack of sleep and from the additional two dives they had made during the afternoon after coming across promising possibilities on the bottom scanner. Both dives had been disappointing. It was nearing nine o'clock when Jimmy marked another object on the bottom scanner at ninety-five feet. It was sitting on a ledge right on the edge of the Channel. This time it was Phillip's turn to dive.

Phillip donned his wetsuit and plunged into the water. He had to fight against a strong current and he knew he was using too much air even before he reached the bottom. He glided slowly, just a few yards above the dark, silty bottom, sweeping his light from left to right, right to left, and back again.

Suddenly the bottom beneath him disappeared and he felt a quick jolt of panic, not sure which way was up or down. He spun around and the beam of light stopped on the edge of a jagged cliff. *The Channel! This is the edge of it right here.* He eased over to the edge and shined his light down into the dark abyss. *Four hundred fifty feet straight down*, he thought. *Nope. Don't want to go there.* The object they had charted sat near the edge of the Channel, according to the bottom scanner. He cruised slowly along the edge of the underwater canyon.

A small lump in the silt caught his eye, and he slowed and lowered himself to the mud. It was only a small disfiguration on the bottom about the size of a thermos, but longer. He plunged his gloved hands into the gooey sludge and discovered a burned piece of wood about two feet long. He dropped it back into the silt and shined his light ahead, his excitement and anticipation growing. He checked his gauges again.

The charred remains of the ship crept out of the gloom like a shadowy, obsidian ghost. It was resting on the extreme edge of the Laurentian Channel and a portion of it hung over the cliff itself, protruding over the blackness of the ominous depths.

Son of a bitch, Phillip thought excitedly. He was breathless. *This has to be it!* The wreck was covered with silt and sand and was nearly unrecognizable. Were it not for a few exposed areas of blackened charred wood, it would be almost invisible. It appeared to be lying on its side, but it was so badly mangled and burned that Phillip thought it might even be upside down.

He moved closer to the wreck and peered through a large hole in the rubble, shining his light inside. *Hot damn and holy shit!*

Here we go! The inside of the wreck was littered with burned and broken wooden crates about eighteen inches square. The silt layer wasn't as thick in the hold as it was on the outside of the ship and Phillip could make out the forms of the boxes clearly in the penetrating beam of the flashlight. He counted a dozen boxes.

When Phillip surfaced, Jimmy was standing on the *John Galt* and Ed was standing on the Bayliner, illuminated by only a tiny light in each of the boats' cabins. Phillip could see the outline of their shapes as he crawled awkwardly through the water towards the trawler.

Don struggled to get to his feet when he was certain that the fat man wasn't watching, but his efforts were fruitless. Next to him Kari struggled continuously, regardless of whether the big man was watching or not. *This wouldn't have happened if you hadn't been so stupid,* Don told himself. *If I hadn't spent the night on the boat, I wouldn't be here, and neither would anyone else.*

Aboard the trawler, Eric lay on the cabin floor, surrounded by piles of dive gear and equipment. Like Don Garrity, he also struggled to wriggle his hands free of the sticky adhesive tape, without success. Phillip hadn't payed much attention to him, certain that Eric would be unable to release himself. When the boat stopped and Phillip donned his wetsuit and jumped into the water, Eric took the opportunity to rub the duct tape vigorously on the edge of the chair. His efforts were cut short by Phillip's shouts from the water. *"I found it! At ninety-five feet! A burned ship! There's wooden boxes all over the place in one of the holds!"*

Christopher Knight

chapter 194

Ed Belmont stepped into the cabin of the Bayliner and shined the beam of his flashlight into the grim faces of his captives. "Them are 'deer in the headlights' looks if I ever saw 'em," he said, as he inspected the bindings on Don and Kari's face, hands, and feet. Satisfied that the two prisoners were going nowhere, he picked up his gear bag and left the cabin.

Don and Kari could hear the three men talking in soft voices. The three boats came alongside one another and the men tied them together. Jimmy Durand shouted something about lowering the anchor on the Bayliner. Then, a short time later they heard a splash, and then another, followed by another. *They're diving*, Kari thought. *We're alone on the boat!* She began to struggle with renewed energy, pulling and pushing her hands behind her back and Don began to do the same.

Eric lay on his back, the wood planks uncomfortable beneath his shoulder blades. His duct-taped hands were under his rear end. Worse, now he couldn't see either. Moments ago, Phillip had returned and placed a six-inch piece of duct tape over Eric's eyes. "See no evil, speak no evil," Phillip laughed, as he left Eric alone in the confines of the small cluttered cabin.

Three splashes. The men were diving.

Think, he commanded himself. *Come on, think. THINK!* He rolled to left side and his head bumped something. *The ladder. I can use the edge of it to cut the tape.* He brought his knees up and squirmed closer to it and positioned his bound wrists against the coarse metal edge of the lowest rung. A sharp pain shot through him and he could feel warm blood running down his arm. *I'm going to look like I've been fighting with a meat cleaver before I'm through.* Ignoring the pain, he concentrated on rubbing the duct tape around his wrists against the sharp edge of metal.

"*Son of a bitch! We found it!*" Phillip exclaimed, nearly beside himself with excitement. All three men had completed their first dive and were leaning over the side of the Bayliner, straining and groaning as they pulled a heavy canvas bag aboard. It weighed almost two hundred pounds and its contents tinkled and clanged as it crashed to the fiberglass deck.

There were four more lift bags floating near the boat, giant red nylon bobbers billowing beneath the surface. The second bag was even heavier than the first, but a few moments later that bag too tumbled over the gunwale and crashed to the deck.

Ed shined his flashlight on one of the bags. He untied the nylon rope binding the neck of the bag and its contents tumbled to the deck. Wordlessly Phillip reached down and with one finger, rubbed away the silty covering from one of the gold bars. The golden surface gleamed in the beam of the flashlight. *Awesome,* Phillip thought, *totally and unbelievably awesome.* The relatively shallow depth of the wreck—ninety-five feet—enabled them to dive and surface without decompression stops, making the salvage that much easier. There were several more crates in the remains of the ship; one more dive would be all that was necessary.

Jimmy seemed unmoved by their find. After glancing at the treasure, he began replacing his spent air tanks with fresh ones. "Let's go back and get the rest of it and get the hell out of here."

Ed's flashlight beam revealed Don and Kari to be still securely tied. Satisfied, he nodded to Jimmy and the three made quick preparations and plunged back into the water to make their final dive.

chapter 195

Sharon awoke on the floor in a dark motel room. *On the floor again,* she thought. *This is becoming a habit.* After a moment she took a deep breath and tried to sit up. The shaft of pain in her abdomen returned immediately. The rage she had felt earlier in the day returned to her in waves, rolling through her, exploding, crashing on top of the other, building to a crescendo of hate. She used the rush of emotion like a crutch, helping her to sit, then stand, then slowly walk to the bathroom. After a long hot shower, the pain relinquished its grip a tiny bit and she was able to move a little more freely without the searing stabs to her stomach.

Eleven o'clock? she thought, glancing at the clock on the top of the dresser. She wasn't sure what time it had been when she had returned from the marina but she was certain that it had been early or mid-morning. *I've been out for over twelve hours?*

She carefully slid into a pair of jeans and an over-sized bulky blue sweatshirt. She stuffed the gun in the front of her pants and inspected herself in the mirror. Her swollen lip was still puffy, but not nearly as much as it had been earlier in the day. Her left eye had a large dark splotch beneath it and her cheek was still swollen and red. After a half-hearted attempt to cover up the bruises on her face, Sharon took one last look in the mirror and stuffed her hair into a baseball cap. The pain she had felt earlier had mostly rescinded and for the most part she was able to walk normally.

I'll try the marina first, and if he's not there, I'll find him somewhere else. The elevator doors opened and she moved carefully through the lobby and stepped into the warm night air. The gun caused her discomfort as it pressed against her belly, but it was nothing compared to what she had felt the last time she had traveled Huron Street. The gun made her feel powerful. It gave her an edge, an upper hand against the menacing Beast from the Flaming Abyss. Jimmy was no longer a person to her. He was no longer human. He was a monster created in the bowels of hell, let loose to run rampant over the face of the earth, laying waste, creating mayhem, gloriously and arrogantly triumphing over the weak and helpless.

Sharon felt a brief moment of panic as a car exploded from the marina, its tires squealing as it rounded the turn, and blazed up the street towards her. The car flew past with the sound of music and laughter blaring from the open windows.

She crept into the shadows behind the harbormaster's office and peered around the corner, her eyes scanning the parking lot. She spotted Jimmy's car and Ed's truck. *So, you* are *here, you son of a bitch.* She eyed the boats in the marina but didn't see their big white boat. *Well, your car is here and you'll be coming back for it sometime. And you're in for a big surprise.*

She felt the gun pressing firmly against her skin and thought about the bullet in the chamber leaving the barrel in an explosive fury, meeting its mark and disintegrating the brains of one soon-to-be-dead Jimmy Durand.

I take that back, Jimmy. It's not a BIG surprise. It's actually very small. Very small and hard. And it travels awfully damn fast.

She slipped into the bushes and disappeared.

And waited.

chapter 196

Eric heard the joyous exclamations of the men and the heavy bags as they clanked on the deck. His hands were still bound tightly behind his back by the duct tape, but he was sure he had made some progress. When he heard the noises, he rolled away from the ladder and lay on his back, in case one of the men came to check on him. He held his breath, praying that they would not check his bindings. They were sure to show signs of wear, signs of him trying to escape. In a few minutes, he heard the sound of three splashes again. Immediately, he rolled back over to the ladder and continued the process of rubbing the duct tape back and forth. The tape felt a bit looser and he paused for a moment to try and snap the sticky bondage, but it still would not give. *For crying out loud. No wonder they use this crap for everything.*

He forced himself to go faster, no longer caring whether he cut himself in the process. Warm blood ran over his hands and the duct tape, lubricating the sharp metal edge.

He heard a disturbance from the water as one of the men returned from the dive, and the boat rocked as someone climbed back aboard.

He was running out of time. Yet, now, if one of the men entered the cabin, they were sure to see the evidence of Eric's attempt to escape. He was sure that there would be a telltale pool of blood at the base of the ladder and on the rungs.

More noise on deck. One of the men was coming.

Come, on, he thought, wincing. His wrists sawed frantically back and forth, back and forth . . . .

Just . . . a . . . little . . . .

Eric gave one last desperate heave on the bindings. The duct tape gave way with a popping sound and Eric's hands were free.

chapter 197

This is incredible, thought Phillip, as he rose to the surface. *We did it! Even if our plans had been a little screwed up by Randall and his Musketeers.* The trawler was dark as he climbed aboard, took off his vest and tanks and dropped them carelessly to the deck. All three vessels bobbed in the water with their lights off. Phillip snatched up his flashlight and shined it into the cabin.

Randall was gone.

"What the *fuck?*" he said, snapping the beam around the room. "Where in the fu—"

Eric leapt up from his hiding spot next to the ladder, grabbed Phillip roughly by the neck and pulled him down into the cabin. Phillip's flashlight crashed to the floor and immediately went out and the two men struggled in the darkness. Phillip blindly swung his arm up, catching Eric in the side of the head. Eric tumbled sideways and Phillip jumped to his feet, lunged toward Eric, catching him around the waist. Eric brought his fist down squarely onto Phillip's ear. Phillip howled in pain and stumbled back and slammed into the wall of the cabin.

In the process, he knocked over a can of gas, a half-filled quart of oil, and a box of tools. Like a cat, Phillip regained his feet and came at Eric again. Eric could hear the gentle *chuggachuggachugga* of the gas as it slowly drained from the nozzle of the overturned can and the thick smell of gas filled the cabin.

Phillip pulled his dive knife from its sheath and lashed out at Eric. Eric rolled to the side and the blade struck the floor, and he seized the opportunity to grab Phillip's knife hand and held on with all his might as he groped on the floor for a weapon of his own of any kind. His hand wrapped around a large wrench and he brought it to the side of Phillips head with a crushing blow. Before he could recover, Eric struck him again, and Phillip, still clad in his wetsuit, went limp. Eric pushed his body off him and took the knife from his hand.

Ed and Jimmy surfaced. Hearing the commotion aboard the trawler, they immediately inflated the BC vests and shed them, leaving them to bob in the dark waters. The two men swam toward the Bayliner. By the time they got there, Eric had bounded off the boat, stumbled across the *John Galt* and leapt aboard the Bayliner. The cabin of the Bayliner was dark, but he could see the outline of two shadows against the wall.

Don and Kari.

They struggled fiercely and tried to speak through the duct tape. Eric cut Don's bindings first. Don's hands were free for only a second before Eric was sent flying, thrown against the opposite wall by some unseen, monstrous entity. The knife scattered and Eric immediately got back on his feet to face whatever it was that had blind-sided him. A huge, wet hand groped out of the darkness, grabbing Eric's shirt and throwing him to the floor.

Don stripped the duct tape off of his mouth with a muffled curse and began frantically unwinding the sticky bondage from around his ankles. The tape had been wound around his ankles nearly forty times. He finally got his legs free and knelt down immediately next to Kari to untie her hands.

Eric and the monster crashed into Kari's chair, sending both Don and Kari sprawling. Don's hand bumped something and he grasped it. *A flashlight!* He clicked it on and the cabin of the Bayliner lit up. The interior of the cabin was in a shambles and Eric and Jimmy Durand were wrestling in a corner. Kari lay on her side still bound to the chair by the duct tape around her feet. Her eyes signaled Don to do something. *Do what? What am I supposed to do?*

Four hundred pounds made up his mind for him. Ed Belmont was struggling up the ladder of the Bayliner. Don hurtled across the gap between the Bayliner and the *John Galt* as Ed battled to heave his huge body up the ladder. He shined the light in the cabin and saw a tightly-bound Mike Felsing sitting in a chair, squirming and twitching. He flew inside the boat and found a pair of scissors in the first aid kit and cut the duct tape that held Mike's hands together. He gave the scissors to Mike to finish releasing himself, remembering what he had forgotten about in the chaos—the shotgun. He had hidden it in one of the lower compartments in the cabin of Dave's trawler.

Don jumped the gap to Dave's trawler, tripped and tumbled onto the deck, only to spring instantly to his feet. He leapt across the deck and shined the light down into the cabin. The small room was a mess. Tools lay all over the floor and the pungent odor of gasoline clawed at his nostrils. Phillip was sitting on the floor, shaking his head. Still groggy, he tried to get to his feet as Don jumped down into the cabin. Don easily brushed him aside. Phillip tumbled to the floor again and Don opened a wood compartment door and began tossing aside the extra lines and life vests. Phillip rolled away, shook his head, and was on his feet again, but Don was only vaguely aware of him as he searched furiously for the weapon.

There you are! Duane Everett, I love you.

The Remington pump lay uncased at the bottom of the compartment. He grabbed it and pulled it up to his waist and turned to point the gun at Phillip, but Phillip was already upon him and he knocked the barrel away and held it with one hand. Both men fought for possession of the gun. Don was not about to release his grip on the weapon, and fought to hang on to it. He pulled and struggled back to the short ladder, trying frantically to wretch the gun from Phillip's hands. If he could get above Phillip he would have the advantage, and he placed his foot on the second rung of the ladder. In two steps he could be out of the cabin, but Phillip showed no sign of relinquishing his hold on the Remington. He tried to swoop the barrel around but Don pulled back, inching up the ladder even more. Phillip stepped on the first rung. The two men were locked together, and Don twisted the firearm in yet another vain attempt to pull it away from Phillip. Arms flailed, nails scraped and scratched. Legs kicked furiously.

Suddenly, Phillip's foot slipped from the rung. He lost his balance and instantly began to fall back into the cabin. He was not about to relinquish his grip, and he would pull Don Garrity into the cabin with him.

Don, knowing that falling back into the cabin would be to his disadvantage, released his grip on the shotgun. He would have mere seconds . . . *seconds* . . . before Phillip would be on his feet. Don needed to put as much distance as possible between himself and the barrel of the shotgun.

He spun and sprang out onto the deck. Behind him, Phillip hit the cabin floor with a heavy, tumultuous thud.

A sudden, powerful explosion lit up the cabin starkly as the twelve-gauge went off prematurely. The spilled gasoline ignited in a sweeping *whoooooooooosh,* and instantly, the entire cabin was completely aflame in a roaring concussion blast. The powerful eruption sent Don across the deck of the trawler where he scrambled to his feet and leapt back to the *John Galt.*

Phillip was completely afire. The wetsuit only added fuel, and the neoprene burned and bubbled with an intense fury. His arms were outstretched and he was screaming—a horrible, sickening wail—as the searing flames ate away his flesh. He pawed his face with his hands as if he could somehow wipe the fire from his eyes. Flames crawled up the cabin wall and smoke billowed from the hatchway. Phillip's burning frame slumped to the floor, fell over, and burned, lifeless and still.

Don stared into the raging furnace. The outline of Phillip's body disappeared, lost in the burning embers and inky-black smoke. Orange flames licked into the night sky, and the stench of burning flesh was repulsive.

Shouting from the Bayliner awakened Don from his dazed state. The fire aboard Dave Shandler's trawler was almost certain to spread to the *John Galt* in a matter of seconds. In the darkness, Don frantically battled the thick smoke and untied the trawler, pushing it away from the *John Galt*.

The noise from the Bayliner intensified. In the struggle with Eric, the stitches on Jimmy's leg had ripped open. As the pain shot through his body Jimmy reeled away, giving Eric a split second to get his breath and prepare for another onslaught. *Eric Randall,* he thought to himself, *you are fighting a losing battle this time.* Kari still lay on her side in the corner, but Eric didn't have the time to even look her way, let alone attempt to free her.

And things were about to get worse.

chapter 198

The pain in his leg infuriated Jimmy and he grabbed Eric again and threw him to the floor. Both Jimmy and Kari saw Phillip's knife at the same time and she tried desperately but ineffectively to warn Eric. Jimmy grabbed the knife while keeping Eric pinned down.

"Hurry it up!" Ed shouted. *"Just get rid of him!!"* The engine of the Bayliner roared to life. *"Get rid of him!"* Ed bellowed again. *"Just get rid of him and let's get out of here!"*

The flames from the cabin of Dave's trawler now enveloped the entire boat. Ed Belmont was still barking orders from the Bayliner. A loud, painful scream from Eric pierced the air and Don turned. Jimmy had plunged the knife into Eric's stomach. Eric doubled over, on the deck, holding his abdomen, screaming in agony. Kari looked on, horrified, powerless to do anything.

"Toss him overboard!!" Ed wailed. "Let's get the hell outta

here! Somebody's gonna see that fire!"

"Lift the anchor!" Jimmy shouted.

"FUCK THE ANCHOR!!" Ed boomed. *"LEAVE IT!! CUT THE LINE!! CUT THE LINE AND CUT US LOOSE FROM THEIR BOAT!!"*

Suddenly Jimmy saw Don as he emerged from the other side of the *John Galt*. He snatched the handgun from his bag and fired off a shot, sending Garrity diving for cover. Mike Felsing had finally released himself from his bonds and was about to get up when the gunshot sent him to the floor in retreat.

Without even straining himself, Jimmy grabbed Eric's arm with his free hand and jerked him to his feet. With a single heave, pushed him over the railing and into the dark water. Eric was conscious, but the gash to his stomach made him dizzy. The cold water woke him up, but it was difficult to tread water and favor his deep laceration at the same time. He swept the water with one hand, keeping his head just above the surface and held his stomach with the other. The pain was numbing, and it was a difficult struggle just to remain afloat.

Jimmy raced to the bow and sliced the anchor line. The boat was free. He sent another bullet into the cabin of the John Galt, just to let the two men know that they wouldn't be heroes tonight, then cut the lines that held the two boats together.

Eric coughed and sputtered struggling to stay afloat. His stomach seared with pain.

"Hey Randall." The sneering arrogant voice caught Eric by surprise and he looked up. Ed was standing at the stern of the Bayliner. A line was in his hands, and he was tying one end to the

manifold bar of two air tanks. "You know," he continued, his breath heaving. "I've had a change of heart." His hands whirled about the manifold bar, spinning the line and tying it off. "You've fucked things up so bad, you know I really shouldn't be this nice. But just so's you don't get *too* lonely, I'm gonna make sure that your lovely wife gets to spend some time with you." He glanced up. "Jimmy . . . go get her."

"Ed, we don't have the fucking time to—"

"*I SAID GO GET HER!!*" he bellowed. Jimmy disappeared into the cabin and returned, dragging Kari and the chair with him. Her hands and feet were still taped tightly to the chair and a large piece of duct tape still covered her mouth. She was struggling to free herself, pleading and begging, but the only sounds she was able to make came through her nostrils. Her eyes were wide and filled with tears, unable to comprehend the unspeakable act that was about to befall her. Ed's hands whirred as he tied the other end of the line around Kari's ankles, then around the legs of the chair. With a forceful shove, Ed pushed Kari over the railing and over the side of the boat. She tumbled sideways, landing headfirst in the water—followed by the snaking white line. Kari bobbed face down in the water. She rolled onto her back, but she knew she wouldn't be able to continue floating for more than just a few seconds. Already the weight of the chair alone threatened to pull her beneath the surface.

"Say hello to your wife, Randall," Ed wheezed arrogantly. He picked up the two air tanks and cradled them in both arms. "*Say hello to your wife in fuckin' Weeezeeeanna.*" He dropped the tanks.

. *"No!"* Eric screamed, wincing painfully in the water. *"No! Don't—"*

The two tanks made a giant splash as it hit the water, and the remaining line sizzled off the deck and slithered rapidly into the dark waters below. In another moment, Kari would be jerked from the surface by the sinking tanks to vanish to the depths of the Channel.

A sudden, jolting jerk caught Ed totally by surprise. He looked down.

"Awww, *SHIT!*" The rope had tangled around one of his feet, wrapping a loop around his ankle. He shook his leg and tried to slip out of the winding snake, but it was too late. The rope snapped taut and jerked Ed's tree-trunk size leg into the air, pulling him off balance. Ed pitched forward onto the thin metal railing, which snapped like a toothpick under his enormous weight. He tried to catch himself, but it was too late. Jimmy sprang to assist, but he missed grabbing Ed's arm by mere inches. The huge man tumbled overboard to the hungry, eager mouth of Lake Huron. There was a loud splash, and Ed disappeared beneath the churning, boiling waters. A split second later, Kari, who had been fighting to remain on her back on the surface, snapped below the swirling waters. The line was tied to her, wrapped around Ed's foot . . . and tied to the two air tanks that plummeted toward the bottom of the lake.

chapter 199

Jimmy leapt to the wheel of the Bayliner, threw the engine into forward and sped off into the night, leaving Eric in the water clutching his stomach and screaming. *"Oh Jesus! Oh my God! "Don! Go!! Go!! Jesus, Don!! GO!!!"* Eric coughed and sputtered, choking back sobs.

Don stood on the deck of the *John Galt*, frozen in place. *"DON! FOR GOD'S SAKE!! MY WIFE IS DOWN THERE!! PLEASE!"* Eric choked as he swallowed a mouthful of water. He made it to the ladder of the *John Galt* and he clung to the rung of the ladder with one hand, looking up at Don, pleading. "Don!! I can't do it! Go! *GO NOW!!"* Don leaned down to help Eric out of the water, but Eric protested. *"LEAVE ME ALONE AND GO GET MY WIFE!! PLEASE!!"*

What? Don thought. *Me? Oh no. Can't. Can't do it.* Eric continued to scream at Don with everything he had. Horrified, Don realized that it was up to him. He looked frantically about the deck. "Where's your vest and tanks?"

"Just get a mask and fins!! Jesus, Don, hurry!" Eric cried.

Don dashed into the cabin. Mike was already out of the cabin and he pointed towards a pile of gear. "Over there! Right there!"

Don grabbed a mask and a set of fins. He slipped on the fins, placed the mask over his face, and plunged feet first into the water. In an instant he was at Jimmy's inflated vest and tanks that bobbed in the water a few yards from the boat.

"Use their gear!" Eric choked, swallowing a large amount of water and coughing it back up. "Get the vest on!"

"Mike!! Get him a dive light!!" Eric shouted. Mike returned a moment later with a flashlight. Don spent a few precious seconds struggling to don the vest. Mike tossed the light to him but it splashed into the water a few feet away from him. Eric lunged for the light and handed it to Don.

"Go! GO! GO!! GO NOW!! GO!!" Don popped the regulator in his mouth, took a breath, and in an instant he was gone.

Mike dove into the water and surfaced next to Eric. Blood was still pouring out of Eric's wound, and Mike helped him up the ladder. On the deck, Eric lay on his side, choking and gasping. "Oh God. Oh no. Kari . . ." he sobbed.

Mike found a towel and pressed the cloth to Eric's stomach, trying to stop the bleeding. Eric coughed and his body shook. *"Don . . . please hurry. God . . . please hurry. Jesus, please. Please, Jesus,"* he whispered painfully.

Christopher Knight

chapter 200

This can't be happening, Kari thought in horror. But it was happening, and Kari was powerless to do anything but watch in terror as the huge behemoth of a man threw the two air tanks into the water. *It's over. This is the end.*

She had heard another splash, this one much larger, and then she had suddenly been jerked beneath the surface. It was impossible to see, and her body froze rigid as she passed through the thermocline. Now the water was intensely cold, but she hardly noticed as she was pulled deeper into the dark depths of the Laurentian Channel.

Damn it all to hell anyway! Ed struggled to reach down and loosen his leg from the rope, but the combined pull of the tanks plus the fact that he had a hard time bending over prevented him from reaching the line. *Damn it! Damn it to hell!* He was panicking now as he fell faster and faster into the depths. He could feel his lungs tightening as his air began to run out, and he knew that if he didn't get his leg free soon, his number was going to be up.

Then, whether it was a memory or an imagination, a voice began speaking to him. At first he ignored it, but it spoke louder and louder as Ed sank further and further into the Channel.

Hello Ed, the voice cooed. *It's been soooo long. It's nice to have you for a visit. I think you'll like it here, Ed. I think you'll like it very much. Oh, it's a little lonely and maybe a little cold, but I'm sure you'll get used to it. Yes, I'm sure you will.* Ed tried to shake Paul Sprague's voice from his head, but it seemed to permeate the water around him, filling his ears and seeping through his brain. He began to flail about wildly in the dark waters. *Come on Ed. You're disappointing me. I want you to feel very welcome in your new home. Welcome. Welcome, Ed.*

Welcome to Weeezeeeana.

Abruptly, Ed's body slowed to a stop. The tanks had hit bottom. Reaching down, Ed felt for the line that entangled his leg and easily slid the rope from his ankle. He began swimming frantically for the surface. He bumped into something that moved and realized that it was Randall's wife. Pushing her away from him in the inky black, he kicked his legs in a frenzy, unsure exactly which way was up. He wasn't going to be able to hold his breath much longer.

This is it. I'm screwed.

He opened his mouth and the escaping air exploded out in hundreds of tiny bubbles. Ed's natural reflex was to breathe in.

Christopher Knight

Paul Sprague whispered to him from the depths. *See, Eddie boy? It's not so bad. I think you'll really like Weeezeeeana. I think you'll really like it here* . . . . Then Ed saw a light—it was only a flicker—far away. It was the last thing he saw as he slipped into unconsciousness.

At the same time that Ed was inhaling a deep breath of fresh clean northern Michigan water, Kari, who hadn't had much of a chance to catch her breath in the first place, could hold it no longer. She exhaled through her nostrils, and the water rushed in.

chapter 201

Barracudas. Thousands of them. Don couldn't actually see them, but he knew they were there, just out of the beam of the flashlight, waiting for him. *No. No. That's in my nightmare.* Music began to play in his ears and he felt very hot, even though he had just hit the thermocline and the frigid cold should be almost painful to his unprotected skin. Yet he slipped into the cold almost without noticing it. The music grew louder, but he continued his descent.

The snake began to slither at his mouth, slowly at first, and then faster, working his way down Don's throat. The snake's forked tongue licked at his palate and slithered between his teeth. *Still here, Donny boy,* a voice told him. *Still here. And it's . . . SHOWTIME!* Don grasped at the regulator, repulsed by the intruding viper. It came out of his mouth and he almost dropped the flashlight.

No!!! This is not real!! This is not real! But then the pounding music began to fade and the snake in his hands went limp. He put the regulator back in his mouth and took a long, easy breath, glancing at his air gauge. There wasn't much left.

He forced himself deeper. He hadn't had a chance to put on a weight belt and the natural buoyancy of his body wanted to pull him back to the surface. It was a fight to continue the descent, but at least the tormenting visions had left him. He looked at his gauge again. Ninety feet.

A shape loomed in his flashlight beam. *There she is! There she—*

His heart sank when he saw the distorted, grotesque face of Ed Belmont. His eyes were open, bulging and wide, and his gaping mouth bellowed a silent scream. Ed still had his wetsuit on and he looked like a blown-up beach toy, its arms and legs spread apart as if it were overinflated. *Ed Belmont, the Incredible Sinking Balloon Man, on sale now at your favorite toy store for just . . . .*

Kari must be nearby. He spun frantically, searching for her.

There! Kari's motionless body lay sideways on the bottom. The line was still tied to her feet and the anchor sat buried in creamy-brown silt just a few feet from her.

He shined the light in her face. Her eyes were blank and half open. He took the regulator from his mouth and shoved it between her blue lips. She did not respond. He shook her and then realizing the futility of the action, replaced the regulator in his mouth and went to work untying the line from around her ankles.

"Where is he? Where is *she?!?!?!*" Eric still lay on the deck in a fetal position, holding his stomach. The pain of his wound was nothing compared to the emotional battle he was fighting. Mike Felsing knelt by his side, scanning the depths with a flashlight.

A brilliant flash of light filled the sky as Dave Shandler's trawler exploded. The fire had reached the gas tanks and hundreds of small flaming pieces of debris burst into the air. A few landed on the *John Galt* and Mike kicked them into the water.

"Oh Jesus!! Where is he?" Eric demanded again. It had been almost two minutes since Kari had been thrown into the water.

"He'll find her," Mike told him. "He'll find her and bring her back up."

Bubbles rose to the surface near the boat, and Mike shined the light into the water.

"What is it?" Eric squeaked out. "What do you see?"

"Nothing yet. Hang in there, Eric."

Agonizing seconds ticked by. Mike kept his light trained at the water, looking for bubbles or movement. Nearly three minutes had passed. Then, without a word, Mike sat the flashlight down and dove headfirst into the water. Eric strained and struggled to his knees still clutching his stomach. After a moment Mike reappeared.

Followed by Don and Kari.

Her lifeless body, still bound by duct tape, was lifted to the surface by the two men. Eric reached both arms out to help and they lifted her limp form to the deck. Eric stripped off the four-inch piece of duct tape that covered her mouth.

"Kari!" he shouted to her. *"Kari! Dammit! Listen to me!"* He

turned her onto her side and slapped her on her back. Don unwound the duct tape from around her wrists. *"CPR!! She needs CPR!"* Eric cried, and rolled her onto her back.

"Eric!" Mike shouted sternly. *"Eric!! ENOUGH! Take it easy! She's going to be okay!"* Mike leaned over and turned his head, putting an ear to her chest. "She has a heartbeat." He put his ear to her nose. "But she's not breathing." He turned Kari on her side and slapped her hard in the center of her back to dislodge anything that may have gotten caught in her throat. He rolled her gently onto her back, took a breath, and put his mouth to hers.

The whirring blades of a helicopter sounded in the distance. Don looked up and saw the blinking lights of a chopper coming from St. Ignace. And a boat, its occupants undoubtedly seeing the flames and explosion, was hurrying towards them from Bois Blanc Island.

"Kari," Eric pleaded. "It's me, baby. It's me. Come on, honey. Breathe. Please breathe, Kari."

Mike bent his head down and gave her another breath. Kari's motionless body snapped and recoiled as the spasm rocketed through her. She vomited and Mike turned her to her side. She continued to vomit, each heave spewing forth water. Her eyes were closed, and she stopped, her body once again going limp. Mike again laid her slowly on her back.

"Kari," Eric pleaded. "Kari, it's me. It's Eric." As Eric gently held her face with both hands, Kari slowly opened her eyes.

chapter 202

The Bayliner raced past the breakwall and into the mouth of the Cheboygan River, disregarding the *No Wake* signs. Jimmy was about to pull the Bayliner into their rented slip, when he saw an empty one closer to the shore. He drifted in and guided the boat into the slip just a few feet from the grassy bank. The closer he was to the shore, the less distance he would have to carry the heavy bags to the car. Although they had been forced to leave a large portion of the treasure floating in the water buoyed by the lift bags, they had retrieved a sizable amount.

And now with no one to share that with . . . .

Jimmy shook his head as he leaped off the boat. Phillip getting toasted, well that was one thing. But Ed's freak accident—that was just too much. *It's like I'm supposed to have all this shit myself.*

Like some kind of karma.

He walked across the parking lot and stopped at his car, wondering how on earth he was going to be able to fit everything into the Trans Am. He looked back at the boat and then at his car. *Yeah,* he thought. *That'll work. I'm not going to need this thing anyway. After this I can buy ten Trans Ams.* He walked over to Ed's truck grasped the door handle.

"Jimmy."

The voice was so soft he thought he had imagined it. He didn't even glance up. As he opened the truck door, it came again.

"Jimmy." He turned and looked to see where it came from. The harbormaster's office was dark, and a small light glowed from above the restroom sign. Shadows slept quietly and nothing moved. The voice came again, this time louder, more forcefully. Sing-song.

"Jim-meeeeee . . . ."

Jimmy strained his eyes and then he saw her standing in the shadows in front of the hedges.

Sharon.

He strode up the lawn and stopped ten feet away from her. Sharon was smiling at him. "You're dead, Jimmy." Sharon reached beneath her sweatshirt and pulled out the Smith & Wesson. Jimmy stood, surprised, staring.

"Well, aren't you cute," Jimmy sneered. "You found my gun int the car. Tsk, tsk. You sure you can handle that thing?"

Sharon raised the gun, leveling it at Jimmy's head. Her hand shook slightly.

"You know, I always thought you were pretty smart," Jimmy

scolded. "I mean . . . pretty smart for a *dumb* bitch, but this surprises me." He stood his ground. *"Go ahead, Sharon. Pull the trigger. Pull the trigger right now."* He stepped forward.

Sharon pulled the hammer back and readied the weapon.

"You don't have the guts," Jimmy said evenly. He crossed his mammoth arms. "Go ahead. Pull the fucking trigger."

Sharon hesitated for a moment, wrapped her finger around the trigger, and pulled.

Click.

"Aww, what's the matter?" Jimmy teased. "You look shocked. Now normally the gun under my seat would be loaded but . . . ."

Sharon pulled the hammer back again.

Click.

"And *normally* it would be loaded. But I took the bullets out, Sharon. I took them out because I might need them." He unfolded his arms. "I might need them . . . for *this* . . . ."

chapter 203

Jimmy reached around behind him and pulled his .38 from his back pocket, stepping towards Sharon as he did so. "But you know what? I'm not going to shoot you, Sharon. Oh, don't get me wrong. I'd *like* to. I'd like to splatter your brains all over the grass, but I'm not going to. That would make too much noise. We don't want to wake anybody up, do we? So instead, I'm just going to bash your skull in. I'm going to bash your head in so hard that you'll be able to wear that fucking baseball cap as a neckwarmer. I think we'll both be so much happier that way."

He lunged for her, but she leaped back out of his reach and quickly vanished into the dense six-foot shrubbery. It was impossible to see through the thick branches.

"Come out, come out wherever you are," Jimmy mocked, and

slowly walked along the edge of the shrubs, listening for the sound of movement. He leveled the gun, sweeping it back and forth. "I know you're in there," he sang lightly, his voice high pitched and sweet. "Come on out and let's play, huh? Whaddya say, Sharon?"

No sound.

"Okay Sharon," he said, his voice growing louder and more impatient. "I'm *going* to find you. And when I do . . . ."

Yes, Sharon thought, watching carefully. *Yes, just a little bit further. Just a little bit . . . .*

She could see his shadow as he crept around the perimeter of the bushes, slowly stalking her. *Just a little more. Come on, Jimmy.* She was certain that he must be able to hear her heart beating. It pounded at her chest, and she desperately tried to conceal her heavy breaths by holding them in, then slowly releasing them.

Jimmy was only a few feet away. He had no way of knowing exactly where she was and Sharon prayed that he could not see into the dense greenery. He stopped. "I know you're in there, Sharon." He stepped further along the line of bushes, closer to her silhouette.

Yes, that's it, Jim. That's it. A little more now . . . .

"I see you, Sharon."

He bent down, his face near the cedar branches, peering into the darkness. *"I can seeeeee yooooou."* He slowly brought the gun up.

Oh yes, Jimmy. It's me. I'm here, all right. You got me. Just come a little closer. She tightened her grip on the stainless steel trigger. Jimmy was bent over, squinting into the darkened brush. She could see his eyes, his nose, his cheeks. *What do they call this, Jimmy? 'Poetic justice'? I think that's what it is.* A mosquito buzzed by her ear. She ignored it. Suddenly, Jimmy's eyes found hers.

"There you are, you little—" his words fell. Then, in a voice that sounded so juvenile, so full of fear:

"Oh *fuck*—"

Sharon pulled the trigger.

The four-inch razor sharp tip of the speargun exploded inches from his nose. The last thing Jimmy heard was a click and a snapping *whoosh!* as the shaft exploded from the brush. The spear caught Jimmy just above his right eye and embedded in his brain. He stood rigid for a moment, the steel arrow piercing his skull. Blood sprayed out of the point of entry, ran down the shaft, and dripped onto the grass. Jimmy's clothing, from his shirt to his sweats, were drenched in blood. Still he stood, his mouth gaping, his eyes wide and staring. The gun fell from his hand and he began to shake. He finally fell forward like a tree crashing to the earth.

Sharon emerged from the bushes as Jimmy's body tumbled forward. The shaft of the spear stabbed the ground, causing Jimmy's head to snap back unnaturally. The spear exploded out of the back of his head, and the shaft held fast, entrenched in his skull. Another geyser of blood sprayed out the back of his head. Bluish-gray tissue dangled from the tip of the spear, and a chunk of it broke loose and fell free, tumbling to the ground. Sharon looked on, numb and motionless.

When the police arrived fifteen minutes later, that's exactly how they found her: standing quietly, speargun dangling from her hand, staring at the now departed Jimmy Durand.

epilogue-
one year later

The evening sun hung low in the western sky and Eric reached for his drink. The four—Eric, Kari, Mike and Evelyn—were dining on the deck at *Leggs Inn* in Cross Village overlooking Lake Michigan. Far to the southwest, a large freighter was lumbering towards its destination. The late-evening July sun was still warm, and Eric raised his glass.

"A toast," he proclaimed, "to another successful novel."

"Here, here," Kari chimed in, and all four clinked glasses and sipped their cocktails.

"Well, just remember," Mike offered, "it's not successful yet. It's only successful if it sells."

"Who's not going to buy it?" Kari asked, smiling.

"Me," laughed Evelyn. "I think I deserve a free copy." The comment brought a chuckle from all. Mike had spent the better part of the year working on his second novel, and to his surprise, it had come quite easily—after he had gotten rid of his computer. The empty white screen with its taunting blinking black cursor had teased him one too many times and he had sold it to a college student for $300. *A pad of paper and pencil is much more user-friendly*, Mike thought. The pencil didn't sit there and blink at him when he wasn't doing anything. Pencils don't crash, and they don't get viruses.

The novel was another murder mystery. Although the story had nothing to do with shipwrecks or treasure, Mike credited the events of the previous summer with jolting his creativity. His agent forwarded the manuscript to a large publishing company, which had just yesterday agreed to publish the work.

"Have you spoken with Don lately?" Mike asked.

"Last week," Eric replied, nodding and setting his glass down. "He's on an expedition in the Galapagos islands, doing some underwater research and photography. He called to say that he wouldn't be back for a couple months and if we didn't hear from him, not to worry."

"Anything from your lawyer yet?" Mike asked.

Eric shook his head. "It'll probably be another year. This thing is going to be wrapped up in court for a long time. But she's positive that this is a winner." The gold and silver bars, gemstones, and Colombian emeralds had been confiscated as evidence by the State of Michigan. Eric and Kari were suing for the rights of ownership as they had discovered that the treasure lay just outside of the boundaries of the Straits Area Shipwreck Preserve. The total value was estimated at a staggering $100 million dollars.

If anyone is entitled to it, it's us, Eric thought. *And Abigail Jewell.* Jewell had been amazed to learn of the massive fortune that her great-grandfather had amassed, and even more stunned to learn of the strange circumstances surrounding its discovery. *Yeah, she should certainly have a chunk of it*, thought Eric. *And Don and Mike and Evelyn. They certainly deserve their share.*

They said their good-byes and Eric and Kari departed, promising to get together again next week.

The river was busy, and a steady stream of boats followed one another. The evening was mild and pleasant.

"So, Mrs. Randall? How 'bout an after dinner cruise?"

"Sounds lovely," Kari replied, slipping her arms around his waist. "You might even get lucky."

"In my wildest dreams." He kissed her forehead.

They boarded the *John Galt* and cruised up the river, out of the mouth and into the dark sea of Lake Huron. The sun had just set and the brilliant orange-yellow sky was fading into charcoal. Eric lay back on the bow and Kari snuggled close to him. The *John Galt* sat motionless in the water as one-by-one, stars began to appear overhead. Eric got up and went into the cabin to open a bottle of wine. There was an audible *pop!* as he uncorked the bottle. Glasses tinked. "Hey," he said curiously. "Come here and check this out." Kari stood up and joined him in the cabin.

"What's up?"

Eric was looking at the depthfinder. There was a large jagged mountain on the screen, protruding up from the depths.

"Right here," he continued, his finger following the up and

down lines. "What do you think?"

"I think," Kari said, reaching out and clicking off the depthfinder. She slipped her arm around his waist. Her voice softened. "I think we both have better things to do." She took a sip of wine and the two kissed and returned to the deck to stare at the stars.